THE NORTH TOWER

MICHELLE N. HAGOOD

First edition April 2022

Cover design by Michelle N. Hagood and Natalia Junqueira

Jacket Design by Natalia Junqueira

Book Interior by Emily Snyder

ISBN 979-8-9854798-0-5 (hardcover)

ISBN 979-8-9854798-1-2 (paperback)

ISBN 979-8-9854798-2-9 (ebook)

For Jess.

*For believing in this story
almost as much as you believed in me.*

Contents

Prologue
The Queen and King

If the world had corners, this would be the darkest.

At least that's what Elizabeth Rose thought.

She was told the day she graduated school she would feel the most accomplished. The day she got married she would feel the most loved. But the day she had her first child would be the happiest moment of her life. Instead, it was the closest to hell she had ever been.

There was nothing joyful about sitting on a stained comforter in a rundown hotel she booked with a fake name. There were no celebratory balloons, just a couple moths that fluttered around the dim lights. There were no grinning family members, just two friends with heavy hearts and downcast gazes.

No matter how hard Elizabeth tried, she couldn't look away from the small face in the crook of her arm. Her fingers gently stroked her daughter's pale cheek as a trickle of tears streamed from Elizabeth's red, rimmed eyes.

Just for a moment she let herself imagine what it would be like to be her mother. What would her voice sound like when she said her first words? Would she be a natural at walking or would it take her a while? Would she be a laughing baby or one who cooed occasionally?

Elizabeth reluctantly lifted her teary gaze. Clearing the thickness from her throat she announced, "I have to go."

"Please don't do this," Vera protested as Elizabeth struggled to her feet. "I admire your optimism, but you're wishing for something that isn't there."

"I agree. He's a lost cause," Steel said. His somber tone made his voice deeper than usual.

"I have to try." Elizabeth rose from the bed and placed the baby into Vera's arms.

"No, you don't." Steel shook his head. "Let Kale deal with this."

Elizabeth smiled sadly. "He's my husband. I have to believe there's still good in him."

"When are you going to realize there isn't any?" Vera asked.

"He's been through a lot. He's just forgotten who he used to be. I can get him to call this whole thing off. I just need to remind him of who he is."

Vera bit her tongue, clearly struggling to keep her thoughts to herself. Crossing his arms, Steel shook his head at the carpet. Both knew the king would give up his mission when glaciers caught fire.

Elizabeth looked down at her daughter. She was wasting time on a conversation they had had a hundred times. "You shouldn't wait more than an hour." She turned toward the door. "If anyone comes who isn't me, assume I'm dead."

"What about her?" Steel asked, nodding toward the sleeping newborn.

Elizabeth stopped. Another wave of tears flowed down her cheeks. Against her better judgment she turned back. "Keep her safe."

"Aren't you going to name her?" Vera asked softly.

Elizabeth cupped her hand over the baby's head, gently stroking her wispy hair. "She'll make a name for herself." She looked up to her friend. "Thank you . . . both of you. I wouldn't have made it this far without you. I owe you everything."

Vera clutched Elizabeth's hand. "I'd do it all over again."

Steel nodded in agreement. "My loyalty is to you, my queen. Forever and always."

"I'll see you in the next life, my friends." Elizabeth's gaze dropped to her daughter. "And I hope to see you too, little one. But take your time." With a shaky breath, she pulled her hands to her chest. She looked at the tall, silent man beside her. "Protect her."

Steel nodded once. "With my life."

Before she could change her mind, Elizabeth turned on her heel and Ported from the hotel.

When she appeared in her own room, she crumbled to the floor. Clutching her empty belly, she screamed into the carpet. Light bulbs shattered and picture frames rattled against the walls. With her forehead pressed to the floor, a sob ripped out of her throat.

Breathing deeply, she willed herself to sit up and dry her face. Rising to her feet, she went to her closet and put on a gown as red as an open wound. She tossed her clothes soiled with the evidence of the birth into the fireplace and watched them burn.

Turning her attention to the vanity, she took extra care removing weakness from her face. With practiced hands, she smoothed blush over her cheeks, bringing life back to their dull complexion. She framed her eyes with dark colors to cover the exhausted red.

When she was done, she was as cold as the room around her. Straightening her spine, she grabbed her pearl crown from the dresser and placed it on her head. Then she walked from the room.

She used to love this mansion, the way the sun streamed through the skylights, the afternoon glow in the sitting room, the smells of the orchard out back that carried through the open windows. It was a place of life and color. The halls were meant for running bare feet, the ballrooms for dancing, and the kitchen for homecooked meals. It would never be used for any of those things.

Maybe that's why it felt more like a coffin than anything else. Elizabeth didn't know how something so beautiful and filled with promise could become nothing but a hollow reminder of everything she wanted and would never grasp.

Gliding down the sweeping staircase, Elizabeth entered what used to be the ballroom. A few of her husband's followers acknowledged her with a slight nod; most ignored her completely. Steel was among them, blending into the ranks.

She didn't give them her attention. She was, after all, their queen. She wasn't required to give them anything. Instead, her eyes locked on the far end of the room where a large wooden table stretched between two thrones atop a raised stage.

Her stomach rolled at the sight of the woman in green at his side. Elizabeth didn't bother to remember her name.

A dry smile tugged at Elizabeth's lips when the woman's envious gaze locked on her crown. It was oddly satisfying knowing she was his queen and wife, while that woman would only ever be his mistress.

Ignoring the sneering blonde, she focused her attention on the man at the head of the table. A wave of fear surged through her veins as she took the place opposite him.

Between them, maps and documents littered the long table. Sections of the maps were scorched, probably from moments of anger, while others were circled. He was still looking for it. Always looking.

"What about here?" The king waved his hand over a mountainous region.

"The search was inconclusive, my lord." The soldier nervously shifted his weight from one foot to the other.

"Inconclusive." The king rolled the word over his tongue. "I gave you a hundred men with some of the best magic. *Inconclusive* wasn't part of your objective."

"It was Kale, my lord. He was waiting for us."

At the mention of the name, Elizabeth looked closer at the messenger, noticing for the first time the state of his uniform. His armor was splattered with blood and crusted with dirt. Dark purple bruises colored his swollen face.

"Very well," the king hissed through clenched teeth. He made eye contact with Steel across the room and gave a silent command. The crimson-armored man responded by stepping forward and grabbing the wounded soldier. Steel dragged the screaming man from the room.

"Elizabeth, my love."

Her heart slammed against her ribs. She jerked her eyes from the doomed messenger to the king, but he wasn't even looking at her.

"How nice of you to join us," he said dryly. He braced his hands against the table as his eyes combed over the layout in front of him. She was used to this cold tone. She looked at his handsome face for any sign of the man she fell in love with so many years ago. When he did look up, his eyes, which their daughter now had, gave her the chilled look of a stranger.

"I'm here now," she said as she joined him on the platform.

His attention returned to the tabletop. "And what did I do to deserve this rare pleasure?"

His mistress snickered.

"I wanted to speak with you."

"Later, my love."

"I'd like to speak with you now. Alone." She clenched her shaking hands, praying he didn't see them.

The room fell silent. Even the air stilled.

He looked up, his gaze narrowed with mild annoyance. After a beat, he said to the room, "You heard your queen. Leave us."

No one hesitated. Not even his mistress in emerald. The room emptied quickly. Doors slammed behind the departing party.

His eyes flickered to her trembling fingers. "What's so important, my love?"

She had practiced this speech for months and chosen every word carefully. Taking a deep breath, she kept her tone cool and unassuming. She even pulled her lips into a soft smile. "I want to tell you something, but before I do, I need to know. When will this end?"

Confusion contorted his handsome face. "What do you mean?"

"This." She waved her hand over the table. "When will this mission of yours end?"

"Once the world is as it should be, strong and without weakness." He tilted his head. "You know this."

"Would you be willing to give it up?" she asked, strangling her last shred of hope.

His confusion transformed into surprise. "Not for anything. We aren't safe until this threat has been neutralized."

"My darling . . ." Taking a deep breath, she stepped forward and collected his hands, so battle worn and so familiar. "You don't have to keep doing this. With our combined power and our alliances, we have nothing to fear."

He shook his head, pulling his hands from hers. "I believed that once and it cost me dearly. I won't lose you to this sickness too."

"But you are losing me. Can't you see that?" Emotions threatened to clog her throat. "I can't do this anymore. I won't watch you leave and come back covered in blood. I don't want to keep wondering how many people you've killed."

"I'm doing this for you. To protect you."

"No. You're doing this for your family."

"You are my family."

"Really?" Heat rose to her cheeks. "Then who is that woman that stands by your side more than I do? I'm starting to think you can't function without her."

"You know who she is connected to."

Elizabeth shook her head.

"She's essential to this fight. She has a lot of influence with—"

"I don't need to hear your same old speech." She crossed her arms over her empty stomach. "I'm sick of this. I can't stand by and watch you go down this road."

"You knew who I was and what I did from the moment we met. What changed?" he snapped.

"I'm pregnant."

He flinched as if she had thrown something at him. In that moment, all of her worries were confirmed. The man she married would've fallen to his knees in joy, not recoil with disgust.

"I thought you would be happy," she whispered. "We always talked about having children."

"A lot has changed since then."

"It doesn't have to." She stepped forward to cup his face. "We can put this behind us and find a place where no one knows our names. We can start over. We can go back—"

"I don't want to go back," he said quietly. "I don't understand what changed. You loved me when I had the license to kill for any reason, and now when I'm actually doing something *good*, you want me to quit?" Shaking his head, he flattened his hand against her stomach.

Her heart leapt to her throat. "I can't feel anything, which means the child is still small. Get rid of it."

Elizabeth's heart crumbled. "Lawrence—"

"I've done everything for you. I started this so nothing would ever happen to you. I would give you the world if you asked. You can have anything—"

"I want this. Every king needs an heir," she reasoned. "Someone whom you know is worthy to stand beside you. Someone born with loyalty in their veins."

"No." His reply echoed around the room. "You assume I need someone to stand beside me."

"You used to." Silently, she begged the man from her past to come back and warm his face.

Her silent plea fell on deaf ears as he turned his back to her. "Get rid of that child or I will."

She watched him round the table and focus again on his work. Vera and Steel were right. He wasn't her school sweetheart. The love of her life had died long ago. Or maybe it had happened gradually and she had been too blind to see it. She was done ignoring it now.

"I'm done." Her voice matched his in every frigid pitch as she tossed her crown on the table. The heavy rim clattered onto the wooden surface as it skidded across the pages of maps.

His startled gaze jerked up to hers. "What are you doing?"

"Leaving. Your mistress can have that." She gestured to the crown. "I tried to understand in the beginning. I tried to grieve with you, but all you wanted was justice. This has always been your fight. So when you're done playing god," she placed her hand on her stomach, "your family will be waiting for you." With her heart fracturing in her chest, she started down the steps.

Just as she reached the bottom, he Ported in front of her. "You can't leave."

"There's nothing for me here." With nothing else to do, she played her final card. "Just let me and the child leave. We won't bother you."

"That child could be used against me. Everything I've worked for."

His hand wrapped around her throat. "I won't let an old dream get in the way of our future."

"The only one getting in the way of it is you."

Desperation quickened his breathing. "We vowed to stay with each other, to be loyal to each other."

Elizabeth had her last brush with fear. A dragon of fury uncoiled in her chest. Around the room the lights flickered. Instead of trying to remove his grip, her fingers encircled his wrist. Blisters bubbled over his skin.

"You only had my obedience through fear. You killed any chance of loyalty the moment you walked into our home covered in the blood of innocent people. Because of that, Kale will destroy you."

His gaze flickered to his wrist. The magic seeping from her fingers darkened his skin to a horrid red. "Don't make me do this."

"I'm not making you do anything," she hissed.

He clenched his teeth with such force they might have shattered. With a strangled cry and a cruel crack, he snapped her neck.

She fell to the floor as lifeless as she entered. Lawrence Hart stood over her, staring at his empty hands.

Vera waited an hour and one minute, holding on to a shred of hope that her friend would come back.

She chided herself for being stupid. Knowing the man Elizabeth had gone to, there was no hope. She looked at the sleeping child in her arms. She hated that the baby would never know her mother. It would be a blessing she would never know her father.

She stood, the child safely cradled to her chest. It was time to disappear.

Screams erupted from the hallway as the walls shook. The door flew off its hinges. Three men dressed in red bumped shoulders as they scrambled into the room.

If they were here . . . that meant Elizabeth had been proven wrong. She wasn't coming back.

Lawrence had acted more quickly than she expected. He was erasing his queen from the world, starting with the last place she had been. How he had found her so quickly, Vera didn't know. And she wasn't about to stop and ask.

Magic swirled from Vera's wand, tearing the sheets from the bed. Like the fins of a betta fish, they undulated through the air and tangled around the men. The mattress and box spring launched across the room, knocking them back into the hall.

With a moment or two gained, Vera blasted the window from its frame. She leapt through the smoking hole into the parking lot.

Cool Kansas air bit at her skin. Shouts for her to stop followed her across the street. Golden orbs of light crashed into the ground, narrowly missing her heels. The baby cried as dirt and rocks flew around them.

Vera tripped to a stop at the end of the parking lot. Crimson-armored guards swarmed the street, waiting for her. She turned on her heel and tried to Port. When her feet spun across the asphalt instead of taking her out of Kansas, she cursed Lawrence's tricks.

She swung down a neighborhood street and jumped into the shadows between houses. Muffling the child's cries with her jacket, she waited. Breathing hard, a squad of Crown guards ran past.

Peering from her hiding place, she counted the armored soldiers. Curses ran through her mind as their numbers grew.

Keeping the child on her would mean when she was caught—and she knew it was only a matter of time—that both of them would be killed. She wasn't about to let her best friend's daughter be slaughtered just like her mother. No one could help her. Not even Steel.

She had to hide the child. She glanced around wildly for literally anything to help.

The alley between houses was bare except for a chain link fence and a tall trashcan. The thought of putting the baby inside went against every cell in her body, but she had no other option.

Vera shrugged off her coat and removed the lid. She placed the garment over the trash. As she lowered the child onto the coat, the baby started to cry. Her little arms flailed out of the hotel towel she was swaddled in. Vera quickly replaced the lid.

Grabbing her wand, Vera ran back into the street. Just as she expected, Lawrence's soldiers caught up to her a short time later.

Not long after, the baby girl was lifted from her hiding place.

1

Salina

My eyes darted to the snowflake clock for the eighth time.

Cheese and rice, why is this taking so long?

I grabbed another menu and wiped the damp towel over the fingerprints and smudged ketchup.

Quiet Christmas music played throughout the nearly empty restaurant, adding to the illusion of the sleepy hour of night. It did nothing to placate the feeling of time ticking by—time that I desperately wished to spend elsewhere.

I finished the stack of menus and tucked them against the back of the booth with the salt and pepper. Circling the towel over the tabletop, I swiped the remaining crumbs to the floor and jumped to my feet to sweep under the table.

The moment the last french fry was trapped in the dustpan, I wove my way through the restaurant, avoiding the lingering table of college students dressed in black, to the kitchen.

As I turned the corner, the cheery rendition of Jingle Bells was knocked back by a pulsating beat. The back of house staff got to play whatever they liked to make the after-holiday shifts pass faster.

In the back of the kitchen, my manager stood in front of the cash register. A train of tickets printed from the machine in a tangled waterfall to the freshly mopped floor.

"You're still here?" Tee called over the music. She tapped her glittering acrylic nails across the screen. The cash drawer slid open with a clang.

"I just finished cleaning my section." Reaching into my apron,

I thrust my checkout sheet toward her. I couldn't stop myself from glancing at the clock on the corner of the screen. Only a couple minutes had passed since my last peek, but it felt like twice that.

Tee backed up through the kitchen doorway to peer at the freshly cleaned booths. Finding them to her standards, she returned to the computer and picked up my checkout sheet. Focusing on the bottom number, she began taking bills from the cash drawer.

Come on, come on. Let me get out of here, I pleaded silently as she counted through the money.

"Have you thought anymore about being an opener?" she asked as she handed my tips to me.

A wave of excitement somersaulted through my stomach.

"Yeah," I said casually. Bending down, I popped open the cabinet in front of her and grabbed my light blue hoodie. "I'd love to, but I have to ask Denny first."

"Don't take too long." Tee slammed the cash drawer closed and collected the small mountain of receipts. Her glittering nails clicked across the screen once again. "Austin and Melinda have been asking about it and we need to make a decision soon."

"I'll have an answer by the end of the week. I promise." She flashed me a warm smile. "Have a great night, sweetie."

"You too!" Dashing from the kitchen, I untied my apron, barely pausing to shove open the front door. The crisp December air greeted me with zero friendliness and all bite. Quickly, I struggled into my hoodie.

I was an hour later than I thought I'd be. Tucking my apron under my arm, I dug my ancient and cheap cellphone from my back pocket. Even though it was past eleven, he answered before the first ring finished.

"Charlie! About bloody time. I was starting to wonder if I should just go to bed."

I grinned at the sound of his voice. Blake Johnson and his family moved from London to Salina, Kansas five years ago. When I asked him why, Blake said that his mother, Dorothea, demanded to see a sky so big that when she looked up even her peripheral vision saw blue. His father, Finley, had been more than happy to oblige.

Blake attended some really expensive boarding school in London, only coming home for holidays and summer break. For reasons beyond my understanding, Blake chose to spend his holidays with me.

"It's eleven on a Friday night," I chuckled. My breath created clouds in the frigid air.

"I'm fighting jet lag. What took you so long?"

"I had a large party that wouldn't leave. Half were kids who had epic sword fights with their french fries. It took a while to sweep it up." Shivering beneath my hoodie, I crossed the darkened street toward the neighborhoods.

"Well, next time you're going to take forever, let me know so I can take a nap."

"If Tee caught me on my phone, I'd be out of a job."

"That's fine by me. Then we'd actually *see* each other."

I rolled my eyes. "Do you still want me to come over?"

"Do you have to ask?"

My smile grew. *I've missed him.* "You're the one talking about calling it early on a Friday night."

"When you come visit me in London, you'll understand that jet lag isn't kind to anyone."

"Let me change first."

"Oh, come on!"

"I smell like steak sauce, tequila, and mashed potatoes." I laughed. "I don't want to offend your polite British nose."

"Now that's just bloody insulting," he said, but there was a smile in his voice. "If you take longer than five minutes, I'm coming to get you."

"You can time me." I flipped the phone closed just as I turned on to Haven Avenue. In the silence of the midnight street, reality came crashing back.

Haven Avenue was run down like everything else in Salina, Kansas. The never ceasing wind peeled the paint off most houses and the constant sunlight faded every color to a shadow of its original self, creating a mosaic of beige and grey. The sidewalk under my feet was a mess of cracks as I headed for a house in the middle of the row.

Denny's house was unassuming and squat. A large oak tree protruded from the center of the yard. It broke through the soil, pulling it up around the trunk as it twisted toward the ceaseless sky. Years of weathering Kansas' conditions caused it to lean dangerously close to the house. When the summer storms rolled in, I often hoped it would tip over and crush the house.

Outside the front door, I kicked the snow off my shoes. I had been eager to leave the restaurant, but standing outside 3366 Haven Avenue all I wanted was to stretch out every second before heading inside.

My hands shook as I unfolded my apron and removed my tips from the night. Hunching my shoulders, I peeled a few dollars from the stack and slipped them into the back of my shoe. I shoved the remaining bills into the pocket of my hoodie.

Facing the door once more, I closed my eyes. *You can do this.* Taking a deep breath, I pushed my way into the house.

The plastic Christmas tree greeted me from the corner. Every year, the living room was rearranged to accommodate the huge pine. This put the couch right next to the front door and, without fail, I always stubbed my toe on the corner.

Biting back a curse, I kicked the door closed and wiped my feet on the mat. The rush of December air shook the gold ornaments, making them twinkle on their branches.

Where is everyone?

Most of my housemates were night owls, except for Kelly. The small house had three bedrooms and a converted study that managed to hold six people—well, five as of last week. Arielle left in the middle of the night and never came back, leaving me a room to myself.

At this time of night, I expected Jamal to be watching TV, and either Hannah or Edmond to be making a snack. But the house remained eerily quiet. The only lights on were the multicolor strands on the Christmas tree and the hall light of the second floor.

If I don't have to talk to anyone, I can get to Blake's sooner.

Rising on the balls of my feet, I padded soundlessly up the stairs and down the sleepy hallway. Tugging the hoodie up over my head, I pushed into my room.

"You're home late."

I stumbled back into the wall. My foster dad sat on the end of my bed with his ankle crossed over his knee.

Denny was just under six feet tall, although he acted as if it was the other way around. He tried to dress like he didn't belong in this small house by wearing ironed shirts and pants he couldn't afford.

"I had a party camp out in my section." My nervous fingers, needing something to do, pulled my hair out of the tie at the base of my neck. Curtains of long brown hair fell on either side of my face. A single lock, red and bright as a maraschino cherry, weaved in and out of the crimped, tangled mess. "What are you doing in here?"

"This is my house. I can go wherever I want." He watched me expectantly with his dull brown eyes.

True, but he never came in *here*. I pulled the tips from my pocket and handed them over. If this was why he was here, he would leave as soon as he counted it.

Denny's gaze broke from mine as he took the money. I always thought he looked like a dragon as he counted his way through the bills. His shoulders hunched protectively forward and there was a greedy gleam in his eyes.

When he finished counting, he tucked my rent money into his shirt pocket. But he didn't leave. Instead, he reached into his jeans and took out a familiar folded envelope.

My gaze snapped over to the floor vent by the window. My stomach plummeted at the sight of it popped out of place.

Denny opened the envelope and removed my secret stash of cash. "I found this when I was cleaning the vents." He slapped the stack against his knee. "Care to explain?"

Panic seized my chest. "I was saving to move out," I whispered.

Denny looked up at me. "You've been taking money out of your rent?"

"Not much," I blurted, with shaking hands. "You always get the majority."

"I thought we agreed, in order for you to stay here, what you make comes to me." He rose to his feet, dropping the dollars to the bed. "All of it."

I stepped back. "I only took a few dollars at a time."

"That wasn't a part of the deal." He undid the clasp of his belt and pulled it free from the belt loops. "You lied and hid it from me. You know the punishment for that." He folded the well-used belt in half.

"You can have the money." The apron tumbled from my paralyzed fingers as I dared to back up toward the hall.

"If I let this go, what will the others think? That they can get away with it too?" He pulled the belt taunt between his hands. "Turn around and face the wall."

"Denny, please—"

"If you're not careful, I'll add to what's already coming."

I looked over my shoulder to the empty hallway. Now I understood why the house was so quiet. They all knew. After Arielle ran away, they weren't going to risk tipping me off.

My body went into autopilot as I tugged my work shirt over my head. My heart galloped around my chest as I turned and braced my forearms against the wall.

Every nerve across my ribs and spine went on high alert. I squeezed my eyes shut as his shadow covered my shoulders.

The stiff material of his shirt rustled. The belt clinked as it arched over his head.

I stopped breathing seconds before the tough leather struck my shoulder.

The force of it nearly knocked me headfirst into the wall. Fire stroked across my back. I barely felt the trickle of blood spill down my spine.

I had just enough time to lock my knees before the next strike came. This time he slashed upward, slicing from my side to the opposite shoulder.

The lights brightened as my arms gave out. My forehead struck the wall. A familiar, horrible hum started deep within my chest. It came alive with a billow of fire, rushing around my ribcage. Breathing through my teeth, I stamped the feeling back until it dulled. The lights returned to their usual glow.

That was two lashes. When Denny wasn't angry, he only gave three. Tonight, I predicted I would have five new wounds when he was done. The belt clinked again, signaling the third blow. Clenching my teeth, tears stung my eyes. My shoulders shuddered with pleas I knew better than to voice.

Before the next blow fell, the bedroom door burst open.

2

I Want to Forget

A blur of color flew by me.

Seconds later, something heavy hit the floor. Weakly I looked over my shoulder. It took me a second to understand what I was seeing. Denny was on the floor, clutching his eye as curses spat through his lips. The belt lay coiled and lifeless beside him.

The man standing between me and Denny had his fists clenched tight. One was raised before him like he was contemplating delivering a second blow. Breathing heavily, the man turned to look over his shoulder at me. My heart jumped when I met his gaze of candy apple green.

Blake.

In all the years we had known each other, I had never seen him look anything less than comfortable. In every setting, he leaned his lanky build against the closest vertical surface as if he didn't have a care in the world. His height had never been a bad thing, it just guaranteed great hugs.

But in my small bedroom, standing over Denny, Blake's towering height could be *felt*. There was nothing casual about his stance now. His shoulders were pulled tight as a bow string. Even his breathing, slow through clenched teeth, had an edge. His brilliant green eyes boiled with a storm of emotions that were foreign to his good-natured soul.

"What do you think you're doing?" Denny hollered. "You can't just break into my house—"

Blake's gaze snapped from me to the man on the floor. "You're lucky I'm not throwing you out the bloody window."

"I'll call the cops!"

"Go right ahead, mate," Blake said, icicles dripping from his words. "I bet they'd love to hear just how much of a twisted son of a bitch you are."

Denny laughed, a low rasp that crawled over my skin. "I've got friends in high places, kid. You'd be the one walking away in chains."

Blake's hands clenched until his knuckles were white under his dark skin. Breathing hard, he snatched my light blue hoodie from the floor and offered it to me, averting his gaze.

Dizzy with lingering fear, I struggled to pull it over my head. Before my arms were in the sleeves, Blake ushered me into the hall.

"Where do you think you're going?" Denny scrambled to his feet. My heart jumped as I cowered behind Blake.

"Away from you," Blake snarled.

"You can't just take her—"

"Watch me. If you think of following, I'll punch you so hard that you'll wake up tomorrow." Taking my hand, Blake pulled me in front of him and herded me out of the house. He didn't bother to close the front door.

Blake led me across the street to the only house that seemed un-affected by the harsh Kansas conditions. The yellow paint was bright, the lawn was full of sleeping yellow grass, and the driveway was free of cracks or oil marks. The Johnson's house looked like it belonged on a different street, maybe even in a different city.

Slowly turning the doorknob, Blake ushered me inside. Moving past the glittering Christmas tree, he took me up the garland draped staircase and went straight for the bedroom at the top of the stairs. To his parent's room.

I stopped, digging my heels into the carpet. "Where are you go-ing?" I whispered.

"To get my mum," he said at normal volume.

"You can't tell them."

"Why—"

"Keep your voice down." I glanced nervously at the door behind him. It remained closed.

"My mum," he said quietly, "can help with your back and my dad can phone the police. That maniac should be in jail."

I wish it were that simple. "You can't do that."

"Why the bloody hell not?"

"Because then we'll all have to find a new place to live. That house, if you follow the rules, is by far the easiest one to live in."

His bright green eyes stormed with conviction. "I can't just not do anything."

"I'm asking you to."

He looked over his shoulder at the closed door. After a few seconds of silence, he faced me. "At least let me take you to the hospital. You need stitches."

I shook my head. "They aren't that bad." The split skin across my back called me a liar. "I can take care of them myself. Do you have a first aid kit?"

He nodded. "Yeah. I think there's one in the linen closet." Quickly he turned and went deeper down the dark hall.

Out from under his watchful eye, my shoulders sagged forward. I closed my eyes against the searing pain. Keeping my breaths shallow, as not to tear the skin further, I made my way to Blake's room.

Pushing open the door, I flicked on the light. The sudden change of brightness stung my eyes.

His suitcase was open at the end of his bed. Laundry burst over the zipper and textbooks lay scattered on the floor.

A wave of guilt rolled down my spine. *He comes home for the holidays and I immediately ruin it by being stupid. Why did I have to take the money?* Living at Denny's wasn't the worst thing in the world. Most of the time at least.

Crossing the room, I stepped into the bathroom and carefully lifted the thick hoodie material over my shoulders. I twisted my back to the mirror to assess the damage.

The two new lashes were surrounded by angry red skin. Smudged with fresh blood, the new wounds stood out against the mosaic of old scars covering my back. Fortunately, these new wounds weren't the worst ones I'd received.

"Bloody hell, Charlie."

Dropping my hoodie, I met Blake's horrified gaze. A thousand lies rushed up my throat at once. I knew which ones would placate him and which ones might downplay what he'd seen. But the look on his face, heartbroken and dejected, caused each one to fall apart.

Wordlessly, I dropped my gaze and took the first aid kit. He opened his mouth, probably to offer to help, but I quickly closed the door before he could. I stood there for a moment, with my eyes closed and forehead pressed to the wood.

You knew the rules. Why did you have to be so stupid?

Because you can't help but run.

A warm trickle of blood followed the curve of my spine. I brought up the hem of my hoodie and trapped it firmly between my teeth.

Using a handful of Kleenexes, I mopped up the blood the best I could. My hands trembled from the aftermath of the adrenaline so I ended up smearing it more than cleaning it.

I grabbed the gauze from the first aid kit and squeezed a thick layer of Neosporin on it. I winced as I placed the cool cream on my skin. Swiftly, I ripped a strip of medical tape with my teeth and secured the gauze in place.

Once all the wounds were covered, I pulled my hoodie from my mouth and met my reflection in the bathroom mirror. My eyes, a tepid combination of light blue and grey, were lined with the fine red line of exhaustion and unshed tears.

I thought of my best friend on the other side of the door and what was going to happen next. I had two tricks up my sleeve, lie or run. I couldn't lie my way out because he saw the scars across my back—the truth of my situation across the street. Cornered in that small bathroom, there wasn't a way for me to sneak quietly away. I was trapped with only one way out.

I had to face him . . . and watch the best thing in my life crumble. There was no coming back from this. Taking a deep breath, I steeled myself and opened the door.

Blake jumped to his feet.

In the time it took for me to patch myself up, Blake had shoved his still packed suitcase into his closet. Dirty clothes stuck out from underneath the door. His impatient hands had moved little things around, a stack of textbooks here and a pair of shoes there. Now that we were face to face, he stared.

My feet acted as if they were glued between the bathroom tile and the carpet of his room. I wanted to say something. I needed to say something, but as I looked at him no words came.

"I made you some hot chocolate." He gestured to the mug on the nightstand.

My eyes followed to the mug on top of a stack of books. Rich coils of steam curled up from the rim.

The gesture was sweet. Knowing it was my favorite drink, he must have thought it would comfort me. But I still couldn't get my mouth to open. I dropped my gaze to my hands. My fidgeting fingers went to work removing the blood from under my nails.

"Can I get you anything else? Aspirin, maybe?" I shook my head.

He crossed his arms. More silence ticked by. "Why didn't you tell me he . . ."

"I didn't want to bother you with it," I mumbled.

"That's rubbish."

"It really wasn't that bad." I gave him a smile as fake as American cheese. "It looks worse than it actually is."

His eyes narrowed further. "How many times has he done it?"

"It doesn't matter."

"How many bloody times?"

I turned back to studying my hands. "Three or four. But I was being stupid. He has a very specific set of rules."

"Bloody hell!" He said it so loud I wondered if his parents heard him down the hall. "Don't ever say something like that again. You should've told me. Then I could've done something other than punch the wanker across the room."

"And how was that conversation supposed to go?" I demanded. "Oh, hey Blake! Welcome back from school. What's new with me? Nothing really. I'm still a nineteen year old high school dropout. I still work my two deadbeat jobs. And, oh, I almost forgot, I got three new scars last month. What's new with you?" I took a moment to calm myself. "I didn't say anything because when I'm out of that house I want to forget."

"How's that working out for you?"

It wasn't.

"You should stay here." He looked down at his red knuckles. "My parents will let you have the guest room until we figure something else out."

"We aren't telling them," I said firmly.

"You can't go back there."

"I don't have a choice. It's where I belong."

My shoulders sagged upon hearing that statement out loud. I never took Blake's friendship for granted. I always knew we were from two different worlds. He was a prep school genius with doting parents and a bright future. I had none of those things. I never felt the differences between us more sharply than I did in that moment.

"You can't seriously believe that," he said softly.

"I was found in a trashcan as a newborn and labeled as cursed by every family I've ever been assigned to. If that isn't a message from the universe, then I don't know what is."

Blake shook his head. "We'll figure something out, but you're not going back there." He moved toward the door. "I'm going to crash on the couch. Let me know if you need anything."

The door clicked shut behind him.

Alone, I walked stiffly over to the bed and perched on the side. The knots in my stomach tightened at the smell of the hot chocolate.

Carefully, I curled up on my side, hugging my knees tightly to my chest. What Blake didn't know was I had tried to figure something out. Nothing worked. Nothing panned out.

At fourteen, three weeks into living on Haven Avenue, my short fuse and quick wit got the better of me. Denny called me a street rat. I called him a fat bastard. He broke my skin right there at the kitchen counter.

From then on, I plotted and schemed how I would make a break for it, where I would go, and how I'd duck out from the search parties.

I ran when my first wounds were still healing. The police found me a week later sleeping in a spillway pipe.

I tried to tell a social worker about Denny's punishments, but no one believed a kid with a record of destruction—fires, burns, broken windows, and shattered lights. Denny simply told them that the marks on my back were the result of self-harm as a way to get attention. He repaid my plea for help with five lashes.

Like clockwork, every few months I was out the door. Each time I managed to stay hidden a bit longer. A week and then two. My longest stretch was a month. I learned from the older kids, with more breakout stories, how to blend in, how to stay hidden, where to find food and shelter. But no matter how many tricks I learned or how far I roamed, someone always returned me to Haven Avenue and my back bled with the consequences.

At sixteen, I asked to move to another house, but with my history, no matter how hard I tried to explain that none of it was my fault, no one wanted to take me in. It was easier for me to stay with Denny. The social workers hoped the stability of staying in one place long term would mellow me out. The terror of my living nightmare had the same effect.

So, I stayed. My escape attempts dwindled as I learned to keep my head down and follow the rules. Even after I aged out of the program, I stayed. At least I had a roof and food. On my own those things weren't guaranteed.

I squeezed my eyes shut and wished for the umpteenth time I was strong enough to leave. I was a good liar, but not good enough to convince myself that would ever happen.

3

I Don't Break Easy

The alarm on my phone sang from my pocket.

I peeled my eyelids back and squinted around the room for a clock. My groggy mind was confused when I didn't see the other twin bed or the bleak grey walls. Instead, I was looking at the eclectic collection of posters on the navy blue walls that made up Blake's room.

The night before rushed in with no mercy.

Denny.

The money.

Blake.

Groaning, I buried my head under my arms. The stiff scabs across my back tightened painfully over my muscles. With a grimace, I breathed slowly as not to agitate the wounds further.

How am I going to get out of this one?

When kids in school started to notice the blood stains on the back of my shirts, I found a seat in the back or ditched class. When coworkers questioned it, I found a new job. But I didn't want to run away from Blake. He was the saving grace of Haven Avenue.

Rolling into a sitting position, I dug my phone out of my back pocket and silenced the alarm. It was five in the morning and I had to get to work.

My clothes reeked of broiled burger patties and spilled bar drinks. I thought about going back to Denny's to change but the thought was fleeting. I wasn't ready to go back. No one had ever stood up to Denny like Blake did. I could only imagine just how pissed he was . . . and where the blame would then fall.

Tiptoeing across the room, I grabbed one of Blake's shirts from the floor of his closet. Carefully, I pulled myself free of my bloodied hoodie and tugged Blake's shirt over my head.

With no other coat, I pulled on my hoodie to fight against the December cold. Crossing the room, I eased the bedroom door open and peered down the darkened hall.

The front door was right beside the living room. With Blake sleeping on the couch there was no way I could sneak past him and not wake him up. I was too tired and too sore to face him again, even though I knew it was inevitable.

Softly closing the door, I moved to the window on the other side of Blake's room. It framed a dreary street view of Haven Avenue. From where his window sat, it looked right across the road to my room at Denny's.

That explained how he knew to come over. He must've been watching to make sure I didn't take longer than five minutes after my restaurant shift.

I looked away and unlatched the window. It slid soundlessly open. A wave of cold, unforgiving winter air rushed over me. Cars on the interstate whispered in the distance.

I popped the screen out of the frame and set it on the floor beside the sill. Ducking down, I stepped through, careful to avoid the lingering patches of snow. It took me a few minutes to wiggle the window closed.

My breath clouded the air before me as I turned to face the street.

My room at Denny's faced a large oak tree. The branches reached toward the small house as if it wanted to engulf the whole thing. Years of patient growing, weathering storms, and pruning had directed a thick branch to parallel the roof outside my window. That branch was my accomplice in many escape attempts.

Blake's yard had no such tree.

I crept to the edge of the roof and peered over the gutter. Maybe it was the early morning darkness, but it didn't look that far.

If I can lower myself over the edge, I thought, *the drop won't be so bad.*

I looked at the gutter and calculated what I would hold on to and how I would swing myself over. Not wanting to be late for my shift, I inched closer to the edge. I shifted my weight, preparing to lay on my side. My thought was to then roll my legs over the edge and grab the gutter to lower myself down.

But I didn't notice the shingles beneath my Converse were covered in ice. The moment I shifted, my feet slipped out from under me. My legs shot over the edge with no time to grab the gutter.

My heart jumped into my throat. A spark, hot and shocking, burst at the center of my chest as gravity pulled me down. I squeezed my eyes shut—*Not here.*

The fiery warmth filled my chest, wrapping around my ribcage, pressing against my skin. The pressure built, pressing against my lungs, filling me with dread.

My shoulder slammed into the sidewalk. The impact threw my head down next. Behind my eyelids there was a bright pop, followed shortly by the sound of falling glass. The freshly scabbed wounds on my back howled as I rolled into the lawn.

Squeezing my eyes shut, I forced the fiery warmth back into my chest. I didn't realize I wasn't breathing until my lungs ached.

"Charlie!"

Crap.

"Let me call you back, mate." Footsteps pounded against the sidewalk seconds before sturdy hands rolled me on to my back. Blake stared down at me, appalled. "What the bloody hell was that?"

"I didn't want to wake you," I wheezed.

"So, you climbed out the damn window?"

"I do it all the time." Sucking in a deep breath, I placed my hands against the frozen ground and pushed myself into the sitting position.

"What are you doing?" Blake's voice echoed down the empty street. "Charlie, stay down before you hurt yourself. Let me call an ambulance."

"I'm fine." Ignoring his pleas, I staggered to my feet. "See?"

My shoulder hurt like I had lost an arm wrestling match with a freight train and my head was going to smart for the rest of the day, but that was it. To demonstrate, I patted myself down, checking all the important bones. Nothing ached any worse than it already did.

"You fell off the *roof.*" Blake twisted around to look at the offending ledge.

"It's not that high," I assured him. I glanced around to make sure he was the only one who saw that. There was no one, but the light across the street was dark. *The pop and the sound of breaking glass—*

"Not high?" He spun back to face me. "It's high enough for you to break something important. I'm going to call an ambulance."

I grabbed the sleeve of his jacket before he could reach for his phone. "I'm *fine,* Blake. I can do a cartwheel if that will convince you."

"No, you bloody won't."

"Relax. I don't break easy," I said with a soft smile that I hoped would put his concerns to rest.

At that, memories from the night before must have crept into his mind. The concern I saw there doubled. And then I saw the one emotion I never wanted to see flitted across his handsome face—the number one reason why I didn't talk about the shitty cards that fate dealt me. Blake looked at me with pity.

Releasing his sleeve, I stepped back. "I need to get going or I'll be late for my shift at the coffee shop."

"What are you going to do after that?"

"I have a shift at the diner."

"And after that?"

I knew why he was asking, but I couldn't bring myself to say it. I had disappointed him enough already.

He made a distressed sound in the back of his throat. "You can't go back there. Let me talk to my parents. We can—"

"Do you really think Denny is just going to let me live across the street?"

"Then I'll get you out of town. I was just on the phone with one of my friends. He might have a place—"

"You don't get it." I shook my head. "I'm cursed."

My hands clenched around each other until my fingertips dug into the spaces between my bones. The confession was lined up on my tongue, ready to be uttered with only the push of a breath. But my dearest friend was already looking at me in a different light. I didn't want to hand him the nails to fasten the lid over the coffin of what we once were. Or maybe the lid was already in place and it was just a matter of putting it to rest.

"I'm going to be late." Ducking my head, I turned to the street. "I've already been late once this month. I can't lose this job. Denny likes the extra cash. It keeps him off my back."

"Charlie, please—"

"I have to go." I shoved my hands into the pocket of my light blue hoodie. "You should get some rest," I called over my shoulder. "Before jet lag gets the best of you."

I took off, leaving his protests behind. My jogging steps took me across the snowy sidewalk and around the corner. The ache in my shoulder and the torn skin on my back stung with my hurried steps.

By the time I covered ten blocks north and three east, my cheeks were flushed, and the cold only clung to the tip of my nose and the crests of my ears. I pulled my long hair into a knotted twist at the base of my neck and pushed through the glass doors into the coffee shop. For once I was on time.

I traded my light blue hoodie for a green apron and ducked under the counter. I threw myself into the familiar routine of pulling shots and pumping syrup. I hoped the quick pace of the shift would help me forget last night, at least for a while.

A wave of laughter rolled through the drive through window. As I waited for the milk to heat, I looked toward the sound.

A minivan of college aged girls giggled at the barista handing them their drinks. No matter how early it was, Troy always managed to make the drive through window a fun place to be. With a wink or a perfectly timed compliment, he charmed everyone who came by. Our tips doubled when he was on the shift.

I looked at the car full of girls as they handed over a couple crumpled dollars. Even though the sun wasn't up, they looked ready to face the day. They smiled easily and laughed without reservation. Their personalities just sparkled out of them.

I couldn't help but wonder what would have happened if someone had found me who wanted me. If, when I was lifted out of Tuesday's trash, a nice, quiet family had taken me in. Would I be going to college, fumbling my way through classes I didn't want to take?

But that wasn't the problem.

Plenty of couples wanted to rescue a baby with a sad backstory. What was more heroic than saying they wanted a baby someone threw out with the leftovers? It was the curse under my skin that forced me out of homes and welcome arms.

I turned my back to the drive through window as the girls pulled away. My gaze dropped to my hands, small and unassuming.

"Let me go!" I cried.

"Jane, honey, you have to come out," the woman said sweetly. Her fingers tightened around my hands. "You haven't eaten anything since you got here."

"Leave me alone." I leaned back into the corner of the closet, trying to break her hold. At the age of eleven, I had some strength behind my scrawny form.

But she continued to hold on. And she continued to pull and smile, but she didn't understand. I was hungry, starving even, but there were too many lights to shatter, too many nice things that would break around me.

In my attempts to protect her perfect little home, my anxiety flared. Warmth broke through my chest and hummed through my ribcage. It flushed down over my shoulder before I could warn her.

The lightbulb overhead shattered. Glass sparkled through the dimming light to the floor. The mother fell back with a scream.

Her husband came running.

"She burned me!" she cried. "She burned me!"

He turned her soft, delicate hands toward him. The hallway light flickered in time with my heartbeat. Lit by that flashing light, both of us saw the crimson blisters covering her hands.

In unison they turned their gazes to my small, empty hands.

The steamer spit and fussed, spraying my apron with milk. Snapping to the present, I jumped back into work. Memories drifted back to the past where they continued to haunt. Even the rising pressure in my chest dulled under the routine of working the bar.

4

The Ticket

"Hey, Charlie!"

Haleigh stuck her head into the kitchen. Propped on her shoulder was a tray topped with six burgers and their corresponding sides of fries. She stood with one hip cocked, like she wasn't holding anything at all.

As soon as my shift at the coffee shop ended, I walked to the other side of town back to the diner. At this time of the afternoon, the place roared with lively conversations and Christmas music. If Haleigh wasn't standing a few feet away, I wouldn't have been able to hear her.

"That British kid of yours is asking for you at the front." She spun around; her ponytail swung between her shoulders as she left the kitchen.

I finished filling a glass of lemonade and looked over the crowded bar. Sure enough, Blake stood by the host stand surrounded by a small group of grinning high school girls.

Cheese and rice, he looks so out of place.

He wore an off-white turtleneck sweater that contrasted pleasantly with his dark skin. Over the sweater was a fine grey coat with a row of shiny black buttons. Embroidered in silver thread on the right lapel was a tree with a mess of roots encased in a circle. He brushed a hand over the top of his tight curls as he searched the restaurant staff moving quickly from table to table.

With a sigh, I stepped into the crowded room and handed out the refills to one of my tables. Unable to avoid it any longer, I weaved my way toward the front door.

Blake saw me coming and met me at the least populated corner of the bar. A neon *Budweiser* sign hummed beside us on the wall.

"Is that my shirt?" he blurted.

I looked down at the oversized graphic tee. It was smudged with barbeque sauce and . . . either mashed potatoes or butter. Since it was so big, I knotted the excess material in the front. The creases held the remnants from dirty plates.

"I'll wash it before I give it back," I said in a rush. "I would have worn my hoodie but—well, you know there was blood . . . on . . . it."

Nicely done, idiot.

Blake scratched the top of his head, dislodging his ebony curls. "And," dropping his voice, he leaned forward, "how are you feeling?"

I closed my eyes, wishing to go back in time. "Just sore."

"Are you certain? After that fall, something could be bleeding internally and you'd never even know."

"I've been on my feet for over twelve hours. I think I'd notice if I were bleeding into my abdomen."

He shook his head.

Over Blake's shoulder, Tee exited the kitchen. She raised an eyebrow at me just standing there. "Blake, I'm grateful that you want to check up on me, but I really need to get back to work."

"I can't have you go back to that house." He reached into his coat pocket.

"I'll be fine. Denny probably burned himself out by now. I'll get a strong lecture and that'll be the end of it." The lie made my spirits sink lower.

"You won't be here long enough to see the end of it. You're leaving." He slapped an envelope on the counter and slid it toward me. "I don't want you anywhere near him ever again, so this is the only solution I could come up with."

Curiosity jerked my hand toward the envelope. Apprehension kept the stark white paper trapped between my fingers and the bar top. There was an intensity I had never seen before in Blake's eyes.

Slowly, I lifted it up. It hardly weighed anything. Turning up the flap, I pulled out a single slip of paper.

It was a bus ticket to Vegas.

One that left at midnight.

"No." I crammed the ticket back into the envelope and shoved it back at him. "Do you know what Denny would do if he found that on me?"

"That's why you're going tonight. He won't find out until you're gone." He pushed it back.

"I can't."

"You will because if you don't show up, I'll put you on the damn coach myself."

"It's called a bus." I clasped my hands, refusing to touch the envelope. "I can't just leave. I have jobs. Everything I know is here."

"Be honest with me, do you really want this?"

No. Of course not. But I dared not say anything in case fate decided to screw me over again.

"Your life doesn't have to be like this." Blake leaned closer as another server walked by our hushed conversation. "Take the ticket and get on the coach or bus or whatever you call it. I have a friend who said you can use his flat and he could give you a job at his café. Problem solved."

I looked back at the envelope. As if my body was reminding me of the punishment I'd face for leaving, the wounds on my back ached. Besides, there were worse things than that house. Like sleeping under a bridge.

"If Denny knew you helped me—"

"I can handle myself."

Blake snatched the envelope from the bar top and stuffed it into the front of my apron. When I reached to pull it out, he snagged my wrist.

"I meant what I said. If you don't come, I will drag you out of that house. Please don't make me do that, Charlie." Reluctantly, he turned away. The bell above the door chimed as he exited the restaurant.

I yanked the ticket from my apron and went back into the kitchen.

Away from prying eyes, I held it over the trashcan. My hand trembled, making the white paper shudder. No matter how badly I wanted to, my hand wouldn't release the envelope.

Fate had practically handed me what I always wanted. But I couldn't tell if it was a miracle or a live wire.

Cursing, I stuck it in the front pocket of my jeans. For the rest of the shift, the ticket poked my leg, and the same question ran through my mind.

Could I really leave?

As much as I couldn't get freedom out of my head, I also couldn't forget my throbbing back.

After work I pulled on my hoodie and trudged back through the snow. With each step, my heart grew heavier. I stopped outside Denny's house and pulled the ticket out once more. I was tempted to rip it up and throw it into the snow.

Out of habit, I pulled my foot from my shoe and placed the ticket on the bottom. As I slipped my foot back in, I opened the door.

Just like the night before, the house was silent. I quickly ducked toward the stairs. *Maybe everyone's asleep—*

Denny waited for me at the top.

The overhead light pulsed once as my heart skipped. I squashed the burning pressure before the lights could flicker again.

He hadn't thrown anything at me. That was a good sign. He didn't seem eager to get too close either. Maybe Blake punching him in the face had worked.

The bruise on his cheek was dark blue and lined with a mixture of red and purple. His eye was horribly blood shot. A small seed of satisfaction bloomed inside me at the sight of it.

I placed one foot on the bottom step. When he didn't stop me, I climbed up to meet him. At the top, I unfolded my apron and placed my tips in the palm of his hand.

He still didn't move. "Are you hiding any?"

The wounds on my back tingled. I had learned that lesson. "That's all of it."

He glanced down at the wad of cash. "You had more last night."

I shrugged and winced. "It was a slow shift."

He leaned down so we were face to face, searching for any sign of a lie. The strong smell of cigar smoke plagued my nose, but I didn't dare move. Every muscle in my body stiffened as his hand dipped into my pockets.

My toes curled around the envelope in my shoe.

When he found nothing but lint, he stepped back. "I don't want to see that British kid here again. If I do, you'll be sorry." Shouldering his way past, he headed down the stairs.

"And if I left?" The words blurted from my mouth. My heart slammed into my ribcage.

"You leave?" Laughing, Denny turned on the stairs. "And where would you go? Need I remind you of what you are? A drop out." He stepped up toward me. "A runaway." Another step. "Something someone threw out with the trash."

He was in front of me now. Eye to eye. "No one even bothered to name you. Accept it, Jane Doe. You keep fantasizing that what's outside of this house is better. And that's all it is. A fantasy. The sooner you accept that, the happier you'll be. This house is the best thing that'll ever happened to you." Turning away, he continued down the stairs and into the kitchen.

No. He's wrong.

I rushed into my room and slammed the door behind me. In the dark, facing two empty beds and a floor scattered with piles of clothes, I paused.

He's wrong . . . right?

Kicking off my sneakers, I pulled out the envelope and peered at the ticket inside.

No matter how hard I tried I wouldn't be able to keep my mouth shut or keep my temper in check or plot some escape route, inevitably breaking one of Denny's rules. Everything that made me *me* would bring me right back here, taping wounds. The only thing here was a hell I had become frighteningly familiar with.

The answer was so simple. All I had to do was get on that bus.

Is Denny right? Had I been romanticizing life outside of these grey walls? Who was to say that it would be any kinder than life here? What could life offer someone like me?

Drop out.

Runaway.

Something someone threw out with the trash.

Something no one even bothered to name.

I chose the name Charlie. It was one of the few things that was truly mine, through and through. But maybe I was just trying to put lipstick on a pig, dressing something up in hopes that it could pass as something that belonged.

What did the world outside of Kansas have to offer me?

I set the ticket on the bed opposite mine, the miracle, my escape. I crawled into bed and curled myself around my pillow. I stared across the room at the small piece of paper until my eyelids grew heavy and I fell into a restless sleep.

5

Everything's Going to Be Ok

Knock knock knock.

I jolted upright. Shoving the hair out of my face, I looked for the guilty party. My room was empty and the door was closed. The light in the hallway was even shut off.

The sound came again.

I jumped to my feet so fast the sheets tangled around my legs. Just as my tailbone connected with the hardwood, I saw Blake sitting outside my window.

My panic evaporated instantly. Kicking the sheets off my legs, I moved across the bed and shoved open the window.

"Do you have any idea what time it is?" I snapped as crisp winter air rushed into the room.

"Funny, I was going to ask you the same thing." Shoving past me, Blake dropped to the floor. "Your coach was supposed to leave ten minutes ago. I paid the driver to wait." He stopped, his eyes scanning the room. "Where's your bag?"

I shoved my hands into the pocket of my hoodie. "I'm not leaving."

When he faced me, his eyebrows were pulled together, not in pity, but concern. "You *have* to get out of here, Charlie."

"I can't."

"You mean you won't." When I didn't answer, Blake looked helplessly at the window. "I go back to school in a week. I can't leave you here."

"You have for the last five years."

"And I hate myself for it. I should have—" He took a composing deep breath. "Let me help you now. Please let me get you out of here."

My door flew open.

"How many times have I told you to keep that window shut?"

Denny stumbled into the room. His words were slurred as he struggled to wake up.

Blake and I froze as his eyes moved from the open window to me. For a moment, one stupid moment, I thought he wouldn't see Blake at all.

When Denny saw him, he became fully conscious. "What the hell are you doing in here?"

Blake didn't even flinch. I, on the other hand, jumped behind Blake without realizing I moved.

"I thought I told you I didn't want to see him again, Jane." Denny's eyes never left my human shield.

"Oh, you won't see me anymore. I'm taking *Charlie* out of here."

My heart flipped inside out. "What are you doing?" I hissed. My eyes flew to Denny.

"If you won't leave, then I'm taking you. Where's your bag?"

Denny's eyes narrowed. "What's he talking about?"

"Exactly what I said." Blake turned toward me. "Grab your bag."

"That's not how this works." Denny moved to side step Blake. Every muscle stiffened as I prepared for him to grab me. Closing my eyes tight, I hugged my arms, hoping it would block whatever he was planning.

But he never touched me.

Blake stepped forward, right in his path. He stood a few inches from Denny, staring boldly into the older man's eyes.

"I should call the police for what you did to her," Blake said quietly, but that didn't mean his tone lacked an edge. "Or at least break your hands so you can never hold a fist again. The only reason I'm not, is because *Charlie* asked me not to. But that only extends so far. You can either let us go or I can beat you into the floor right here."

"You can't lay a finger on me in my own house."

"I already did." Without breaking eye contact, Blake inclined his head toward me. "Charlie, get your bag, please."

Dropping to my knees, I reached under my bed. Ages ago I had cut a hole in the underside of the mattress. At first it was to hide tiny treasures like chocolate and fruit from the other kids. Now, it held only one thing. Reaching into the old mattress, I yanked out my escape bag.

"We have a bus to catch," Blake said once I was standing. "You're going to stand there and let us leave. If you follow, both of your eyes will be the same color."

Denny's black eye twitched.

"If you try to follow her or call the police to bring her back, I'll be on your doorstep. And trust me, mate, I can do more than bruise your face. Do I make myself clear?"

Denny's face flushed as if fire smoldered under his skin.

Blake shifted forward. "Do I make myself clear?"

"Do you know that she was left out with the trash?" Denny seethed. "Her own flesh and blood didn't even want her. But if you do, fine. Good luck with the demons under her skin."

My gaze flew to Blake. Had Denny's declaration swayed him to leave me here? Relief flooded down my spine when Blake turned to me and ushered me to the window.

Keeping his body between Denny and me, Blake helped me on to the roof. The shingles groaned under my weight as I tiptoed to the overgrown tree. Carefully grabbing the branches, I let myself down into the powdery snow.

I looked up to the window where Denny watched us. He held my gaze for a moment and then he pulled the window closed.

Cheese and rice, he's really letting me go.

Blake dropped beside me and kicked the snow off his shoes. Placing a hand gently on my back, he guided me down Haven Avenue.

I craned my neck to look over my shoulder. My brain couldn't process it all. Was this the last time I was going to see that house? To be on this street? To be in this sunbaked city?

When we stepped onto West Crawford Street, the bright red and blue colors of the 24/7 gas station came into view. A long, tall dark blue bus was parked in front of the station. A cloud of exhaust plumed around the bumper as the engine rumbled.

Blake didn't waste a second. He herded me to the doors. A sleepy-eyed bus driver looked down at me.

This was it.

I was leaving.

No one was going to come looking for me.

I was getting out with no strings to pull me back.

I couldn't comprehend it. I looked over my shoulder, down the street to the way we had come, expecting Denny to be barreling toward us. But the only thing to occupy the sidewalk were heaps of dirty snow.

Blake dug into his jacket and handed me another envelope; this one was thicker than the last.

"I assume you got rid of your ticket, so you'll have to use mine. In there," he pointed to the envelope in my hands, "is my friend's address. It's just in case he doesn't pick you up at the station. There's also some money if you get hungry on the road."

My eyes jerked up to meet his. "You were coming with me?"

"Of course."

I stared up at him. Gratitude and adoration swirled through my chest, choking off a reply.

"I'll stay a couple days here to make sure Denny doesn't do anything stupid, then I'll make my way to you." He leaned down to meet my gaze, making sure he had my full attention. "Everything's going to be ok."

Those last six words burst the tension rising in my chest. I actually believed him.

"Off you pop." Blake nudged me toward the steps. "I'll see you soon."

A grin stretched over my lips. *This is happening.* Taking a deep breath, I stepped up to the driver. As I stood there waiting for him to process my information, I glanced back at Blake. He smiled up at me. The driver handed my ticket back and gestured for me to find a seat. His old wrinkled hands reached for the lever to close the doors.

"Wait!" Dropping my bag to the floor, I rushed out of the bus and threw my arms around Blake's neck.

"Thank you," I whispered into his shoulder as I squeezed him tighter. "*Thank you.*"

Blake held me just as tight. "I wish I had done it sooner."

"You're doing it now." My voice trembled as moisture seeped into my eyes, blurring my vision.

He pulled back and smiled down at me. "You were made for more than this. And I'm going to prove it to you when we meet up, ok?"

I nodded with a watery smile. "Ok."

He tipped his head back to the bus. "Go on then."

Wiping the moisture from my eyes, I climbed back on to the bus with more *life*. Breathing easier, I picked up my bag and floated down the aisle. While other passengers saw their seats as the dotted line between two places, I saw freedom, possibilities, a fresh start.

I sank into the only window seat left and peered down at my best friend.

Shivering against the cold, Blake waved.

My heart pounded against my ribs. I felt like a goldfish who had spent its entire life in a bowl and was just released into a lake. Salina was my fishbowl. The vastness of the world expanded around me making me feel unbearably small.

But it was going to be ok. Blake said it was going to be ok.

With a roar that rumbled through the cabin, the bus jerked away from the curb. I gripped the armrests as the bus driver pulled away from the gas station. My best friend grew smaller until we turned, cutting him from view.

As we accelerated on to the highway, I settled back into my seat and hugged my backpack to my chest. For the first time in my life, I felt like I was moving forward.

6

Excuse Me, Love

Of course, the first time I left the state, it was in the middle of the night.

The midnight hour hid everything but passing cars and the brief glimpses of yellow and white lane paint. After a few hours I assumed the bus was nearing the Kansas-Colorado border, but there was no proof.

The inside of the bus wasn't better. Most of my fellow passengers were taking advantage of the late departure to sleep. I was too wound up to close my eyes longer than a blink. Only a few were awake. A man a few rows up had his phone flashlight directed toward a book in his lap. Across from me, an older lady was knitting a pair of socks. The rhythmic clicking of her needles could just barely be heard over the roar of the engine.

Resting my chin on my backpack, I stared out the window. *I wish I could see something.* I had been in Kansas nineteen years. I just wanted a peek at what the rest of the world was like.

Carefully, I leaned back into my padded seat. The cushion, while stiff, was kind to the tender scabs on my back. Staring at the passing darkness, I tried to picture what Vegas would be like. What anything would be like.

"Excuse me, love. Is this seat open?"

Jerking away from the window, I looked up at the stranger smirking over me.

He had an unkempt look of shaggy dark hair and scruffy cheeks. Multiple earrings dangled from the curves of both ears. One was in the shape of a human molar.

The tall man was dressed completely in black with a leather trench coat wrapped snugly around him. Tattoos peeked out from around his clothes; the hilt of a sword was on his neck. He had a black heart inked on the back of one hand and a curved spine on the other.

"My seatmate has been snoring ever since we left the station," he said with an Irish accent. "I'm surprised you can't hear him from here."

How was I supposed to react? Obviously normal would be the best choice . . . but I couldn't remember what that even looked like.

"I know I look rough," he said, catching my assessing gaze. "Would you believe me if I said it's laundry day and this is all I've got?"

No. He looked like the type that broke bones for a living, but his wide grin said otherwise. There was a spark in his whiskey colored eyes that simmered with hidden laughter, as if we were a part of a joke that only we knew about.

"Or not," he said, straightening to his full height. "I respect a lass who likes her space. But I will warn you, I'm excellent company and you're sending me back to hours of endless torture at the hands of that man's nasal cavity."

He paused. "Did the guilt trip help at all?"

Against my will, I found the corners of my lips lifting. "A little."

"Brilliant." His eyes lit up. "I am a damsel in desperate need of rescuing. Please, save me from my misery."

"You hardly look like a damsel."

He followed my gaze to his thick leather trench coat, his ripped, and mended jeans to the heavy combat boots. "Like I said, love, it's laundry day."

Against my better judgment, I shifted closer to the window. "The seat is open."

"You're a godsend." Without missing a beat, he dropped into the seat beside me with a grin. The faint scent of cigarette smoke wafted from his jacket. "What's your name, blue eyes?"

"Charlie."

He held out his tattooed hand. "Arthur Atlas, but you can call me Atlas."

I placed my hand in his just as we went over a bump. He ripped his hand out of mine to catch himself against the seat in front of him.

He shot an annoyed glance at the driver. "Where are you going?" He tugged his phone free from his coat and started typing.

"Vegas."

He nodded and slipped his phone back into his pocket. "Not bad. What for?"

I hesitated. Why did this Irish god care about an average girl from Kansas? I fought the urge to pinch myself.

He picked up on my slow response. "I don't mean to be nosy."

"No!" *Ah, too loud.* "Sorry, um." *Cheese and rice, Charlie, can you even form a sentence?* "I'm staying with a friend of a friend."

"What made you—" His phone rang from his pocket. "Excuse me for a moment. It's my boss." He unlocked the phone and answered in a language of drawls and rolled sounds. With one more smile, he turned to the aisle, putting his back to me.

I quickly turned to my reflection in the window. Frantically, I combed my fingers through my hair. I made sure my hair was as flat as it could be and I didn't have anything hanging from my nose before I turned around. He still had his back toward me.

I glanced at my reflection and mentally kicked myself. My light blue hoodie was splattered with stains, not to mention the number of holes in my jeans. I looked homeless.

Cheese and rice, what am I doing? Remember the last guy you thought was nice? He put scars on your back.

With a sigh of defeat, I decided not to make a fool of myself.

Hugging my backpack to my chest, I continued to watch the mile markers pass. A black sedan pulled alongside the bus and coasted by my window.

I was about to turn away from the car when the window rolled down.

A blond man smirked up at me.

That's it? I expected something cruder.

Just as Atlas hung up something flashed outside my window. The blond guy shined a light from his hand. He mouthed, "Hold on," and sped to the front of the bus.

"Alright." Atlas replaced the phone in his pocket. "Where were we?" He followed my gaze through the window.

The sedan's brake lights flared as the vehicle slowed alongside the bus driver's window. The blond extended his arm out of the sedan and aimed something at the driver. He was too far ahead and the night was too dark for me to see what he held.

Atlas cursed as a flash of gold shot from the blonde's hand and struck the front wheel.

A loud pop sounded from the front. Passengers startled awake as the bus swerved sharply to the right. Following the momentum, Atlas slid into my seat, crushing me against the window. Screams rose over the noise of thumping rubber. Car horns blared. Pressed against the glass, my eyes widened as the asphalt drew closer to the window. The bus was tilting.

Squeezing my eyes shut, I screamed as the bus fell on its side. Glass shattered. Sparks lit behind my eyelids as the metal grated across the interstate.

Then the bus started to roll.

Atlas was ripped away as I tumbled out of my seat and landed on the roof. I was thrown back into the seats seconds before someone landed on top of me. My head struck an armrest and everything went black.

7

Molten Sunlight and Scars

Light pierced my eyelids.

A sharp ache pulsed from behind my ear. With each heartbeat the pain enfolded my skull. Prying my eyes open, I flinched back from the bright track lights.

I was on the ceiling of the bus. Hanging above me were rows of empty seats. Cool air seeped through the gaping windows of jagged glass.

Motionless, bloody bodies were scattered all around me. Some hung out of the windows, but most were piled on top of each other. The air was thick with the scent of spilled gasoline and metallic blood.

Rolling onto my side, I pushed up to my elbows. Glass tumbled out of my hair and clinked against the ceiling beneath me. The pounding in my head doubled, forcing my eyes shut.

Breathing slow, I pulled my attention from my screaming skull to the rest of my body. My back ached, but that could have just been from Denny. My knees and palms stung from the broken glass beneath them.

Forcing my eyes wide, I looked down the length of my body. Nothing was jutting out of me. A few patches on my blue jeans were dotted with blood, but it wasn't major. The old woman who had been knitting across from me lay over my feet. Her head was nearly twisted all the way around. The right side of her skull glistened with red. The yarn from her knitting was tangled around her.

I patted down the front of my hoodie. Nothing felt broken.

Mumbled voices broke through the eerie silence.

With a shaky hand, I pushed my hair back, searching for the sound. I thought it would be the police, but there were no blue and red flashing lights coming from outside.

"This is a fucking mess, dude." A man ducked through the warped hole that used to be the windshield. With a scrunched nose, he kicked a bloodied limb away from his boots.

Another man, shorter by several inches, followed him in. "I didn't see you coming up with any better ideas on how to deal with the hunter."

Ice poured through my veins. The short one was the blond from the sedan. *Did he shoot the front tire?*

My eyes snapped to his hands, expecting a gun. The only thing clutched in his meaty fist was a slender piece of black wood. I thought the track lights of the bus reflected on its surface, but then the reflection should've been icy white. Beneath his fingers, the surface of the stick glimmered a warm, vibrant gold. The fine tip of the stick glowed with it too.

"Any sign of him?" the tall one asked.

"No. If we're lucky, he was thrown from the bus and killed."

"Please . . ." A moan came from one of the bodies by their feet. A feeble, bloody hand reached toward the cuff of his pants. "Help me."

The blond lifted the stick from his side and aimed the glowing tip at the battered man before him. A bright, golden flash left the stick and slammed into him. With a choking cry, he went limp and silent.

What the hell?

The tall man stepped over the body as if it were a log in his way. The short blond smirked as he toed the bloody hand away from him.

The pair picked their way through the bodies, pausing only to roll over prone figures. Each time, when they didn't find who they were looking for, they aimed the gleaming stick and a violent wave of gold added to the silence of the wrecked cabin.

With each flash of molten sunlight, my heart leapt. *They're killing them.*

I twisted around to look at the heavy body pinning my feet. Ignoring my pulsing head, I worked my feet out from under the old woman. My aching skull pleaded that I move slowly, but the men were getting closer.

Once free, I grabbed the window frame and pulled myself toward the shadows of the interstate. Glass bit into my palms and broke through my jeans, cutting into my hip.

"We've got a live one!"

My gaze broke away from the darkness to the lit interior of the bus. The smirking blond looked right at me.

I dug my heels into the bodies around me and launched myself out of the window. My back landed hard on the asphalt, agitating the wounds there. Flipping onto my hands and knees, I scrambled to my feet and stumbled away from the wreck.

The blow to my head caused my vision to double; overturned cars, blaring headlights, and flickering flames multiplied before my eyes. Dizzy, my fleeing steps turned into a drunk man's stumble.

"Where are you going?"

I whirled toward the voice. Rough hands grasped my shoulders and slammed me against a nearby minivan tipped on its side. The metal groaned beneath my back.

The blond braced his forearm against my chest.

He's going to kill me. Oh, my God, he's going to kill me.

Grabbing my arm, he shoved the sleeve of my light blue hoodie over my elbow and grasped my bare wrist. As soon as his skin touched mine, he dropped my arm. Curses spewed from his mouth.

Over his shoulder he called, "Jackpot!"

"User?" the voice of the tall man asked from the other side of a crushed Accord.

"Hell yeah," said the blond. "And a Royal too. At least an eight."

The tall one jogged around the car with a hungry gleam in his eye. That terrifying look was directed at me.

"That must be why the Horsemen are interested in her." His head whipped to the right and then to the left, searching. "We better go before his boss gets here."

"Come on, sweetheart." The blond man grabbed my other elbow, the one still covered by my sleeve, and yanked me away from the minivan.

The movement threw my throbbing head for a loop. I could either voice my objections or keep myself standing; not both. I chose to remain vertical.

The blond dragged me across three lanes of traffic. The only thing lighting the interstate were the beams from the headlights and flickering flames of totaled cars.

That's when I noticed something about these men. Although they were in the middle of chaos, they were untouched by it. They weren't bloodied or bruised. No shards of glass glittered from their clothes. Even their car, parked upright and safely on the shoulder, didn't have a single scratch.

The headlights flickered. The blond and his tall companion froze.

I blinked. In the time it took for me to open my eyes, we weren't alone.

Four figures stood among the smoke and destruction, three men and a woman. All I could make out through the smoke and the fog in my head were their silhouettes backlit by fire. Each with their own glowing stick.

The blond released my arm with a curse. I barely caught myself before I stumbled to the asphalt. Gravel cut into my already torn-up palms but the feeling barely registered.

Flashes of gold, much like the ones from the bus, lit up the air. My body buzzed with a familiar energy—the scalding pressure that pushed from my ribcage, but this was different. It slipped over my skin like burning honey.

Sore and groggy, I pushed myself to my hands and knees.

The two men from the sedan were dancing around throwing lights at the new arrivals. Every time the golden light struck the ground, it shook like an earthquake. Thunder billowed from each impact as cracks shot through the concrete.

I was hallucinating. I had to be. Shaking my head, I pushed myself to my feet.

I stumbled away from the men. Over the years, shadows had proven to be my friend. They hid me when I needed it most and the only thing they demanded in return was silence. I was counting on that tonight.

A flash of gold, bright as sunlight, streaked over my shoulder and slammed into the asphalt. It broke the earth with a loud crack that sounded as if it went down for miles.

I flinched back as the fracture spread and widened. The pavement groaned, stone against stone, as gravity pressed in. I scrambled back from the widening hole, but not fast enough. The highway caved in right under my feet.

Screaming, my nails drug across the asphalt as I went over the edge. Someone grabbed my forearm, halting my descent. My shoulder wrenched in its socket. Tearing my eyes from the drop, I looked up into the face of my rescuer.

The firelight battled against the darkness to unveil his face. All I could make out was the firm set of his jaw. Another flash of gold overhead highlighted a slash of scar tissue marring the side of his face.

His grip loosened for a fraction of a second.

He's going to drop me. My eyes flew to his and found only darkness. There was no glint of color. It was as if the shadows themselves looked down at me.

Before I could utter a plea for my life, he pulled me up and over the edge. Once on sturdy ground, he didn't let go. He dragged me away from the bus and crashed cars.

The blond from the bus rounded the corner. Raising his glowing stick at us, a burst of light flew across the lanes of decimated traffic. The golden orb struck my shoulder. With a *pop*, it broke me away from the man with the scar.

I landed flat on my back. All the air ejected from my lungs.

A thin thread of light wrapped around my ankle. With a sharp yank, it drug me across three lanes of traffic to the other side of the bus. The blond man from the crash was waiting for me.

"What's in Vegas?" he snapped. He shot a fearful glance behind him.

"Please don't hurt me." I scrambled back, pressing the glass deeper into my palms.

The blond jumped forward and kicked his boot into my stomach, pinning me to the asphalt. "Why were you going to Vegas?"

"F—for a job!" I exclaimed.

His eyes lit up. "What job?"

My mind raced, but fear kept me from remembering what Blake told me. "I don't know."

"Don't lie to me. You wouldn't have the Horsemen tailing you if it wasn't important. What are you to Achilles Heel?"

"What are you talking about?"

"In Vegas, were you meeting with Michael Kale?" he asked earnestly.

"I don't know his name! It was just someone my friend knows."

His expression reminded me of one of the foster kids I knew a few years back. When he caught me hiding snacks, his face would twist with emotion—anger that I was keeping something from him— but with an edge of urgency because it would soon be his.

He raised his arm and pointed the glowing stick at me. Gold light illuminated the designs carved into the shaft.

My body exploded with fire. I screamed as I patted my arms and legs to douse the flames, but there weren't any. Writhing against the asphalt, it felt like my skin was melting away from my skeleton as my bones shattered.

Then the pain stopped.

Panting, I looked down and didn't see a single mark on my skin. *What the hell was that?*

"Let's try again." He pointed the stick at me.

"What is that thing?"

"What's your mission?" He looked behind him again, searching. A bead of sweat rolled down the side of his face.

"I don't know what you're talking about!"

That wasn't the answer he was looking for. He flourished the stick again, but this time, the pain was worse.

The frightening hum awoke in my chest. It reverberated against my ribs as the fire that consumed the surrounding cars brightened and flared.

"Tell me what Michael Kale is planning!"

I racked my brain for any memories of Achilles Heel or Michael Kale. My stomach went cold when I couldn't think of anything. "I don't know! I swear! I've never heard of them before."

With a wave of his arm, the fiery pain returned.

Heat swirled inside me. Pressure started to build, thumping in my chest like a loud speaker. *No! Please don't!*

But the cursed feeling didn't listen. It never did. It just demanded to be heard, to be felt, to be released.

The boiling pressure broke. It rushed out of my chest like an exhale. Bright, golden light erupted, blooming toward the midnight sky. It rolled over the chaos of the highway, melting metal and obliterating the blond man where he stood. Fire swirled into the air like it wanted to char the sky. I covered my head, expecting the fire to consume me too, but the flames rolled harmlessly over my skin.

Peeking between my arms, I watched the bus and surrounding cars melt and sag beneath the heat.

Then I wasn't alone.

A man stood in front of me, the flames flowed harmlessly over his leather jacket. He locked his fingers around my wrist. The flames retreated from us, leaving me cold. He pulled my arm over his shoulder and scooped me up from the asphalt. My unfocused eyes could just make out a scar slicing across his cheek.

He turned sharply on his heel. The next second, the air around us turned cold too. The man in the leather jacket shouted, but my brain was too fuzzy to register the words.

Gravity shifted as I was lowered onto something soft. The smell of mint wafted across my face and the darkness pulled me under.

8

Do You Know This Man?

I felt like a well-used punching bag.

My chest ached with each heartbeat. My ribs protested with each breath. I swear I could feel the blood scraping through my veins.

Cheese and rice, what happened?

I couldn't remember the last time I felt this sore. I thought of Denny and his belt, then of the fall off the roof . . . The bus crash came back with memories of broken glass, cracking asphalt, and molten sunshine that burned through my body. Phantom aches circled through my limbs and ribcage.

My eyelids creaked as they opened. Bright lights hissed across my vision, stinging my eyes. What was above me confused my pulsing head. There was a darkness, starless and thick, yet, there was light strong enough to cause me to squint.

I blinked rapidly, forcing my eyes to focus. As they did, my confusion only doubled. The blackness took shape in high arches, forming a ceiling of sleek black stone. The glittering light condensed into a chandelier of a thousand crystal pieces, intertwined with intricate gold fixtures.

What the hell?

With stiff movements, I pushed myself upright. My head threatened to sprout wings and fly off my neck. Breathing slow, I turned my gaze about the rest of the room.

Tall windows framed by deep red curtains patterned the walls. Bright lanterns were perfectly spaced between them, bathing the gym-sized room in warm light.

Beds with black metal frames, like the one I sat on, outlined the perimeter. The wall directly on the other side of the room was comprised of shelves from floor to ceiling. Each housed medicinal bottles of different sizes, shapes, and colors.

I stared at the obsidian stone beneath my shoes. Scattered images of the interstate—the cracked asphalt, the fire, the melting wreckage—paraded through my mind. But I couldn't remember getting here . . . wherever *here* was.

Feet shuffled behind me.

I twisted around. Four people, three men and a nurse, stood a couple paces from the bed I was on. Each of them stared at me.

My eyes were drawn to the member of their group that stood out like a sore thumb. He wore all black, from his jeans to the black fitted Henley top. Two of the three buttons were missing from his throat. He wore a black leather jacket that had obviously seen better days. In places it was so worn the shine was gone. In others, there were crudely stitched repairs. A double holster peeked out from under the sad garment. Even the thick locks of his short cut hair were shades of starless midnight.

On the left side of his face, from his cheekbone to his jaw, ran a thin scar. The jagged line pulled up a moment on the interstate. This was the man who kept me from falling when the ground gave way.

His eyes held my attention the longest—if you could even call them eyes. They were so dark I could hardly distinguish the pupils from the irises. It wasn't just because they were dark in color. They were hard as obsidian and brimming with such rage that my heart skipped when our eyes met. It was the look of a man seconds away from bloodying his fists—and all of that was directed at me.

"Hello, dear."

My eyes snapped away from Mr. Leather Jacket. The man who spoke was the oldest of the group. He had large, distinguished eyebrows. While Mr. Leather Jacket was in casual attire, this man wore a tan suit with a gold tie and matching pocket square. The biggest difference between the two was that he was smiling at me.

Eyebrows stepped toward me with his hand extended.

I jumped to my feet, putting the bed between us.

My legs wobbled under my weight as a groan erupted in my throat. I braced myself against the wall, locking my teeth around the cry. Gravity seemed to tug my organs apart and shift them around my torso. My vision swam as my knees threatened to buckle.

"Careful," Eyebrows said earnestly. "You were in a terrible accident. We've just managed to reverse the damage. Well, that was Helen."

The woman, dressed in deep maroon scrubs with an embroidered gold compass over her heart, moved around the bed toward me. A fluffy off-white cardigan hung from her shoulders.

I plastered my back to the wall.

Helen stopped and held her gloved hands up between us.

"I'm not going to hurt you, sweetie," she said with a kind smile. "I just want to make sure your skin is holding the potions."

Potions?

Moving slowly, Helen reached toward me and took my hands in her gloved ones.

"Are you in any pain?" she asked, turning my hands palm up.

I shook my head. My eyes darted over her shoulder. Mr. Leather Jacket continued to glare. Eyebrows' smile was still locked in place. The third and shortest man with slicked back hair, hadn't said a word. Actually, I don't think he had even blinked.

Behind the group was a set of tall gold doors. My heart tripped.

That's my way out.

"You sustained an intense blow to the head and massive internal organ failure. Are you being truthful that you're not experiencing any pain?"

My gaze snapped away from the doors. *I—what?*

My pounding head begged me to tell the truth as my entire torso sang in agreement. My head hurt . . . actually, all of me hurt. But I nodded, wanting to get out of here as quickly as possible.

Helen's eyes narrowed on my face. No doubt she saw the fine layer of sweat glistening over my clammy skin and the tightness of my clenched jaw.

Reaching into her apron, Helen took out a small bottle and

pressed it into my hand. "Your body is still healing from the flare, which is causing the body aches. This will take care of the pain." Clasping her hands in front of her, she nodded for me to drink.

The bottle fit in the palm of my hand. It looked like it barely contained a mouthful. But I wasn't concerned about the mysterious substance. What I was concerned about was the smoothness of my palms.

I remembered glass cutting into my skin on the interstate. But there was no proof. The skin should've been scabbed or scratched. I shoved the sleeve of my hoodie up to my elbow and found no bruises or scratches there either.

This is it. I've finally snapped. I'm going crazy.

Helen gently cleared her throat and nodded back to the bottle. "I'm not drinking anything." I tossed the bottle to the mattress. "Who are you people? Where the hell am I?" There was no way this was a hospital. There was too much grandeur in the deep red curtains, too much shiny black stone—it was just too *much.*

"My name is Henry Lenin," Eyebrows said with a smile. "And you're in my school, the Magisterium of Magic."

The Magisterium . . .

. . . of Magic.

My pulsing headache kept the words from being processed and understood.

"I shouldn't be here." That much I knew. "Thank you for the, uh, help or whatever." I looked down at my unscathed palms. *Did I imagine being hurt?* I shook my head. "But I need to get going. I have someone waiting for me."

"Whoever is waiting for you thinks you're dead," Mr. Lenin said gently. "With the amount of damage from the fire, I'm sure they will find no survivors."

My mind flashed to the blond man and his companion with their glowing sticks as they made their way through the bus . . . the heated buzzing in my chest that fed the fire . . . the explosion . . .

I tried to swallow my growing fears, but my mouth was dry.

"It was a good thing we were already looking for you, Jane.

Otherwise, there would have been a very different outcome." Mr. Lenin gestured to the bed between us. Unbuttoning his jacket, he perched on the mattress next to mine.

I didn't move. "My name isn't Jane. What do you mean you were looking for me?"

Mr. Leather Jacket's eyes narrowed at my tone.

"No?" Mr. Lenin ignored my question. "Your foster file says that your name is Jane Doe."

I tried not to cringe at the lazy name my first pair of foster parents gave me. "I go by Charlie."

"Well, Charlie," Mr. Lenin continued, "it's no accident you're here. However, we were hoping to meet under better circumstances. We've been looking for you for about a week now."

I peered toward the doors again. They were too far to run to. I would have tried it if Mr. Leather Jacket and Slick Hair weren't in the way. Mr. Leather Jacket was still glaring and Slick Hair was still staring, wide-eyed.

"I strongly suggest you drink this," Helen said, once again offering me the tiny bottle. "You'll feel a lot better. I promise."

"Please." Mr. Lenin gestured to the bottle as well.

Tentatively, I took the bottle and brought it to my nose. It smelled like the inside of a spice cabinet, although none of the fragment notes were ones I was familiar with.

Against my better judgment, I tipped the bottle into my mouth. A thick glob fell on my tongue. Just as I was about to spit it out, the sweet taste of fresh peaches filled my mouth.

I forced myself to swallow. The glob tingled down my throat and heated my belly. The warmth spread up my chest and down my aching legs. The brutal pounding in my head softened and then quieted all together. In a matter of heartbeats, I was in no pain and my body hummed with contentment that can only be achieved by being wrapped in a blanket fresh out of the laundry.

"Better?" Helen asked, taking the bottle from me.

"What is that stuff?" *No pain killer worked that fast.* I shook my head. "Forget that. Why were you looking for me?" I directed the question to the glaring man.

Mr. Lenin reached toward the man with the slicked-back hair. "The photo please."

As if he just realized he had been staring without blinking for the past five minutes, Slick Hair's gaze snapped toward Mr. Lenin. He handed him the large yellow envelope he held at his side.

Mr. Lenin pulled out a photo and offered it to me. "Do you know this man?"

Unfortunately, there wasn't a nice way to say, *Hell no. Can I leave?* So, I stepped closer and took the picture. The room was so quiet a mouse's burp could've been heard in the next room.

The man in the photo was a contradiction. He exuded power. It was in the unrelenting stare of his light blue eyes and the downward tilt of his head. But his expression was kind, paired with a coy smile. His golden hair, combed without fault, gave the illusion that he was untouchable, unreal. But the gravity of his gaze, whispered of wonderful promises and dreams that you wanted to lean in and learn. I couldn't tell if I wanted to toss away the picture or continue to study him.

Pulling my attention from his face, I found yet another contradiction. He wore a maroon suit made of rich, smooth fabric. Even his tie was a dark shade of contrasting red. That look on anyone else would have been pretentious, but he wore it as if it was his favorite t-shirt, casually and with ease.

I shook my head. "I've never seen him."

"Are you sure?"

I nodded. *I'd remember a man like that.*

"What do you know about your father?"

"You're going to have to be more specific." I dropped the picture onto the bed between us. Maybe one of my foster parents finally got arrested and the police wanted my statement.

"I was asking about your biological father."

My gaze leapt from the picture back to the man questioning me. "Why do you want to know about him?"

"Answer the question." Mr. Leather Jacket demanded. Each word was rimmed with steel.

I shifted away from him. The backs of my knees touched the bed behind me. A shudder rolled through me—I was cornered.

Helen cleared her throat. "Perhaps there's a better time to do this, sir."

Mr. Lenin waved off her concern and waited for me to answer.

"I don't know anything," I said slowly.

Mr. Lenin pointed to the upside-down picture on the bed. "That man is Lawrence Hart. He's your biological father."

A laugh snorted from my nose. "Yeah, right."

The two men stared back at me with puzzled expressions. Mr. Leather Jacket's glare intensified at the sound of my laugh.

"He's too expensive to be around my lifestyle," I quickly explained. "He probably doesn't even know where Salina is."

"We ran a blood test while you were unconscious," Mr. Lenin said. "Your DNA matches."

My eyes dropped back to the picture. While I dyed my hair brown with a lone red streak on the left side, my natural color was the same golden blond as his. Looking more closely, I saw that our eyes were the same too, a cool combination of light blue and grey.

But that was where the similarities ended. He looked so strong, so sure of himself. It was the kind of confidence that spoke of the will of the world bending to his. Life was a simple chess game, and he was winning by three moves. Meanwhile, life constantly used me as a doormat.

My fascination quickly soured. He looked rich enough to at least drop an unwanted kid at an orphanage, not a trash can.

"So?" I crossed my arms. "Did he pay you to look for me? Because he can rot in hell for all I care."

"We didn't find you because your father wants to meet you," Mr. Lenin assured me. "On the contrary, he has no idea you exist."

"If he did, we wouldn't have found you." Slick Hair looked very pleased with himself.

"There's no *we* in this situation, Magee." Mr. Leather Jacket looked completely disgusted that he had to address the other man. "*We* would imply that you got off your ass and did something."

Mr. Lenin cleared his throat. "Master Kale, please."

Master? I looked at Mr. Leather Jacket. *What the hell does that mean?* I shook my head and prioritized my curiosity. "If he doesn't know about me, then why am I here?"

"Master Hart is our," Mr. Lenin paused, searching for the right word, "society's most powerful Magic User, a Royal. In addition to the blood test, we confirmed that you inherited his impressive magic status."

My eyebrows pulled together. "Did you just say magic?"

His head moved up and down with slow deliberateness. "I did."

"Does that . . . stand for something?"

Mr. Lenin straightened his tie, switching gears. "I'm going to be blunt. You're not human. You've subconsciously noticed this. You don't get sick, you've never broken a bone, and it takes a lot to wear you out. Correct?"

He rushed on without giving me time to respond. "That is because you're a Magic User. Meaning, you're a part of a race born with the ability to control and use magic."

I gaped at him. Either I stumbled into an insane asylum, or I was in purgatory. Why else would someone be able to say that with a straight face?

Then it hit me. "Did Denny put you up to this?"

"Denny?" He sent a questioning glance at Mr. Leather Jacket.

"The Regular back in Kansas that we first suspected to be Hart's offspring," he answered coolly.

"Ah." Mr. Lenin turned his attention back to me. "No one put us up to anything."

Ok. Then this is a loony bin. "Magic doesn't exist."

"It does. Regulars just have no knowledge of it. Since you grew up with them, you've adopted their thinking." Mr. Lenin leaned forward, resting his elbows on his knees. "You can use magic. The evidence is in what happened on the interstate moments ago."

"Did Blake put you up to this?" I asked in a small voice.

"I promise, no one put us up to anything. This situation has no room for humor."

Really? Because from where I'm sitting, this is ridiculous.

"You see, Charlie, your status is . . ." Mr. Lenin redirected himself. "Without proper control, you're unstable to the people around you."

"Over the years, have there been situations that you couldn't explain?" Magee interjected, studying my expression. "Sudden fires, broken lights? I'm guessing you've noticed."

Magic . . . Was that the reason the lights flickered when my heart skipped? Or why the pressure in my chest made things crack. Was this the answer to my curse? No. Magic was sparkly and for small woodland creatures with pink hair. What happened around me was dark and twisted. It was something I feared.

"I've lived with kids who have as many issues as there are words to describe them." I clenched my fists until my knuckles turned white. "Of course something's going to be on fire."

Magee shrugged. "But do the other kids burn someone with nothing in their hands?"

"No one can prove that." My heart seized, igniting a humming spark in my chest. The light over the bed flickered. Breathing slowly to douse the fire in my chest, my eyes shifted toward the doors again.

Magee tilted his head. "What do you remember from the crash?"

I clamped my mouth shut. I wasn't sure I had seen anything other than what adrenaline and a knock on the head made me see.

"Two magic poachers crashed your bus. When they captured you, they provoked you into releasing a magic flare—an uncontrolled blast of magic. That's what killed all those people, not the crash."

The lights flickered again, drawing Mr. Leather Jacket—Kale's— obsidian gaze.

"You're wrong," I said. "Those men with the glowing sticks did something. Magic doesn't exist. If it did, I would've left Kansas a long time ago."

But no matter how badly I wanted to, I couldn't deny what I saw. On the interstate, the hum that vibrated through my chest with the heat of an inferno, I saw it burst out of me in a wave of golden light.

I saw what it did to the fire, making it burn brighter and hotter to the point where it could melt metal. And that wasn't the first time it had happened either.

"I know this is hard to understand," Mr. Lenin said smoothly. "But give us a chance to explain—"

"You've said enough." I rounded the bed, heading for the doors. "I don't know what game you're playing, but I don't want any part of it. My life is a circus enough as it is."

Mr. Kale stepped between me and the exit. He towered over me with a look so dark, I thought he was going to crush my bones into the floor.

"Miss Hart."

I broke my gaze from the dark eyes of the man in black to look at Mr. Lenin. *Hart.* I looked back at the picture on the bed. *Is that my last name?* The confusion and need to run overwhelmed me to the point where I couldn't decide if I liked the name or not.

Mr. Lenin rose to his feet and stepped between me and the seething Kale. "How about we prove it to you?"

9

You Have My Attention

"You're going to prove magic to me?"

Mr. Lenin nodded.

"Ok. But it better not be a card trick."

A low chuckle made the hairs on the back of my neck shiver.

Kale's eyes were no longer on me. "Gentlemen, if I may?"

My moment of confidence faltered. *What did I invite him to do?*

Reaching under his black leather jacket, he pulled out a stick—I guess I could call it a wand—from the holster beneath his arm. Under his calloused and scarred fingers, the black wood lit with molten sunlight, just like the men on the bus.

With a wave of his hand, a thread of gold shot under the bed and pulled a stool into view. The legs shrieked against the black stone as it came to a stop in the middle of the room.

He flicked his wrist, directing the tip of the wand toward the stool. A small, golden spark shot forward.

As soon as it made contact, the stool broke into a million splinters. The sound of splintering wood filled the air as it formed a cloud of kindling no bigger than pine needles. The shards floated in the air suspended by nothing. With another golden spark, the splinters spun back into the stool like nothing happened.

"Touch it." Kale stepped out of my way. "It won't break."

He didn't have to tell me twice.

Moving around him, I reached for it with shaky hands. The cool material didn't crumble or even creak. I gave it a firm shake. It clattered against the obsidian floor.

It was a solid, normal stool.

My mind whirled.

Maybe whatever Helen gave me was making me hallucinate. I glanced back at Mr. Lenin and Magee. There was a wand peeking out of Mr. Lenin's suit jacket. Magee had one tied to his belt. Helen's protruded from one of the pockets in her cardigan.

The lights flickered in time with my racing heart.

In the shadows of what I just witnessed, I paid more attention to the rhythmic flare of the lights. Before, it was just a precursor to chaos, but was that magic? *My* magic?

"This is crazy." I shoved my trembling hands into my hair. Bits of glass and dirt poked into the pads of my fingers as I pressed them into my skull. I needed to ground myself, but the world was spinning out from under me.

I closed my eyes, squeezing them tight enough to press them back into my skull. *I'm dreaming. I fell asleep on the bus and I'm dreaming. I need to wake up. I need to wake up. Ineedtowakeup.*

I didn't realize I said all of that out loud until the man in black sighed. The sound was sharp with irritation.

Stepping forward, Kale took hold of my wrist, wincing when our skin touched, and pulled my hand from my hair. Before I could pull back, he slapped the hilt of his wand into my palm and closed my fingers around the black wood.

Immediately, the burning hum in my chest flared. All around the room, the lanterns on the walls and the crystal chandeliers brightened until there wasn't a single shadow. Helen, Mr. Lenin, and Magee's hands covered their faces to block out the onslaught of light.

My gaze, however, was riveted on the wand in my hand. Beneath my white-knuckled grip, the wand was shining. Bright as sunlight, gold and alive, the hilt glimmered between my fingers.

My mind warred with what I was seeing. It tried to convince me that it was a trick, that Kale was doing something.

But he wasn't touching the wand. One hand was still locked around my wrist, holding me in place, while the other held my fingers around the shaft—without his grip I would've dropped the thing.

This was coming from me.

I could feel it.

The hum in my chest—the magic—sang through my ribcage, flowing over my shoulder and down my arm. My hand tingled with a million pinpricks, as it leached from my skin and into the black wood. For the first time, the buzz in my chest wasn't a feeling I wanted to squash. As it warmed through my body, it seemed to seep into my muscles and fortify them with steel. My bones hardened to granite with an intoxicating feeling of pure *power.*

I pulled my gaze from the wand glowing under *my* fingers and up into the obsidian gaze of Kale's glowering face.

I released a shuddering breath. "Ok . . . you have my attention."

10

Control or Consequences

"Excellent."

Simultaneously, Kale released my wrist and yanked his wand from my hand.

The moment it was free from my grasp, the lights dropped back to their normal shine. The storm of heat slithered up my arm and over my shoulder. Back in my chest, the hum quieted, leaving me cold, light-headed, and breathing hard.

Stepping back, Kale twirled the wand across his palm and caught the hilt. Magic surged back into the shaft.

With a quick flick, the stool spun around me and back under the bed where it came from. Without breaking eye contact, he replaced the wand in the holster under his arm.

"Why am I here?" I asked.

"We have a proposition for you." Mr. Lenin's eyes danced with excitement. "Your magic status is extremely rare. As you've noticed, without proper training, you have a dramatic effect on the world around you. Because of your unique circumstances, I'd like to offer you a place, here, at my school, where you can learn to control and use your magic."

My eyes narrowed. "What do you get out of it?"

"By enrolling you at the Magisterium, I'd get the pride of calling you my student."

"Bullshit."

Magee and Helen's eyes widened. Their gazes snapped to Mr. Lenin, gauging his reaction. As for Kale, his glare softened for a fraction of a second as if my contradiction impressed him.

"I can't pay you," I said. "And you can't tell me that you want me for my sparkling personality."

Mr. Lenin's smile didn't falter or dim. He just dismissed my words with a wave of his hand. "I can afford to scholarship students now and then. And if you choose to stay, you'll come to understand the importance of us having you on our side."

It was an answer, but it was vague enough not to answer anything at all.

"What do you say, Miss Hart?" Mr. Lenin asked.

Years of experience and scars filled me with unease. The house on Haven Avenue was perfect, homey and warm, until the monsters shed their sheep's wool. All I could see when I looked at Mr. Lenin's fancy suit, Helen's kind eyes, and Magee's blatant fascination were shadows, secrets, and hidden agendas—all of which could and would inevitably be wielded as a weapon against me. The only one being truly honest was Kale with his black apparel and simmering obsidian gaze.

Mr. Lenin's smile dimmed as I shook my head. "I've lived this long without . . ." I couldn't get myself to say it—*magic*—without breaking into a fit of laughter. So, I gestured vaguely to the room. "Any of this. I'll manage just fine without it. Now, if you'll excuse me, I have someone who I need to tell that I'm not dead."

"Miss Hart." Mr. Lenin was once again standing between me and the gold doors. "I don't think you understand the gravity of your situation. I'm offering you a chance to learn at one of the best schools in the world with zero consequences for your actions, on the interstate and before. We know this wasn't the first time you've flared like this."

My heart tripped. "You can't prove that."

"We did. That's how we found you. Over the last few years, you've been flaring more and they've been getting more and more potent," Magee said. "It only takes someone paying attention to magic reports, as we were, to follow the signs to you."

"What signs?" *Maybe I can hide them.*

"The flare that happened a few months ago, in the field by the overpass—"

My stomach dropped.

"—left a mile of barren scorched earth in its wake. A year before that, you knocked out the power of an entire city block. There were two other instances when you were sixteen—"

"I don't think recounting those traumatic moments is offering her any comfort," Mr. Lenin said with a hardened tone.

Magee turned his wide eyes back to me. "They shouldn't be traumatic. On the contrary, they display just how powerful you are."

He said it like it was a good thing. He didn't know that each *flare* left someone hurt, but never me. When the power was knocked out, it was because a man approached me in the darkness of the parking lot after a late shift at the diner. The next morning, they found him tangled in the wires of a telephone pole.

In the field by the overpass, one of the new kids at Denny's house was low on rent money, so he tried to take mine. When denying him didn't work, I ran, but he ran faster. When he caught me, heat poured through my chest and burst out of me, tearing his greedy fingers from my arms. He landed in the middle of the road . . . everyone assumed he had been crushed in a hit and run.

And there were more, so many more. Not all of them bloody, but they all left destruction in their wake. They didn't make me feel powerful, just dangerous. Like a grenade without its pin.

"I could turn you over to the authorities," Mr. Lenin continued somberly as he gestured to Kale. "Your lack of control with your magic is dangerous to everyone around you. The number of people you have hurt, unintentional as it may be, does demand justice. But I'd hate to incriminate someone so young and innocent as yourself."

My attention once more returned to the man in all black. A spark lit in his eyes at Mr. Lenin's words. It made his already fatal stare into something hungry, even starved. He wanted me to be handed over. His hands clenched at his sides, knuckles white with control, as he fought himself not to pull me to him right then and there.

"I didn't mean it," I whispered, taking a step back from the man in black.

"I know you didn't," Mr. Lenin said softly, "But if you choose not to learn to control it, it will happen again. I cannot in good conscience release you back into the world to hurt more people. How many more people do you have to destroy before you realize that this is what is best for you? Maybe if you burn this friend of yours?"

I wanted to say that I would never hurt Blake, but the words wouldn't leave my mouth. Each flare of my so-called curse, happened despite my best attempts to fight it. I had no control.

"People seek out power like yours. It can tip balances and change some very important things in our world. If you continue to flare like you do, it'll only be a matter of time before another group of poachers finds their way to you. You were lucky tonight that Master Kale and his team were already looking for you, or it would've been too late."

My gaze again shifted to the man in all black. Any thanks I might have had shriveled under his heated stare. The disgusted turn of his lips said that he had been there against his will.

"How about this?" Mr. Lenin opened his hands in offering. "Let's take this one step at a time. You stay here and learn to control the power inside you. Here you'll be protected, and I won't have to turn you over for something out of your control."

I wanted to run. Every fiber of my body from the top of my head to the bottom of my feet begged me to.

But what if the next time something happens, Blake is the one that ends up being hurt?

I pictured his kind face and laughing green eyes. That image instantly fell away to an expression of betrayal as blisters bloomed under my fingers. Too easily I could picture the horrors of each flare inflicted upon *him*. I'd never be able to live with myself.

I met Mr. Lenin's sympathetic gaze. I couldn't deny the truth in his words. I needed to control my curse—my magic. A solution, best of both worlds, clicked into place as easily as puzzle pieces.

I could stay, learn to control my magic from flaring, and then vanish. Once I learned to keep it inside my chest there wouldn't be any bread crumbs for them to follow. I could drop back into a life of anonymity and leave this and them all behind.

Then Blake would be safe.

I would be free.

"After I learn to control it?" I asked. "Then what?"

"After that, you can continue to stay as a student to learn more about magic. Here, you will find nothing but comfort and protection and the ability to harness a power unlike anything we've seen for generations. However, if you still wish to leave, I'll personally take you wherever you want to go."

I rocked back on my heels in surprise. No one had ever offered me an exit before. I looked from hopeful Magee to patient Mr. Lenin. I didn't have to look at Kale to know he still wore the same glare.

"Really?"

Magee chuckled. "This isn't a prison, darling. On the contrary, we're offering you a fresh start."

What's your angle? But no matter how my mind whirled, I couldn't put one together.

"Just stay for a couple days," Mr. Lenin said. "I think you'll find that you like it here."

But what about Blake? If he thought I was dead because of the bus he put me on, he'd tear himself apart.

But it'd only be for a short while, right? If it didn't work out, I could appear on his front door and take away his pain like nothing ever happened.

I'd stay just until I learned to control it.

And the moment I saw a red flag, I'd bolt.

Without Denny's favors and friends in high places, I doubted they could find me.

Slowly, I nodded. "Ok. I'll stay."

11

A World Anew

A bright smile crossed Mr. Lenin's face once again. "I'm very pleased to hear that."

Kale remained with his arms crossed. The hungry darkness that had filled his eyes said he wasn't just hoping I'd reject the offer, but he was counting on it.

"You'll start your lessons right away. In preparation for finding you, I secured private lessons with one of our world's finest Users, Master Michael Kale."

My gaze snapped over to the silent man in black. I was going to be stuck with *him*? He looked just as happy with the idea as I was.

My shoulders rounded under his harsh gaze. Quickly, I turned back to Mr. Lenin. "It sounds like you were pretty sure I'd want to stay."

"Just optimistic," Mr. Lenin said. "Since it's nearly three in the morning, I'll show you to your room. After some rest, you can start in the morning."

"If you need anything or feel any discomfort, let me know," Helen said with one last sweet smile. She tucked her gloved hands into the pockets of her cardigan and retreated in the opposite direction.

Mr. Lenin turned and headed for the gold doors. Stuffing my hands into my hoodie pocket, I followed after him. My gaze unconsciously swept over Michael Kale and found his obsidian eyes drilling into me. As I followed Mr. Lenin and Magee toward the gold doors, I felt them dig into the back of my head.

"I do hope you'll join us for the rest of the school year. The

Magisterium of Magic is one of the best schools in the world. All students board here during the school year with the choice of going home for weekends and holidays. Each student has their own apartment on the seventh floor. Classrooms are on the second through sixth.

"The dining room, library, infirmary, and greenhouse are on the first floor. There are two gyms, one in the Southeast Wing and the other in the Northwest Wing. The pool can be found on the second floor of the Northeast and the sports field is in the Southwest. The lowest level belongs to the teachers. There you can find their offices and living quarters. You have free range of the four wings of the castle—except for the North Wing. The grounds outside the castle are off limits."

I raised my eyebrows slightly, feigning a look of mild interest. *Learn to control it and run.*

We passed through the infirmary doors and into a perfectly round stairwell the size of a baseball field. My feet came to a stop as my mouth dropped open.

Around our group sat eight sets of tall gold doors evenly placed around the circle. Each was etched with a name: dining room, West, library, North, East, greenhouse, and South. The doors behind us read *Infirmary*.

Spiraling in opposite directions were two grand staircases with glittering gold railings. Like prowling tigers, they mirrored each other, twisting in opposite directions as they wrapped around the perimeter of the stairwell. A glass ceiling sat above them, framing a crescent moon and thousands of dazzling stars.

At the very center of the stairwell, as if the staircases coiled around a sacred jewel, was a grandfather clock. It rose as high as the first landing without a mite of dust. The body of the structure was carved into three distinct tiers.

The closest to the floor was carefully carved to look like a crowd of people. From different nationalities, they crawled over each other, all reaching up to the next tier. Some glowed with a golden aura while others were so faded it looked like the artist forgot to gloss them.

The second tier of people, significantly less crowded, weren't reaching up. Instead, their glowing heads were bent with their arms reaching out and down toward the bottom level.

At the topmost point stood seven figures, three women and four men, etched entirely in gold. The long layers of their clothing tangled and rippled down to the layer below. Each of the seven figures stood with their hands raised over their heads. Resting in their palms was the clock. The clock face itself was crowded with minute and hour hands. There were so many I could only guess that there was one for each time zone.

No wait . . . there were four tiers. At first glance I thought the black base of the clock wasn't carved so it could blend in with the black floor.

In the shadows of the dark stone, just barely visible to discern from the darkness, were people. They were so faint I couldn't tell if they were reaching toward the higher tiers or if they were gripping the shadows and holding them back.

"You'll have the castle to yourself until after New Year's."

I shut my gaping mouth and hurried after Mr. Lenin.

"The rest of the students are still away for Christmas break," he continued as he started up the stairs. "If you choose to stay, I can enroll you in classes with students your own age."

I didn't plan to stay here that long. New Years was in three days, so I had seventy-two hours to learn what I needed to and bolt.

Mr. Lenin paused on the staircase to look back at me. "It'd be best if you didn't talk about your private lessons, or your childhood without magic. There'll be fewer curious questions that way."

"That won't be a problem." In Kansas, my history was handed out in folders to every house I was sent to. Here, no one knew my story and I planned to keep it that way.

Pleased we were on the same page, he continued. "I assume you don't want anything to do with your biological father. Seeing as you're already in the habit of choosing names for yourself, you can choose a last name—"

"No."

Everyone froze.

Michael Kale leaned casually against the gold railing, but his voice was hard. "You can spell it differently, but we aren't changing it. She's *his* daughter. She should at least sound like it."

I opened my mouth to ask why it mattered, but Mr. Lenin spoke before I could.

"Alright." This was the first time I had seen any real emotion directed toward this guy. Mr. Lenin was actually glaring at him. "How about we spell it with an E? So, it's *H-E-A-R-T*? It sounds the same, but it won't draw as much suspicion."

Crossing my arms, I asked the guy behind me, "Do I have a choice?"

Kale didn't bat an eyelash. "No."

His tone made my hackles rise. I thought about putting up a fight, but only for a second. I wasn't going to stick around long enough to get used to the name. They could call me whatever they wanted, but when I left, I'd be just Charlie once again.

I rolled my eyes and turned back to Mr. Lenin.

He continued up the stairs before the tension could escalate. "Your private lessons will start after breakfast. If you were raised by Users you would've learned to use a wand and control your magic by the age of ten. So, it should be rather easy for you to pick up."

That's what I'm counting on.

We reached the seventh floor and started down a well-lit hallway. I was surprised to see how close together the doors were. Were the apartments just closets disguised as bedrooms?

"We hope to streamline that process a bit." Mr. Lenin took a key ring from his suit jacket. "That way if you choose to stay, you'll be able to fit in with your classmates."

I fought the urge to put emphasis on *if.*

He inserted the gold key into the door between us and pushed it open. Like a gentleman, he motioned for me to step through first.

The room was a lot larger than the hallway let on. Before me was a comfortable living room of plush leather couches and a large red brick fireplace. A small kitchenette with a mini fridge and stove top was to my left, and a study with a huge oak desk and empty bookcases were to my right.

The outside wall, directly in front of me, was made of glass. Displayed beneath a silver moon was a jagged mountainside covered in thick evergreen trees.

Anxiety spiked through me. My escape plan was based off the assumption we were near civilization. Blending into crowds was kind of my superpower, but the wilderness? There weren't many camping spots in Salina, Kansas for me to practice living off the land.

"Where is this school exactly?" I asked, unable to look away from the view. My eyes flew over the evergreen ridges, looking for a hint as to where we were or even better, far off city lights. There was nothing.

"The location is something of a private matter," Mr. Lenin said lightly. "There are other schools who wish to glean some of our curriculum, so I've kept the location undisclosed."

"You needn't worry about poachers tracking you," Magee said, misreading my uneasiness. "The Magisterium is protected by powerful wards."

Was that magic also keeping me here? In the pocket of my hoodie, I curled my fingers into fists, fighting back my rising panic. *One problem at a time. Get control of my magic. Figure out running later.*

Moving across the living room, I peeked through an open door into the bedroom. The off-white carpet contrasted dramatically with the burgundy comforter on the queen bed. Along with a polished white bathroom, there was a closet stocked with clothes, more clothes than I'd ever seen, much less owned: jeans and skirts of every color and cut, long sleeves of lace, cotton, and other fine materials. Every color of the rainbow was represented.

"We assumed everything you owned was burned on the bus. I took the liberty of getting you what you'd need for your stay. They're enchanted to fit." Mr. Lenin leaned against the doorframe.

I gazed around the room. This was far different from the impersonal black stone that made up the rest of the school. The red brick, off-white paint, and warm wood floors made the apartment feel homey.

With a knife and a strong arm, I could pop up some of the floorboards and stash anything I needed to keep hidden.

Since we were seven stories high, the windows would be useless in an escape attempt. I hated that there was only one way in and out. But maybe that could work to my advantage. There would be fewer places to watch if someone wanted to sneak in.

"Do you like it?" Mr. Lenin asked after watching me mentally tear the room apart.

It felt too clean, too nice. I glanced down at my dirty Converse leaving smudges on the white rug. I could almost hear Denny laughing at me.

You don't belong here.

Wordlessly, I nodded.

Mr. Lenin gazed around the room. "We strive for excellence here at the Magisterium. I hope you find that you can feel at home during your stay." He paused and reached into his jacket. "I almost forgot. You'll be needing this."

I nearly tripped over backwards. It was one of those *things*. A wand.

He gave me a reassuring smile. "It won't do anything unless you tell it to. If you don't want it, I can give it to Master Kale until your lesson tomorrow."

Stop being a baby, Charlie. It's just a piece of wood.

It was thin, no bigger than the width of one of my fingers. It was a little longer than my forearm, stretching from the crook of my elbow to my wrist. Plain in decoration, the smooth black surface was flawless.

Holding my breath, I wrapped my fingers around the handle. I expected what happened in the infirmary to happen there. My eyes flew to the lights, waiting for them to brighten enough to sting.

But the lights didn't change. The air remained comfortably cool. No warmth rushed from my chest and down to my hand. I was so worried about the reaction that I almost missed what was happening.

Underneath my fingers, lines and swirls cut into the black surface. Soundlessly, they twisted up the shaft, connecting and creating a backdrop beneath my fingers. It looked like billowing flames curled and engulfed the shaft.

"It's personalized to you. It's yours now."

There were very few things I could with complete certainty call mine. As I ran my fingers along the shaft I was surprised that l liked the feeling. Although I missed seeing it light up like before. No matter how I shifted my grip, the wand didn't light up.

Magee stepped forward. "I'm so glad you're here, darling. Who knew we would find such a rose among the sunflowers of Kansas?"

Mr. Lenin chuckled. "Robert was the one who brought the evidence of your flares to our attention and convinced us to bring you here."

"Why?" I winced at the bluntness of the question. "Thanks for the save and all, but you don't know me. Why look for a stranger?"

Magee didn't seem to mind. "Magic poaching is illegal. I used to work for the Hunter Guard—our version of law enforcement. You know what they say about old habits dying hard." He flashed me a bright smile. "I knew your Royal status would fit in here at the Magisterium with Master Lenin."

There's that word again. Master.

Michael Kale rolled his eyes. "Lenin, do you need anything else from me?"

"No. Thank you."

Kale didn't wait for Mr. Lenin to put a period at the end of his sentence before heading toward the door. As it slammed behind him, I felt every muscle in my body relax.

Without Michael Kale glaring at me, my curiosity woke up. "What's a Royal? You called my father the same thing."

Magee smiled eagerly. Taking his wand from the holster on his belt, he aimed it at the stools before the kitchen counter. A thin golden strand looped two and lifted them into the air. They settled on the floor, one beside Mr. Lenin and the other beside Magee.

"The magical ability of each User is ranked on a scale from one to ten." Magee sat on one of the stools, crossed his legs, and clasped his hands over his knee. "Those with the least magic—levels one to three—are called Deficients. They can do simple magic, but nothing more. Levels four through seven are called Commons. They make up the majority of the magical population, hence the name. Anyone with a status of eight to ten is a Royal."

"Can someone have more magic than a ten?" I asked.

Mr. Lenin and Magee answered at the same time. Mr. Lenin with a firm, "No." Magee said, "Yes."

"They're called Celestials," Magee continued.

"They are also myths." Mr. Lenin's eyes cut to the other man.

Magee was undeterred. "They died out into myth and legend."

"Which is where they will stay for the remainder of this discussion."

The firm edge in Mr. Lenin's tone said that it was time to change the subject. Good thing my curiosity was already on the move. "What's Lawrence's magic level?"

"The correct term is magic status," Magee said gently. "Your father is a Royal Ten."

Cheese and rice. I thought back to the picture they showed me in the infirmary. I knew he looked like he was at the top of the food chain, but it appeared to be in more ways than one.

"What about my mom?"

Mr. Lenin shook his head. "That we don't know. Whoever she is, she went to great lengths to hide her identity and keep you from your father. With how much magic you have, I'd say she could be no lower than a Royal Eight."

Did she leave because I didn't have enough magic? *Stop,* I scolded myself. *The only thing that matters is that she left. I'm not going to pay her any more attention than she paid me.*

"What am I?"

Mr. Lenin's long pause gave me the impression he was holding back. "You're a Royal Nine."

Never in my life was I something other than a kid pulled from a trashcan. Now I was being associated with the word royal.

What's the catch? I looked between the two men, all smiles and niceties. There was no way that they tracked me, rescued me, set up a place for me in this magic school with promises to keep me hidden with no strings. There had to be a catch.

Maybe they want to steal my magic? I looked down at that wand twisting between my fidgeting hands.

No. If they wanted to do that, they would have strapped me to the bed instead of leading me upstairs. But still . . . there has to be a catch.

"You keep saying Master," I said, wrapping both hands around the wand. "What does that mean?"

"It's a title," Mr. Lenin said. "Users study for decades to master a specific craft of magic. The title distinguishes them from the rest of the population. It may be custom to call your elders *Mr.* or *Mrs.* in the Regular world but, here, Masters of a trade are always called by their title. They've done a lot to earn it. As a sign of respect, you'll use that title."

"So, you'll refer to him," Magee gestured to the man sitting beside him, "as Master Lenin."

"Master Lenin," I repeated, testing the new phrase.

Master Lenin nodded. "Correct."

"What trade did you study?"

"All of them." He said it simply as if he had just confirmed that he had brown hair. There was no flare of arrogance or uncomfortable break of eye contact.

"Master Lenin is a School Master," Magee explained. "He's one of seven. Each great school, like the Magisterium, has a Master in charge of it. They spend centuries learning all they can for this role."

Did he just say centuries?

"Anyone can have a high magic status, but knowledge is where true power lies. Since they know the most, they hold the most power. All laws passed and vetoed, titles given and titles stripped go through them. They are the closest thing to royalty that we have."

My gaze slid back to Mr.—or rather Master—Lenin who looked just like any other man, unassuming, maybe even kind. But Magee's description tore apart his practiced smile and pristine appearance.

If he outranked everyone, then he was the one I needed to keep my head down around. All my life I'd been surrounded by the forgotten and the unwanted. But now I was having casual chats and slouching in front of one of the most powerful beings in the world. Supposedly. At the moment, he looked like nothing more than a striking man in his forties with large eyebrows in a fine suit.

"Do you have a title?" I asked Magee.

He shook his head with a smile. "No. I never had the taste for the work it required. You can just call me Robert."

My skin crawled at the intimacy of the gesture, first name versus last. I made the mental note to call him Magee, hoping to add some space and disinterest between us. I noticed the steadiness of his gaze as he watched me take in the information and his readiness to help. His attention felt like I was staring at cracking ice between my feet.

He's a leech. He saddles up to someone who did all the work to get the benefits. I knew a couple of kids like that in Kansas. Hell, I'd been one on occasion to get an extra bone thrown my way.

"You look overwhelmed," Master Lenin said gently.

I looked down at the wand clenched between my hands. "It's . . . a lot to take in."

"You'll get used to it."

If I stay.

"So, tomorrow. . ." I rubbed my eyes. "What will I be doing?"

"Breakfast will be in the dining room at eight. Your first lesson will begin shortly after with Master Kale."

I thought back to the man in black. I shivered as I remembered his intense stare. "What did he master in?"

Magee's smile stiffened. "Hunting."

I tried to picture the brooding man in black stalking through the woods prowling after deer . . . or maybe lions. His leather jacket and steel toe boots hinted at hunting something other than furry creatures. Bears, maybe? Or tigers.

Master Lenin smiled softly as I fought another yawn. "If you don't have any other questions, you should rest. I know healing potions can make you tired, plus it's rather late." He rose to his feet, as did Magee.

"If I have any more questions, who do I ask?" I followed them to the front door.

"Master Kale or myself. I'll make sure to check in regularly." Master Lenin pulled open the door and said with one last smile, "Welcome to the Magisterium of Magic, Miss Heart. It's a pleasure to have you."

"Goodnight, darling." Magee followed Master Lenin into the hall and pulled the door closed behind him.

Immediately I grabbed one of the remaining stools from the kitchen bar and rammed it underneath the door handle.

Lastly, I went into the closet and grabbed one of the many backpacks. Snagging shirts and jeans, I stuffed them inside. Then I slid it under the bed.

Control it and then run.

When the time came, I'd be ready.

12

Breakfast

Despite pure exhaustion, my internal clock woke me up.

In the space between consciousness and not, I expected to feel the world moving beneath me as if I were still on the bus. When I found it still, my mind reverted to the worse.

I sat upright in a rush. I shoved tangled locks of hair from my face, expecting to see the empty twin bed on the other side of the room, the dreary grey walls of Denny's house, and a bitter Kansas winter framed by my window.

A wave of relief rushed over me when I found none of those things.

I was in the middle of a large bed topped with too many pillows surrounded by red brick and fine wood. In the light of day, the apartment of the Magisterium looked less like a dream. Reality rested in the two empty stools near the end of my bed and the wand on the bedside table.

I slouched against the headboard.

Last night was . . . real. *I can do magic.*

I looked at the wand sitting on the bedside table. Reaching over, I carefully picked it up with two fingers and placed it in my lap. With a deep breath, I grabbed the end etched with images of fire.

The wand remained empty and still.

I tapped the tip against my leg a couple times. Nothing. Trying it against something harder, I knocked it against the nightstand. It didn't even spark.

I guess that's what Michael Kale is for.

I returned the wand to the bedside table and dropped my feet to the cold floor. Out of habit, I checked to make sure my getaway bag was still beneath the bed.

Ok. Now I just need to know how to get out of here.

Striding across the room, I dipped inside the closet and took out a t-shirt and jeans. The crispness of the fabric hinted at the newness of the garments. True to Master Lenin's word, they fit as good as if I had picked them out myself.

After my Converse were laced up, I dug through my old clothes for what was left in the pockets: the bus ticket, wrinkled and blood stained, and the envelope of cash that Blake gave me. Last was my cell phone. The screen was cracked and a few of the buttons fell out when I flipped it open. The metal had a burned, brown tint to it. In short, it was deader than a brick.

Everything else was gone.

I tucked the envelope of cash and the ruined ticket into my new getaway bag. For sentimental reasons, the phone also went inside.

Back on my feet, I grabbed my dirty hoodie and tugged it over my head. Just as I was about to leave the room, the wand on the nightstand caught my attention again.

Carefully picking it up, I slipped it into the front pocket of my hoodie.

Leaving the room, I retraced my steps to the staircase. Sun streamed through the glass ceiling, drenching the stairs with early morning warmth. With each step, the sound echoed seven stories below.

On the first floor, I looked around the rotunda at the eight gold doors. It looked less ominous in the daylight. Possibilities gleamed on every surface. The obsidian stone sparkled under the rays of daylight and the golden banisters, clock tower, and doors reflected it around the room.

Like the night before, the clock tower drew my eye. The three distinct layers of carved people—Users, I assumed—now looked different in light of my conversation with Master Lenin and Magee. The bottom and the most crowded layer must have represented Users without titles.

The middle layer of regal carvings were Masters, leaving the layer holding the clock to be School Masters.

Kind of over the top.

The clock's main hand, a golden needle marked with the word MAGISTERIUM said that it was half an hour before eight, which was when Master Lenin told me breakfast was supposed to start.

A little self-guided tour never hurt anyone.

I turned my back to the dining room and crossed the grand stairwell to the gold doors etched *Greenhouse*. Bracing my hand against the cold metal, I pushed the doors open and was immediately enveloped in a rush of humid, floral air.

It was rich with smells that were sweet and robust, like the vibrance of summer, the freshness of spring, and the crispness of fall all at the same time. Pulled by the fresh air, I floated through the door.

Glass walls and ceiling enclosed a maze of organized planter boxes. Some held perfectly round bushes of emerald green with tiny pink flowers. Others contained tall stalks of black reeds that moved without a breeze. Most of the containers held small batches of flowers. I recognized none of them.

Wandering through the aisles, I spotted a short cluster of purple buds upon a wiry yellow stem. I had never seen such a color combination before. Curious, I crouched in front of it for a closer look.

As I watched, one of the buds, no bigger than a penny, started to unfurl. The purple petals darkened to a deep maroon. As they opened, a wave of heat curled from the center. At the very heart of the flower sat a small white flame.

"What on earth?" I mumbled, unable to keep the smile off my face. Staked in the dirt before the plant was a small placard that read, Prometheus Tears.

I stayed at a crouch to watch a few more buds bloom. When I started to lose feeling in my legs, I left the greenhouse behind. There was so much I wanted to see before breakfast started, the most important being the door out of this place.

Exiting the greenhouse, I crossed the stairwell to the doors etched *Library*. I grabbed the gold handle but found it locked. Dropping to my knees, I peered through the keyhole, but only saw darkness.

No matter. Back on my feet, I faced the stairwell. *If I were the front door, where would I be?*

I looked at the doors marked North, South, East, and West. Since I was closest to the West doors, I crossed the black stone floor and pushed them open. Glittering chandeliers and lanterns flashed on the moment I crossed the threshold. In succession, they flared to life, illuminating the long hallway.

Just like the apartment level, doors were lined up almost too close to make sense. Pushing one open, I found a large room with amphitheater seating, a chalkboard, and desk up front.

Magic . . . right.

Moving further down the hallway, I opened one of the last doors. This space was set up like a standard classroom with all the seats on the same level. At the end of the hall sat another gold door, but with no engraved label.

Are you my way out? Quickening my pace, I pushed it open but didn't find the outside world. Instead, I was in a circular room wrapped in windows. A burgundy set of couches and comfy armchairs sat at the center. A spiraling staircase twisted around the perimeter of the room leading to another level and then another and another.

A tower?

I left the tower and retreated back to the main stairwell and headed for the South Wing. It was exactly like the West Wing, lined with classrooms and capped by a door. Quickly I walked by the closed classroom doors to the end of the hall. The door there also led to a tower.

A thought popped into my head, but I quickly dispelled it. *There's no way.*

Back in the stairwell, I tried the East Wing and again only found classrooms and a tower that only led to the higher levels. With one last wing to try, I retreated to the stairwell and crossed under the glass ceiling toward the North Wing.

"You have free range of the four wings of the castle—except for the North Wing."

Master Lenin's off-handed comment caused me to pause before the bright gold doors. Was this wing off limits because it had the door to the outside? I glanced over my shoulder, confirming that I was alone. Then I pushed my way inside.

Unlike all the other wings, the lights didn't turn on when I stepped through the doors. The light from behind me hit the grand chandeliers above, only to illuminate the dust covering the intricate gold and crystal artwork. With no windows to offer any light, the North Wing remained a thick black void.

I was used to shadows. All of my shifts at the diner ended well past the time of sunset, leaving me to walk home in darkness. They were my only allies in my attempted escapes. But what sat before me was different.

Thick and unrelenting, it sent a chill up my spine.

A loud chime echoed through the stairwell. Startled, I spun toward the sound, letting the North Wing doors slip from my fingers. They slammed closed with a boom as I faced the carved grandfather clock.

It was eight o'clock. Time for breakfast.

I looked back at the North Wing doors. If this wing was built like the other three, did that mean this place had no doors that led outside?

Who built a castle with no front door?

Then I remembered how Master Kale brought me to the Magisterium. One second, we were surrounded by fire on the interstate. Then, after turning on his heel, we were in the coolness of the infirmary. They didn't need doors if they could just use magic.

There has to be a way out of here that doesn't involve magic. This place has windows, right?

As the clock continued to chime out eight bells, I jogged back down the East Wing. Right before the tower, I pushed open the door to one of the classrooms where all the desks were on the same level. Just on the other side of the desks was a row of large windows.

Leaving the doorway, I pushed up the windowpane and peered outside. The drop to the ground wasn't too high. From here, it was a clean sprint into the woods.

And then, I'm surrounded by miles of forest. My escape plan wasn't looking very promising.

That's another problem for another time, I told myself as I closed the window and headed back toward the stairwell. *Now I know how to get out. I can figure out the rest when I need to.*

With my exit plan in place, I quickly left the East Wing and crossed over to the doors marked *Dining Room.* Leaking through them was the delicious smell of buttered bread.

My stomach growled. Pushing open the gold doors, I found myself standing in a cafeteria. Not as majestic as I was expecting for a magic castle.

Round tables surrounded by benches were scattered around the large space. Against the back was a stage with a solitary podium. The vast room was only occupied by one man hunched over his breakfast.

My attention was drawn to the left side of the room to a long buffet table. From where I was standing, I could see six different kinds of toast and seven kinds of meat.

"Good morning!" A short woman came around the other side. "You must be Miss Heart. I'm Cassie, the head chef. Master Lenin told us to keep an eye out for you."

"Hi." My eyes wandered to the food behind her.

"I didn't know what you liked so we just made it all. Grab a plate and help yourself." She nudged me toward the buffet. "While I'm thinking about it, is there a snack you like? We want your stay here to be as comfortable as possible."

Instantly my mouth watered. "I really like chocolate covered raisins."

Another smile broke across her face. "I'll have some dropped off in your room this afternoon. If you run out, you can just ring, and someone will bring more. Now come, come. Breakfast is getting cold."

I couldn't help but load my plate up with a little bit of everything. Then I followed her to the only occupied table.

At the sound of our footsteps, the man looked up with curiosity. He wore a thick orange turtleneck under a navy-blue blazer that was a size too big for him. His dark hair seemed to grow up, rather than down, so it was hard to get a read on how tall he was versus what was just hair.

"Charlie, this is Richard While," Cassie said, gesturing toward the man. "He's in charge of the library."

His green eyes brightened with curiosity. "It's a pleasure to meet you. Welcome to the Magisterium."

I awkwardly settled on the bench across from him. "Thank you."

"I thought Master Lenin wasn't accepting midterm applicants anymore," he said to Cassie as he picked up his coffee mug.

She shrugged. "You know how he is when he sees a new penny. He can't help but swoop down to shine it. Plus, with so many students transferring away . . . well, you can't blame him."

My interest piqued. *Why were students transferring away?*

"Master Kale brought her in last night," Cassie said flippantly. But there was nothing casual about her unblinking gaze at her coworker.

Mr. While's mug paused before his lips. The steam clouded the lenses of his glasses.

Mr. While swallowed. "Is that true?"

I assumed he was talking to me. His fogged over lenses hid his searching gaze.

Not seeing what the big deal was, I picked up another piece of bacon. "Yep."

Slowly, Mr. While lowered his coffee and let his glasses clear. "Why? With everything going on, you'd think he'd be too busy. Not to mention running errands is significantly below his paygrade."

Cassie gave me a sympathetic look. "No offense, dear, but you know how things are."

Not really.

"What's he too busy with?" I asked, reaching for the butter. *Probably glaring at people.*

Before either could answer, *he* walked in.

13

This Is Going to Be Harder
Than I Thought

As soon as Master Kale stepped into the room everyone launched to their feet.

The man in black nodded to Cassie and Mr. While as they awkwardly bowed their heads.

"Good morning," he said tightly. His obsidian gaze swung over to Mr. While, who was sweaty and flushed. "It's nice to see you're still around, Mr. While."

Stiffly they clasped each other's forearms.

The librarian nodded. His eyes were wide behind his glasses. "Good to see you as well, Master Kale. H—how's work these days?"

"Manageable." Then his lip twitched in disgust at the sight of me. "If you're finished eating, I'd like to get started." Judging by his tone, he didn't care if I was done eating or not. He was leaving and I was going to follow, by myself or dragging behind him.

Rising to my feet, I gave Cassie what I hoped was a smile. "Thanks for breakfast." Having no other choice, I stepped toward him.

Master Kale stuffed his hands in his pockets and headed straight for the doors. As soon as we passed into the stairwell, Cassie burst into a flurry of excited whispers. Mr. While wordlessly watched us leave.

Passing under the grand staircases, Master Kale moved down the South Wing. He made sure to stay two strides ahead of me. For the entire walk, the only sound was our footsteps bouncing around the empty hall. He didn't bother to look or say anything to me.

At the very end of the wing, he shoved a door open and gestured for me to step inside.

The floor was clear, except for a stack of dusty chairs shoved in the corner. Beside it sat a lonely desk. The windows let in the winter sunlight, as well as most of the cold.

Master Kale slammed the door behind us. The sound clattered around the room, echoing and reechoing. I was very aware we were alone and as far from another human being as the castle would allow.

With a locked jaw, he took his time looking me over, like he was peeling back my skin, looking for imperfections.

"Why are you here?" he asked. "Why stay?"

My feet moved me back from his tone rimmed with broken glass. A couple equally sharp rebuttals flew to my mouth. I swallowed them all and, instead, told him the truth.

"I don't want to hurt anyone anymore. I want to control this."

He tilted his head back, peering at me down the length of his nose as if I were something on the bottom of his boot.

After a moment, he grunted, unconvinced. "Lenin wants me to make magic seem interesting to persuade you to stay. "Magic is objective and unapologetic," he said looking at his wand. "It's not a party trick. It's not something to use lightly. Just because you can use a sword as a walking stick, doesn't mean it won't chop off your leg if you trip over it.

"The first thing you need to know is that there is a cause and effect directly associated with its use. Magic affects its surroundings —brightening or dimming lights, wilting plants, heating or cooling the air. Or it affects the User, most of which is internal. Our organs are created with an extra layer to protect our insides against normal use, but large doses erode that layer, leading to internal damage. Depending on the amount of magic, it can affect both.

"Last night was a perfect example of that. You burned five miles of interstate, killing everyone on it, and you nearly gave yourself massive organ failure. So, every time you use magic, ask yourself if it's worth it."

He raised his wand then. The creases between his fingers

brightened. Shining from the tip of his wand, almost too bright to look at, was what looked like molten sunlight. The air slowly left my lungs.

Magic . . . That's magic.

With his wand, he directed the golden glow into an anatomy model, rounding out the head and pulling out the shoulders. It shifted between translucent and opaque as the magic continued to twist and curl.

"Users aren't too different from Regulars. We have a heart." He gestured to the bright red organ. "And a brain—some forget that. What makes us different is that we have a core."

In the figure, the heart and lungs moved over to make room for a slender colorless organ.

I stepped forward for a closer look.

"That is where our magic is stored. When we use it, it flows down the arteries to our dominant hand. There, our wands draw it from our skin and we're able to perform charms, enchantments, and wards. Magic makes us stronger, more durable."

More durable? My eyes flickered to his.

"Have you ever broken a bone?"

I shook my head.

"That's why."

So, when I fell off the roof, or when Jamal pushed me down the stairs, that's why nothing broke. I thought back to all the times someone uttered, "You're lucky to not have broken something."

Every riddle of my life was so easily answered with the word *magic.*

"If magic makes me stronger, why can I be cut?" I thought about the number of scars crisscrossing over my back. My eyes turned to the thin scar running along the side of his face.

"It's all about proximity. The same lining around our organs protects our bones. Our skin doesn't deal directly with magic, so it has no need to be stronger than a Regs."

Master Kale slashed his wand through the figure, dissolving it. Without the glow, the room dimmed considerably.

"Lay on the floor."

"Why?" My eyes moved toward his wand.

"In order to use magic, you have to connect to it. Or else you're just an idiot waving around a stick. Lay down."

"I didn't need to lay down last night."

"That's because your magic was already out of your core. You need to learn how to draw it out in a safe way that won't break every lightbulb in the area or kill you." He let out an exasperated breath. "Either you're far more stupid than I first thought or your hearing is impaired." He raised his wand, just barely from his side. "Do I need to make you?"

No, but you could say please. I dropped to the floor and stared at the ceiling.

"Close your eyes."

Did he even know the word please? Biting back my throbbing temper, I closed my eyes. Uneasiness slithered into my chest when I realized I couldn't see where he was or what he was doing.

"Concentrate on your chest, where your heart should be." A couple seconds passed.

"What do you feel?"

"My heartbeat," I said. "And the air moving my lungs."

"Push aside everything. Remember where the core sat on the figure? Concentrate on that area."

Slowly, a heaviness settled into my chest. I had never noticed it before. It was right where the terrifying feeling started. As I held my attention there, a low hum vibrated through my chest, hot and alive. But it wasn't teeming like before. This time it was smooth, almost timid as it awoke.

Butterflies flew around my stomach. Along with the feeling came memories of shattering lights, blisters, fires with no warnings. My hands fisted at my side involuntarily.

In order to control it you have to face it. Get it together.

Somewhere to my left, there was the sound of a match striking.

The quiet hum in my chest exploded with fiery excitement. It flared forward with a sting that I felt all the way around my ribcage.

I jerked upright with a gasp. The burning magic snapped back into my core leaving me cold. My lungs expanded but no air filled them.

My eyes watered as I choked. "What was that?"

"Congratulations." His voice held no joy. "You just connected with your magic."

"Damn, that hurt." I rubbed my chest, trying to scrub the pain from my bones. "It didn't do that last night."

"Because you didn't hold it." He held up the spent match. "Energy attracts energy. The energy of the flame pulled your magic, but since your grip was weak, it snapped out of your grasp." He dropped the match and took out a new one.

"If you want to learn to keep your magic from flaring, you first need to have a good grip on it. Or else anytime you pull for it, it'll head for the nearest energy source. Try again, but this time don't let go."

"How do I do that?" I looked down at my hand. It wasn't something that I could *hold.*

"No one taught you how to breathe, right?"

"No, but—"

"Then I won't waste my time teaching you something so instinctual. Lay down."

"But—"

"I thought I just said I wasn't going to waste my time. Yet, here I am wasting it," he said sharply. "Lay down."

Control it and run.

Taking a calming deep breath, I rolled onto my back and closed my eyes.

Again, warmth bloomed out of the center of my chest. It poured through me like the first swallow of hot chocolate. I could picture the golden light from the night before, twisting and rolling through me . . . only to scald my organs black, to singe skin, and shatter lights.

Master Kale struck the match.

When my magic flared toward the tiny flame, I recoiled from the scalding rush, pushing it down like I had done every time I felt it rising up. The rush of magic snapped back into my core. The lights closest to me popped. Glass clinked to the floor, dousing half the room in darkness.

Master Kale regarded me with bored eyes. "What was that?"

I could only wait for my lungs to unfreeze from the shock of it. My eyes watered. My vision blurred. Finally, I sucked in a deep breath, coughed, and then drank in another one.

"You're getting in your way." He flicked the spent match toward my shoes. "You're afraid of it—"

"No, I'm not," I croaked.

He tilted his head at the interruption. "Really? So then why are four lights broken?"

"It slipped—"

"Or you're letting your fears get the best of you. You won't hurt anything in this room. Well, no one but yourself anyway."

I sat up, glaring at him through a loose lock of hair. "I'm not afraid." But wasn't I though?

Master Kale shrugged. "Prove it. If you're not afraid of your magic, you'll call it and hold on. If not, I'll get to watch you gasp like a fish and hope you choke on your own tongue." He took out a fresh match. "Ready?"

He lit three more matches.

Three times I was left gasping for air.

By the fourth I almost blacked out.

The fifth broke more lights.

Each time, it got harder and harder to concentrate over the ache circling my torso. My hands began to shake, and my head started to feel hot and light. The pain only made me think of the people who had been on the receiving end of these flares . . . which did not help me grip my magic. It deepened my fears toward the feeling.

He struck the sixth match. With a hiss, the flame ignited.

I curled my arms around my chest. With my eyes squeezed shut, I mentally shoved the burning feeling away as if I could pitch it from my body. There was only a second of relief.

In that second, the closest furniture skirted away. Fractures split up the window. The remaining lights brightened and blew.

Then the magic came back. With a furious rush it scorched through my ribs, burning the air in my lungs. I rolled over and threw up my breakfast on the black stone floor.

"Well." Master Kale flicked the smoking match toward me. "That settles my case. You're an idiot."

He tucked the match book into his pocket as he watched me empty my stomach completely. Wordlessly, he turned and headed for the door.

"Wait." I wiped the bile from my lips. "Where are you going?"

"As entertaining as it would be to watch you kill yourself, I'm not going to let you waste my time. I told you what you needed to do. You're the one hellbent on ignoring it."

"I'm trying—"

"This," he gestured to the room, the broken lights, the overturned chairs, and cracked windows, "says otherwise."

"What if I tried while holding my wand?" I asked, fumbling to pull it out of my pocket.

"Your wand will only use the magic you connect with. If you can't hold on to it, nothing will happen." Again, he turned to the door.

"Just give me a second."

"No. If we continue, you'll do some internal damage. Go see Helen for the pain." Without looking back, he opened the door. "Try not to be such a disappointment tomorrow."

The door slammed closed.

In the dark, broken room, I rolled onto my back. I kept my breath shallow, afraid that my ribs would snap.

This is going to be harder than I thought.

14

Control It

Helen gave me three potions.

A red one that fizzed with pink bubbles. The second was a thick, blue syrup. The third was both colorless and odorless. She gave me strict instructions to take them lying down and in a specific order of color to: colorless, blue, then red.

As soon as I swallowed the last of the red potion, my eyes rolled back. I woke up the next morning with my eyes nearly glued shut and my mouth dry. But the pain in my torso was just a memory.

The only thing that kept me from being truly grateful was that I knew I had to do it all over again.

I skipped breakfast, just in case, and waited for Master Kale in the classroom in the South Wing. Sometime during my potion induced coma, the room had been mended. The lights gleamed brightly as I walked in. The windows were clear of cracks. My mess on the floor was also gone.

At the middle of the room, like a brooding, dark centerpiece, stood Master Kale. The morning sunlight seemed to bend around his shoulders as if it were afraid to touch him. The darkness of his eyes were twin blotches of ink accenting his steely expression.

"Ready to actually do something today?" he asked, pulling the matchbook from the pocket of his leather jacket.

I nodded.

"I guess we'll see." He nodded to the floor. "Lay down."

My stomach sank to my toes as I laid back against the black stone. Taking a deep breath, I closed my eyes.

My magic responded without hesitation. As soon as I turned my mind to it, it awoke. Warmth spilled through my chest, twisting toward my shoulders, begging to be directed and channeled.

I'm not afraid.

Master Kale struck the match, but the flame didn't catch.

I'm not afraid.

A flame blazed to life with a sputtering hiss.

The magic in my chest sharpened, humming in on the new energy. I held my breath, squeezing my fists together as my magic rushed to meet it. Behind my eyelids, the lights flared.

"Hold it," Master Kale directed.

But it was too much, too sharp and hot. My concentration slipped into memories and the magic broke free. A lightbulb shattered and the wave returned with severity back into my core.

Over my gasping breaths, I heard Master Kale release a long, disappointed sigh.

"Get out of your head," he spat. "Or don't, if you enjoyed the events of yesterday. Then we can continue this meaningless cycle."

"Maybe if I had a teacher without a tree branch stuck up his ass, I might be able to do something else," I snapped.

He flashed me a smile as sharp as knives, all teeth and mirth. "This has nothing to do with me. This is *your* magic. *You* control it, not the other way around."

"Oh, really?" I snapped. "I don't remember *wanting* to burn someone with my hands. Or *wanting* a light to explode by someone's face. And I sure as *hell* didn't mean to blow out a wall because I was standing too close to a fireplace. I didn't want to do any of that, but it happened."

"That's because your magic was reacting to you. In all those moments, you thought you were in danger, right? Magic follows the thoughts of the casting User. You were thinking of ways to protect yourself or to get away, and your magic responded."

"But I'm not in danger now! So why is it flaring?"

"Because you're allowing it to. Energy calls to energy. If you stood in the middle of a superstore and pulled on your magic, it would rush toward the fluorescent lights. If you pulled on it near a candle, the same thing would happen. It will respond either to you or whatever's around you."

"I don't want it to respond."

"Then *hold it,*" he stressed. "Don't shy away from it. Embrace it. If you keep shying away from it, it will make poor interpretations of your thoughts and you'll continue to hurt yourself and others."

How could I embrace something that I wanted nothing to do with?

Master Kale didn't give me a chance to verbalize the question, let alone think of an answer for myself. He took up a fresh match and poised it against the box.

Dropping back to the floor, I closed my eyes. Magic slithered from my core, buzzing through my chest like a hive of bees.

He struck the match but it didn't light.

Hold it.

Don't shy away from it.

This is your magic. You control it.

There was another strike and a light.

I expected my magic to flare toward the flame. I knew that it would burn before it snapped back. Instead of getting the scared, tightening in my stomach, I clenched my fists. I turned my mind to the feeling of rolling flames swirling through my ribcage.

This is my magic.

I control it.

I willed it to settle and remain. I expected there to be resistance, that I would have to coax it back, but the flames stilled and cooled. I expected the rush and the burst of pain. But nothing happened. No pain came.

I opened my eyes and found Master Kale holding a lit match. All around the room, the lights pulsed with each of my heartbeats. It was calm and rhythmic, not frantic and flashing.

"Easy," Master Kale said quietly. "Can you feel it? You're holding it."

I nodded. My magic was firmly locked in my chest. I felt warm and energized. Like my first night, it spun through me, coiling my body in power. I felt like I could run the length of Kansas in a single day.

"Now, you're going to release it and let it return," he said. "Take a deep breath and slowly breathe out. If you don't do this right, you'll feel the same pain as before."

I did not want to feel that again. I rolled my shoulders and took a deep breath. As I exhaled, I felt the heat slowly fade and the hum quieted. In response, the flame grew smaller and smaller until it was a smoldering tip. The lights went back to normal.

"Do you have your wand with you?" He pocketed the matches and came to crouch before me.

Nodding, I reached into my hoodie and pulled out the length of black wood. He snatched it from my hand.

"Connect with your magic. Don't lay down," he said brisky as I started to lean back. "Connect with your magic and direct it down to your dominant hand."

"How do I do that?"

"How did you keep your magic in check?"

"I just . . . thought it."

"Then there's your answer." He arched an eyebrow expectantly when I didn't immediately move to follow his direction.

As soon as I turned my mind to my magic, it surged forward, eager and ready. With a stinging spark it jutted between my ribs toward the lights encircling the classroom.

No, you're staying with me. The surge of magic lapsed back. Completely under my control, it remained a comforting warmth.

Keeping my breathing even, I turned my thoughts to my right hand. The magic bled over my shoulder and down my arm. A faint glow gleamed under my skin as it reached my hand. There it pooled, prickling like a thousand tiny bubbles dancing in my fingers.

Master Kale placed the hilt of my wand into my upturned palm.

Instinctively, my fingers gripped the shaft. The etched flames lit up and smoldered with molten gold. My magic rushed toward the end, and there it waited, glowing and ready.

"Do you feel the difference?" he asked, staring down at the glowing wand.

I nodded. It wasn't an enemy. Or a weapon. It was . . . me.

My thoughts and will manifested into something tangible, brilliant. Something that crackled with raw unadulterated power.

"Release it," Master Kale said as he rose to his feet. He spoke with the same bitter edge as if the glowing victory in my hands meant nothing.

I was mildly surprised that I didn't want to. The rush, the intoxicating surge of power—I didn't want to release it and go back to being just *me*.

Drop out.

Runaway.

Something someone threw out with the trash.

Something no one even bothered to name.

I liked the feeling that I could do *something*. I wasn't sure what that something was but it was better than the gaping hole of nothing at all.

But that wasn't a part of the plan. Control it. Check. Now, it was time to run.

I released my magic as if it were a coiled snake. It sped back into my core with enough force to make my breath hitch. A dangerous thought started to bloom at the back of my mind. I hadn't even realized the seed had taken root. A part of me, a minuscule sliver, wanted to *stay*. To learn. To lean into this new world. To use the power glowing beneath my skin. To be something.

The new, sparkling idea was crushed swiftly and without mercy under the familiar drum that beat at the back of my head for years.

Run.

Run before this place breaks you.

Run before fate turns this new leaf into a dagger and slips it between your ribs.

Run before your fears are proven right.

I had been to too many houses, been welcomed into too many families, met too many two-faced individuals to be comfortable. Staying in one place meant getting stagnant, letting your armor soften which led to attachment. Attachment always led to bruises and scars.

Blake was my one attachment. Without him, maybe I would have tried harder to leave Salina. I certainly wouldn't have taken Master Lenin's offer to stay in a black stone castle with no doors. Attachment was an anchor. Love was the thing that drowned you. I already had one anchor. I couldn't afford another.

No. I wasn't going to stay and wait to see if fate had found a new way to shatter me. I had learned to control my magic. I was getting out, only this time without the fear of hurting someone.

I cleared my throat and looked up at Master Kale. My expression revealed nothing but that I was bored with his abrasive tone.

"What's next?"

He rose to his feet, eager to retreat a few paces as if being too close made his skin burn. "Now, you do it again. But this time, you'll be standing."

15

And Run

If someone had asked at the start of the day if there was anything worse than lying on the floor having my magic snap in and out of my core, I would have said no. The pain was enough to make me throw up, to make breathing—the most natural and easy thing in the world—difficult.

Master Kale found something worse.

At first, he simply had me stand and draw upon my magic. It was a bit more difficult. I found more things demanding my attention, balancing being the most prominent one. Every time I drew on my magic, and he lit the corresponding match, I was tugged toward the energy source as my magic begged to join it.

The tug came as if a string were wrapped around my spine. It yanked me forward before my feet knew what was happening. The cold stone bit into my knees each time I fell.

My knees were black and blue by the time I figured out how to hold on before it surged. But that only took about a half an hour.

He then had me move. First at a casual stroll, and then at a jog.

Years of sneaking over creaking floors and dipping into shadows had made my steps sure and light. I couldn't afford to be clumsy. Clumsy got you caught and getting caught meant bruises.

But Master Kale's test caused my feet to rebel against countless hours of practice. With each light of a match, my attention strayed, my balance shifted, and my toes knocked into the opposite heel. With each attempt, I was surprised to find that there were still new ways that I could trip myself.

It took hours to keep my feet steady beneath me. By then, my knees, hips, and shoulders hurt from their forced meetings with the floor. Sweat clung to my hairline.

The final tier of his educated torture was to bring me into the hall outside the classroom. On either side of the hallway, bright lanterns burned against the walls.

"Pull," he barked.

When I drew upon my magic, it didn't just tug in one direction. It went in *every direction.* Like a child in a candy store, it rushed from my chest eager to burn each lantern brighter, hotter.

My grip slipped. My magic snapped back into my core seconds before my head struck the obsidian floor. It took a few moments to find my way back to my feet. All the while Master Kale stood silently, watching.

He took an involuntary step forward. But I could tell from the hunger darkening his gaze that it wasn't to help me to my feet, but to keep me there. His knuckles were white at his sides.

I scrambled to my feet and backed out of reach. My skin sang with fresh bruises, but I didn't dare flinch. His black eyes reminded me of a shark's, hovering until it smelled weakness.

"Again," he bit out. Forcefully, he stepped back.

This time when I pulled on my magic and the lights flared to a blinding degree, I kept my magic close. Reveling in the strength it gave, I held it in my chest like a shield. Not that I knew what to do with it, but the heat and low hum vibrating through my ribcage were a shred of comfort against Master Kale's bottomless stare.

The way he looks at me . . . it's as if I've taken everything from him.

The lights returned to their normal shine. I remained on my feet and met his gaze. At that point he knew the last box had been checked.

"Release," he said. His voice cold and hollow.

Reluctantly, I did. His harrowing gaze kept me from celebrating my victory.

"What's next?"

He shook his head.

"We're done?"

"For today." He replaced the matchbook in his pocket.

I rolled my eyes. Turning down the hall, I mumbled under my breath, "Smartass."

In a blink he appeared in front of me. My shoes squeaked against the obsidian floor as I stopped to keep from ramming into him. My heart slammed against my chest as he loomed mere inches in front of me.

How did he do that?

Master Kale leaned down into my breathing space, bringing us eye to eye. The smell of ground sage, cool and earthy, plagued my nose. "Disrespect is something I've killed for. Pair that with your unique ability to waste time and the fact that I hate literally everything about you, it's a miracle I haven't killed you already."

Stepping closer, he said softly, "Just because Lenin thinks you're special, doesn't give you a free pass to act how you choose. Rein it in or I'll remove your voice box. You don't need to talk to do magic."

"What's your problem?" I snapped.

"You."

"You don't even know me."

"And I'm all the better for it. Do us both a favor and tell Lenin you're done." With a rumble of leather, he turned on his heel and disappeared, leaving a faint glowing circle on the floor.

How was he doing that?

"Well, *Master Kale*," I sneered at the space he used to occupy. "Don't make it sound like such a dare. I just might stay to spite you."

Might being the key word.

"*Masters of a trade are always called by their title. They've done a lot to earn it. As a sign of respect, you'll use that title,"* I remembered Magee *saying.*

Master Kale. I shook my head, making my way out of the South Wing. *Like hell, I'm going to give that douchebag any sign of respect. He thinks he can act that way for no reason?*

My next thought made me smile. *I should've just called him Michael. Or Mike. The biggest slight to a guy like that would be to not acknowledge all of his hard work.*

I tried to picture his reaction if I had thought of this sooner and called him by his first name. That was almost enticing enough to stay one more day.

Almost being the key word.

The aches and pains of the lessons faded as the excitement of a run slipped into my blood. I quickly climbed back to my apartment and retrieved my getaway bag from under the bed. I grabbed a couple more pairs of socks and the thickest coat inside the closet, just in case. Lastly, I raided the kitchen for any snacks in the cupboards.

When I was fully stocked, I peeked into the hallway. It was empty, like it had been every time I stepped out the door.

Gently, I closed the door, even though there was no one around to hear it. My footsteps were feather light as I padded down the stairs. As quiet as a shadow, I made it to the main level and slipped between the large gold West Wing doors.

Out of sight of the main artery of the castle, I quickened my pace, careful not to run because I didn't want to waste my energy. I had a long night in the woods ahead of me.

At the end of the wing, just before the tower, I stepped into one of the classrooms where the desks were all on the same level in neat rows, instead of tiered levels.

I closed the door with a soft *click*. The vast hallway carried the gentle sound all the way to the main stairwell. Weaving my way through the desks, I hitched up the window.

A rush of winter air, smelling of evergreen and future frost, stole the warmth from my skin. Undeterred, I hopped onto the window ledge and swung my legs up and over.

My feet hung over open air. Freedom.

I pushed myself off the ledge and dropped to the ground. The window slid closed as I landed in a crouch outside the school. The soil beneath my shoes was black with a thick coating of old yellow pine needles. Patches of muddy, hard packed snow lingered at the base of trees and never moving shadows.

Rising to my feet, I adjusted my heavy bag across my shoulders.

In the open air, my blood sang a single note.

Run.

Run.

Run.

I took a step toward the shadows, the unknown, toward freedom.

And then I hesitated.

I looked back at the black stone structure. The fading daylight streamed through the evergreen branches, painting the dark stone with ribbons of yellow. The glass of the classroom windows reflected the sunset colors as if they contained fire. The tower at the end of the wing stretched up and up, high above the trees, piercing the sky with its gleaming, pointed roof.

The outside was remarkably plain. The siding was smooth, with no seams between the stone as if the whole thing was carved out of a single slab. There were no fancy embellishments or window trims. It was as if the castle was never meant to be seen from this angle.

Despite that it really was something straight out of storybooks and myths. Even as I looked at it, I couldn't quite wrap my brain around it.

My hands moved on their own, slipping into the pocket of my hoodie. As soon as my fingers met the etched hilt of the wand, my magic warmed and hummed through my chest. The wand glowed through the fabric.

Stay and learn.

Stay to use the power glowing beneath my skin.

Stay to be something.

I pulled my hand from the wand and turned my back to the school. Shouldering my backpack, I headed deeper into the woods.

Run.

Run.

Run.

For the first time since I woke up after the crash, it felt like I was truly breathing. The cool outdoor air felt richer, sweeter than anything I'd ever breathed. I was running with no strings attached. No longer a kite, but a bird.

I moved quickly, avoiding mud and snow patches. I left no trace in my wake, save for a few broken pine needles under foot.

The air was still and quiet. There were no bird calls or animal chatter. The soft pine needles cushioned my feet, adding to the thick layer of quiet. I had never heard something so absolute.

In Kansas there was always something, a car motoring by, whispers of someone talking in the next room, restaurant chatter, or coffee beans being ground.

I followed an incline until it plateaued, leading to another sharp ridge. Breathing hard, I crested the top and stepped *through* something.

One second the air was a degree away from crystalizing. In the space between footsteps, it boiled, flushing across my skin. The air glimmered with specks of gold as if something tore around my body.

Magic.

When my foot landed, I turned, but found nothing out of the ordinary. There was no evidence of a burning wall of magic. Or anything.

I looked around, twisting over my shoulders searching for something that was other than trees and black dirt. I found none.

Turning to the nearest tree, I grasped the branches and hoisted myself off the ground. I scaled higher and higher until the needle covered limbs hid the ground. I reached and pulled my way to the top. There my hope started to slip.

In my first exploration of the castle, I wondered if the school was in the middle of nowhere. Now, I had proof.

The castle was nestled in a valley of evergreens surrounded by jagged purple peaks—or that's what I suspected. I couldn't see the school anymore. There were no roads in and out. No other buildings. The forest stretched on and on without a seam or an end that I could see.

I moved to the other side of the trunk. The orange streaked sky highlighted a dark rocky ledge. Snow clung to the crevasses of the mountain side, looking like silver veins in the fading light.

Maybe if I go over that next ridge?

There was no guarantee that I'd be any closer to finding something.

I cursed under my breath. It sounded too loud in the quiet wood. My thoughts churned with my next steps as I carefully climbed down to the forest floor.

"Did you enjoy the view?"

16

Give This a Chance

Master Lenin stood a few paces away with his hands in his pockets.

He wore a navy suit with gold pinstripes. At the end of the day, he must have removed his tie, but a gold pocket square still poked out of his jacket. He looked like an immaculate doll that had been dropped and forgotten in the middle of the woods. He was so put together, so neatly groomed that my brain warred against seeing him next to stoic evergreen trees.

"If you wanted a great view," he continued, "I have four towers back at the Magisterium that offer the same overlook, with significantly less work."

My eyes flickered to the growing shadows, expecting Michael or Magee to be lurking there. But it was just him.

"How did you find me?" I asked.

Master Lenin pulled one hand from his trousers and gestured with a casual flick of the wrist to the space behind him, to the invisible wall of burning magic.

"The Magisterium is heavily warded to stay hidden. Those exact same wards also let me know when someone walks off the property." He returned his hand to his pocket. "And just so you know, we're a couple thousand miles from civilization or even a camping tent. I doubt you packed enough food for that journey." His gold flecked gaze dropped to my shoes. "Or warm enough clothes."

I wiped my runny nose and remained silent.

"Did you feel that you wouldn't be taken care of here?" Master

Lenin asked. "Were you not comfortable? Was there something missing?" He lowered his head to catch my eye more directly. "I'm trying to understand why you are miles from the school, Miss Heart, without so much as a departing word."

"Don't take it personally. I can't—I don't want to be here."

"Even if you belong?"

"I don't belong anywhere."

"You've been here for barely thirty-six hours. That doesn't seem like you gave it a real chance."

"Yeah, well, I go with my gut."

The corners of his mouth turned down. "What are you running from?"

Nothing.

Everything.

The potential in your eyes.

Another anchor.

I shrugged.

"Master Kale told me that you have a grip on your magic. Now that you have more control you can begin learning to use it. If you ask me, that's the fun part of being a User." He smiled.

"But that's the thing. I don't want any of this."

"Of course not. Who in their right mind would want literal magic at their fingertips?"

My cheeks heated under the jab.

"You can't keep me here."

"I didn't think I was. Last I checked, I offered you an invitation." He nodded to me. "I see no chains or leashes on you."

"But you're keeping me from leaving."

"I'm saving you from starving in this forest. Or worse." He cast his gaze around. "Did you wonder why it's so silent? There are monsters out here. The magic in your veins will only make you a tastier treat."

My eyes snapped to the lengthening shadows. Once more my ears strained to pick up a whisper, a chirp, or chatter of nature. But there was nothing. A shiver tiptoed up my spine.

"Come back and give this a chance," he said, nodding back the way I'd come. "A real chance. If you still don't like it after, let's say, seven days, I will personally take you wherever you wish to go."

"I don't believe you."

"Then I guess you'll have to trust me."

"I don't do that either."

His expression softened, not under the effects of pity but of understanding. "Come back to the Magisterium and let me make you a cup of tea. Let's clear the air. Somewhere where it's warm and we're not being stalked for an evening meal."

Again, my gaze flickered to our dusky surroundings.

Moving slowly, Master Lenin took his hands from his pockets and extended one to me. The only callous on the offered hand was between his index and middle finger from holding a pen for long hours.

I knew defeat when I saw it—or rather felt it. My fingers and toes were numb. My nose ran from the cold. The deepening shadows only added to my unease. Shadows were usually my friends, but here . . . they wouldn't just be hiding me.

With a sigh, I stepped forward and placed my hand in his.

He winced as soon as our skin touched. He moved to pull away, but at the last second, he wrapped his hand around mine. He took a round black stone the size of a gumball from his pocket. It glowed bright with magic seconds before our feet left the frozen ground of the forest.

It was replaced by a lush burgundy rug. The outside chill was immediately exchanged for the cozy warmth of a well-lit office.

Master Lenin quickly released my hand.

The only thing that really made it an office was the large desk. Other than that, it resembled more of a portrait gallery. The wall closest to the door was covered with photographs of stellar students. Each one displayed their name and the year of their greatest achievement. On the opposite wall to my right, hung portraits of the school's highest ranked and most praised teachers. Directly behind the desk was the third collection.

Each frame was hung with the greatest care in chronological order.

On each frame was a small plaque identifying the students by name with the additional title, "Trial Winner," and their year of glory.

The walls were painted a dull gold, making the real gold of the door even more brilliant. Short bookcases lined the room, filled with ornate tomes and knickknacks. A globe, a couple statues, and frames with pressed flowers or certificates. On top of the shelf directly behind him sat a collection of pictures all with the same woman and small girl.

Master Lenin shook his hand as if it pained him. Rounding his desk, he flexed his fingers.

I looked down at my hand, still red from the cold, and found nothing wrong with it.

Master Lenin, cradling his hand to his chest, used his other to press a button on the desk.

Not more than a second passed before the gold door behind me opened. A woman in an electric blue pantsuit stepped inside. Her black hair was cut short, right under the angle of her jaw.

"Can you bring in a pot of tea, Miss Baker?" Master Lenin asked.

"Of course, Master Lenin." Her gaze brushed over me standing before the desk, flushed with cold and streaked with dirt and sap. "I'll bring two cups."

"Thank you. And I'll clean it up."

"Are you sure, sir?"

He smiled. "Yes. Go home and say hello to Elias for me."

"Thank you, sir. Have a good night." She pivoted on a bright orange heel and pulled the door closed behind her.

When she was gone, Master Lenin gestured to one of the two plush chairs before the desk. "Please. Have a seat."

I pulled the backpack from my shoulders and perched on the edge of one of the chairs. The cushion sank under my weight, making me want to lean back and let the softness fold around me.

"What happened to your hand?" I asked.

"You."

"I didn't do anything," I said in a rush. *He isn't going to pin something on me, was he? He couldn't do that. There was—*

"Not intentionally." His kind smile returned. "Your magic is strong enough for certain Users to feel when they come into contact with you. The higher the status the more magic they can feel. I am a Royal Eight, so I can feel even the slightest bit of magic. If a Regular or a Deficient three were to touch you, they wouldn't feel anything. A Common Six might feel a slight sting."

"A sting? You mean it hurts even when I'm not flaring?"

Nodding, Master Lenin looked down at his hand. "It was like putting my hand to a live flame. But now it's numb, all the way up to my elbow."

"I'm sorry—"

"Oh, don't apologize. I knew what was going to happen the moment I offered you my hand."

"Then why did you?"

"I wanted to feel it for myself." He flexed his fingers into a fist. "It's extraordinary."

"You're talking about pain."

"I'm talking about your power. The pain is a warning to anyone with opposing strength who might want to harm you. Feeling that — *this*," he raised his numb hand, "will deter them from taking you on as an enemy."

"I don't want to be anyone's enemy."

"What do you want, Miss Heart?"

The office door opened. Miss Baker stepped into the room with a tray *floating* in front of her. Standing in the doorway, she directed her glowing wand toward the desk. The tray followed the movement as if attached to an invisible string. The teacups didn't even rattle as the tray settled between us. Wordlessly, she pulled the door closed.

"You were running toward something." Master Lenin shifted forward in his seat and took up the teapot. "What was it?"

I didn't have an answer. Was it Blake? Did I even have a destination or did I just want—*need*—to feel my legs carrying me away from here?

Master Lenin poured the dark brew into two ivory teacups. A sugar cube clinked in each. He didn't say anything until he added a healthy splash of milk and set one on the desk before me. Then claimed the other for himself.

"I can offer you safety, a warm place to live out the rest of the winter, food, clothes, and the chance to hone and use the power inside you."

His words drove my arms to cross tightly over my chest.

Run.

Run.

Run.

"Don't you want to see what you're capable of?"

No.

. . . yes.

Reluctantly, I nodded.

"Then *stay.* You won't find any better teachers than those under this roof. All around the world, people beg to be let into this school but I'm offering you a slot because I think you're worth the effort."

"You don't know me."

"No, but I'd like to." He took a sip of tea. "Everyone here only wants what's best for you. Just give us a chance to prove that."

Warning bells shrilled through my head. Looking at his warm, twinkling smile, all I saw were sharpened wolf's teeth behind a coat of sheep's wool. But for the first time, I didn't want to listen to the suspicions pulling my muscles tense. I wanted to see where this went. I had *magic.* I'd be crazy not to want to use it.

But I couldn't shake the need to run, not fully.

Maybe I could stay, just for a little while. If I saw any red flags, then I could run.

But there was still the fact that the school was in the middle of nowhere.

My mind fished for an escape route or a lifeline to keep me sane. Then I remembered the way Michael disappeared from the hallway and how Master Lenin took me out of the forest and into his office.

If I could learn to do that . . . then it wouldn't matter if I was surrounded by thousands of miles of monster-filled woods. I could just disappear and reappear somewhere else.

With a new escape plan blooming, I found the tightness in my chest start to deflate.

"If I stay," I said slowly, "can I at least have a new teacher? Michael hates me."

Master Lenin took another sip of his tea. "Master Kale is a complicated man, I'll give you that."

"No, anger is a very uncomplicated emotion. It's always directed toward something or someone." Realizing I said too much, I dropped my gaze to my lap. "It's never without a reason."

Master Lenin gave me a gentle smile. "Things aren't easy in this world. Master Kale's job is demanding and unforgiving. He's doing his best to tread water while simultaneously keeping others afloat. He's a good man. Albeit, he forgets that sometimes."

"He told me he'd cut out my voice box."

Master Lenin winced. "Just give him some time to warm up to you."

I had a feeling the possibility of that happening would be right after the sun turned purple.

"He is a brilliant User, the best in his field. Despite his . . . rough attitude, you won't find a better teacher. I could find someone with a better temperament, but I fear you won't progress as fast as you have been."

"So, he's my fastest way to learn magic?" *And get out of here.*

Master Lenin nodded. "I'm afraid so."

Well, that sucks. I sat back in the plush chair. My fingers drummed against my bent elbows. His *rough attitude,* as Master Lenin called it, was just another Tuesday in Salina. I could handle Michael Kale with his double-edged words and soulless eyes.

"Can you do something for me?" I asked.

"Of course." Master Lenin sat up straight. His large eyebrows pulled together over an intense gaze.

"That friend I was going to meet in Vegas, can you give him something for me?" I reached across the desk and grabbed a piece of paper. Not in my best handwriting, I scribbled a quick note to Blake.

I'M OK. I'LL SEE YOU SOON.
~C

I folded it roughly down the middle. But before I handed it over, I wondered if I should call him. Who knew if Master Lenin would actually give it to Blake?

How would I explain all of this to him? Magic, hidden black stone castles, and my father . . . he'd think I was insane. I could lie, but I knew once I heard his voice I'd drop everything, consequences be damned, and immediately go back to him. He wanted me to have a better life, and as much as I hated to admit it, this was the way to get it. To be in control. Without fear of my own touch.

With a deep breath, I offered the note to Master Lenin. "Blake— the guy that lives across the street from me. He gave me the bus ticket. Can you give this to him? I just want to make sure he knows I'm alive."

"Of course." Master Lenin took the note and placed it beside his elbow. "Does that mean you'll stay? No more evening walks through the woods?"

I dropped my chin and shifted in my seat. "I'll stay until I know how to use magic."

"There's a lot to learn," Master Lenin said honestly.

I shrugged. "I'll know when I've had enough. And you'll take me back to Kansas?"

"Whenever you're ready to leave, I'll be waiting." He paused. "But I do hope you stay. You can do so much with your magic, if you only take the time to learn."

Seeing that I wasn't going to enter into a debate with him, Master Lenin set down his teacup. "Since you'll be staying with us a little longer, that means you'll be here when the rest of the school returns from their holiday. I'd like to enroll you as a student. There'd be less suspicion as to why you're here."

My stomach dropped. "I don't think you want me as one of your students. I haven't been in school for three years."

"These classes won't be anything like what you endured in Kansas. They are, after all, about magic and the other incredible things of this world."

"I don't know."

"I'd only enroll you in classes that will assist your lessons with

Master Kale. With the student body returning, you won't be able to meet all day anyway since the classrooms will be occupied. So, you'll meet with Master Kale after curfew."

He always has the perfect excuse lined up, I thought eyeing him warily.

"I was also thinking of enrolling you as a Common Six."

Confused, I said, "I thought you said I was a Royal Nine."

"You are. But since you'd like to keep away from attention, especially your father's, we'll have to lie a little bit. A Common Six is still a good deal of magic, since the majority of Users range from a Deficient Three to a Common Seven. This will just ensure that your time here is uneventful."

My stomach dropped. "Because someone will want to steal it?"

"You are quite safe here," Master Lenin assured me earnestly. "It's just that a Royal Nine hasn't been born in some time, and a status like that will draw all kinds of attention." He picked up his teacup and drained the rest of the brew. "I can imagine after the day you've had that you're rather tired."

He set the ivory cup down with a clink and rose to his feet. "I had a thought that you might like to know more about the world you were supposed to be born into."

Turning his back to me, he took care looking over the short bookcases running around the perimeter of the room. He pulled out one book and set it on the desk. Then he grabbed another and another, each varying in thickness.

A real smile stretched my lips. Books. Something normal. "You have no idea how nice that sounds."

"These aren't as detailed as what the rest of your classmates have gone through, but they should give you an idea of what they've been learning. If you have any questions, Mr. While in the library will be able to help you." He grabbed one last book and set it on the stack.

He pulled open the drawer on his left and took out a black marble the size of an egg. "This is for your night lessons with Master Kale. The transporter will beep and illuminate yellow when it's time for your lessons. When you're ready, grab it and you'll be Ported to the classroom.

When you're dismissed, it will Port you back to your apartment." He offered me the rock with a mischievous smirk. "This gets you around the curfew rule, but only for lessons."

"Ported?" I asked, slipping the marble into my pocket.

"It's short for teleporting. Master Kale Ported you here the night of the accident." He rose to his feet and turned on his heel. In a blink he appeared next to me.

I flinched away from him. "When will I learn to do that?"

"All students learn it in their final year." His grin turned sheepish. "If you chose to stay, you would learn it with your class next year."

"It sounds like you're trying to bait me."

"That sounds too conniving. How about let's go with enticing? I'm enticing you to stay longer." He paused. "Is it working?"

The corner of my lips twitched. "Maybe a little."

His grin broadened. "Here, take these." He pushed the books close to me. "Read and relax for the rest of the evening. I believe it should be calming after lessons with Master Kale."

"Anything that doesn't involve him would be calming."

He chuckled. "I can imagine. Now get some rest." He nodded to the door. "You look like you need it."

I shifted my arms under the books and stood. As I made my way to the door, he called, "Happy New Year, Miss Heart."

I turned toward the door and stopped. "How do I get to my room from here?"

"Oh, right!" He escorted me to the door and stepped into the hallway. Both directions curved as if it belonged to a large circle. Directly across from Master Lenin's office was another door, although unmarked.

"Follow the hallway to the stairs," Master Lenin said pointing to the left. "It'll take you to the main stairwell where you can make your way to the apartments on the seventh floor."

"Thanks." Hugging the stack of books to my chest, I followed his directions down the curving hallway.

17

Get Your Shoes On

Kicking the door shut, I set the stack of books on the coffee table with a thud.

I returned my getaway bag under my bed and quickly hunted down a container of chocolate covered raisins. With a full bowl, I dropped onto the couch and browsed the spines of the tower of books.

Essentials of Wand Technique
Organic Chemistry
Wand Structure
Magic Hierarchy in Tiers
User Anatomy and Physiology
Fundamentals of Magic Management
History of the Magical Arts; Volume One
History of the Magical Arts; Volume Two
Introduction to the History of the Magical Arts
Evolution of Magic Use Through the Ages

Tossing a chocolate covered nugget into my mouth, I flipped open the first book and thumbed through a few of the pages.

Bang!

With a golden flash, the door flew open and slammed into the wall. Chocolate covered raisins leapt out of the bowl as I startled in my seat. The gilded book flipped to the floor.

"Cheese and rice." I gripped the front of my sweater as my heart flipped into my throat.

Michael Kale stepped into the room with his wand drawn.

"Have you heard of knocking?"

"Knocking would imply that I care." He kicked the door shut behind him. "Get your coat and shoes on."

With his leather jacket zipped up to his chin, he looked ready to brave the snow. "Why?"

"Lenin wants me to take you to the New Year's Festival." His lips twitched into a sneer. He looked like he would rather eat his own leg than take me anywhere besides the morgue.

That made two of us.

I stooped to pick up my scattered chocolate raisins. "He didn't say anything about it when I saw him."

"It's a spur of the moment thing." He glanced at the door. "He thinks it'd be a good idea for you to celebrate your choice to stay."

"Tell him I don't want to go."

"I was instructed to be as persuasive as necessary. Personally, I think you'll be killed within the first five minutes. Get your shoes."

His words registered as he grabbed a coat from the closet. "What?"

"I'm tempted to call Helen to fix your pathetic excuse for hearing." He threw the coat in my face and turned to the door.

"Stop!" I kicked the fallen book out of the way and stumbled after him. "Hold on a second. Someone might kill me?"

He shrugged. "Maybe. If they feel your magic. If they don't, no one will look twice at you."

"But I could die."

Again, he shrugged. "Maybe. Maybe not." He glared down at me. "Don't make me throw you over my shoulder. Unlike you, I actually do what I'm told."

I knew he would do it. "Well, I don't want to go."

"I don't care. Get your shoes on or you can walk in the snow barefoot."

"Michael—"

The look on his face stopped the words from exiting my mouth. "It's *Master* Kale to you. And this is the last time I'll ask."

Ha. I bit back a smile. "I'm not kidding. I want to—"

"You mistake me for someone who gives a damn." He stepped closer and dropped his voice. "Get your shoes on."

I wasn't in the mood to be beaten senseless, so I ran and pulled on my shoes. As I walked back into the living room, I struggled into my hoodie. "Where are we going?"

"Do you ever pay attention?" He stepped into the hallway. As soon as I was out of the room, he slammed the door shut. "Every year the European Academy hosts a festival for New Year's. It's supposed to be fun." That last comment sounded like he was swallowing acid. Either he didn't think so or he didn't know what fun was. My bet was on the latter.

"What's the European Academy?"

"It's one of the seven great schools," he said, like that explained everything.

"Are there only seven magic schools?"

"Living in the Regular world has made you annoyingly dull."

I dug my nails into my palms.

To my surprise, he answered the question. "There are three phases of magical education; the first to learn the basics, the second to find out what you're good at—if anything—before you study for five years at one of the seven great schools, like the Magisterium."

"So, they're like colleges?"

"In ignorant terms, yes. Only these schools teach specific elements of magic. The Magisterium specializes in the magical arts. Others teach organic magic or pathetic enchantments. If you get good enough grades, you can apprentice with a Master."

Suddenly, he turned.

I was two steps above him, which brought us to eye level. "I'm only going to say this once. Don't talk to strangers, don't let anyone touch you, and control your magic."

"Gee, we could just hang out in a graveyard all night," I said dryly. "That might be just as much fun."

"This isn't a joke. I'd like to reach my three hundredth birthday, not die because of your immaturity."

My mouth dropped open. "*You're three hundred years old?*"

He rolled his eyes. "Of course, that's the only thing you got from that." Sighing he said, "No. I'm two hundred and seventeen. Do you understand what I'm asking of you?"

"Two hundred and seventeen! You don't look a day over thirty-five."

"I'm a Magic User. Do you really think I'm going to walk around looking like an old man?"

"How old is Master Lenin? Is he as old as you? What about Magee—"

"I asked a simple question." His voice whipped around the stairwell. "Do you understand?"

My curious excitement cooled. "Yes."

"You should think before you speak. It would waste less time."

His eyes locked on mine and, again, his lip twitched in disgust. "Don't look anyone in the eyes either."

"Why?"

He continued down the stairs. "Because they're just like your father's."

Why did that matter? I valued my life too much to ask, so I chose a different question. "How long do magic people live for?"

"Magic User."

I stuck out my tongue at his back. "How long do *Magic Users* live for?"

"It depends on their status. Deficients can live for a couple hundred years. Commons live longer. I knew a High Common who lived for six hundred years."

"And Royals?"

"Royals live until something kills them."

"So that means . . . ?"

"If you play it safe, you can live forever."

Cheese and rice. In Kansas I was convinced I wouldn't live to see twenty-five. Now I had the possibility to live for *centuries*?

"Most Royals kill themselves around nine hundred years. Living forever is overrated."

"What's your magic status?"

He completely ignored me. Mental note—don't ask him personal questions.

Reaching the first floor, he paused before the gold dining room doors. He lifted his hand, displaying a ring on his middle finger. The stainless steel was hammered into the shape of a moaning skull. He twisted the ring around once. A shimmer of gold glazed over his skin, distorting his appearance.

A scrawny teenager took his place. There was nothing remarkable about him. His new form would be easily overlooked in a crowd, which I guess was the point.

No matter how hard I tried, I couldn't forget what he actually looked like. It was like putting a rattlesnake inside a teddy bear, even though his unassuming appearance shouldn't have given me such feelings.

Taking his wand from his holster, Michael tapped each side of the door frame and ran it along the underside of the gold door. Instantly the air warmed and metal began to shimmer.

Sheathing the wand, Michael pushed open the dining room doors. Cold air rushed through my hair. Instead of seeing a room filled with round tables, there was only darkness so thick I couldn't see through it.

He stepped through but paused when I didn't instantly follow. He almost blended in with the shadows. "Come on, we haven't got all night."

Shaking myself free of shock, I stuffed my hands into my pockets and walked into the cold. Michael latched his hand onto my elbow and pulled me through the darkness. I had no choice but to trust him to be my eyes.

One second later, it was like I was stepping through burning syrup. It itched across my skin. In a blink it was gone, just like when I tried to run from the Magisterium.

Michael answered the question on the tip of my tongue. "It's a magic shield. It keeps Regulars from seeing or hearing anything that happens here."

He waved his hand toward the scene in front of us. "Welcome to the New Year's Festival."

18

The New Year's Festival

A Ferris wheel as tall as a skyscraper towered over the festival.

It flashed with every color, erupting in bursts like a firework. Each car painted a different color was strung with hundreds of little lights.

Before me, booths lined the streets of packed down, muddy snow. Some housed games, while others sold contraptions that shot out fire or sparkles.

Music played cheerfully from deeper in the festival. Smells of strange foods filled my nose as I tried to take it all in. On a stage to my right, dancers in tight gold leotards leapt through floating rings of blue fire.

"What—" I took a step back, pulling myself from Michael's grasp. I spun around expecting to see the stairwell of the Magisterium behind us. But there was just a moonlit landscape.

"How did we—" I twisted back to face the festival. "What did you just do?"

"Portal. I didn't want to Port and then have you puke on my shoes." He shoved his hands into the pockets of his jacket and turned his wary gaze to the milling crowd.

I had half a mind to tell him that I had Ported with Master Lenin without puking, but I didn't want to give him an opportunity to berate me further. Plus, I was rather distracted by the scene in front of me.

A thousand conversations bubbling with laughter and excitement converged into an incoherent mess. People exclaimed over won prizes or failed attempts. Out of sight, I heard shrills of excitement from people being spun around on wild rides.

No one looked older than the prime age of forty. Cultures of colors and different fabrics blurred together. Some shivered in silk, others wore heavy wool coats. Accents and different languages broke through the muddied noise of the crowd. I had never seen so many people, and for them all to look so different.

"They're all Magic Users?"

I could practically feel Michael roll his eyes. "Obviously."

"But how can you tell?"

"Other than the fact that we're in an enchanted bubble that *only* Magic Users can enter?" He pointed at the passing people. "He has a wand. She has a wand. So does she and he. Use your damn eyes."

I tracked his pointing finger and found the hilts of black wands sticking out of purses and backpacks. Most of them had a pocket sewn into the side of their pants just wide enough for the wand to rest against their thigh.

My fingers slid down the sides of my new jeans and found a small opening just wide enough for a wand.

"They just look so . . . normal," I blurted.

"What were you expecting?"

"Robes? Pointy shoes and cobwebs."

"Don't be ridiculous."

"Says the man dressed in all black."

His gaze snapped to my face. Even though the facade he was wearing was significantly less abrasive than his actual glaring expression, it didn't mean he looked any less severe.

"It so happens that my title demands that I wear all black. Not that you'd know anything about it since you have the intelligence of a sunbaked caterpillar."

"What? Are the animals that you hunt scared of color?" I asked dully.

He grinned, a flash of white teeth and malice. "Yes."

I had a sinking feeling that we weren't talking about animals.

His shoulders shuddered against the cold. "I'm going to get a cup of coffee. Go play a game. That's what kids do, right?"

I jerked around, ignoring the fact that he just called me a kid. "Or I could just go with you." I didn't like coffee, but there had to be hot chocolate in the magic world.

"That's not what I suggested," he said.

"You're *leaving* me?"

He gave me a dry look. "Did you think I was just going to walk around with you?"

"Yes!"

He gave me an incredulous look. "I'm not a babysitter. When you're ready to leave, meet me back here." He turned toward the nearest food shack.

Grabbing his sleeve, I pulled him around to face me. "You can't just leave me here!"

"Let me make something very clear." He ripped his arm from my grasp. "Don't *ever* touch me."

His black eyes burned into mine. I flinched back from his scalding glare and tucked my hands into the pocket of my hoodie.

"Besides," he continued. "Nothing will happen to you while you try to win a cheap toy."

"But you said someone could kill me."

"That was just me being optimistic," he said with a cruel smirk. "Meet me back here in an hour." He sharply turned and stepped into the crowd.

My legs locked. Should I go after him? Was this a test? As soon as he stepped into the crowd, he disappeared.

With my heart pounding against my ribs, I forced myself to move forward. My gaze bounced from one magical display to the next.

The people on the stage weren't in gold leotards. It was their *skin* that was gold. Their long, agile bodies leapt through rings of blue flames. As I wandered closer, I realized they had cat eye pupils and hairless tails protruding at the end of their spines.

On the other side of the muddy path was a stand of miniature animals. I thought they were figurines until one of the unicorns neighed to another across the display.

The carnival rides were suspended in the air by magic. One shot the riders past the clouds while another dropped the car miles into the earth's belly.

I was trying to take it all in so fast that it made me dizzy. My hands clutched the insides of my pockets. I scanned the crowd again for Michael. I couldn't believe I was wishing that leather- jacket-wearing jerk was with me.

Get a grip, Charlie, I scolded myself. *This is your new reality. You need to get used to it. Besides, without Michael, you can probably enjoy yourself.*

Slowing my breathing, I located what looked like a safe enough game. When I got closer, I peered over the shoulders of those already playing. The goal was to throw a ball at floating bottles. The more you knocked down, the more points you got for a stuffed animal that hugged you every time it was squeezed.

Seeing as I sucked at throwing balls at stationary things, I turned and scanned the more difficult games. One booth wanted you to use magic to direct water into different cups. Another had you choose which floating ring was the disguised bird feather. There was even one where you had to solve a riddle and turn a cup into a cat.

Good to know that Michael hasn't taught me anything useful.

I was about to go find him when I saw a face-painting stand. The poster above it showed the paintings moving on the skin. There was a flying bird that glided in lazy circles, a tree that danced in the wind, and even a fire-breathing dragon.

That actually looked pretty awesome. But Michael and Master Lenin cautioned me not to touch anyone. Did that mean no one could touch me?

To my delight, the woman at the stand was wearing gloves to fight the cold. With determination in my steps, I joined the end of the line.

When I saw the artist was counting change for the person at the front, I cursed. What little money I had was at the Magisterium under my bed.

Old habits pushed to the front of my mind as I focused on the couple in front of me. The guy was too distracted by the swooning girl leaning heavily against him. As he stared into her face, I knew all of his attention was on her.

My hands were small, but my fingers were long. I used one finger to open his coat pocket. I eased his wallet from the fold and slipped it into my own. I feigned looking over the colorful design choices, while my fingers worked the wallet open. Creeping into the folds, I extracted several bills.

I slipped his wallet back into his coat, undetected. Pulling the money out, I counted my loot. Twenty bucks, not bad.

The couple stepped forward and I watched the girl get a blooming rose painted on her cheek. I held my breath when the man pulled out his wallet to pay. Noticing nothing, they left.

"What would you like, honey?" the painter asked as I stepped up to her chair.

I glanced back at the options board. "Can I have a butterfly?"

"I actually just ran out of blue paint." She smeared a glob of blue across the thigh of her jeans. "I do have a lot of yellow and red. How do you feel about fire?"

My mind flashed to the interstate. The brilliant, blinding flames that encroached over everything. My magic hummed through my core and vibrated along my ribs. I clenched my hands into fists— *never again.*

"You have the complexion for it," she continued without noticing my hesitation. "The colors will really pop."

"I don't know—"

"Trust me." She smiled. "It'll be fun."

Michael told me to have fun. "Go for it."

She dipped her brush into a jar of shimmering paint. "Good. Take off your hoodie."

With stiff fingers, I pulled it over my head. I barely settled into the chair before her paintbrush landed on my neck. Warm paint glided up my skin to my cheek.

Her brush moved in swirls up to my temple. Reaching behind her, she dipped the brush into reds, yellows, and oranges. All the while her eyes were locked on the side of my face.

With a smile, she straightened. "Ready to take a look?" She reached behind her and handed me a small mirror.

Brilliant flames of ruby and burnt orange swirled up my neck to my temple. Every time my blood pulsed under my skin, the paint twisted and curled as if the flames were real.

"I love it." The deep oranges made my skin look smooth and pale, while the bright yellow highlights made my eyes look brighter.

She smiled. "Good! Thanks for stopping by. Happy New Year's."

"Thank you. You too!" I slid out of the chair and handed her a couple bills. With my hoodie pulled back over my head, I stepped into the cold. I wasn't as nervous as before. I was actually enjoying myself.

If Master Lenin wanted me to celebrate, I was going to celebrate. I had ten dollars left and my stomach was begging for a hot chocolate. As I wove through the crowds trying to locate a hot drink stand, the Ferris wheel caught my attention. I had never been on one before. Why not now?

I snatched a couple more wallets and bought a large hot chocolate with as many marshmallows as the cup could hold. Sipping the treat, I headed for the ride.

Bathed in the flashing lights, excitement warmed my stomach almost as much as the hot chocolate.

A loud whistle broke through the noise of the crowd. All around me, people stopped what they were doing and turned their eyes skyward.

Following their gazes, I looked up into the darkened sky and saw three streaks of gold climbing higher and higher.

With a mighty bang, they burst into lovely hues of pink. The glowing array of sparkles took the shape of two roses. Gravity took its toll, causing the bouquet of fire to begin their descent. But the sparkles didn't fade. They drew closer and closer, and then fluttered to the ground.

One dazzling sparkle landed on my shoulder. It was a rose petal. Laughing out of disbelief, I plucked it off my hoodie. I rubbed my fingers over the soft petal. It felt so real, so normal even though it glowed as bright as if it were still in the sky.

The rain of petals grew steadily heavier, coating the ground in a brilliant pink glow.

"Two more hours till midnight!" someone yelled to my right.

The fireworks are a countdown? I grinned up at the sky.

"Blue Eyes?"

The Irish accent jerked me around. Arthur Atlas, tattooed and swathed in black, walked toward me with his long black trench coat swishing around his knees.

"Charlie, right?" Atlas asked. "What are the odds of seeing you here?"

19

The Ferris Wheel

A rush of relief swirled through me.

The last time I saw him, it was right before the bus crashed. I assumed that he had been killed by the poachers or the fire. But he looked fine.

Then my blood ran cold.

The only people to survive that crash were Magic Users—me and the poachers. If he was standing here . . . did that mean he was working with the poachers who crashed the bus?

I took a step away from him. "It's a small world, I guess."

"I thought you were dead. That crash was brutal."

"I was lucky." Dropping the glowing rose petal, I slipped my hand into my pocket, seeking out my wand. "I didn't know you were a Magic User."

"I guess we were both in the dark there." He grinned.

I took another step back. "Well, I'm glad you're ok. Maybe I'll see you around."

"Ah, come on, love." He closed the space between us. "Don't be like that."

My heart jumped. Magic hummed through my chest. The lights near us started to flicker. "I have to get going. My friends are waiting for me in line. I'm sure you're here with someone too."

"Actually, I'm here for you." His charm dissolved.

I turned to bolt.

He grabbed my elbow with an iron grip, stopping my retreat.

My hot chocolate hit the snow, spraying the scalding liquid across our shoes. I threw my elbow back into his nose.

Cursing, he clutched his face with both tattooed hands.

I pushed through knots of people, gripping the wand in my pocket. I needed to find a way to get to Michael or hide or—

Atlas appeared in front of me. "Now, love, is that any way to treat a friend?"

"We aren't friends. I don't even know you." I stumbled back. My mind raced for a way out.

"You're not wrong." He unsheathed his wand. "Pity."

I opened my mouth to scream. His hand moved so fast, that if I wasn't looking right at him, I would have missed it. From within the folds of his coat, he fired. A small spark of magic flew from the tip and collided with the side of my neck.

My head went light. My eyes rolled back as magic vibrated through my body.

Just as my knees buckled, he scooped me into his arms. With a thousand-watt smile, he charmed his way by curious onlookers.

"Too much to drink," he said with a chuckle. "She's from sea level. Can't hold her liquor up here."

I couldn't do anything but groan.

He carried me between two game stands to the shadows behind. Through my blurry vision, I could barely make out an alley of sorts behind the vendor stalls. Completely hidden from the rest of the festival, he dropped me into the snow.

The moment I slammed into the ground the electrifying spark in my neck fizzled out. I sucked in a deep breath as his magic left my body. I sprang to my feet, feeling for my wand in my pocket. My fingers only met fabric.

Atlas held up my wand. "Give me some credit. I'm not thick."

With a sweeping kick, Atlas knocked my feet out from under me. I landed with a grunt on my shoulder. The hard-packed snow bit through my coat. Inside my chest, magic flared with a deep heated hum. Clenching my teeth, I tightened my grip on my magic, begging it to behave. It wasn't just me and Atlas. I was surrounded by thousands of people, and just as many lights—there were so many things that could draw my panicked magic, causing a flare. If what Master Lenin said was true, if I didn't control my magic, I could destroy much more than an interstate.

Atlas's foot slammed into my stomach, knocking the wind out of me. Fear choked my lungs as he raised his wand. Just as the tip flared, my grip slipped.

The hum of magic sharpened and flared. I squeezed my eyes shut as brilliant, golden magic flooded from my core, scalding the air. Wood cracked and metals shrieked. People screamed all around me.

With a whoosh, the flare of magic retreated back into my core. The sudden rush of heat pulled me upright with a gasp.

The snow around me had melted. Atlas was sprawled on his back, not moving. Steam rose from his black leather trench coat. The booths around us were flattened and the ground was littered with motionless people. But the thing that made my blood run cold was the cracked base of the Ferris wheel.

The wheel whined and tipped toward the earth. I jumped to my feet and watched in horror as it began to fall. The night, once filled with sounds of merriment, erupted in screams.

No, no, no!

I remembered the people on the interstate, those still alive on the bus. Some of them might have made it if it hadn't been for my magic. I stayed at the Magisterium to keep this from happening again. But I had failed after one field trip.

The flashing wheel halted in its downward descent with an ear splitting squeal.

Metal groaned and whined as it slowly started to move back into its upright position. Wildly, the cars full of people swung back and forth.

My gaze flew around. There, at the base of the grand structure, were two men bathed in the flashing multicolor lights of the Ferris wheel. Golden strands of magic erupted from their wands, directing the ride back into its upright position.

Relief flooded into my lungs. *Thank God.*

With a final groan, the wheel came to rest on its base. The bottom glowed as it melted back together. The lights flashed cheerfully, and the wheel started to spin once again.

My knees shook with the rush of adrenaline. Stumbling through the snow, I picked up my wand and broke into a run, away from the ride. I joined the crowd rushing away from the scene. Streaked with mud and snow, I blended into the fleeing masses.

I passed the hot chocolate stand and the face-painting booth. The crowd became less fearful and more curious as I neared the meeting place at the edge of the festival. Most of the groups of people were moving toward the ride to see what was going on.

I rounded a group of teenagers staring at the Ferris wheel. Michael stood behind them, one hand stuffed in his pocket and the other holding his coffee. His eyes narrowed when he saw me.

"Took you long enough," he said dryly.

"I—" I stopped.

If I told him what happened, would he think I was too dangerous to teach? *I need him to teach me.*

"I got lost." I jerked my thumb toward the Ferris wheel. "Do you know what happened?"

Sipping his coffee, he shrugged. "Someone might've been drunk and used too much magic. It happens."

His gaze remained steady, as if he could see the truth cowering behind my eyes. But he didn't call me out. He just continued to hold my gaze.

"There's another reason never to get drunk," I laughed weakly.

"Good to know you're not a complete idiot." He took another swallow of his coffee. Without another word, he turned and started into the darkness.

My hands shook in my pockets as I followed him, but it wasn't from the cold. Just before we stepped through the magic barrier, I glanced back.

The Ferris wheel spun like nothing had happened.

20

A Lie Laced With Gold

Knock knock knock.

I sat upright, instantly awake.

Dreams of fireworks and monster-filled woods slipped out of my memory. Before I even knew I was moving, my feet touched the floor. As I stumbled from the bedroom, I stepped over discarded chocolate covered raisins from the night before.

I dragged away the chair jammed under the doorknob and un-twisted the deadbolt. Opening the door just a crack, I peered into the hall.

It was empty.

Did I dream that someone was knocking?

Opening the door wider, I leaned out. Both directions of the brightly lit hall were deserted.

Just as I was about to go back to bed, my gaze dipped toward the threshold. Sitting right outside the door was a flat box topped with a gold ribbon. A steaming teacup of clear liquid sat beside it.

It couldn't be from Michael. That man didn't know how to knock.

I stooped down and collected the morning surprise. I looked around once more, before nudging the door closed behind me.

Setting the box and teacup on the counter, I uncoiled the gold ribbon and pulled off the lid. Nestled on a bed of white satin were three items.

The first was a silver bracelet made up of plain, delicate links. There were no charms hanging from the loops or any studded jewels.

The second item was a gold pin no bigger than a quarter. A black and gold compass rose was engraved into the surface and at its center was the number six. The final item was a card.

Good morning,

I hope this note finds you well rested. I would have delivered these items personally, but with students making their way back to the Magisterium this afternoon, I have a full docket.

Helen asked that I pass along the bracelet. The metal is enchanted to read your vitals to make sure there are no lasting effects from your previous flares. Injuries to the core take a good while to heal so we need to be cautious.

The pin is a visual of your magic status. Since you have chosen to stay with us for a little while longer, you'll need it for your classes when you join the student body. Please wear it to all of your classes.

If you need anything, please alert myself or my assistant, Miss Baker. Your fellow classmates will begin to arrive before dinner. Your lessons with Master Kale will continue tonight at 10:00. After your exciting evening last night, I thought you could use the day to recharge.

Sincerely, Master H. Lenin

Ps. I couldn't help but notice your untouched tea last night. I suspect that it might not be your drink of choice. I hope this beverage makes up for it.

I looked at the cup. The steaming liquid was as colorless as water and just as fragrant. Confused, I lifted the teacup from the saucer.

The moment my hand closed around the porcelain sides, the liquid darkened to a rich, creamy brown. In that instant, the warm scent of hot chocolate drifted to my nose.

Tentatively, I took a sip. As the sweet drink played across my tongue, it reminded me of nights spent with Blake on his breaks. With one small sip I was swaddled in comfort and homey memories. I clutched the small cup between my palms and, hoping to savor the treat, I looked back at the box of gifts.

"My exciting evening," I mumbled, slipping on the silver bracelet. *Did that mean my failed escape attempt or the New Year's Festival?*

He didn't mention the New Year's Festival in the card. If he was going to discard the event, then so was I. Besides, the Ferris wheel was fixed, and no one was seriously hurt, at least not that I saw, and Master Lenin said the Magisterium of Magic was the safest place in the world. Atlas and the other poachers couldn't find me here. I took great comfort in that.

Sipping my hot chocolate, I plucked the pin from the box and rolled it between my fingers.

A lie laced with gold, I thought idly.

I had been to so many schools that if being the new kid were an Olympic sport, I would've won gold. My goal was to delicately balance being invisible enough not to be noticed, but sharp enough that if I was noticed any attention would be redirected.

In three days I had left the only place I'd ever known, survived a bus crash, been attacked by magic poachers, woken up in a black stone school, gotten exposed to magic, learned about my father, and been harassed by a jackass in all black.

Being around teenagers with normal problems and class work sounded like a nice break. I found that I was actually looking forward to it.

Leaving the pin on the counter, I took my hot chocolate and returned to bed. It was the first time I had had a day with nowhere to go. I was going to make good on it.

I set the petite cup of hot chocolate on the nightstand before throwing myself back into the comfort of the mattress.

I finally left my room around noon because my stomach demanded real food.

I took one of the books Master Lenin gave me and tucked it under my arm. As the door slammed shut behind me, I stuck the compass pin through my shirt and clipped it in place over my heart. Stepping into the stairwell, the shiny surface gleamed in the sunlight that poured through the glass ceiling.

As I walked down the stairs, I peeked down at the number six pinned to my shirt. From my upside-down vantage point, it looked like a nine.

Clever. While the world saw the lie, every time I looked down, I would see the truth.

Not that it'd be hard to forget I was a Royal Nine. Not with the constant flashing lights or the accidents I managed to get in and out of without a scratch. The bus crash, falling off Blake's roof . . .

My steps slowed as I stepped onto the third level landing. I leaned over the railing and looked down three stories to the main floor. The only thing below was the lonely grandfather clock.

I wonder . . . It was higher than Blake's roof.

Don't be ridiculous. Below was a floor of unforgiving stone, not a snow laden lawn. Pushing away from the railing, I continued down to the next level. With each step, my gaze returned to the drop. On the first landing, I again stopped before the railing.

Curiosity itched under my skin as I leaned over.

"Magic makes us stronger, more durable."

With Michael's sharp tone in my head, I set down Master Lenin's book. Carefully, I swung one leg at a time up and over to the other side. I gripped the gold railing with white knuckles as I turned myself to face the floor far below.

My stomach dropped.

This is stupid.

That thought was shushed by the memories of falling through open air and walking away fine. Michael said magic makes us stronger, but how much stronger?

Taking a deep breath, I let go of the railing.

For the split second I was airborne, I wondered if I had made a mistake or maybe I had misinterpreted Michael's explanation of magic. Leave it to him to plant false information in my head in hopes that I'd try it and willingly throw myself off the nearest height.

My heart jumped into my throat but before I could scream, my feet slammed into the obsidian floor.

The impact rolled up to my knees . . . with zero pain.

I straightened to my full height, breathing hard. A breathless giggle escaped me as I looked up to the landing where I had jumped.

"Good to know Michael's not full of shit," I mumbled.

Quickly I retreated back up the staircase to retrieve the book. I was about to go back down, taking the stairs this time, when my gaze was drawn to the original landing where I had first thought of jumping.

How far could I fall before I broke?

I set down the book once more and climbed up to the third floor. It didn't take nearly as long to convince myself to climb over the gold railing. As I swung my legs over, one at a time, a thrill of excitement shot through me. This time, I straightened my arms as I leaned over the open air. Curtains of unruly hair framed my view of the drop.

My fingers relaxed, and I plummeted three stories.

My shoes slapped against the floor with a loud clap. The impact jarred my hips. A sharp bite of pain flared in both feet, but it was mild. Nothing more than a stubbed toe in comparison.

And I was standing.

Immediately my gaze swung back up the staircase, not to where the forgotten book sat, but to the higher levels.

Could I make the jump from the fifth landing?

What about the sixth?

Could I just walk out of my apartment on the seventh floor and bypass the stairs all together?

I chuckled at the thought. Alone in the stairwell, the sound crept up the stairs toward the glass ceiling.

It was ridiculous and stupid. Or was it? The thrill of falling twice sang through my veins. It called to higher floors, to dare to do something more dramatic.

My feet pulled me back toward the stairs. Once more I climbed up, passed the third landing to the fifth.

"Miss Heart?"

I spun toward the gentle voice and found Cassie, the head chef, standing at the base of the stairs.

"Are you alright?" she called up to me. "I thought I heard something fall."

"I'm fine!" I had a feeling that jumping from three stories was frowned upon. My mind raced for an excuse. I found it sitting on the first landing. "I just dropped my book."

Cassie turned her worried gaze to the staircase and found the neglected book a step or two from the landing.

I raced down the steps to collect it before she could see that it wasn't damaged. I hugged the book to my chest and, for good measure, crossed my arms over the cover.

"What's for lunch?" I asked as I moved down the remaining stairs toward her.

The topic of food thawed her concern. She turned to the dining room with a smile. "We've got a lot going on for the welcome back dinner tonight so I don't have anything fancy. I hope a grilled cheese will do."

Her version of a grilled cheese consisted of cheddar and pepper jack cheese with onions, tomatoes, and basil leaves. While it wasn't fancy to her, it was a treat to me. I asked her for a second, which she was more than happy to oblige.

With a second sandwich in hand, I crossed the stairwell to the greenhouse. In the shade of a purple fern with white blossoms, I sat on the floor and opened Master Lenin's book.

After a few hours, a low rumble pulled my attention from the pages to the door. Ducking out of my hiding spot, I followed the sound until it grew into an incoherent mass of voices.

Stepping through the greenhouse doors, I got my first look at my classmates.

As they trickled into the dining room they greeted their friends. Bags drifted in the air as they floated behind their owners. Paper airplanes zoomed around in loops, never losing momentum. Girls changed their hair color with a simple tap of their wand, trying out new shades as they stood in circles.

Each one was flawless. Their hair was smooth. Their teeth were straight and snow white. The lack of acne and pimples made them look alien. No one stood out with the normal teenager things like braces, poor hair choices or facial features that were too big for their developing bodies. Anyone of them could've rocked the cover of a magazine.

I remembered what Michael said about using magic to change how you looked. Every one of these kids had mastered that skill.

I reached up and touched the splitting ends of my hair. I winced when I noticed chocolate under my nails and the wrinkles crisscrossing over my t-shirt. Flying under the radar might not be so easy here. I stood out like a frizzy cat in a dog show.

My gaze flew from one group to the next, looking for their wands. One girl had the long piece of black wood stuck through her top knot as if it were an accessory. A boy by the stairs twirled it between his fingers like a drumstick. Another had it stuck up the sleeve of his sweater.

On and on it went. They were in hidden pockets along the seams of their jeans. They stuck out of boots or bags. One wore it around her neck from a chain. Each one looked so *comfortable* with it, as if it wasn't something that performed magic.

Slowly my apprehension melted into pure fascination.

I leaned against the doorframe of the greenhouse. A few paces in front of me a guy pulled on his magic. Molten gold swirled from his wand and pooled under his large suitcase, lifting the bag a few feet off the ground. As the boy walked toward the stairs, the bag followed close behind.

A small spark of magic zipped across the rotunda and up the stairs.

The golden blip struck the bag, bursting the zipper. The boy's neatly folded clothes cascaded down the stairs. His irritated groan was lost in the chatter of the room.

As the boy began collecting his things, I looked for the offending User but found that no one was really paying attention to the boy on the stairs, save for the occasional laughing glances.

I looked back. The boy now had his arms full of clothes.

Why isn't he using magic to pick it all up?

I squinted, focusing on the pin on the left side of his shirt. Just barely, I could make out a three.

Another boy broke away from a group by the library doors and, taking the stairs two at a time, started to help the other gather his things. The new User also didn't use his wand. With a smile framed by dimples, he helped the flushed student shove everything back in the bag.

With the zipper ruined, he hoisted the suitcase up and hugged it to his chest. Grimacing with effort, he started the long trek up to the seventh floor.

The helpful boy's smile dropped as soon as the other's back was turned. His eyes scoured the crowd below as he looked in the direction of where the assaulting spark came from.

Taking in the whole room, his gaze came to me. The accusing edge disappeared as if a switch had been flipped. Eyes as rich and warm as chocolate stared down at me from the first landing.

I snuck a glance over my shoulder but only found the rows of planter boxes behind me. I ran a hand over my face feeling for leftover cheese from lunch on my chin.

Finding nothing, I snuck a glance at the cute, helpful boy on the stairs. But the landing was empty.

That's probably for the best. I tucked Master Lenin's book under my arm and headed for the dining room.

"Hello."

I spun toward the greeting and found the cute boy standing a couple feet away. Up close, his eyes were the perfect shade of chocolate brown and filled with just as much sweetness and warmth. The fading afternoon light caught in his neatly combed sandy brown hair. He wasn't more than a handful of inches taller than I was, but he carried it well.

"I didn't mean to sneak up on you." He took a step back with an easy grin. "I help Master Lenin as the Records Keeper. He told me to keep an eye out for you. I'm Daniel Phillips." He held out his hand.

Instinctively, I reached forward. In that split second before our hands touched, I remembered Master Lenin's saying that my touch stung.

Without hesitation, Daniel reached past my offered hand and grasped my forearm. I was relieved when my fingers wrapped around the sleeve of his burgundy bomber jacket and his fingers locked around the frayed sleeve of my light blue hoodie.

"Charlie," I said. "Uh, Heart."

Daniel dropped his hand immediately with an eyebrow cocked with surprise. "Heart? How do you spell it?"

My eyes narrowed at his reaction. "Like the thing in your chest."

"Of course." His smile returned, but a watt dimmer. "I bet you get asked that a lot."

"Why?"

His smile dimmed again, but this time with confusion. "Because of Master Hart . . . Your names sound sim—I'm sure there's no relation." His gaze flew around the room looking for a life raft.

Before I could offer up a lie assuring him that there wasn't, he found a way to change the topic.

"Cornelia!" He waved toward the doors.

Standing between the golden doors of the dining room a pair of eyes, deep and blue as sapphires, turned our way. A pretty blond grinned when she saw Daniel's waving arm. She left the doorway and quickly made her way toward us.

"Hey!" She rushed toward him with her arms stretched wide for a hug. She pulled up short when she saw me beside her friend.

"This is Charlie," Daniel said, sliding his hands into the front pockets of his pants. "Charlie, this is Cornelia."

"Hi." I clumsily grasped her forearm.

"She just transferred to our year," Daniel explained. His brown eyes hardly left mine as he introduced me.

"Nice to meet you," Cornelia said brightly. "Welcome to the Magisterium."

"Oh, I'm not really—I'm only here on a trial basis."

"So that's why Master Lenin asked me to seek you out." Daniel's dimples deepened. "Let me guess, you're deciding between two schools and he's trying to convince you to choose his."

Does it count as a lie if it was so close to the truth? "That's exactly what he's doing."

"What other schools are you deciding between?" Cornelia asked as she fiddled with a bumblebee pendant resting at the hollow of her throat.

Crap. My mind scrambled for one of the names Michael mentioned before the New Year's Festival.

"The . . . European Academy?" *Crap. Or was it the European University?*

Cornelia's eyebrows rose. "You have an offer from the Academy, too? Good for you."

Daniel shook his head. "You should choose the Magisterium. If not for the food, then at least for the relaxed dress code. The Academy has all their students in suits. Master Lenin doesn't care much about what you wear as long as your grades are solid."

"It's true," Cornelia piped up. "One guy in our class showed up in his pajamas for a month. I think Master Lenin would have let him continue if he didn't keep falling asleep."

"I'll add that to the list of pros and cons," I laughed.

"Would you like a tour of the castle?" Daniel asked. "I'd be happy to show you around before dinner."

"Is this part of Master Lenin's plan to convince me to stay?"

"Ah, no." He looked down with a sheepish smile. "This one's all me." When his gaze returned to mine, it twinkled with a secret wish for more time. His eyes flickered between mine as if he were trying to decipher the color.

You're not staying, I told myself. *Making friends isn't a good idea.*

"Thank you, but I already looked around this afternoon." The lie flowed smoothly over my tongue. "I have a meeting with Master Lenin in a few minutes. I should make my way down there."

"Oh, yeah, sure." His gaze dropped, barely hiding his disappointment. "Well, if Master Lenin asks, tell him that I did my best to convince you to stay."

"I definitely will."

Cornelia grabbed Daniel's arm. "It was nice to meet you. I'm sure we'll see you around!" Dragging Daniel after her, she pulled him toward the dining room.

Daniel looked back twice before they disappeared into the crowded room. Each time was accompanied by a dimpled grin.

As soon as they were out of sight, I pivoted toward the stairs. I could get more reading in before my lesson with Michael. My plan was thwarted when I saw the golden doors marked *Library* were open for the first time.

I glanced back at the dining room to make sure I wasn't still being watched and headed for the newest addition of the castle.

The ceiling rose a hundred feet in the air. Shelves of books went up half that height, letting the black ceiling dome over the shelves. Multiple chandeliers the size of minivans glittered with crystal and gold. The shelves stood in neat rows, going far back into the room until the farthest ones looked to be the size of my thumb.

I wandered about, enchanted by the rows of different colored spines. I didn't have much time to read in Kansas. There were a couple bookshelves in the coffee shop I worked at, but most of the titles were teen romance.

The fine leather covers, while carefully preserved, looked to be older than Michael. Tentatively, I pulled out a book about the magical uses for sunflowers.

"Are you finding everything alright?"

My heart jumped to my throat. I spun around, dropping the book covered in sunflowers. Mr. While stood at the end of the aisle.

"Careful with that," he said with a shy smile. "These books are one of a kind."

"Sorry." I scrambled forward and collected the fallen tome. I flipped it over, looking for scuffs or dented corners. Thankfully it remained unscathed.

"Is there anything I can help you with?" Mr. While asked, striding forward and taking the book from my hands.

"I'm just looking around."

"I'd be happy to give you a tour if you'd like. After all, the Magisterium of Magic is known for its library."

A few beats of silence followed as he continued to watch me with an expectant intensity.

"Alright. I'll bite. Why?"

He flipped open the book. I jumped as a brisk voice filled the aisle.

"Every book is enchanted so the author reads it to you. You can change the volume by stroking the spine." He ran his hand over the glossy cover, reducing the voice to a near whisper. He snapped the book closed and returned it to its shelf.

"The books you'll need for class are different because they show you how things are done." He walked a little further and pulled out another one twice as thick. Opening to the center, a small orb shot from the middle of the spine. Hovering over the pages, an animation demonstrated the magic that made a plant grow faster. "The Magisterium has the largest collection of instruction manuals. We have manuscripts spanning back to the first civilization."

So, some of these books *were* older than Michael. Centuries older.

"If you're not sure what book you need, just ask me. If you know what you're looking for but don't know where to find it, just look up." He pointed at a pulsing blue light hovering over us. Behind it was a thin trail that went back the way we had come. "That light appears as soon as you enter the library and it will lead you to any book you're looking for. When you're finished, it'll lead you back to the door. The back of the library is set up with tables for intense studying. There are computers there as well."

He must have noticed the glaze over my eyes because he smiled. "Don't worry. You'll get the hang of it. Besides, once school starts, you'll have more to do than wander around this dusty old boot." Closing the demonstration book, he replaced it on the shelf. "How are you settling in? Master Lenin said you transferred from a smaller school. I know going from small to big can be difficult."

I shrugged. "I'm doing fine."

"I'm glad to hear that." He glanced behind him. "If you ever have any questions, I'm always happy to answer if I can."

I hesitated as curiosity wrestled for control of my tongue. "Master Lenin mentioned something about the North Wing. Why isn't anyone allowed in there?"

"You don't know the story?" He shrugged when I shook my head. "I can't blame you. It's not one most people like to tell. And when it is told, it's been changed so much it's hardly like what happened."

He leaned against the closest bookcase. "The North tower is haunted. A couple decades ago, a Royal snuck into the tower after curfew and never came out. The tower caught fire and the door was jammed shut. No one knows exactly what happened. She either killed herself or her magic was stolen, but she's not too talkative on the subject to say what happened."

My heart tripped against my ribs. *Master Lenin or Magee didn't say how often people stole magic.*

"The ghost has acted violently towards students in the past. She destroyed a lot of the classrooms that are too close to her. That's why the wing is forbidden."

Master Lenin forgot to mention that in the 'Persuade Charlie to Come to My School' speech.

"Isn't there something he can do to get her out?" I asked.

He shook his head. "Ever since that night, the tower has been sealed. Nothing can open it, not even magic. We've all learned just to work around her."

"And here I was thinking that the front door was down there," I grumbled, doing my best to sooth the goosebumps running down my arms.

Mr. While chuckled. "The Magisterium doesn't have a front door or any door to the outside. Everyone either Ports or uses a transporter."

My interest flared. *Porting. That's my way out of here.* "Do you have any books on how to Port?"

"Of course. That's an advanced subject. You'll be learning that next year in Miss Van Davis's class."

"I'm not trying to jump ahead," I said, feigning a look of innocence. "Some of my friends were talking about it and they said you had to jump twice before you Ported. Cornelia said you had to mutter something."

He tipped his head back and sighed toward the ceiling. "The ignorance of young people amazes me. Truly."

"I knew it sounded wrong, but I wanted to be sure before I told them"

"I admire that." He turned and headed down the main aisle. "Not a lot of people will challenge their friends or even look for the right answer."

A few rows down he stepped between the shelves and scanned the titles. He gestured to the shelf closest to the floor. "Everything you'll need is here. The best one is *The Art of Teleportation.* The instructions are clear, but it does use some advanced magical techniques and terms. *Porting for the Ignorant* would be my second suggestion."

"Thank you." I dropped to my knees and pulled out the books.

My fingers tingled with the possibility of freedom, true freedom. *Think of where I could go with just a turn of my heel. No one would be able to catch me, ever.*

"I know you're just looking for the techniques," Mr. While continued, "but *365 Ports in a Year* has great ways to use Porting other than just going across the room when you're lazy." He bent down next to me. "This one here is great for—"

"Mr. While!"

Two girls came around the corner and excitedly made their way over. He took a step away and was instantly enveloped in questions.

While he was distracted, I tucked *The Art of Teleportation* under my hoodie. Following the blue dot hovering over the ceiling, I quickly left the library and reentered the stairwell.

The North Wing doors drew my attention, as they were the only ones closed. I remembered the impenetrable darkness on the other side. With the story of the Royal girl twirling through my mind, chills prickled over my arms.

21

Ensuring an Escape

Flying up the stairs, I returned to my room and locked the door.

Just for good measure, I closed my bedroom door before I removed the book from under my hoodie.

My fingertips tingled with anticipation as I sat on my bed and flipped open the cover.

The moment the introduction page was displayed, a smooth voice blared across the room. *"Porting is one—"*

Startled, I slammed the book closed. Remembering what Mr. While told me, I twisted the book around and stroked the spine, lowering the volume. When I opened the book for a second time, it was much more manageable.

> Porting is one of the hardest magical achievements a User is able to perform that does not require a wand. Instead, a User must rely on clear thoughts and a substantial amount of magic. Depending on the magical status, some Users might not be able perform this act at all.
>
> If you are a Deficient, seek the professional advice from a magic consultant before attempting to Port. Other options may be available to you.

Well, I didn't have that problem.

Skimming the introduction, I flipped ahead until I found instructions. A bright orb shot from the crease between the pages. At the center a figure demonstrated the steps of Porting.

The key to Porting is movement. The User's magic wraps a portal around themselves. Moving gives the User the momentum to throw themselves into another space.

The most common and effective way of generating this movement is spinning on the heel of one's foot. Others include jumping, stepping, or falling, depending on what is most comfortable for the User.

The first step to a successful Port is to have a clear mental picture of the destination. Having seen the place before keeps Users from Porting into solid walls or into open air. This mental picture should be as detailed as possible.

Faulty or incomplete mental pictures have been the cause of Users Porting miles from their desired destinations and 3% of User casualties to date.

Not using enough magic can cause the User to go unconscious. Many studies have shown Users who do not use enough magic suffer brain trauma due to the rush of blood that floods the brain.

Users under the status of a Deficient Four should not attempt Porting for this reason. Ineffective Porting by a Royal can be equally destructive as their unused magic floods the air around them, killing anything within five feet of the User.

Cheese and rice.

The knots in my stomach doubled. Rolling the tension from my shoulders, I set the book on the mattress and rose to my feet.

I thought about trying to go to the other side of the apartment, but I settled on the other side of the room.

From where I stood, I faced the windows overlooking the evergreen mountains. To the left of the window was a bedside table topped with a lamp wearing a gold shade. On the other side of the windows was the closet door.

I flipped to the next page in the textbook.

With the mental picture of the end destination as the sole focus of the mind, the User must pull magic from their core. Once filled with magic, use the preferred method of movement to throw oneself toward the chosen destination.

When a Port is successful, the User's magic scorches the surface they leave behind. These are appropriately named Porting Circles. Depending on how far the User is Porting will determine the depth of the Porting Circle. How strongly the circle glows indicates when the Port was made. For more on Porting Circles, refer to page 27.

The final step to completing a successful Port is the landing. Many Users do not maintain their footing beneath them, resulting in a loss of balance. This is not for lack of trying. The sudden change in terrain shocks the mind. With practice, this can be overcome.

"That doesn't sound too hard," I mumbled.

I watched the orb illustrate a person filling with magic, turning, and then appearing on the other side of the bubble a few times.

I stepped away from the bed and took a deep breath. Closing my eyes, I focused on the center of my chest. My magic awoke instantly, filling my ribcage with a deep, scalding hum.

Gritting my teeth against the sensation, I formed my mental picture of the other side of the room. I turned sharply on my heel.

The magic in my chest burst like a balloon, striking my ribs. All around the room, the lights glared brightly. My head went light, knocking me off balance. I landed hard on my hip.

On the floor, I opened my eyes with hope.

I was exactly where I was before—just sprawled on the floor.

Did you really expect to get it right the first time? Shaking off the disappointment, I tried to sit up, but my vision twirled like a merry-go-round. I waited a few seconds until I could see straight.

Stumbling to my feet, I re-read the instructions and watched the orb again. *Maybe my mental picture isn't detailed enough.*

Closing my eyes, I painted the other side of the room across my eyelids: the clothes scattered on the floor, the chipped bricks under the window, and the creases in the curtains. I focused on the open space in front of the window and pulled on my magic again.

I breathed slowly against the fire billowing through my body. Again, I turned on my heel. This time my feet flew out from under me.

My bed shoved away from me as I smacked my head against the floor. Half the lights in my room went out before slowly blinking back on. Dazed, I stared at the ceiling for a few minutes.

Crawling toward the bed, I jerked the book into my lap. *What am I doing wrong?*

I muted the blabbing author entirely and read the passages out loud to myself, saying each word carefully to make sure I comprehended the sentence. Returning the book to the bed, I mirrored the little person in the demonstration bubble. I pulled on my magic and when the little figure turned so did I.

This time when I hit the floor, I passed out.

I woke up with my face pressed into the rug. My body was twisted in an awkward angle, putting a kink in my neck. Worse was the pounding in my skull and the sourness in my chest.

I sat up slowly, my ears ringing. My vision swam with flashing colors and black dots. Breathing slowly, in through the nose and out the mouth, my vision stilled and solidified, but the flashing didn't go away.

That's because something *was* flashing.

Fisting my hands in the comforter, I dragged myself up right. Now more awake, I found that the ringing in my ears wasn't from being thrown to the floor.

Next to the clock on the nightstand was the large, black marble from Master Lenin. Glowing bright yellow, it let out a ceaseless shrill. The longer it went the louder it became.

It only agitated my aching head further. I reached out to silence it or, worst case, throw it into the hall. But the moment my fingers wrapped around the marble my feet left the carpeted floor of my room.

The warmth of the apartment vanished. In the next second, I was standing in the middle of a cold, empty classroom.

"You forgot."

I whipped around and found Michael Kale standing with his arms crossed tightly over his chest.

22

Using a Wand

I forgot about night lessons.

"Sorry, I—" I clamped my mouth shut. He couldn't know that I was learning how to Port. "I fell asleep."

As my eyes adjusted to the lighting of the room, I noticed a dark purple bruise peeking out from under the collar of his shirt. I was familiar with bruises, but this shade of purple, a dark plum, was new to me.

"Are you ok?"

"Of course not. I'm with you." He tugged his collar up with his right hand, favoring his left arm close to his side. "Did you bring your wand?"

I nodded, holding it up for him to see. Lucky for me it was next to the transporter when I was yanked out of the apartment.

"Tonight, you'll start with the basics. You know how to connect to the magic in your core. Now it's time to use the magic you connect with." He looked at my wand and rolled his eyes. "First, you need to learn how to actually hold it."

He stepped toward me and roughly twisted the wand from my grasp. "Which hand is your dominant?"

"My right."

He held my wand up. "When you connect with your magic, it'll travel from your core, down your arteries, and into your hand. Make sure you always have your hand over the designs. The designs pull your magic into the shaft so it can be used." He snagged my wrist again, careful to keep his fingers wrapped around the cuff of my hoodie.

He took my wand and placed it back in my palm. "Hold it like this." He turned my wrist and adjusted my grip so my index finger curled around the shaft and my palm faced down.

"This way, when you cast, your arm will snap back and you'll be ready to cast again. Keep your hands away from the tip." He slid my hand lower. "You could lose a finger."

"Cheese and rice," I mumbled.

"What does food have to do with this?"

I flushed. "Nothing. Keep going."

His eyes narrowed. "The chest is the broadest part of the body. That's where you should aim. The bigger the target, the better chance you have of hitting it. Most of the time, you get one chance, and you can't afford to miss."

"Will I be firing at someone?"

He shrugged. "You never know. The first charm I'll teach you—a simple one—is to move an object." He pulled out his own wand. It could've been an extension of his hand; he looked so comfortable with it.

He pointed it at a chair on the other side of the room. On top of this chair was a shiny, red apple. With a flick of his wrist, a small glowing dot flew from the tip of his wand. It hit the apple and knocked it to the floor.

"The key is to keep your movements sharp and to move quickly." He stepped forward and slashed his wand through the air.

The chair skidded to the right. He dipped his wand in the other direction and the chair followed like it was connected on a string. He jerked the tip toward the ceiling. Just as the chair rose in the air, he turned in a tight circle and threw his arm forward, like he was physically throwing the magic from the wand. The chair broke apart. The pieces clattered to the floor.

"The less time you give your opponent to think, the greater your chance is of winning." He made a quick loop and the chair reassembled. "If you have a floppy wrist, you will lose control of the shot and it won't accomplish anything." With a flick of his wand, the apple jumped back onto the chair. "Point your wand at the apple."

I looked down at the eleven-inch piece of wood. Running my fingers over the carved designs, I tried to picture myself using it.

How was I supposed to use it without it flying out of my hand or looking like a complete moron?

Already feeling pathetic, I raised my arm and pointed my wand at the apple.

"What did I just say about the chest?"

"It's the biggest target on the body."

"So, you do listen." He smirked. "Look at how you're standing. You're facing your target head-on. You're giving them a clear shot."

"It's an apple."

"This time." His hand struck my shoulder, spinning me so my body was in line with the apple. He reached over and realigned my wand with my target. "Grab your magic and be very clear what you want it to do. Let's just start with you saying it out loud."

"That's it?" I blurted.

His eyes became instantly bored. "Yes, that's it. Concentrate, tell your magic what you want it to do, and it'll do it. With enough practice, all you'll have to do is think and your magic will act. Now, go ahead and try." He stepped back and continued to analyze my movements.

Nerves set in as I took a deep breath. This was worse than doing a demonstration in front of an entire class.

Lifting my arm, I looked at the apple, then at the tip of my wand, and back at the apple. There was a perfect line between the two. It couldn't be that hard, right?

Clearing my mind, I focused on my core. Magic awoke in my chest and spilled down my arm. As the heat pooled in my hand, the flames engraved in my wand glowed like live embers.

"Move." A bright wisp left the tip.

The apple wobbled . . . and remained on the chair.

"That was painful to watch." He grabbed my fingers and began prying them from the shaft. "You aren't allowing your wrist to move or your magic to flow. Relax and try again. You won't kill anything in this room. Do what feels natural."

Raising my wand, I tried again. "Move."

The designs on my wand barely glowed and the apple rolled across the seat of the chair.

Michael let out a frustrated sigh. He stepped into my line of sight. "You need to concentrate—"

"I am."

"—and stop interrupting me," he snapped. "Concentrate on your magic. Feel it burning in your chest. Tell it what to do. Don't ask. Command it." He stepped back. "Try again."

Shifting my wand to my other hand, I flexed my fingers before grabbing it again. Lifting my arm, I aligned my wand with the apple and concentrated on my magic. The carved designs in the black wood smoldered with molten sunlight.

"Move." Instead of holding stiff, I twisted my wrist.

This time I could feel that it worked. My hand tingled and went numb as a spark blew from the end. It collided with the apple, kicking it off the chair, and smashing it against the wall.

I stared at the remains of the poor apple. My wand slipped from my numb fingers and clattered to the floor.

Reaching up, I rubbed my chest. *So that's what using magic felt like.*

"Is your hand numb?" Michael asked.

Trying to re-wet my mouth, I nodded. "Is that normal?"

"This is your first time correctly using magic, every other time it's been an uncontrolled flare. Your hand isn't used to it. The numbness will last for a couple minutes and should only happen the first few times."

"And the light-headedness? Is that normal too?" The floor was starting to tilt.

"For you, yes." He plucked my wand from the floor and offered it back to me. "Your core is used to having the pressure of unused magic inside you. When you get familiar with your status, it will only happen when you use too much." He used his wand to put the apple back together and tossed it back on the chair. "Do it again."

Quickly I pulled on my magic and, with a flick, I said, "Move."

Instead of being thrown into the wall, as soon as the spark hit the apple, it exploded.

"You're using too much magic," Michael coached. "Regulate the amount that leaves your core."

My hand was so numb I had to concentrate to keep my fingers wrapped around the shaft. This time I didn't pull on my magic as hard as the time before. When the spark hit the apple, it rolled off the chair and bruised against the floor.

With a flick of his wand, the apple jumped back on the seat of the chair. "Again."

We had an hour left in the lesson when Michael walked over and picked the apple off the chair.

Thoughtfully, he tossed it from one hand to the next. After a couple of times, he stopped.

"Deflect this." Then he threw it at me.

The apple smacked into my shoulder—hard.

"Ow! You never told me how!" I picked up the fruit and chucked it back at him.

He caught it like a pro baseball player. "When an object comes toward you, slash your wand like you're going to cut it in half."

"What do I say?"

"Nothing. Your wand knows what to do." I swear I saw him smirk. The bastard was going to enjoy throwing things at me.

"Then why did I have to tell it to move an apple?"

"Because that was a charm . . . You know what that is, right?"

Oh, for crying out loud. "Why on earth would I know what that is?"

His eyes narrowed at my tone. "Magic is divided into three categories based on the amount of magic required. Charms are the easiest. All Users can cast them like levitation or disarming. Enchantments are . . ." he struggled to articulate his thoughts, "the intermediate level of magic, like illusions. Wards are the most powerful. Only High Commons and Royals can use them."

"Like what?"

"Offensive magic, Porting—" he ground his teeth together. Giving up on his explanation, he turned back to the apple in his hand. "Deflecting is hardly a charm. You're not manipulating the object. You're only altering its trajectory."

He threw the apple as hard as he could toward my face.

My mind's eye transformed the crimson skin of the apple into five clenched fingers. I dropped to the floor seconds before the apple made contact with my face.

"Use your magic," he said. With a swish of his wand, the apple flew back into his hand. "You look like a toddler trying to use a stick as a sword."

My heart hammered in my ears as I staggered back to my feet. *It's an apple. It's just an apple.*

I pulled on my magic again. My eyes watered as it burned down my arm.

He threw the apple.

I dropped to the floor so quickly that my knees bruised. It didn't do any good. The apple clipped my shoulder as I went down. I felt the impact throughout the scars on my back.

"You have the power to stop this," Michael said, reclaiming the apple. "Plant your feet. You're a Magic User. The world bends to you."

I focused on the apple in his hand. I forced myself to take in the shape and color to remind myself that it was a harmless fruit. But every time it flew toward me, I felt the cold terror that settled into my stomach right before Denny's belt landed.

The apple struck twice more. Then five times. My hands were shaking so hard I could barely keep my wand from slipping out of my hand.

Drop out, Denny's voice hissed through my skull.

Runaway.

Something someone threw out with the trash.

Something no one even bothered to name.

I stepped out of the way of Michael's rocket throws. My foot caught around my own heel and knocked me to the ground. I landed hard on my hip. Anger sizzled in my chest.

My name is Charlie Heart.
I'm a Magic User.
A Royal.
The world bends to me.

Breathing through clenched teeth, I pushed myself up and planted my feet. Magic poured down my arm and into my waiting wand. The lights flickered and danced as the next apple left Michael's hand as a blur.

As it flew toward me, I saw Denny's stupid, cocky face. I thought of all the times he knocked me down and broke the skin on my back. In those moments, I so badly wished I could stop him. Now I could.

I slashed my wand through the air. Magic streaked forward. The apple split in half; one half going to the left and the other to the right. The halves smacked into the ground and rolled to opposite corners of the room.

A moment of silence followed.

Breathing hard, I looked at Michael, expecting him to say something smartass, but he remained silent. Before I could gloat, he took another apple from his pocket.

How deep were his pockets?

As soon as the clock struck midnight, he stopped. "That's all for tonight. You're dismissed." He turned his back to me and started picking apple pieces up off the floor. His collar shifted, revealing the purple bruise.

I stepped forward to help.

"Go," he snapped.

Clamping my mouth shut, I pulled the transporter from my pocket and appeared back in my apartment.

I collapsed on the bed, rubbing one spot on my shoulder that the apple had landed particularly hard on. Despite my headache, my unsuccessful Porting attempts, and Michael's radiant personality, my mood wasn't sour. I was grinning at the ceiling.

All I could see was the approaching apple, the rush of magic, and the split halves flying around me.

I had kept something from hurting me. For the first time, I protected myself.

And I could do it again, and again, and again.

I told Michael I would leave the moment I could control my magic . . . now I wasn't so sure I wanted to. I wanted more.

23

First Day

The next morning my wake-up call was another knock at the front door.

This time the teacup of transformative clear liquid was accompanied by a leather satchel filled with crisp, new textbooks, notebook paper, and black ink pens. Master Lenin even had my initials embroidered on the corner of the bag.

I stuck my status pin through a thick off-white sweater. Taking a deep breath, I knotted my hair at the base of my neck, hoping it would tame some of the frizz. I draped the new bag over my head and let the wide strap settle comfortably on my shoulder. I dropped my hand to my hip where my wand was safely stowed in the little pocket running down the length of my jeans.

I had everything I needed to start my first day in a school that taught *magic*. A grin lit across my face.

I'm going to learn about magic today from someone not in all black and who knows how to act like a human with real feelings. Are Magic Users considered human? I guess I'll learn that today!

Throwing open the door, I stepped into the hall.

"Thank God, you're a Common."

I jumped back and bumped into the door just as it slammed closed.

A short figure straightened from her slouch on the other side of the hall. To say she was five feet was pushing it. Her ridiculously high ponytail tried to add a couple inches, but somehow it made her look even shorter. Four-point diamond frame glasses held her shrewd gaze.

Pinned to the front of her sweater dress was a status pin with the number seven.

Beside her, with a dimpled grin, was Daniel. His gaze was as warm and inviting as it was last night.

"I swear if I had to escort *one more* stuck up Royal, I was going to lose my mind." She shouldered her backpack higher on her shoulder.

"What she means to say is good morning," Daniel said.

"If I wanted to say that, I would have." The short girl turned down the hall. "Come on. If we're lucky, there'll still be cinnamon rolls left."

"Who are you?"

"Aanya Moose, but everyone calls me Moose. Master Lenin asked me to show you the ropes before class," she shot over her shoulder.

"Of course, he did," I mumbled. Seeing as we were heading in the same direction, I fell in step with her.

"And you know Daniel."

I peeked over at him. My heart danced a little when I met his gaze. "Yeah, we met last night."

Daniel opened his mouth, but whatever he was going to say was cut off.

"Let me see your class schedule," Moose said, holding out her hand.

I rummaged through the pockets of the new bag. I found the schedule printed on cardstock, in its own thin slot in the back. In my haste to pull it out, I tore it in half.

You've got to be kidding me. I put the pieces together and scanned the first line.

<u>Creature Studies, Harrison, E5534</u>

Moose swiped the schedule from my hand. Without missing a beat, she pulled her wand from the side of her boot and pressed the glowing tip to the torn edge of the paper. The seams fused together without so much as a wrinkle of evidence that it was torn.

I stared at the whole piece of paper. I could perfectly picture the page in pieces. *How cool was that?*

"You have the same class as us," Moose said.

"How can you tell?" I asked through my shock.

Daniel reached over Moose's shoulder and pointed at the page. "The first letter is for the wing it's in. The first number is the floor, and the last three numbers are the room number."

Moose shot him a side glance and handed the schedule back. "East Wing, fifth floor, room five, thirty-four."

My shoulders sagged with relief. "I thought it was going to be like hacking into a safe."

Daniel chuckled. "I thought the same thing on my first day."

"The hardest part is remembering which direction you're going in and that you're using the right staircase." Coming into the stairwell, Moose stopped at the top of the staircase and pointed. "The left staircase goes to the odd floors and the right one goes to even floors. If you need to go up one level in the same wing, use the tower staircases so you don't have to keep coming back to the main stairwell."

With that, she started down the stairs. At this point in the morning, the only students on the stairs were the stragglers rushing down to the main level.

"Master Lenin gave us a whole spiel of things to tell you," Moose said gesturing between her and Daniel. "You should be flattered he wants you so bad."

I gave her a tight smile.

"The Magisterium is one of the best," Daniel said, peering around Moose. "Technically we're second out of the seven, thanks to the last Master's Trial. Our curriculum is unmatched in the magical arts—although I can tell you which classes to avoid if that's the title you want. Sixty percent of each graduating class gets apprenticeships with Masters, which is the most of all the schools."

"I don't think that has anything to do with the school itself," Moose cut in. "It's just that the other schools teach their students to be assholes."

Daniel shrugged one shoulder in agreement.

Her honesty surprised me. "Noted."

"I could let Daniel go on, but I don't want to bore you or me."

Daniel looked a little disappointed to not be going over all the talking points, but he quickly covered it with another easy smile. "If Master Lenin asks, tell him we were thorough, warm, and friendly."

Moose snorted. "Maybe don't use the word warm. He'll know you're lying."

"I think I'm being plenty warm," Daniel said, turning his attention to me.

I nodded. "Very."

Daniel's smile deepened. It was such a cheery look that I found my own lips wanting to mirror his expression.

"I'm talking about me, smartass," Moose said dryly.

Daniel chuckled. "And here I thought you were in a good mood this morning."

"That depends on if there is any good food left." She shot me an accusatory look. She quickly faced forward, continuing down the spiraling stairs.

After a couple seconds of silence, I cleared my throat. *Act normal.* "I'm Charlie, by the way."

"I know. Charlie with the last name of an organ." Her dark brown eyes cut to the new bag resting on my hip. "You really lost the name lottery with that one, huh?"

"So everyone keeps alluding to. Is Lawrence Hart a bad guy?"

Daniel awkwardly scratched the back of his neck.

Moose laughed once, a dry, sour note. "Depends on who you ask. But he couldn't have gotten the nickname of '*Lucifer*' for nothing."

Cheese and rice.

"Which school did you transfer from?" Daniel piped in.

"Just a private school in Kansas."

Interest narrowed Moose's eyes. "How'd you transfer to the Magisterium?"

"I got lucky."

"The Magisterium is the school for the best, the richest, and the biggest brats," Moose continued. "You either have really rich parents or you had good enough grades to draw Master Lenin's wallet. Besides, no one transfers to this school anymore—only out of it. So, which one is it?"

"It doesn't matter. I might not be staying." Again, I saw another question. "Why do people transfer out?"

"You know, because Master Hart doesn't like Master Kale and Master Kale is buddy-buddy with Master Lenin. Personally, I think people are overreacting. Or they transfer with no reason at all." She said the last bit with a bitter edge.

I wonder what Lawrence mastered in. "Why don't they get along?"

"Now that's the question of the century," Daniel mumbled.

"It has to be something more than just conflicting worldviews, although neither is willing to talk about it." Moose shrugged. "I guess when your best friend won't back you up, you have to prove that you're right to everyone else."

My eyes bulged. *Michael was best friends with my dad? You think someone would have mentioned that.*

She laughed at my expression. "Surprising, huh? I heard they went to school together, like, forever ago."

"My dad told me they went here," Daniel said.

I looked around the stairwell at the black stone stairs, the black stone walls, and the black stone floor below. *Maybe that's why Michael wears all black.*

"You *still* haven't answered my question," Moose said.

"Which one? You ask a lot."

She shrugged. "Why beat around the bush when you can kick it in the ass?" Stepping off the last stair, her short legs quickly crossed into the dining room. From the door, I noticed that about a good fourth of the room was empty.

"You'll have to forgive Moose," Daniel said quietly as we followed after her. "She's not a morning person." He paused. "Or a night person for that matter. I saw her smile once at four, so maybe she's an afternoon person."

I laughed at that and Daniel grinned.

Moose led us across the room toward the buffet line. Taking two plates, she handed one to me and then cut in front with the other, leaving Daniel to fend for himself.

"So, I've gone through all the talking points Master Lenin wanted me to cover. Now I'm going to tell you how to actually survive here." She grabbed a large cinnamon roll and dropped it on to her plate. Her keen eyes peered over the rims of her glasses at the rest of the room.

"Breakfast starts at eight. Eight-thirty is when all the good stuff gets picked over. By nine you're lucky to get burnt toast and a brick of eggs. When the kitchen makes cinnamon rolls, always get a cinnamon roll." To prove her point, she took the second largest on the tray and placed it on my plate.

"Royals sit close to the stage and at the front of the classrooms. Commons get the middle and Deficients get the back. *Don't,*" she stressed, looking me right in the eye, "sit with another status or you'll be eaten alive. If you can avoid the Royals, do it. They have double the magic and double the problems and, worse, they have Master Lenin's blessing. So, if anything happens between you and a Royal, you'll take the fall, no matter what."

I glanced at Daniel for confirmation. He nodded sadly.

"Is it like that at all the other schools?" I asked.

"I heard it's worse at the Russian University," Daniel answered. "Deficients aren't allowed to ask questions during class."

Leaving the buffet with only a cinnamon roll, Moose headed for the row of beverage dispensers marked with different types of coffee. Daniel meandered down the line, looking over the slim pickings.

I looked over the room toward the tables closest to the stage. The students there were the most polished and put together. There was an air about their posture that said they knew they were untouchable.

I was glad for the fake status pinned to my shirt. If I were enrolled with my real status and had to sit among them, they would tear me apart. Their confidence alone would smother me.

A pleasant chime rang from the stairwell.

Around the room, students got to their feet and headed for the door. The steady stream poured up the stairwell.

Moose and Daniel looked at their watches, confirming the time. I was surprised when both of them collected their food and drink and headed for the door.

"Are we allowed to bring food?" I looked down at the huge cinnamon roll on my plate. I could try to eat the whole thing, but it'd be a terrifying sight for my new classmates to witness.

"Mr. Harrison doesn't care," Moose said over her shoulder. "As long as you don't make a mess."

"I guarantee he's eating when we walk in." Daniel sipped at his coffee.

I followed Moose and Daniel up the left staircase to the fifth floor of the East Wing. As we walked down the long hallway, students peeled off into different classrooms. Moose's confident strides took us to classroom five, thirty-four. Long rows of tables and chairs sat on risers of varying height, making the back of the classroom higher than the front. Everything curved in a semicircle around the teacher's desk and blackboard.

Just as Moose said, every student knew where to sit. All the Royals migrated to the front, and the lower statuses filled in behind them. Worried I'd sit by the wrong status, I followed her to the middle of the room and took the empty seat beside her. Daniel took the seat on the other side of me.

"Welcome back, everyone."

Leaning against the desk was a wide shouldered man with shaggy blond hair. A status pin with the number five pierced through his chunky beige cardigan. Just as Daniel predicted, there was an avocado loaded bagel on the corner of the desk.

With a flick of his wand, Mr. Harrison shut the door. "I'm interested to hear about everyone's holiday. Mr. Chessmen, I can see you thoroughly enjoyed your time in the Bahamas."

I turned with the rest of the laughing class to look at a guy in the back of the room. His sunburn was rivaling the tone of a tomato.

"Mr. Phillips," Mr. Harrison called over the snickers. "How was your trip back home?"

Daniel shook his head. "Let's just say I'd rather switch places with Chessmen. I spent it with my father."

Mr. Harrison chuckled. "Family drama?"

"Always."

Mr. Harrison addressed the rest of the room. "Come on, someone had to have a good holiday."

"I was on the Ferris wheel when it almost fell over," a redheaded girl said a few rows behind me.

Guilt dropped into my stomach like a brick. But the class turned with mild interest, and no one looked accusingly at me.

Mr. Harrison's eyebrows rose. "No kidding. Was anyone hurt?"

She shrugged. "My neck hurt, but it wasn't anything a potion couldn't fix."

"Well, I'm glad you were able to join us for the rest of the semester, Miss Jackson. Did they find out what went wrong?"

Miss Jackson shook her head. "It was probably a couple Royals screwing behind a game tent."

The knots in my stomach eased a little when the class snickered.

"Royals," Moose grumbled under her breath.

"On that note, let's pick up with where we left off." Mr. Harrison combed his fingers through his thick golden locks. "Please, take out your copy of *Dark and Rare Creatures* and flip to page six hundred and seventeen."

As I reached into my bag, his voice echoed around the room. "Miss Heart with an E."

I froze as every eye swiveled toward me.

But he was smiling. "Welcome to Creature Studies. It's always nice to have a fresh face around here."

I almost fell to the floor with relief. Worried that my voice would crack with nerves, I just smiled back.

"I know it's been a while, but can someone tell Miss Heart what we were studying before the break?" He hopped on the desk and rocked his feet back and forth. Reaching over, he grabbed his bagel and took a bite.

Moose's hand hit the air in record time. On the other side of me, Daniel's hand was just as high.

Another smile graced Mr. Harrison's handsome face. Silently, he mouthed "eeny, meeny, miny, moe" between the two. "The floor is yours, Miss Moose."

Moose sent a smirk in Daniel's direction before facing the teacher. "Demons," she answered smoothly.

Mr. Harrison nodded. With a flick of his wand, the chalk sprang to life sketching a cute creature with horns and a spiked tail. I even found myself smiling.

"If they looked like this, I think they would be more of a nuisance than something to fear." His smile dimmed as the duster erased the image. "The true form of a demon is far different. You'll most likely never see one in its true form. At least, I hope you never do."

Again, he waved his wand. Instead of the chalk moving, black smoke curled from the end and formed a tall man. Aside from his pointy nose and glowing red eyes, the man's facial features were hard to discern. It was more like a three-dimensional shadow than anything else.

"There's a story about the first User," Mr. Harrison said. "He had two faces, four arms, and four legs. He took care of the world like a garden. Until he realized he was the only one of his kind.

"Using branches from around the world, he tried to create someone like him. However, all the beings he created didn't contain any magic. Some think that's where Regulars came from."

He took up his coffee mug and took a sip.

"After decades, the man used his magic and tore himself in two. Taking his second face, two legs, and two arms, he created a woman. Because the limbs were from him, they contained magic.

"There are legends that say the world runs on magic, like a light bulb runs on electricity. Miles beneath our feet, too far for us to reach, is a surplus of replenishing magic. In the story of the first Magic User, back when creation was young, that magic could be harvested from certain locations."

The way Mr. Harrison told the story was like he had known it his whole life. I sat back as I realized, he had.

"As the story goes, our young User found something rare, pure magic, possibly from one of these locations. Out of curiosity, he touched it. When he did, the magic latched on to the shadows of his darkest thoughts and secrets and amplified them. Magic can do funny things to anything, but pure magic *creates* something. In this case, it created evil. It created demons."

At this point, his charming smile was gone. The time for jokes and nostalgia was over.

"Demons are the embodiment of evil. They are the only beings with our kind of power because they were once Users. Does anyone know how the transformation from User to demon can happen?"

Daniel was quicker to raise his hand. "You said that pure magic creates something. There's pure magic in our cores, so the transformation takes place inside the User. A complete transformation requires a lot of magic, which is why Royals are more susceptible. I read a book that used that as the reason for why there aren't as many Royals around."

"I think some of our classmates might be undergoing that transformation." Moose shot a withering look at a black haired girl several rows in front of us.

A girl in a bowtie on the opposite side of Moose smothered her laugh with a cough.

"You'll have to tell me the title after class," said Mr. Harrison. "You're correct that Royals are more prone to the transformation."

"What starts the transformation?" the girl with the bowtie asked.

"No one knows exactly. Users who've completed the transition aren't exactly talkative." Mr. Harrison leaned back against his desk. "Some think it begins when the User's thoughts go dark, when they only feel things such as envy, loathing, and bloodlust. Their magic, directed by their thoughts, kills all moral reason and pure emotions such as love and compassion. Then there's nothing left in them but darkness."

I knew a man in all black who was pretty freaking close to that description. Too bad Michael's eyes weren't red or else I would have been convinced.

"When the transformation from User to demon is complete, the User's body dies. The body will continue to function as long as it has magic but not like before. A study in New Zealand showed a demon body doesn't need rest, food, or even to breathe like we do.

"Royals aren't the only ones who can undergo the transformation. All it takes is enough magic inside a User. Does anyone remember our lesson from last year about curses? Which curse pertains to what we're talking about?"

Behind him, the chalk lifted from the desk and floated over to the chalkboard.

Moose's hand shot into the air so fast she almost launched out of her seat. "A Binding Curse. It enables a User to take another User's magic and absorb it into themselves." As she spoke, the chalk took notes.

Mr. Harrison nodded. "And what's so important about this use of magic?"

Daniel blurted from his seat. "It's dark magic."

"Why is that?"

"Magic is pure when it comes straight from the core and is channeled through a wand. Dark magic finds other ways to manipulate magic without a wand," Daniel explained. "Like using herbs and enchanted objects to obtain your goal. It has detrimental effects on all Users involved."

"Good job, Mr. Phillips. I can tell you've done your research." Mr. Harrison hopped off the desk.

Moose rolled her eyes.

"Anyone can do dark magic—Deficients and Royals alike. The act of combining herbs or using an enchanted object to casts of magic bends the laws of nature. For example, let's say I'm a Deficient Two and I want to levitate my house to the other side of my property. I don't have enough magic to do it, so I gather various herbs and amplifying stones to strengthen my cast. Seems like a good idea, right?"

I found myself wanting to nod. *Why not get a little help?* But from the corner of my eye, I saw Daniel shake his head.

"But the moment my magic joins the herbs and stones, my magic goes sour. Sure, I moved my house, but the foundation is riddled with burns and cracks. Not to mention my organs are shutting down after being subjected to too much magic.

"Luckily, nature likes to keep things balanced, so nothing is all powerful. For example, Dellamora hate sunlight, so they keep to the shadows. Wolfin can be killed by silver. Even we have limitations. Without a core to contain our magic we wouldn't exist. Without a wand, we can't perform magic, and we have to wait for our magic to regenerate if we've used too much at one time.

"In your first years of school, you learned each of us has a certain amount of magic we can draw from at any given time. For example, while Miss Heart," he gave me another smile, "can do more than Miss Montgomery," he gestured to Cornelia a few rows back, "she can't do more than Mr. Phillips."

I snuck a glance at Daniel's chest. He was a Common Seven.

"Once the demon transformation is complete, the outer lining of the core disintegrates, leaving the flexible inner layer intact. It becomes like a stretchy balloon." The chalk quickly sketched a diagram of a core and named the two layers. Then it drew a demon core, which looked like an ameba.

"Meaning," Mr. Harrison continued, "the more magic the demon steals, the higher their magic status rises. But unlike Users, demons cannot regenerate their magic because that side of them died. They have to keep stealing it in order to live.

"Because their bodies are essentially dead, they are extremely hard to kill. Can someone tell me which magical cast can kill them?" The whole room was silent. Even Moose and Daniel remained still. "Good, because that's what we're going to be talking about today.

"There are only a couple ways to kill a demon. The first is fire. I'm not talking about the reaction you get when you strike a match. I'm talking about magic in the form of fire, also known as the Infurnous ward." The chalk wrote the word in all caps and underlined it. "It's one of the greatest weapons we have but very few can cast it. Why?" Mr. Harrison's eyes scanned the room. Surprise raised his eyebrows when he called on the next student. "Yes, Mr. Hardy."

"Not all Users have enough magic to do it. Only Royals can. If a Deficient or low Common tried, it'd kill them."

I looked around for the speaker with the southern drawl. A few rows below me was a black haired boy slouched so low in his seat that I could only see the top of his head.

"Correct. The Infurnous ward is the closest a User will ever get to performing pure magic. Charms and enchantments are too diluted to do any damage. There are some wards that might have the correct potency, but the Infurnous ward is guaranteed to destroy the unnatural magic binding the demon to this earth and end their reign of fire. Yes, Miss Montgomery?"

"You said there were a couple ways to kill a demon," Cornelia said, lowering her hand. "What are the others?"

"I've heard decapitation works rather well. If the body sustains enough damage, that can do the trick. Even then you can't be entirely sure. There once was a case in Brazil of a demon who lost all of its blood mass and continued to walk around. Nothing is as effective as the Infurnous ward. I'll admit, there's a lot we don't know about these creatures," Mr. Harrison added, crossing his arms. "Because of their decaying nature, they're difficult to study and even harder to get information from. But what we do know is that they're dangerous. And if I had a chance to kill one, I would."

Mr. Harrison launched into a detailed discussion about the Infurnous ward and its effects on both the User performing it and its victim. Cinnamon roll forgotten, I copied the chalk and scribbled down as many notes as I could.

The clock tower sounded, cutting into Mr. Harrison's explanation of Infurnous ward side effects.

"Please read the rest of the chapter," he called over the sounds of students grabbing their bags. "We'll discuss it next week."

No one lingered in the classroom. Everyone quickly collected their books and pens and headed for the door. Cornelia made her way from the back of the room and stepped into our row behind Daniel.

With a sigh, Daniel slung his bag over his shoulder and rose to his feet. "Good job today. I almost had you a couple times."

Moose smirked. "You wish."

"One of these days, I'll answer a question your brilliant mind hasn't heard of yet."

Moose got to her feet. "When that happens, I'll buy coats for everyone in hell."

"You better start saving then. Our Testing Year is right around the corner."

Moose pulled her shoulders back. "You say that like it's supposed to scare me."

Daniel just shook his head. To me he said, "Be careful around this one. She's the smartest kid in our class and she's not afraid to remind you."

Moose grinned.

"I don't know how you find the time to read ahead," Cornelia said with a shake of her head. "I barely survive with the current workload."

"It helps when you have no life," Mr. Hardy said as he stopped beside our group. Being this close to him, I saw that his right eyebrow was split by a jagged scar. The pin on his shirt said that he was a Royal Eight.

He turned his cool gaze of dark blue my way and nodded once. "Clarence Hardy."

Remembering for the first time I had a last name, I said, "Charlie Heart."

"With an E." He raised his split eyebrow. "Pleasure."

A tick of uncomfortable silence followed.

I cleared my throat. "That's a cool scar."

His hand lifted to touch the thin line. "My older sister threw me across the room and my head hit the desk. Of course, she's our father's darling, so she didn't get in trouble for it."

"I didn't know you had a sister," Moose said.

"That's because you never asked," he replied with a tight smile. "Listen, darlin', you should really get some better company than this stick-in-the-mud and pain-in-the-ass." He vaguely gestured to Daniel and Moose, like either insult could be applied to them.

"Are you implying that you're the better company?" Moose scoffed.

"She has higher standards than you. Even if you are an Eight." Moose looked at me. "The only reason he's here is because he got kicked out of all the other schools. Master Lenin had no choice but to take him to keep him under control."

Clarence rolled his murky blue eyes. "Or so the rumor mill spins it."

Daniel cleared his throat. "What did you think of your first class at the Magisterium?" he asked me.

Thankful for the change in conversation, I said, "This is totally different than what I'm used to."

Daniel smiled. "Mr. Harrison is the best in the school."

"Second to Mrs. Paylor," Cornelia piped in. "That's only because she has cookies on her desk."

"If you liked this class," Moose said, "just wait until we get to chapter twelve. We're going to be talking about dragons. I heard from one of the older students that he brings in miniature ones for us to dissect."

"I heard we're going on a field trip to the Dragon Farm, which would mean the whole day off," Cornelia said brightly.

Daniel sent her a skeptical side glance. "Master Lenin would never waste a day on that tourist trap."

"Why did you transfer here?" Clarence cut back into the conversation as if Daniel hadn't spoken. "Or is Master Lenin letting in just anyone?"

"Do you have to be a constant asshole?" Moose asked dryly.

"I was just asking a question." Clarence's blue-eyed gaze didn't waver from mine.

"In an asshole-y way."

"I'm here on a trial basis," I said, matching his casual tone.

"She's choosing between here and the Academy," Cornelia added, bringing up my lie from the night before.

Clarence huffed with disbelief. "Sure. Word of advice, get out while you can. The Magisterium tends to break the weak."

"You would know," Moose grumbled.

Clarence's gaze cut to her. With a lopsided grin, he tapped the eight pinned on his shirt. "Remember your place, Moose."

"Oh, I remember. Was it last month or the month before when Master Lenin named me the best in our class? Where were you on that list?"

Daniel smothered a smile with his hand. "I'll see you guys later." He bent in a mocking bow to Moose. "Until next Thursday, Moose."

"See you later, Second Place," Moose said, continuing to pin Clarence with an icy glare.

Cornelia waved, and the pair trotted down the stairs and out of the classroom. Moose collected her bag and followed after them. Surprisingly Clarence fell into step with us.

As we stepped out of the classroom, Moose came to a dead stop in the doorway. Blocking our exit was a group of tall girls. All three were chatting too intensely to notice they were clogging the doorway.

Moose pinched the bridge of her nose. Taking a deep breath she barked, "Hey! Out of the way!"

The trio turned. The girl in the middle looked as if her features were carved out of ice, smooth, polished and impossibly cold. She held her head back to peer down her nose at everything and everyone before her. On the left side of her sweater was a number eight. Another Royal.

Moose's shoulders stiffened. "Janet, how terrible you survived Christmas break. I prayed every night that you would be kicked in the head by a reindeer."

My eyes bulged. *Damn, Moose.*

Janet didn't even give her the time of day. Turning her bored gaze to Clarence she smiled, a look of mild amusement. "Hey, sugar. What are you doing with this Common?"

"We're just walking in the same direction," he said dryly.

Then her grey eyes zeroed in on me. Laughter sparkled in her gaze at the sight of the six on my shirt. "Welcome to the Magisterium. Hopefully, you have enough magic to handle it."

Without waiting for a response, she stepped into the hall. The two others in her party followed close as if they were her shadows. As soon as the doorway was clear, Clarence too stepped out into the moving crowd.

Moose sighed. "Royals. They can't go extinct fast enough."

I looked at the six pinned on my shirt, an upside down nine in plain sight.

"Yeah," I said. "They're the worst."

24

The Substitute

Master Lenin's plan worked flawlessly.

With the six pinned on my shirt, I was invisible to every class of the day. With Moose's warning about the unspoken seating arrangements, I flew under the radar.

That night, I took my dinner back to my room to get a head start on my homework. For the first time in my life, I was looking forward to it. I had to read two chapters on the healing properties of fairy tears. *Fairies.*

I was so swept up in the work that when the transporter beeped for my lesson with Michael, I was actually disappointed I had to trade the quiet enchantment of my room for the glaring, rough man.

Not wanting to be late, I grabbed my wand and took up the transporter.

"Hello, darling." Magee beamed when I popped into view.

I had completely forgotten about the fourth member of my welcome party when I first woke up in the Magisterium. Robert Magee wasn't much taller than I was. His dark hair, an awkward shade between dirty blonde and brown, was slicked back from his face. The product in his hair glinted from the surrounding lights.

I wasn't sure what his roll was in all of this. Master Lenin mentioned that he convinced Master Lenin and Michael to look for me. It wasn't exactly a point in his favor. But he wasn't Michael, so he had that going for him.

"Hi!" I sputtered. "How—how are you?"

"Very well, thank you." He extended his hand toward me. "It's a pleasure to see you again." He reached past my hand and grabbed my covered forearm.

For once I didn't fumble through this new greeting. I grasped his sleeve confidently.

"What are you doing here?" I scanned the room for any sign of the brooding man in black, but Michael was nowhere to be found.

"Master Kale was pulled away last minute. So, Master Lenin asked me to step in for the night." A smile spread across his face at my expression. "I'm guessing you like that idea?"

"Anything that doesn't involve Michael, I like."

Magee laughed, which was strange to hear in a room that was normally filled with insults. "I'll agree with you there. If you're ready, we should get started."

Eagerly I took out my wand. Whatever took Michael away I hoped it would happen again.

"What has Master Kale been teaching you?" He took his own wand from the inside of his jacket. I could just barely make out the designs of what looked like broken glass on the hilt.

"He's taught me to move and deflect."

His eyebrow rose in surprise. "Are you any good?"

"I'm getting better."

"That's all that matters," he said. "One of the most useful things I've ever learned is how to disable someone. Tonight, I'm going to teach you to be on the offensive. You can only defend yourself for so long before you start running out of magic. Being on the offensive at least moves you into the place where you can win."

"Why are you guys teaching me so much fighting magic? Isn't there something more practical?"

"With your status, we all agreed it would be smart for you to learn how to effectively protect yourself first. It's better to be prepared than have no way of saving yourself." With a flick of his wrist, a chair slid to the center of the room. "Aim your wand."

I leveled the tip of my wand at the center of the chair.

"Here." He stepped closer. Sliding his fingers down my sweater, he bent my elbow. "Don't lock your arm. It takes away from your flexibility. When you're ready to fire, cast a short burst of magic."

I pulled on my magic. A flood of fire rolled from my chest and into my arm. With a slow exhale, I fired.

A bright orb flew from my wand and slammed into the chair. The back disintegrated into splinters against the wall, cracking the stone beneath it. The remaining pieces scattered across the room.

"Beautifully done." Patting my shoulder, Magee moved to stand beside me. "You used too much magic, but that will come with practice. That was excellent for your first try."

I didn't share his glowing satisfaction. Horror filled my lungs. No matter how hard I tried, I couldn't look away from the place of impact. Yes, it was just a chair, but it stood in the place of a living, breathing person.

Another chair moved into the place of the first. "This time, try not to release as much magic."

Shaking my head, I stepped away from the new target. "I can't do that again."

"Sometimes, we have to do things we don't like in order to survive."

I shook my head harder.

"Think about it like this: by taking care of the problem, you're saving others from that problem."

There had been many nights in that cursed house in Salina when I held my pillow over my head. The walls kept people out, but that was it.

Sounds from the other kids' rooms always made their way through, and it didn't matter how hard I squeezed the pillow. I could always hear it. With every cry and whimper, the scars on my own back burned. A hundred times I wished I could do something. If I only had the courage.

I looked at the wand in my hand. Now I had a chance, but I wasn't sure I wanted to take it.

"You just need to get used to it, darling."

I wasn't sure I wanted to.

Reluctantly, I raised my wand. Knots twisted in my stomach. A light sweat covered my forehead and palms. *It's just a chair. You're not hurting anything.*

Magic rushed into my wand again and a burst of light the size of a golf ball blew from the tip.

It slammed into the chair and ripped it away from its legs. Splinters scattered across the obsidian stone as the broken frame clattered to the floor.

"What the hell are you doing?"

Magee and I spun toward the door. At the sight of the man in black, I dropped my wand. Quickly I stepped away from Magee.

Michael's eyes flickered to the cracks in the walls and the crumbled chair. Then his dark eyes locked onto my substitute.

"Master Kale. You're not looking so well." Magee didn't sound the least bit concerned.

The bruise I'd seen last night was nothing compared to the color of his skin now. The same dark purple moved up his neck, accenting each cord of muscles. It leaked onto his face, shadowing his cheekbone. His left eye was nearly bloodshot. Blood smudged the sleeves of his leather jacket and dirt caked his shoes.

"I'd offer you a chair," Magee gestured to the broken wood on the floor, "but Miss Heart and I—"

"What the hell are you doing here, Magee?" Despite his injuries, Michael's question whipped across the room with severity.

"Henry called me saying you were unavailable."

The muscle in Michael's jaw pulsed as he clenched his teeth. The lights dimmed as a chill seeped into the room.

Was that because of him? I watched as Michael took in a slow breath. The lights brightened a bit, but the cold remained.

He struggles with his magic like I do. Then he has to be a Royal too, right?

Michael took his phone from his back pocket, dialed, and pressed it to his ear—all without taking his eyes off Magee.

"Get your ass up here," he snarled into the mouthpiece.

No one moved or breathed in the seconds that followed. I wasn't even sure either man blinked. I didn't know how Magee wasn't shriveled up on the floor. I almost was, and that look wasn't even directed at me.

The door opened and Master Lenin stepped in with a nervous air around him. "Master Kale, I wasn't expecting you back until later." He approached him like he was walking around landmines. "I assumed your problem would keep you until the morning."

"It was easily handled."

"Is that why parts of you look like a plum?" Magee taunted.

I took a second larger step away from Magee, just in case Michael decided to blow his head off his shoulders.

"What I want to know," Michael turned his wrath to the School Master, "is why you thought it would be a good idea to bring *him* here."

"Oh, come on, Kale." Magee rolled his eyes. "You're not the only person capable of teaching magic. I can prepare her, same as you."

"You can't tell your wand from a stick."

I winced in sympathy for the other man.

Magee's eyes narrowed. "She has a lot to learn if she's going to do anything. She needs to learn to attack. All you've been teaching her is how to defend herself."

"You haven't fought a day in your life. What I teach and how I teach is none of your damn business."

"Fine. I won't teach her." Magee slipped his hands into his pockets. "But when we lose, just know you're the one who didn't trust anyone to help you."

My ears perked up. *Lose what?*

"I trust people. Just not you." Michael leveled an accusing finger at Magee. "If it were up to me, I wouldn't trust you with the air you breathe."

"Gentlemen, please." Master Lenin took a cautious step between the two. "Miss Heart, I think it's best to call it a night. You can continue this lesson later." He reached forward like he was going to escort me to the door.

"War doesn't guarantee there'll be a later," Michael snapped. "For all we know, Lawrence could kill us tomorrow."

At the mention of my father, I whirled toward the man in black. "What?"

Master Lenin opened his mouth but both of us could see the lie sprinting up his throat.

Michael rushed to beat him. "We're fighting a war. One your father started."

25
Achilles Heel

"Kale." Magee's tone was as sharp as broken glass. "There's a better time for this conversation."

"And when would that be?"

For once, and I hoped this was the only time in my life, I agreed with Michael. "What are you talking about?"

Michael again beat the other two to the punch. "The reason you're really here is because we want you to use your magic to destroy The Crown, your father's gang of merry assholes, so I can kill your father."

My jaw hit the floor.

Master Lenin shifted uneasily from one foot to the other. "I was hoping to avoid this until later."

"Avoid what?" I squeaked. "*Plotting murder?*"

"It's a bit more complicated than that."

"Not really," Michael muttered.

"You said yourself that you don't like your father," Magee said.

"That doesn't mean I want him dead!" I looked back at Michael. "I don't get it. Weren't you two friends?"

Michael's gaze darkened as his hands clenched. "That was a long time ago."

Magee took pity on me and turned away from Michael. "We're on the brink of a civil war. Your father—the Crown, or Lucifer, as he is often referred to now—is on one side. We, Achilles Heel, are on the other."

Achilles Heel. The poacher on the interstate mentioned that.

"Why?" I recalled the picture they showed me when I woke up. He looked nothing short of charming.

"Your father's ideals reflect a time when high status Users dominated the earth," Magee said. "He wants to restore our world to those days. In order to do that, he has to eliminate those with little or no magic at all. For years he did just that. He wants to cleanse the world for his version of paradise.

"Your father is the most powerful player in this war," Magee continued gently. "If he wins, he'll completely change the face of the planet. We found you because we believe you have enough power to help us find his Achilles Heel before he does more damage."

The impact of Magee's words knocked the air right out of my lungs. "You—you want me to fight him?" All around the room, the lights shuttered.

"It's more complicated than that," Magee said. "If we aren't careful and he dies in combat, he dies a martyr and people will grasp on to his legacy. We have to break him down to the foundation, which means bringing down those he's working to recruit and most of all, by shrinking his current numbers. You're not here to kill your father, but his army."

"Because your father is mine to kill," Michael growled.

Master Lenin shifted again. "We were hoping you would be willing to help us when the time comes."

"You mean that after you fed me, housed me, and taught me how not to be a safety risk, that I would owe you." His silence made me realize something else. "You were never going to let me leave."

Master Lenin shook his head. "I'm afraid not."

"I knew it." I looked from one man to the next. They had dangled the perfect bait: starting over, empowering me to protect myself—all of it clouded my vision. I ignored the voice telling me it was too good to be true because I was starving for a clean slate, to become something other than what I was.

Michael's black eyes locked on Master Lenin. "I told you. The coward's way was too much like Lawrence. We should've told her up front."

"That was a risk we couldn't take." Master Lenin lowered his voice. "You know that."

"And this is better?"

"If you know anyone else with her status and no ties to Hart, please give me a name. Everyone else is too afraid of the man to even speak against him."

My lungs refused to let in any air. The lights pulsed with my racing heartbeat. "I—I can't fight anyone."

"My thoughts exactly," Michael said. "She even agrees that she's a waste of time."

"That's not true," Magee jumped in again. "The magic flares she released in Kansas, before the crash, and what she did a minute ago is proof that she can."

Michael shook his head. "She's still unstable. She'll do more harm than good."

"You don't know that."

"I took her to the New Year's Festival and had Atlas provoke her. She flared like I expected. She would've taken down the Ferris wheel if Went and I hadn't been there to catch it."

My eyes narrowed on his mouth. "You *know* Atlas?"

He nodded. "He's an associate of mine."

Everything he said quickly added up, knocking me back another step. "You—you planned that?"

Again, he nodded.

"Holy shit, Kale." Magee stepped forward like he was going to strangle him. "What were you thinking?"

"Calm down." Michael waved away his words. "I was watching her the whole time."

"You know better than anyone what you were risking." Master Lenin spoke like he was still wrapping his mind around what Michael had done. "If you hadn't been just teaching her to hold on to her magic, she could have killed thousands."

"If that had happened, would you have finally given up on this stupid plan?"

"No. Because you know what this chance means to us, to our cause."

"To *your* cause," Michael corrected icily. "All I want is Lawrence's head."

"When are you going to realize that's not enough?"

"When are you going to realize that I'm only in this for one thing?" Michael hissed. "You knew that from the beginning."

"How could you?" I breathed.

Michael turned his indifferent expression to me.

"How could you do that to me?" The light blared, filling the room with so much light the men shielded their eyes.

"I needed to prove a point," Michael replied coolly.

"You tried to kill me!"

The bastard narrowed his eyes. "I never *try* to kill someone. That word doesn't exist in my vocabulary. I was simply testing you."

Anger rushed over me like a tidal wave, causing the lights to flash again.

"You jackass!" I tangled my hands into my hair to keep myself from doing something stupid, like smacking the smug look off his face. "Do you have any idea what I could've done? I could've killed someone!"

"Thus, the reason for the test. I wanted to see if you could control yourself in a dangerous situation." The corner of his lip twitched into a gross smile. "You failed." He turned to Master Lenin. "Proving my case. She'll do more harm than good."

"A case I've told you to forget," Master Lenin snapped. "She's the only Royal equal to your status, not on Lawrence's side. We need her, unless you have some other brilliant idea of how to bring this war to an end."

"I can get to him if you would just give me the time. With this," he jerked his hand toward me, "we're walking around with an atomic bomb with a broken timer. I can't kill him if I'm dead."

"I would love to hear what other options you seem to think we have," Magee said dryly. "Your bloodlust scares off any other possibilities, and your lack of bedside manners deters the rest." Magee paused thoughtfully. "We could drain her magic."

Fire blazed in Michael's eyes. "Those are *his* methods. I don't play by Lawrence's rules."

"Maybe that's why we're losing so dramatically. When are you going to realize you're not enough, Kale? You can't save us."

Michael's hand twitched toward his wand.

"I can't do it." I shook my head.

Master Lenin clasped his hands loosely in front of him. "I know this sounds extreme. But this war is not just affecting our world. It's also affecting the one you left. Your father has spent decades killing low status Users and Regulars—"

I shook my head. "Another lie."

"I wish it were."

"Then where's the proof? Huh? Show me the gravestones."

"You'll find them throughout history," Master Lenin continued softly. "Regulars just call these events by different names. Look through the genocides of history and you'll find his fingerprints."

"I think someone would've noticed one man behind all of that."

"History is written by those who live to tell it. For now, Master Hart has been content to stay in the shadows and pull the strings. His followers are bold because they know no one would dare defy them with a man like Lawrence Hart in charge. Master Kale has been trying to bring them to justice but he's one man against our world's strongest."

Was that the reason for Michael's dark purple bruises? He may have been the best in his field—hell, he could have been the best in the world—but it wouldn't matter if he was outnumbered.

"Once this war breaks into the open, we won't be able to withstand your father's forces. If he steps forward and declares himself king, we lose and there'll be nothing we can do to stop him. We need your help to keep that from happening."

My heart raced. My hands trembled. "I don't want any part of this. Please, just let me leave. I promise I won't say a word to anyone."

Master Lenin stepped forward. "Miss Heart—"

I slapped my hands over my ears. "No! My name is Charlie. Just Charlie. I haven't had a father or a last name for nineteen years and I sure as hell don't have one now. I don't want any part of this."

"Whether you like it or not," Master Lenin said sadly, "you're a part of this."

"If I choose to do nothing, I'm remaining neutral." My hands clenched around each other, praying for it to be my third option.

"Not doing anything is the same as helping him. You might as well hand him a crown," Magee said flatly.

I hated the hope in their eyes when they looked at me. "No good will come out of me fighting your war."

"How do you know?" Master Lenin asked. "Miss Heart—"

I bristled at the name.

"I wouldn't be surprised if within a year your father has all the support he needs to complete his mission. We only ask that you try. To give us the hope to win. You could save generations." Master Lenin spread his hands. "Nothing has changed. You can continue here at my school to learn about magic. In return, we ask you to help our cause. Once the war is over, you can go and do as you please."

Was any of it true or was this just another trick laced with pretty words?

"With your magic and enough training, you can do a great deal of damage," Master Lenin persisted. "If you make even a small dent in this war, I'll be happy. I agree that hiding this from you wasn't the best idea, but we wanted to give you time to adjust."

"You mean trick me."

He stilled at my words.

I looked from one to the other and found myself shaking my head. "I can't help you. I can't kill someone—evil or not. That's not who I am."

The emotions that flickered across their faces ranged from sadness to disappointment. The only one who kept their neutral expression was Michael.

Smoothly, he reached under his arm and took his wand from its holster. "Then you forfeit your life."

I choked on my spit. "What?"

"Now, hold on a second—"

"No, Lenin. She needs to hear this." Michael aimed his wand at my chest. "Magic is dangerous. With the amount you have, there's triple the risks. There are plenty of people who would drain you for this war. I won't have billions of lives resting in your hands just because you're a coward and you don't want to use what you have. I don't have time for that shit."

I felt no fear when he finished. Death had been my roommate for nineteen years. Facing it now was just like greeting an old friend.

"Then kill me," I said. "I accepted death long before you entered the picture, buddy."

Michael's dark gaze searched my face almost desperately. Then an idea lit in his eyes.

"Fine," he spat, lowering his wand.

He walked calmly to the window. Tapping his wand against the frame, the glass distorted as it began to move. When it settled, the image upon it knocked the wind from my lungs.

It was Blake.

Surrounded by grey stone, he sat at his desk with his headphones on. Tapping his pencil to his music, he scanned his homework. He wore his old grey beanie paired with a button up and slacks. He must've been back at school. He looked so real I thought I could reach through the glass and touch him.

Michael took a phone from his pocket. After punching in a number, he said a couple words to the person on the other side. In a blink there was a man standing behind Blake. The shadows of the room hid everything but his long black coat. My heart fell to the floor when I saw him take out a wand.

Covering the mouthpiece, Michael turned to me. "If you refuse, I'll kill him."

"Y—you can't do that."

"There are very few things I can't do, and this isn't one of them." For the first time, a full smile spread across his face. It was as cold and heartless as the rest of him. "You help Lenin, or I end Pretty Boy's life."

"Now hang on a minute." To my great relief, Master Lenin stepped forward. "You can't—"

"Despite popular belief, I can. Or have you forgotten what it means to be a Master Hunter?" Michael peeled his gaze from the School Master to fix on me. "Once I kill him, I can kill you, if you wish. The choice is yours."

"Please." I couldn't take my eyes off the window. "He has nothing to do with this."

He shrugged. "What's one more life lost in a war?"

I looked at Master Lenin and Magee. They had to do something! My heart swelled when Magee stepped forward. "Leave the child alone—"

Michael swung his wand toward him. Magee flew across the room and flattened against the wall. He slumped to the floor with half closed eyes.

"Lenin, if you interfere, I *will* kill the boy," Michael growled. His glare intensified. "You better choose. I'm about to lose the last of my patience."

I looked back at the window. Blake was the reason I got out of Kansas. He got me through the empty life of foster care by simply knocking on my door every time he came home from school.

Now, his life was thrust into my hands.

I didn't want to hurt anyone, not even a man who had apparently been killing people for decades! But it was either help destroy my father or watch my best friend die.

Impatient, Michael muttered a couple more words into the phone. The figure in the shadows raised his wand toward the back of Blake's head.

"If you don't make a decision when I'm done counting down from three, I'll have his head blown open."

I stepped toward the image, unsure what to do. Words clogged my throat. The lights flickered like hummingbird wings. A panic I had never felt before started to drown me.

"Three."

My mouth opened. Nothing came out.

"Two."

He's serious. "Yes! Yes, I'll do it! I'll do whatever you want—just stop!"

Michael said one word into the phone before replacing it in his pocket. Immediately, the man in the shadows Ported. The glass rippled and it resumed its normal job of viewing the outside.

I stared at the window with the image of Blake burned into my eyes.

"I'll know where he is at all times." Michael sheathed his wand. "If you change your mind, I'll have his head so fast it'll still be dripping when I give it to you."

Master Lenin reached toward me. "Miss Heart, this wasn't—"

"Don't touch me." I jerked away. My magic flared, shattering the lights with a shower of sparks. The room plunged into darkness.

"I'm . . ." Numb and cold, I stepped toward the door. "I'm going to go to bed."

They didn't stop me as I pulled open the door, letting light from the hall flood the room. Everything was a blur between the classroom and the apartment. In a blink, I stood in the living room, breathing hard.

I have to get out of here.

I stepped toward the bedroom where my getaway bag was stashed underneath the bed. But I stopped short.

If I bolted into the forest, I'd die before I got very far, and Michael would kill Blake out of retaliation.

My gaze zeroed in on *The Art of Transportation* sticking out from under the corner of my mattress.

Yes! I could Port to Blake and . . . then what? We'd go on the run together from a magical man and his magical war? *Blake will think I've cracked.*

I can think of how to convince him when I get him safe.

I pulled on my magic with a violent tug. It seared through my chest, filling my body with a storm of fire. With tears brimming in my eyes, I turned on my heel, thinking only of Blake.

Please work. Please, please work.

Like all my attempts before, my magic flared out. Furniture skidded away from me. All around the living room, lights burst into a shower of sparks. The room dropped into darkness with only the full moon as a light.

With the wind knocked out of me, I crumpled to my knees and pressed my forehead to the cold floor.

26

What Keeps a God
From Smiting Nations?

I stared at the black stone ceiling.

Last night's sleep danced just out of reach. Instead, a single question tornadoed through my mind.

Could I help kill a man I knew nothing about—my own father—to save my best friend?

No matter how I worded the question, I couldn't find an answer. I would do anything for Blake. But this . . . every cell in my body screamed in protest.

I woke up in a fog and that cloud followed me down to breakfast. In autopilot I collected a bowl of oatmeal and located an empty table in the middle of the room. Despite the early hour, my classmates were bursting with energy. A couple of guys were having a loud conversation across three tables.

I sat down in the center of the noisy room and kept my shoulders hunched low. I hoped people would take it as a hint to not disturb.

"Look at you." Moose plopped onto the bench beside me. A cup of coffee and cinnamon roll accompanied her. "Already learning to get here early for the good stuff. Although, I distinctly remember saying to get the cinnamon rolls. Oatmeal was not a part of the official tour yesterday."

I looked at her with her four-point diamond frame glasses and high ponytail. Magic, as wonderful as it had seemed yesterday, came with a paranoid edge. She could be a spy planted by Master Lenin to watch me. Or she could just be a girl my age.

Her eyebrows pulled together. "You don't look so good."

"I didn't sleep well." I turned to my oatmeal and found that I wasn't hungry. Just the thought of swallowing anything made my stomach clench.

"Really? Because I'm exhausted and I don't look that depressed."

I focused my attention on her earnest face. *Was she working for Master Lenin? Or worse, if she wasn't, would Michael use her against me too?*

Time and time again, life had proven that people were weapons. Denny. My foster family before him, and many others before that. And now, looking at Moose, there was an extra sharp edge.

"Master Lenin asked you to show me the ropes. Consider the ropes shown and your responsibilities fulfilled." I turned back to my cooling breakfast. "I'm sure you have friends who you'd rather eat breakfast with."

"My friends transferred to other schools."

"I'm saying you can leave."

"Ok, Miss Doom and Gloom." She got to her feet. "Jeeze, just trying to be nice."

"If you change your mind, I'll have his head so fast it'll still be dripping when I give it to you."

I trembled under the memory of the threat. *Could he even do that? Or was that another lie to keep me running on his wheel of war?*

"Have a good day . . . or semester or whatever." Moose sank her teeth into the cinnamon roll. "See you around, transfer."

"Wait, Moose." I pushed my breakfast away and ran after her. "You're the smartest in the school, right?"

"Technically, it's just in our class, but I'll take being the best in the school."

"What do you know about Hunters?"

Her cinnamon roll paused before her mouth. "What do you mean?"

"Like . . . can they just kill anyone they want for no reason and get away with it?"

"I mean, yeah, I guess they can. But Hunters don't kill without reason. At least, they didn't." Seeing my confusion, she added, "Follow me." Moose shoved the last few bites into her mouth and turned back toward the doors.

Leaving my untouched food, I followed her from the dining room across the stairwell. Her short, determined strides took us directly into the library. She paused in the doorway and looked up at the black ceiling.

Twin blue lights shone from the dark stone directly above us. The marker above Moose brightened and slid across the ceiling, directing us deeper into the library. Shouldering her heavy book bag, Moose followed it down the main aisle, past rows and rows of towering shelves. Finally, the light took a sharp left and went to the far end of the row.

"Ok," Moose mumbled as she scanned the shelves. "I saw on the syllabus for next year that Mrs. Litpath in Magical History is supposed to go over the Hunter Guard before graduation."

She set her coffee on the shelf in front of her and licked the frosting clean from her fingers. Standing on her tiptoes, she took hold of a thin black book with silver lettering. The cover read, *The Hunter Guard and its Origin.*

Pressed into the cover was a ring of silver caging in a simple globe. Crossed over the top were two silver wands. The outer ring read, *Into the darkness to defend the light.* Above and below the globe it said *Hunter Guard.*

Moose stroked the spine, silencing the author before the enchanted pages could speak. Bracing the book against her stomach, she flipped through the silver edged pages. "Did you know there used to be eight School Masters?"

"Uh, no."

She shrugged. "Most people only focus on the seven that founded the schools. When the schools were still new, some thousands of years ago, the School Masters did whatever they wanted."

"Is Master Lenin really that old?"

She snorted. "No. He's, like, the seventh Master of this school—all of which were Lenins. The Magisterium is the only school out of the seven whose Masters have followed a lineage.

"The first School Masters acted more like deities than the scholars we have today. If you slighted one, they'd kill you. If you looked at them wrong, they'd kill you. They thought it was within their rights. Barbarianism was very much in fashion. That was until one of them," she paused on a page and turned the book toward me, "Master Cecilia Wikström, saw that the problem was that there was no one to keep them in check."

The woman pictured had high delicate cheekbones and a furrowed brow. Thick locks of curly black hair whipped around her head in a ringlet crown. Her gaze, fierce and deep blue, nearly jumped off the page.

"What keeps a god from smiting nations or just any random person when they're bored?" Moose asked.

"A soul?"

"Another god. Master Wikström threw off her title—just threw it off—and died." Moose turned the book around and continued flipping through the pages. "Not literally. She signed her own death certificate. Her reasoning was that the dead are accountable to no one. The Users under her command, she ordered to do the same."

"What does that even do?"

"By being legally dead, each User shed their titles, family ties and responsibilities, they gave up property and anything they owned. The only thing they kept was the name their family gave them, but even then, a few Hunters created new identities once they were accepted by Master Wikström.

"The Hunter Guard was a fully independent operation. They belonged to no country, colors, or loyalties. The Hunters only listened to Master Hunter Wikström and her objective was simple—protect life. I mean, how can you charge a crime to someone who is dead in all the ways that matter? You can't. Her Users could go anywhere and do anything to fulfill their assignments."

My stomach dropped. "Anything?"

"Yep. Because they were legally dead, the same rules that apply to us—don't steal, don't murder, don't break into someone's house— they didn't apply to them. The Master Hunter was the judge and jury. Her Hunters were the executioners."

No wonder why Michael smiled when I mistook his title for hunting *animals*. He hunted *people*.

"Master Hunter Wikström created the Hunting Guard in tiers." Once more she spun the book around. On the new pages was a diagram of a triangle.

Moose pointed to the top point. "The highest form of command, being herself, was *the* Master Hunter. Next down were the Master Hunters in charge of the last tier, Hunters. It takes fifty years of training to apply to be a Hunter and be placed into a trio, and just as long to become a Master Hunter. Becoming *the* Master Hunter is as rare as becoming a School Master."

"And then what? They were just released on the world?"

"Under very strict orders from the Master Hunter. The Hunting Trios were sent out on assignments to control unruly Users, creatures who were feeding where they weren't supposed to, and poison crimes. They dealt with it all."

"So, they're like the magic world's version of police." *I am so screwed.*

"Were." Moose turned the book around. "The Hunter Guard's been dead for seventy years."

"What happened?"

Moose shrugged, closing the book. "That's the thing. No one really knows. They just vanished. There was talk in the fifties about shutting the program down because they weren't needed anymore. My mom thinks that's what happened."

"But?"

"But if that were true, why are there only five left, two of which are trying to kill each other with a worldwide war?"

Her meaning hit me between the eyes. "Master Hart is a Hunter, too?"

Moose nodded. "He and Master Kale were the best the program ever created."

"And this war has been going on for . . ."

My ignorance made Moose's eyebrows draw together in confusion. "The Guard fell seventy years ago, which is when I think this all started. Officially, Master Kale joined up with Master Lenin about twenty years after. Did you really not know that?"

"My old school glossed over the exact details of the . . . current state of our world." *Cheese and rice, there has to be someone who can help me protect Blake from Michael.* "Who polices everything now?"

"Each School Master has their own regiment of Users. They take care of the high-level stuff in their designated areas, but it's not as organized as the Guard. Definitely not as efficient."

Meaning Master Lenin was in charge. By how he acted last night, he wasn't going to lift a finger to help me. I had no way of contacting the other School Masters, not that they'd be willing to help against a Hunter, and a Master Hunter at that.

Michael could make good on his gruesome promise. In Kansas, Denny kept me there like a ball and chain. Every time I ran, the consequences fell solely on me. But now, with Michael's blade hanging over Blake's head . . . I was trapped in this haunted black stone school.

Attachment is an anchor. How right I was. And it comes with a razor's edge.

"What brought all of this on?" Moose asked. She replaced the book with great care, aligning it with the others on the shelf.

"I just—" I shook my head. "I heard some of the cooking crew talking about Master Kale. I didn't know what a Master Hunter did."

"Yeah, people talk about him in hushed tones nowadays. My brother used to tell me that if I didn't go to sleep before midnight that Michael Kale was going to come out of my closet to look for evil and if he caught me awake, he'd cut out my eyes."

"That's terrible."

"You don't have to tell me that." She wrapped her hands loosely around the strap of her bag.

"Have you ever met him? Master Kale, I mean."

Moose barked a single, sardonic laughing note. "No one has *met* Master Kale in the last seventy years and lived to talk about it."

"So, he's really as bad as he seems?" When her expression began to cloud again with confusion, I rushed on. "How my parents raised me is the equivalent to abandoning me under a rock, ok?"

She nodded but remained slightly skeptical. "I mean, it's complicated. He's the only one brave enough to confront Master Hart directly but he's . . . well, he's a Master Hunter. He's given himself the assignment of killing Master Hart, that's all he cares about. I read an article that he went into a restaurant to kill one of Master Hart's supporters—he got him, alright, and everyone else in the place."

A chill ran down my spine.

"There's more lore about that guy than there is about Dracula. I heard he does straight up dark magic once a year with dragon hearts and eats them for their strength."

There was almost too much to unpack in that sentence—the first being that *dragons exist?* I remembered Moose saying something about the Dragon Farm yesterday, but I didn't think it actually meant *dragons existed.* And then there was the obvious about eating raw tissue. I wish I could be surprised, but it was extremely easy to picture the man in all black with blood dripping off his chin as he bit into a bleeding organ. Instead, I was just nauseous.

"He's killed so many things—people and monsters—that people call him Hades. They actually think that calling him *the Lord of the Dead* is less scary than using his actual name."

Hades.

And my father goes by Lucifer. Great.

"Why doesn't someone else stand up to Master Hart?"

"Because of his title. You can't oppose another User unless you're matching in status, and most Masters either believe Master Hart or want to avoid conflict so they keep their heads down."

"What about Master Lenin?"

Moose shrugged, unimpressed. "He created Achilles Heel as a way to give Master Kale direction, but it's not enough. With Master Kale in his ranks, any support is scared off, so they've been doing it mostly alone."

And that's why they dragged me onto their sinking ship.

"Because we live so long, prejudices stick around a lot longer than they should. I know Clarence sides with Master Hart. Most of the students that think the same have transferred out of the Magisterium."

"You're kidding."

Moose shook her head. "I wish. The underline is, not everyone agrees with Master Hart, but no one can get behind Master Kale's methods."

Did Michael's methods matter? If he was trying to save the world from Lawrence, who was committing one genocide after another, was it worth it? That question was quickly hushed when I thought of Blake. His only crime here was that he was close to me.

"Is Achilles Heel the good guys in all of this?"

Moose shrugged. "Going against evil doesn't make you good. I think they're the lesser of the two evils, for sure. But . . . like I said. It's complicated."

So, not only am I being blackmailed into fighting a war against my homicidal father, but I'm also being forced to fight alongside another homicidal maniac?

I have to get out of here.

I wanted to ask if Moose had any tips on Porting, but if she was reporting back to Master Lenin it'd tip him off about my next escape attempt. So, I swallowed my questions.

"Thanks, Moose."

"Sure thing." Collecting her coffee, she stepped around me and headed for the main aisle. "Best of luck."

In a matter of seconds, I stood alone. I looked back up at the book Moose had looked through. Its black cover appeared out of place among the warm tones of the surrounding titles like a storm cloud on a beach front.

I reached to take it out again when I spotted the book pressed against it. *The Many Faces of Death; Master Hunters and Hunters.*

Taking that book instead, I stoked my finger down the spine, silencing the enchantment. Idly, I opened the cover to the table of contents. It was a list of names in alphabetical order. My finger flipped through the silver edged pages till I came to the K section.

Kale, Michael was a third of the way down the page.

Quickly, I turned to the assigned page. My stomach clenched when Michael's face appeared. The picture was taken head on, with as much emotion as a rock. I moved to cover his face with my thumb when I noticed . . . there wasn't a scar on his cheek. He was still wearing that leather jacket, although it looked significantly less worn. The leather pictured had more shine and stiffness than the one I knew.

Covering his soulless gaze, I scanned through the lines under his name. There was a brief history of when he joined and who he trained under. Sixty years after he was accepted into the Guard, he earned his Masters title, one of the faster promotions in the Guard. The section ended with a single word, ACTIVE.

The next bit, labeled *Assignments*, was nothing more than a list of names. Some belonged to creatures and monsters of myths, but most were names of people. The list took up nearly three pages, tightly packaged with little space between them. Beside each small printed name was a date.

Are these all the people he's killed?

My hand trembled. They went back over a century, meaning he had been doing this over half of his life.

"What's one more life lost in a war?"

I closed the book with a snap and shoved it back on its high shelf. I backed up until my back hit the other side of the aisle. The black spine glowered down at me until the clock chimed.

27

A School Master's Midnight Stroll

That night, I shouldn't have been surprised when the transporter beeped.

Why would Michael want to take a break? He didn't care about my physical health, which was apparent by the number of bruises he gave me via apples. So why would he care about my mental state or that I was a good deep breath away from screaming and never stopping?

I stood over the bedside table, watching the transporter glow and chirp. My heart ached as I remembered the night before—the war, the lies, no escape, the threat against Blake.

Unable to put it off any longer, I grabbed the transporter and Ported into the classroom. As usual, Michael was already there at its center.

We regarded each other in cold silence.

"Are you incapable of showing up on time?" Stepping forward, he offered me the wand I left the night before.

I didn't take the wand. I searched his face for remorse or any human emotion. I found none. "I was trying to decide if I wanted to be force fed anymore of your bullshit."

He dropped his offered hand to his side. "Would you have agreed to fight if you were told up front?"

"I guess we'll never know."

"When this war breaks into the open, it'll be horrific. Lenin was doing what he thought was necessary."

"By tricking me."

"It was better than forcing you."

"Like you did?"

The muscle in his jaw pulsed.

"How do you sleep at night?" I hissed.

"With a bottle of Hell's Whiskey and dreams of your father's blood." He held out my wand again. "Are you done wasting my time?"

I crossed my arms over my chest. "How can I fight for you when I don't trust you?"

"I never asked you to fight for me. I just want you to kill enough of your father's people to put me next to him. Fight for Lenin, if that helps. Just stay out of my way."

"Why do you hate Lawrence so much?"

His eyes smoldered. "That's none of your damn business."

"Actually, it is, seeing as I'm his daughter."

"That doesn't help your case. If anything, it makes me want to chop you into little pieces and feed you to stray dogs." He stepped forward and uncrossed one of my arms and slapped my wand into my hand. "You don't have to like being here. You don't even have to like what you do. But the faster you learn, the sooner your father will be dead, and we'll never have to see each other again."

Grinding my teeth together, I grabbed my wand. His grip tightened.

"But let's be clear about something. If you think about setting me up for failure to save your precious Britain, if you so much as *think* about getting in my way, I won't hesitate to rip out your heart." He released my wand and stepped back. "And trust me, nothing would make me happier."

He spun on his heel and stalked to the other side of the room. Taking an apple from his pocket, he threw it at me.

The anger heating my blood made my magic easier to call. The only thing that seemed to get me through the night was that I was getting better. I deflected most of the apples, which meant less bruises and headaches.

Without warning, Michael pulled out a baseball and chucked it at me. The ball punched me in the stomach. Before I could hurl it back at him, it flew across the room to his waiting hand.

"Pay attention." He threw it again.

The ball whizzed toward my face. I dropped to the floor before my nose became a speed bump.

The ball snapped back into Michael's hand. Leaning against the wall like he always did, he launched the ball for a third time.

I slashed my wand through the air. The ball ricocheted back to Michael. I didn't have time to celebrate my success before the ball was headed for my face again.

This rapid-fire continued for ten minutes. I spent more time jumping out of the way than actually deflecting.

"Stop!" I exclaimed before he could hurl that ball again. My wand fell as I collapsed to my knees.

Michael regarded me with cold eyes. "Breaks aren't granted in war."

"It's a good thing this isn't a war," I snapped.

"No, but you're preparing for one. What you practice is what you'll perform. If you're lazy here, you'll be lazy later."

"I'm not lazy."

"What I'm seeing says otherwise." He pushed off the wall and stood to his full height. "Would you like some help getting to your feet?" By the tone of his voice, I knew if he helped, I would get more bruises.

I slowly pushed myself up onto my shaky legs. "Can I at least have some water?"

He rolled his eyes. But he walked over to his jacket and pulled a water bottle from the pocket. He quickly tossed it to me. I barely caught it before it socked me in the stomach.

"Have you ever been attacked like that?" I took a sip.

"Yes."

I took another chug of water. "By Lawrence?"

His eyes snapped to my face. I expected the question to provoke a response of anger, but he simply nodded. "Yes, by your father."

"What's he like?"

"Does it matter?"

I shook my head, looking down at the bottle. "I just want to know something about the man I sold my soul for."

Silence suffocated the air between us. I quickly raised the bottle to my mouth, hoping to make the break last a little longer.

"Charming is too light of a word." He stared vacantly at the air in front of him. "He has a way with words. He can talk you into anything before you realize it." He shook his head. "There's no use talking about who he was. That man is dead. Now he only values the lives of those who meet his perfect standard. And if you don't meet it, you forfeit everything." He gripped the ball. "Is that what you wanted?"

I wasn't sure what I wanted.

He looked back at me. "Are you done?"

I had about a thousand more questions I wanted to ask. But judging by how he reacted to that one, I knew it would only be like poking a sleeping bear. I twisted the cap back on the bottle and grabbed my wand. I focused on the ball in his hand.

"Already you're doing something wrong."

Of course.

"Look at your opponent, not their wand. If you look at the wand, you won't know where the ward is going until it hits you. If you look at your opponent, they'll give hints as to where they're planning to strike."

"Hints?"

"Have you ever watched a game of soccer?"

Confused by the sudden change in topic, I shook my head.

"In the game, you can tell where the player is going to send the ball by their body language. Some players might hide it better than others, but there's always something in their movements that tell you."

"What do I look for?"

"Where their eyes are looking, most of their weight on one foot, bracing—anything might be a clue." He lifted the ball and placed his weight on his right foot. "Where am I going to throw it?"

I could draw a perfect line from the ball to my left shoulder. I touched my shoulder. "Here."

"Correct." Sliding his foot back, he tilted his hand. "Where?"

"My head."

He dropped the ball and drew the wand from the holster under his arm. Raising his arm above his head, he put one foot in front of the other. "Where?"

Panic seized my tongue. *He's not going to fire, is he? Can I dodge in time?*

He rolled his eyes. "I'm not going to cast anything. Where would the ward land?"

Trying to ignore the uneasiness in my stomach, I tapped over my heart. "Here."

"Good." Much to my relief, he lowered his wand. Bending down, he picked up the baseball. "Get ready."

I hit the floor seconds before the ball crashed into the wall behind me with a loud pop.

"Plant your feet and watch my movements," he said as I got back up.

He put all of his weight on his right leg as he raised his arm. My mind whirled as I tried to read his body. By the time I put the pieces together, the ball punched me in the shoulder.

Ow! That was going to re-bruise the bruise that was already there.

Two more throws and two more hits followed. While I knew where the ball was going to strike, I was spending too much time trying to figure it out.

With a hiss of dissatisfaction, Michael jerked his wand toward my feet. My ankles locked, keeping my feet firmly in place.

Before I could curse him with every word I knew, he threw the ball. I rocked to the side before it could karate chop me in the throat. I almost tore my leg away from my ankle in the process.

Then it clicked.

Instead of focusing on his arm or leg, I needed to concentrate on his eyes.

I watched him pull back his arm. As the ball left his fingertips, his eyes lingered on my collarbone. I slashed my wand. The ball swerved and hit the wall.

Ha! It worked!

He gave me no time to celebrate. The ball flew back to his hand and left a split second later.

For the rest of January, Michael threw baseballs.

He continued until I could deflect them with one hand behind my back and my feet firmly planted without magic. With each passing lesson, he added more baseballs.

In the weeks that passed, a lonely routine emerged.

I slept in as late as I dared to make sure that I got to breakfast late. By that time, the dining room was nearly empty, as was the buffet. I did it to avoid Moose, Daniel, and Cornelia. I couldn't have anyone become an anchor to keep me here. When I learned to Port, I needed to leave without hesitation. So, to keep my soft heart from making friends, I removed myself entirely.

After a hurried breakfast, I went to my classes and sat close to the door. The moment the class was over, I took the long way to my next one to ensure that I got there right as the clock chimed. This left no time to say hi or for small talk—although Cornelia and Daniel tried. Every time I walked into a class we shared, they waved. Always with an empty seat beside them. After the first couple weeks, they stopped saving seats. Moose never bothered.

I took my lunches into the greenhouse and my dinners back to my room. Every night after I completed my homework, I spent hours trying to Port—or until the headaches got the better of me. Then I took the transporter to the other side of the school for night lessons with Michael. The next morning the cycle would start again.

If I wasn't being blackmailed into fighting a war, I would have fallen in love with my classes. Magic was just so *cool*. There was no better way to describe it.

In my Wand Structure class, I learned that the black surface of our wands was porous. Within each tiny hole was an enchantment that drew the magic through our skin and into the wand. It collected and directed it toward the tip of the wand, all without losing any potency.

It was a marvel, yet every student I saw treated it like it was just an everyday object. One kid used his as a back scratcher constantly throughout the class. I was engrossed in the material and how each teacher used it. If I wasn't me, I would relish in it all. But the same thumping song raced through my blood.

Run.

Run.

Run.

I was close to Porting. I could feel it . . . at least that's what I told myself.

One night in February, during one of our lessons, Michael's phone beeped.

As soon as he heard the sound the balls paused. He waved his wand and they continued to assault me, as if being pitched from a machine.

He walked over and dug the phone from his pocket. His shoulders stiffened. Sheathing his wand, he grabbed his jacket. "You're dismissed."

"What?" I looked at the clock. We had another hour left. "Why?" As he headed toward the door, he swung his jacket over his shoulders. "Atlas needs me to control a situation."

Is he going to the war front? I remembered the bruises he often came back with.

"I didn't think you'd mind an extra hour of sleep."

That was the nicest thing he'd ever said to me.

"Don't be stupid and waste it."

And he ruined it.

"You'll have to walk back to your room. The transporter is set to only work at certain times." With that, he Ported.

"Goodbye to you, too," I muttered to the empty room. I pushed open the door and stepped into the hallway.

Moonlight poured from the glass ceiling, illuminating the stairwell and clock in silver light. I paused just outside the South Wing. Something was different. Where a set of gold doors should've been was a gaping hole of darkness.

The North Wing was open.

Cold air rolled from the darkened hallway. Thinking of ghosts, I quickened my pace toward the stairs.

My foot hadn't hit the first step before a scream ripped through the air. Every cell in my body froze. I knew the sounds of pain. I lived with them for five years and that was definitely one of them.

I didn't think. I sprinted through the open double doors and down the hall all students avoided. Unlike the other wings, the chandeliers and wall lights didn't turn on as I entered. The shadows darkened the further I ran, until I almost believed they were tangible.

The hallway started to narrow. My heart pounded in my ears as I pulled up short at a huge metal door.

Out of breath, I grabbed the handle and pulled. The door didn't budge.

"Hello? Is someone in there?" I tried to push the door, but it refused to move.

Under my hands, the door grew hot. I jerked back seconds before flames rushed from beneath it. As quickly as they appeared, they were sucked back inside the tower.

Shadows moved under the door. Muffled words leaked into the air.

What the hell? No one could survive that.

I inched toward the keyhole and peered inside. Smoke stung my nose.

On the other side of the door a grey form passed, blocking my view of the room. I jumped back as a chill laced the metal.

The muttering stopped mid-syllable.

Not a breath passed before the sounds of heavy footsteps came from inside the tower.

Pressing my eye back to the hole, I watched a figure descend the moonlit stairs and move toward the door.

Toward me.

My throat went dry. Jumping to my feet, I ran from the locked door and threw myself into the nearest classroom. The unrelenting shadows enveloped me as I pushed the door until there was only a sliver to peer through.

The tower door squeaked open. A man stepped out and locked it behind him.

I narrowed my eyes to make sure they weren't playing tricks on me, but it was undeniable.

What was Master Lenin doing in a tower he told everyone to stay away from?

28

Just Hear Me Out!

Late to breakfast, I ran into the dining room the next morning.

Most of the students had already eaten and left, leaving the large room with an eerie layer of quiet. A few muttered conversations came from the remaining occupied tables.

I snatched a couple pieces of cold toast and left the late morning stillness. I kept my gaze locked ahead as I took the stairs two at a time. I wouldn't let my attention drift to the North Wing or what happened last night.

Instead, I ate my toast and put one foot in front of the other.

Halfway up the third flight, I slowed my march behind a large group meandering to higher levels. Nearly halfway through the week, the student body moved slower as if there was no end in sight.

Moose's high ponytail bounced with each step. On one side of her was a girl with spiky platinum hair and on the other side was a tall dark toned girl with a bowtie. I had seen both of them in Creatures Studies with Moose, but I never caught their names.

Clarence was doing his best to distance himself from the trio. He only managed a few steps above them thanks to a group reeking of pool chlorine.

Like every morning, I found myself looking for the charming duo of Cornelia and Daniel. With how late it was, I knew my chances of seeing them were slim.

"What?" Bowtie spun toward Moose so fast that I worried she'd trip right over the railing. "When?"

"I overheard Tiana say it in the breakfast line," Moose said with as much glee as a child on Christmas morning. "Miracles do happen."

"And you just now thought to tell me?" Bowtie would have sounded offended if she wasn't grinning so hard.

The platinum blond next to Moose snorted once. Up a bit closer, I noticed that everything about her was pale. Even her blue eyes were so washed out they almost looked white. The only thing that wasn't pale was her peeling black polish, her ripped jeans and graphic t-shirt, and the cherry red lollipop between her lips.

Moose shrugged. "You would know if you ever showed up to breakfast on time."

"Not everyone functions on three hours of sleep like you."

With a sigh of indignation, Clarence turned to face the trio. "How'd it happen? Did Master Lenin finally look at her grades and force her out?"

The blond grinned around her lollipop. "Nice."

"No idea," Moose said. "Master Lenin must have been up past midnight filing the paperwork."

My attention snapped to the mention of the School Master. I leapt up two stairs, closing the distance between us.

"Who are you talking about?" I asked.

The three turned to face me. Moose's earlier excitement dimmed as her keen brown eyes raked over me.

"Janet Raven," she said. "She transferred out of the Magisterium."

I glanced down and up the twin spiraling staircases. Sure enough, on the opposite staircase stood her two tall friends without their middleman.

"When?" I asked.

Moose shrugged. "Some time past curfew. She must not have wanted to wait until the morning to get out."

My heart took a swan dive toward my stomach. After curfew was when I saw Master Lenin leave the North Tower. Meaning he was nowhere near the seventh floor where Janet was.

"Are you sure it was after curfew?"

Moose nodded. "Positive. I tutor one of her friends and she said Janet was in her room at ten."

"And Master Lenin was with her?"

"He had to be in order to get the paperwork filed this early."

Oh, cheese and rice.

Moose watched me closely as if she knew some ugly thoughts were running through my head. "Charlie, this is Nirean Knowles and Ace Navarro."

The blond, Ace, nodded once. "Pleasure."

Nirean dropped down a step and offered me her hand. Just as I was about to grab her hand, I changed course and grabbed the thick sweater on her forearm. "Did Master Lenin say why she transferred?"

Moose shook her head. "Your guess is as good as mine."

The clock sounded, prompting our group to keep moving up the stairs.

I jumped up two steps to fall in line with Moose. "Is it normal for someone to want to transfer after curfew?"

Moose nodded. "It happens. My friend Holly transferred after curfew. I guess when you want out, you want out as soon as possible."

"Where did she transfer to?"

"Don't know." She paused and when she continued her voice was quieter. "She died the next day." Stretching her stride over two stairs, Moose outpaced in front of me.

I remained frozen on the steps where she left me.

Master Lenin in the tower.

The scream.

Janet transferring.

It didn't add up.

I had the same feeling back in Kansas when I saw the kids didn't smile and there were bloodstains on the backs of their shirts. Something wasn't right.

As Mr. Harrison continued to crack jokes about Moose answering questions faster than Daniel, I could hardly breathe right.

To hell with their war. I wasn't going to stick around and wait for the other shoe to drop.

As soon as my last class was over, I quickly crossed the stairwell under the intertwining staircases. As I stepped into the library, I spotted Mr. While at the front desk with his feet kicked up. His glasses had slid low on his nose as he focused on the book in his lap.

The clamor of the dinner rush covered my footsteps as I tiptoed past him, deeper into the shelves. I retraced my steps to where he brought me a month earlier. It took me a couple tries, winding in and out of the rows, before I found the collection of books on Porting.

I dropped to my knees and skimmed my fingers along the titles.

He said there was a book with simplified terms. I need a dumbed down version because what I'm doing clearly isn't working.

Over the last month, every time I attempted Porting I passed out or blew a lightbulb. I'm pretty sure I gave myself a mild concussion three weeks back.

"Good evening, Miss Heart."

I spun around with my heart in my throat.

Mr. While stood in the mouth of the aisle with an easy smile. "Shouldn't you be at dinner?"

"I already finished," I lied.

"The line's only been open for thirty minutes," he chuckled.

"I was starving." I crossed my fingers.

"Clearly." His green eyes dropped to the row of books before me. "Still interested in Porting, I see."

"Yeah," I said with a nervous laugh. "The ones you recommended weren't as helpful as I had hoped. So, I came back for a second round."

"Well, now you just wounded my pride," he said with a pleasant smile that said the exact opposite of the words that left his mouth. "What do you need exactly?"

"Something with clearer instructions. You were right about *The Art of Transportation*. The terms were out of my league."

"Luckily for you, Porting is a popular topic for instruction. Here are a couple books that might do you better. I think they gloss over some things, but since you're wanting simpler—"

"There you are."

Mr. While and I nearly bonked heads as he looked toward the new arrival. Mr. Harrison blinked upon seeing me beside his coworker.

"Hello, Miss Heart. Why aren't you at dinner?"

"I already ate," I blurted.

Mr. While stood up and faced the teacher. "What can I help you with, Will?"

"If you have a moment, I'd like to hear your thoughts on something." Turning his eyes to me, Mr. Harrison waved. "I'll see you next Thursday, Miss Heart."

Lamely, I waved back. "Bye."

The two men rounded the shelves and disappeared. Alone, I sagged against the wall of books. The lights closest to me shuttered nervously. Shaking the nerves from my hands, I bent down and grabbed *Porting for the Ignorant.* For good measure, I grabbed *So You Think You Can Port.*

I shoved the books deep into my bag before heading toward the library doors. When I got back to my room, I wasn't going to do a page of homework. As far as I was concerned, Porting was my homework. I needed to get out of here. I needed—

"Just hear me out!"

I nearly jumped out of my skin and took a bookshelf down with me. Peeking around the corner, I saw Mr. While standing close to Mr. Harrison. The pair was as far from the main aisle as they could get without being inside the wall.

"You can't say that about a Master of a School," Mr. While said in a voice matching his tense shoulder.

"Just listen, alright?" Mr. Harrison scrubbed a hand over his face. "Another student transferred today."

"Yes, Janet Raven." Mr. While pushed his glasses up his nose.

Too curious for my own good, I slipped down a row of shelves. Peering through the neat rows of books, I watched the pair.

"She's the third Royal to do so in the last three years," Mr. Harrison said. He shot a cautionary look over his shoulder. I was successfully hidden behind a wall of books.

"So?"

"So?" Mr. Harrison laughed incredulously. "Each one of those students wanted to Master in magical arts. None of the other great schools offer the training for that title better than the Magisterium."

"With everything going on, you can't expect them to stay. Besides, not just Royals are transferring. Students of all statuses are doing that these days."

"But how many of them do it late at night and then leave before breakfast. No goodbye and no explanation." Mr. Harrison paused. "I caught a look a Miss Raven's paperwork on Tessa's desk this morning. It was signed off by Master Lenin."

"What are you saying exactly?" Mr. While asked slowly.

"I'm saying that something isn't right here. I think Master Lenin's up to something and he's covering his tracks by saying these students are leaving."

"Why would he do that?"

"I don't know . . ." Mr. Harrison struggled with his next thought. "All I can think is that he's using them for his crusade with Master Kale. Why else would he be targeting high statuses?"

"You think he's draining them for the war?"

"Kind of, yeah. If he really is following Master Kale like he says he is, I wouldn't be surprised. You've seen how dark that man is. He'd do anything to get Master Hart's head."

"I'm sure there's another explanation than *Master Lenin* picking off his own students," Mr. While hissed.

"I thought the same, but I asked around and he started these late night transfers of high status students right around the time he voiced his loyalties to Master Kale."

My stomach chose that moment to growl like a rabid animal. I didn't stay to see if they heard. I bolted toward the entrance.

In a blur of books and towering bookcases, from the corner of my eye, I saw the flash of a man, dressed in a navy suit. He was close enough to be eavesdropping on the same conversation I was. Before I could turn my head to get a good look at him, a flash of gold erupted through the shelves.

The brilliant burst of magic knocked into the bookcases. The shelves fell against each other like a wave of dominos, sending books clattering to the floor. Wood groaned and dust plumed to the ceiling in a thick cloud.

I watched in horror as the bookcase closest to me tipped over. Books rained off their shelves. A hand dragged me out of the way before I was trapped beneath it.

Wood snapped and books rolled like an avalanche. The shelf crashed at my feet, leaving me unharmed but choking on dust. When it stopped, silence thundered through my ears.

29

Forget I Said Anything

Moose, still clutching my arm, gaped at the destroyed library.

"*What did you do*?" she hissed.

"This wasn't me—"

A pile of rubble heaved and groaned.

Moose and I broke away from the door, clambering over the books toward the sound. Drawing closer, I saw a hand sticking out from beneath a broken shelf. I pushed aside blood-smudged books as Moose ran to get Helen.

I grabbed a large textbook and lifted it off Mr. While's face. There was an angle in his bloody nose.

I shoved aside as many books as I could to uncover him, but a bookcase pinned his lower body. I grasped the shelf but stopped. There was no way I could lift something that heavy. I looked at the wand at my hip, but I had no idea how to use it to help him.

Helen ran in with Master Lenin close on her heels. He waved his wand, lifting the bookcase enough for Helen and Moose to drag Mr. While free. A couple feet over was a lost shoe and a bloody tuft of hair.

Slipping on book covers, I scrambled to uncover Mr. Harrison. Dark purple bruises shadowed his chest. His irregular breathing sounded like it was coming from a shredded paper bag.

Helen ran over and froze at the color of the teacher's bruised skin. "Master Lenin. Your help, please."

Master Lenin left Mr. While propped against a dune of dusty, displaced books. Sliding across book covers, he staggered over with his wand drawn. A thin lace of magic left his wand and curled under the bookcase, lifting it off Mr. Harrison. Together Helen and Master Lenin levitated him toward the infirmary.

I looked around the scattered books for something to tell me where the third person was. No one could escape that. I barely did.

"Come on, Charlie." Moose grabbed my sleeve, pulling me toward the door.

I wrenched myself free and continued to shift through piles of books.

"What are you looking for?"

"Someone else was in here." I moved to another pile. "I saw him. He was over here."

"Did you see his face?"

I shook my head, "He was wearing . . ." I stopped and looked at the man that had walked back into the room. "He was wearing a navy suit."

Master Lenin carefully made his way back over to Mr. While. His lips were tight and pale as he talked low to the librarian. From where I stood, I could see the smudges of dust from the books.

Moose followed my stare. "What are you thinking?"

"I saw Master Lenin . . . right before the bookcases fell." But that couldn't be true. I saw him run *into* the room. But he could've Ported out once the books started to fall and then run back in, feigning surprise and panic.

If he heard the same conversation that I did, that means he also heard the same accusation.

"So?" Moose prompted.

Dread attacked my stomach like an angry hive of bees. The blast of magic, the destroyed library, the two hurt faculty members, Master Lenin unhurt . . . all of it came together and added up to answer my previous question from the night before.

"I think Master Lenin killed Janet."

Moose's mouth gaped open like a flytrap. She grabbed the sleeve of my sweater and dragged me from the library. By now the cloud of dust billowing through the stairwell had drawn the attention of the dinner rush.

Students left the dining room and crowded toward the library with exclamations of shock and dismay.

I glanced back. Master Lenin, with his back to the destroyed library, watched me with an expression too far away to read.

Moose yanked me through the growing crowd, across the stairwell, and into the bathroom beside the dining room.

Slamming the door and locking it, she quickly checked all the stalls to make sure we were completely alone.

Then she faced me, her wide eyes framed behind her diamond point glasses. "You're going to explain everything, slowly and clearly. Alright? What the hell do you mean Master Lenin killed Janet?"

"I—" Shaking my head, my hair flew wildly around my face. "Forget I said anything."

"*Forget you said anything?*" Moose shrieked. "You just accused a man—a School Master—of murder. How the hell am I going to—"

"Moose, please. Just forget it." The scars marring my back tingled.

"No! Tell me why—"

"There's nothing we can do!" My voice rose to match hers.

Her eyes hardened. "Stop interrupting me." She took a slow deliberate breath. "And start explaining."

I shook my head, moving toward the door. "I can't."

She stepped in front of me with her arms crossed. "I think you mean you won't. You have a working tongue and functional voice box. The only thing stopping you is you. Janet transferred. Good riddance. There's nothing that says she's dead or that Master Lenin killed her." She paused. Her lips parted just enough for a few words to slip out. "Unless you saw something."

I knew the feeling of thin ice under my feet, and we were treading on it. "It doesn't matter."

"Of course it matters! What did you see?"

"Stop, please," I begged. "I've been in a situation like this. If we try to intervene, we could be next."

"Oh, come on."

"You don't believe me?" I turned and lifted the edge of my shirt to expose the scar tissue crisscrossing over my back. "I tried to stop my foster dad from beating another girl. The only good it did was add scars to my back and the punishment was still handed to her."

"Charlie." Her hand flew to her mouth.

I shook the chills of Memory Lane from my skin. "This is a losing battle. We should quit while we're ahead."

She shook her head slowly. "I can't."

"Well, I can." I reached around her and jerked open the door. Noise from the dining room rushed into the bathroom. My shaky hands gripped my bag as I stepped into the hall.

"So, you're not even going to tell me what you saw?" she called from the doorway.

I glanced back. The look of determination on her face scared me. I had seen foster kids with that look. It was usually beaten out of them.

"Something's bothering you. Let me help."

"I'm not going to be here long enough for it to bother me. As far as anyone is concerned, I have no idea what you're talking about." I turned and didn't stop until I was upstairs in my room with the deadbolt in place.

I dumped the books on Porting across my mattress. The need to get out of here was stronger than ever.

I grabbed *The Art of Teleportation* but it slipped from my sweaty fingers. The lights were pulsing like it was an underground nightclub.

I slid to the floor beside the bed. Curling my arms around my chest, I pressed my forehead to my knees. I took a deep breath before slowly releasing it back into the room. If Michael saw any flinch of panic or tremble of fear, he would know something was up.

Once I had stopped shaking, I pulled out my homework and pushed the library conversation from my mind with meaningless facts about cactus needles in potions.

At ten o'clock, the transporter beeped on my nightstand.

Pushing aside my homework, I gathered my wand and grabbed the transporter. With my feet firmly planted in the classroom, I turned, looking for my instructor.

Master Lenin stood beside Michael.

30

Casualties

Seeing Master Lenin beside Michael, magic surged from my core.

I stopped breathing and tried to wrestle my magic back. The lights flickered once and just barely. Then I arranged my features into a look of surprise.

"Good evening, Miss Heart," Master Lenin said coolly. "Master Kale was just informing me of your progress."

"It must be a short report." I forced the words from my throat, hoping it sounded like a joke.

He smiled, but it didn't reflect in his eyes. "On the contrary, you're moving along nicely."

I looked at Michael. For once, he wore a look that resembled mild curiosity. I followed his gaze to my hands. I was fidgeting with the hem of my shirt. I forced myself to make my hands hang limp at my sides.

"But I do have another reason for being here. I saw you in the library tonight. It's a miracle you weren't hurt as well."

"I guess I was lucky."

Michael's eyes narrowed.

"I was hoping you could tell me what happened." Master Lenin shifted his hands into his pockets.

I shook my head. "I was leaving when the bookcases started falling. I didn't even know anyone else was in there."

Michael crossed his arms. "Why were you in the library?"

Crap! My mind scattered everywhere looking for a lie that would work. "Obviously, I was looking for a book."

His eyes flickered to my shaking hands. "You're a horrible liar."

"I'm not lying! I'm just freaked out. It's not every day a library tries to crush me."

"Did you see anything?" Michael repeated.

I dropped my eyes to my hands and willed them to be still. "Like I said, one minute I was looking for a book and the next a bookcase was trying to squish me."

When he didn't say anything, I looked up. Michael's eyes ran wildly over my face. He wasn't buying any of it.

Instead of calling me on it, he turned to Master Lenin. "If you don't have anything else, I'd like to get started. You've made us late."

"Of course." Master Lenin nodded to the Master Hunter. "Thank you for your time. Have a good night." The liar strolled across the room and out the door.

When the door closed, Michael pulled out a baseball. "Stand with your feet shoulder width apart."

With Master Lenin out of the room, I about melted to the floor. Ready for a distraction, I prepared myself for the ball to fly out of his hand.

Instead, Michael set it on the floor.

"You'll be starting levitation tonight. That way if another bookcase tries to crush you, you can stop it. Just by looking at you, you don't look able to lift a lot of things." He looked at my arms. "I'll tell Lenin to make you start lifting weights."

"Or you could just ask me."

He sent me a cold look. "See the base of the object? The ball is on the ground, yes?"

I nodded. *Duh.*

"Have you seen a car jack?"

"I lived in Kansas. Not under a rock."

His glare reached a boiling point. "Your magic will act as a car jack to levitate the baseball. The more magic you use, the higher it will rise. Level your wand at the base."

My fingers tingled with nerves. I could feel his eyes on me, looking for mistakes. I made sure my hand was low on the shaft, that my elbow wasn't locked and my fingers were relaxed. I aimed at the ball and peeked at him from the corner of my eye.

He nodded in approval. "Grab your magic and direct it to the base. Then jerk the tip up."

That sounded easy enough. At least nothing was being thrown at me.

I pulled on my eager magic, releasing a flood of warmth down my arm and through my hand. Unlike the apple it didn't just twitch. As soon as the golden magic left my wand, the ball shot up and cracked against the ceiling.

Baseball pieces rained down, sprinkling the black floor with grey chunks.

My spirits sank as I looked at the Master Hunter, waiting for his harsh critiques.

But Michael just thoughtfully rubbed the scar on his cheek. Crossing the room, he took one of the chairs from the stack in the corner and dragged it to where the baseball had been.

"The chair doesn't have one base but four legs you need to focus on. Make sure equal amounts of magic are under each leg. The chair is heavier, so it shouldn't shoot up like that."

He couldn't have been more wrong.

If the chair was a living person, I would've killed it. With the first couple tries the chair shot toward the ceiling like a rocket. Sometimes it would go up, turn, and crash into a wall. Or it would scuttle across the floor like a bug.

This continued for half an hour before I was ready to throw my wand across the room.

Finally, I whirled around and looked at the man who had been chuckling the whole time. "What a big help you are." That damn smirk crossed his lips. "What am I doing wrong?"

He straightened. "You don't know how much magic you should be using." He reached for my wrist, careful to grab my sleeve and not my skin, and pointed my wand at the chair again. "Let's try something new. Pretend you're blowing a bubble under each leg."

Pushing my irritation aside, I released my magic toward the chair. It wobbled. Increasing the flow, I pictured the bubbles expanding.

"Keep the same amount of magic under each leg," Michael coached as the chair tilted backward.

Adding more magic under the forgotten leg, the chair started to lift off the ground. As the imaginary bubbles got bigger, the higher it went. The chair floated effortlessly above us.

I cut the flow of magic, letting it plummet back to the floor. My annoyance returned as I faced him. "Why didn't you tell me that an hour ago?"

"It was barely thirty minutes, and I was waiting to see how long it would take you to ask. Pride has no place in war."

"All of that was to teach me I'm prideful?" *I should levitate that chair right up his—*

"That and it was entertaining. I haven't had that much fun in years." With a smug smirk, he walked over to grab his jacket. "The first thing they do in the Hunter Guard is beat the pride out of you. You should be thankful this is all I did."

No, I wanted to levitate him into the ceiling.

"That'll be all for tonight. Levitate one of the chairs in your room for an hour before you go to bed."

"You're leaving?"

"I'm not a babysitter." He dragged the worn leather jacket over his shoulders. "If you think about forgoing practice, I'll know tomorrow night based on how well you perform. So, do us both a favor and don't be as lazy as we both know you are."

I ignored the jab. With the conclusion of our lesson, I had nothing to distract me from the events of that afternoon. Reality settled back in. As I fiddled with my wand, a question popped into my head. If he worked for Master Lenin, could he be helping him kill those students?

"Stop staring." He turned with narrowed eyes. "It's impolite. Especially from you."

Asking, *are you helping Master Lenin be a serial killer?* didn't seem like a good conversation to have with him.

"How well do you know Master Lenin?"

If he was surprised or suspicious by my question, he didn't show it.

"Not well. He was my School Master and now we work together with The Heel." He paused. "Why?"

I shrugged, hoping it looked carefree. "Just curious."

"About?"

"What kind of man he is."

The muscle in his jaw pulsed. "War changes people. When I went here, he was a better man."

So, Mr. Harrison could be right. He could be doing something with the students for his cause. I had to concentrate on my hands to keep them from clenching. "How's Mr. Harrison and Mr. While?"

He looked at me for a couple seconds. At first, I thought he was connecting the dots, but then he said, "Mr. While has a couple broken bones and bruises. Mr. Harrison didn't make it."

Shock made my blood run cold. I blinked, trying to clear my mind but that only brought up the memory of the teacher, smudged with blood and colored with plum purple bruises.

Master Lenin killed him. He heard what Mr. Harrison had figured out and he took him out before he could tell anyone that mattered.

"Is there anything else you want to waste my time with?" Michael asked dryly.

"No." I swallowed my panic and headed for the door.

"What book were you looking for?"

I stopped with my hand on the doorknob.

"When you were in the library this evening."

I said the first thing that came to my mind. "Something to show me how to use magic on my hair."

A cruel smirk crossed his lips. "Good. You need it." He turned on his heel and was gone.

31

What Did You See?

"Mr. Harrison was a long-time member of the Magisterium."

Master Lenin straightened his note cards on the podium before him. He wore a suit as black as the stone around him. A plain white tie hung from around his neck.

On the stage to his left was a picture of Mr. Harrison, smiling with sparkling eyes. A wreath of white tulips surrounded the picture. The morning light made the petals look as if they were glowing.

"Most of you knew him as a brilliant teacher with a jovial teaching style. Some of you knew him as a mentor. I knew him as a friend. He came here over fifty years ago. The Magisterium was better for it the moment he Ported within these walls."

His words sounded sincere, but all of the best liars could. I stood in the back of the room leaning against the wall. Even though it was almost time for the clock to chime, the breakfast buffet was nearly full. Food had been ignored by most students, myself included.

I stared across the room of sniffling students to the School Master on the stage. I barely paid attention to what he was saying— why listen to bullshit?

How could he stand there and speak about a man he killed?

Master Lenin paused in the middle of a sentence to remove a handkerchief and dab the underside of his nose.

He's good, I'll give him that.

"The events of last night are a shock to everyone here. We are still investigating what exactly happened in the library, but please know you are safe. There is no danger here."

Said the rattlesnake.

"There will be counselors available to you throughout the day and the rest of this month. If you need someone to talk to, please go to Miss Baker and she'll set you up with someone immediately."

Master Lenin tucked his cards into the lining of his jacket and looked out to the room. "Magic Users are resilient. We will get through this. Please let me know if there is anything I can do for any of you. You are dismissed."

Master Lenin Ported from the stage. Slowly, students got to their feet. But no one made a move to head directly to class. They moved from table to table to check in and console their friends.

Alone by the doors, I pushed away from the wall and moved to leave the dining room.

I had showed up to breakfast a few minutes before the clock chimed, catching the end of Master Lenin's speech. It was a strategy with the sole purpose of evading Moose. Her keen gaze and direct line of questioning needed to be avoided at all costs. I needed to keep my head down until I could Port the hell out of here.

It was a good plan too. At least I thought so.

As soon as I stepped out of the dining room, I spotted Moose talking to Daniel at the bottom of the stairs. Moose leaned against the gold railing, sipping a cup of coffee. In her other hand was a biscuit smothered with red jam. Daniel, in a thick knit blue sweater, stood with a casual posture, his hands wrapped loosely around the strap of the heavy bag draped over his shoulder.

I thought about sprinting down the nearest wing and using the tower staircase to get to my class.

But, as if she felt my eyes on her, Moose spotted me in the doorway. She broke into a wide grin and held up the biscuit.

"Cheese and rice," I mumbled.

Daniel followed her gaze and smiled when he caught my eye. Without releasing his bag, he waved with just his fingers.

Maybe with Daniel there Moose won't interrogate me.

I clutched on to that hope, and, with no escape, I made my way over.

Daniel's warm brown eyes held mine as I joined them before the stairs. He took in a breath to say *something*, but Moose cut him off.

"Good morning," Moose said with an extra layer of sweetness. "I got this for you. They didn't have cinnamon rolls this morning." She thrust the jam slathered biscuit toward me.

I took it only because I was really hungry. It was barely in my hand a second before I sank my teeth into it.

"How'd you sleep?" Moose asked.

"Great," I lied. My dreams were filled with falling books and navy blue suits that hovered over me without a body to fill them. I quickly turned to Daniel to redirect the conversation. "Hey, I haven't seen you in a while."

"I was thinking the same thing." He brushed a hand through his hair, as if it wasn't already perfect. "I actually thought you transferred to the Academy without saying goodbye."

My stomach swam with guilt. "I've just been busy trying to stay afloat in my classes."

"Daniel and I were talking about what happened to Mr. Harrison," Moose butted in. Her eyes locked onto mine.

The warmth in Daniel's gaze fizzled out. Sadly, he nodded. "I can't believe it. I keep expecting to see him having breakfast with Mr. While."

"Charlie was in the library last night," Moose said. "She was practically in the middle of it when the books started to fall."

The single bite of jam and biscuit hardened into a knot of nausea in my stomach. "Moose is exaggerating. I was by the doors. I didn't see anything." I pinned Moose with a look, pleading her to drop it.

"Pretty hard not to see anything." Her eyes never left mine as she took a sip of coffee. "You were *right there*. You even knew where Mr. While and Mr. Harrison were under the books."

"Are you ok?" Daniel asked. He didn't look over me for injuries. Instead, his gaze remained steadily on mine with genuine concern.

I nodded. "I wasn't hurt."

"Would you look at that?" Moose said with obviously false surprise. "The library is put back together!"

As if on their own accord, my gaze swung across the stairwell toward the gold doors. Sure enough, the bookcases were upright. The vast collection of books were in their rightful places in neat, organized rows. If I put my mind to it, I could have convinced myself that the events of last night were a dream. But Moose wasn't going to let that happen.

"I wonder if Mr. While is working today," she mused. "We should go check."

"Moose." I took a deep breath, a last-ditch effort to calm myself. "I told you, I don't want—"

"Oh, come on. He was practically buried alive last night, and his friend was killed in the same accident." She spun around to face me. "You can't be that heartless not to care how he's doing. Come on. We won't even be late for class." She turned and started across the black stone floor.

I looked helplessly at Daniel. I thought at least he would come to my rescue and pull me away from Moose's best efforts. But he mistook my look for one of dismissal.

"I guess I'll see you around." He smiled his dimpled smile and moved around me toward the stairs.

"Daniel, wait."

He stopped a step or two above me.

A dozen apologies rushed to my mouth. Each one would have done a fine job removing the thin layer of hurt from his genial face, but I couldn't let myself utter a single one. I was going to get out of here and I would do it without saying goodbye. I didn't want to hurt him anymore than I already had.

"Say hi to Cornelia for me when you see her."

He nodded with a small curl of the lips. "I will." Adjusting his bag on his shoulder, he began the slow climb up to his first class of the day.

I didn't let myself watch him go. I thought only of Blake and Porting out of that black stone school. In order to do that, I first had to shake Moose and her relentless nature.

With determined, almost angry strides I crossed the stairwell toward her. My stomach tightened as we entered the library. I followed Moose past the vacant front desk. Up ahead, Mr. While limped as he dragged a simple picture of a black star behind him.

"Mr. While!" Moose ran up to him. "Would you like some help?"

Drawing closer, I saw bruises covering his hands and arms. One arm was held captive in a sling.

Upon seeing us, a smile lit his face. "Brilliant timing." He looked down at his arm, limp in the sling. "My casting arm has been forced into a temporary vacation."

"Here, I got it." Moose pulled out her wand.

He stepped away as she tapped her wand against the large frame. It floated from the ground and rose to align with the wall. Mr. While directed her until it hung straight.

"Thank you." Mr. While stepped back to admire the picture. "I've been struggling with it all morning. Thankfully, it's the only one I have to put up." He ran his hand along the frame. "It needs a new stain but other than that, it looks pretty good for what it went through."

"You look pretty good too for being squashed by a bookcase."

His smile was tight, almost strained as an onslaught of emotion filled his green eyes.

"I'm sorry," I blurted before Moose could say anything else. "You probably don't want to talk about it. We'll leave you—"

Moose cut me off. "It's a miracle you weren't hurt as bad as Mr. Harrison."

Mr. While nodded. "I know. I was standing three feet from him. That ward could've . . ." He pushed his glasses further up his nose. "I don't want to keep you from your classes."

"You said ward." Moose stepped closer. "Was someone else there?"

His kind eyes grew cold. "What are you assuming, Miss Moose?"

"Were you attacked?"

He glanced around the room. Whether it was for an exit or to make sure we were alone, I wasn't sure. "This isn't something I can discuss with students."

"Mr. While, we should know if someone is attacking our teachers."

He sighed. Moose's shoulders straightened with victory, but he shook his head. "It doesn't matter because that man is dead. Mr. Harrison fired the ward that ended up killing himself and almost me. The man was as drunk as if he took a bath in whiskey."

What? I thought back to the events of last night, specifically to when Mr. Harrison joined Mr. While and I in the aisle housing books on Porting. My memory showed a man of sure feet and sound mind. He didn't slur or give off any obvious indication that he was under the influence. I smelled no strong substances on him. On the contrary, I vaguely registered his pleasant evergreen cologne.

Why would Mr. While lie about that?

My own question was answered by another horrifying thought. *What if he was covering up the truth because Master Lenin asked him too?* Moose said that School Masters were regarded as kings and queens, deities.

Mr. While refused to meet my gaze as if I could decipher the truth from his eyes.

"I thought you were friends," Moose said softly.

"He had no truer friend than the bottle," Mr. While replied with a melancholy tone. "You must forgive me, but I'm rather tired. I ignored Helen's orders to remain in bed to make sure my library was put together just right. Thank you for your help."

"Of course." Moose stepped away. "I hope you feel better."

Mr. While moved to leave us but he stopped when he looked at me. "I've been meaning to ask you, Miss Heart. Your first day here, Master Kale escorted you from breakfast. Do you know him?"

Moose whipped toward me with a slack jaw.

And I thought this day couldn't get any worse. I shook my head as a lie tumbled from my lips. "No. That was the first time I saw him."

"Do you know why he was here?"

Again, I shook my head trying to ignore the look Moose was giving me. "No. I haven't seen him since that morning."

He nodded, accepting my answer. "That's for the best. He's not a good man. Doomed men tend to be desperate, and desperate men injure those around them. I encourage you to keep your distance if he comes around again."

If only it were that easy. "I'll keep that in mind."

"Thank you again for your help." He turned and limped further into the library.

I spun on Moose. "What's your problem?" I hissed. "I told you to let it go."

"And I told you I couldn't. And for good reason, too." She grabbed my arm and pulled me toward the doors.

"Moose—" I tugged at her grip, but it was surprisingly strong. "Will you stop dragging me around?"

She didn't bother to respond. She continued her brisk pace out of the library and across the stairwell with me in tow. Her stride didn't slow as she shouldered her way into the humidity of the greenhouse.

The moment the doors closed behind us, she released me. "He was lying."

"Moose—"

"Enough, Charlie!" Moose stepped in front of me so all I could see was her. "I couldn't stop thinking about what you said last night. I started to wonder if maybe this has happened before. So, I wrote down as many students as I could remember who have transferred."

"Moose, please stop." I cupped my hands over my ears.

She jerked them away. "My friend Holly transferred last year."

I froze.

"She was a Common Seven. Janet was a Royal Eight, but they left the exact same way. Holly left in the middle of the night. She didn't tell anyone that she was thinking about leaving—not even me, and we'd been friends before we started walking. She just left. I learned about her transfer from Tessa Baker, of all people, and when I called her home to see what was going on her mom told me she was dead."

Moose's cheeks flushed. She blinked rapidly against the moisture gathering in her eyes.

"Apparently on her way home she stopped to get a cup of coffee and got hit by a car. Her body was so beaten up they had to have a closed casket." Her voice cracked. "I always thought it was weird— her transferring without telling me and how she died—but you know, shit happens.

"This morning I called Janet's mom to ask after her." Moose's gaze hardened. "Janet's dead."

I felt the blood drain from my face. "How?"

"She went to a nail salon and there was an electrical fire in the back. She didn't make it out."

I pressed a hand to my mouth as nausea rushed up my throat.

"I wrote down all the names of the Royals who transferred in the last couple years and guess what? Every single one that transferred in the middle of the night died in some freak accident—transporter failure, fires—you name it. And it always happens when they're on their way home from the Magisterium. Don't you see? *Something* is going on but I can't figure it out if you don't talk to me."

"You have to get me out of here," I said in a rush. "Can you Port?"

"No—"

"What about a transporter? Do you have one of those?"

"Yeah, that's how I can pop home for weekends if I want."

"Can I use it? I don't have any money, but I can pay you back somehow."

My heart fell when she shook her head. "Each transporter in and out of the Magisterium is blood coded. It won't work for anyone but me."

"What if you use it and I'm holding onto you—"

"It's only coded to transport one person. Even if you were holding on, it'd leave you here." She took in my panicked expression for a few seconds. "What did you see?"

My earlier fears came back. *Was* she working for Master Lenin? Was this a way for him to find out what I saw?

"You can trust me," Moose said after a hesitant silence.

How did I know that? It seemed that every Magic User I'd met was a liar.

But Moose's gaze was steady and earnest. She looked up at me as if I were the only person in the world with anything interesting to say.

If she's working for Master Lenin, I reasoned, *then she would have turned me over last night.*

I released a shaky breath and prayed that I was right in trusting her. "I was out past curfew the night before last." Everything in me screamed for me to stop talking. The scars on my back begged me too. "I heard a scream and went to check it out. I saw Master Lenin leaving the North Tower when he was supposed to be filling out transfer paperwork for Janet."

Moose stared unblinkingly at my face.

"I've been asking myself why he would be in the only off limits section of this entire school. When I was in the library, I heard Mr. Harrison telling Mr. While that Master Lenin has been saying that students are transferring away. Mr. Harrison also noticed that the high-status ones were dying. He thought Master Lenin was stealing their magic."

"And you think," Moose continued slowly, "that Master Lenin heard Mr. While and Mr. Harrison in the library."

I nodded. "I saw him hiding in the shelves. He was close enough to overhear the same conversation that I did."

"And he attacked them for it?"

"Who else would have done it?"

"But why leave Mr. While alive?"

"He was defending Master Lenin."

Moose shook the dazed look out of her eyes. "It doesn't make sense. Mr. Harrison would never question the motives of a School Master."

"He would if this has been going on for decades."

Her eyes bulged. "Someone would've noticed . . ." I could almost hear the gears in her head turning. "Ooooh, crap."

I straightened, feeling left out of the conversation she was having with herself. "What?"

"I always thought it was because of Master Lenin working with Master Kale and that's why people were leaving. But I never thought why it was just the high statuses. There are plenty of low statuses who are uneasy, and they're still here. Did Mr. Harrison say how long this has been going on?"

"He said it started not too long after Master Lenin teamed up with Michael Kale."

"So, forty to fifty years ago." Moose began to pace. "Maybe that's his motive," she muttered to herself. "Mr. While said desperate men injure people. With this school, Master Lenin has unlimited access to magic he can drain to make his side stronger."

My stomach sank even further. Didn't Magee suggest taking my magic when they told me about the war? I remembered Michael being aggressively opposed . . . but Master Lenin hadn't said a thing against it.

Moose shook her head wildly. "But Master Lenin's not like that."

"War changes people," I said, echoing Michael's words from the night before.

Moose didn't answer. After a couple paces, back and forth and back again, she turned sharply to face me. "Are you sure you saw Master Lenin leave the tower?"

"Positive." The look on her face said that meant more than she was letting on. "What does that mean?"

"You know about the tower, right?"

"I know it's haunted."

"Some think the girl who was killed had her magic stolen by dark magic, a binding curse."

"What does that have to do with Master Lenin?" I asked. "It's his school. He can go in if he wants, right?"

Moose shook her head. "Ever since that night, the tower's been locked. No one can get in, not even the Master of the school. It's sealed with magic from the inside."

"Isn't there some kind of magic that can open it?"

"No." Moose rubbed her eyes again. "Mrs. French taught us last year that when we die, our magic coats the place of our death. In the case of violent deaths, the magic that remains is so strong that it creates a magical entity. The girl that died in that tower isn't just a ghost. She rebukes each use of magic and conjures up wards of her own. Any attempt into the tower she blocks." She paused, unsure if she should continue.

I crossed my fingers hoping my next question was answered with an affirmation. "Did they ever catch the killer?"

Moose shook her head. "They didn't even have a suspect. Some people think she had a mental break—her room was totally trashed—and killed herself." A shiver worked over Moose's skin. "No one knows what she was doing in the tower in the first place."

"So, Master Lenin could be the killer of the North Tower?"

"No!" She groaned and slumped against the nearest planter. The pink plant leaned away from her. "There has to be another explanation for all of this. All we have are two teachers gossiping. That doesn't prove anything."

Her eyes brightened. "That could be why Maser Kale was here —by the way, why didn't you mention he was *in the school?*"

"I didn't think it mattered."

"You didn't think it mattered?" She rolled her eyes. "Just one of the most powerful Users in the world has breathed the same air as you and you don't think to mention it? Why was he here?"

I shrugged. "He just walked me down to Master Lenin's office. We didn't even talk the whole way there."

"What was he like? Is he really as scary as they say he is?"

"He was a complete jackass."

Moose winced as her gaze swung to the door, as if the Master Hunter would be seen lurking in the doorway. She refocused.

"We can confirm this," Moose said thoughtfully as if she were talking to herself. "If we got our hands on the death records, we could see if Janet and Holly died on school grounds. They're written entirely by magic and are updated automatically when someone dies so no one can tamper with them. If someone tried, they'd get a charm in the face and end up in jail. Then we'd need to cross reference that with the transfer documents to make sure it's not just a coincidence."

I took a large step away from her. "I'm not getting in the middle of this. I have to get out of here."

"Then ask Master Lenin for a transfer. Since you're not in the target bracket, I'm sure he'd let you waltz right out of here. Unlike me." Her gaze dropped to the seven pinned to her shirt.

I looked down at my status pin. "I'm not a Common Six," I blurted. "I'm . . . I'm a Royal Nine."

Moose stood frozen.

"I didn't know that I had magic until a month ago. Master Lenin found me and brought me here."

"Holy shit," Moose breathed. "You're serious? You're a Royal Nine?"

I nodded.

"But why go through the trouble of enrolling you? Why not just drain your magic?" Her eyes lit with the answer. "Of course. He brought you here for Achilles Heel. Why drain someone once when you can recruit them and use their status continually?"

"Now you understand why *I have to get out of here.* Please, you have to help me."

"It doesn't sound like you can. You're in the perfect prison. Even if you did tell someone, all of the teachers and staff are loyal to your captor."

"Thank you for so elegantly summing up my hopeless situation," I snapped.

Moose was unfazed by my curt response. She stared at me for a moment. The gears in her head were working overtime.

"The only way out is through," she said after a pause. "If we can prove what Master Lenin is doing, we can get him stripped of his title and locked up. Then all of this stops and you can skip out of here as free as a bird."

"And how do we do that?"

"The first step is to cross reference the death records with the transfer documents."

"Where are those?"

"In the Records Room, I'd guess."

"Where's that?"

"Across from Master Lenin's office."

Of course.

"Getting in there won't be easy," she said. "Those documents are probably locked up tighter than spandex on a fat man. If we get caught, we'd be expelled, and no school would enroll us. Our futures would be completely over—or worse, Master Lenin would just add us to his body count."

My heartrate spiked at the thought.

But Master Lenin and Michael lied to me. They said my father was the most evil man alive. But if Master Lenin really was picking off his own students to change the tides in his favor, would that make my father the good guy? No, Lawrence Hart was killing thousands of Regulars and low statuses . . . maybe no one was the good guy here.

"So, we be discrete," Moose continued. "If we can get the key to the Records Room, we can pop in and out without anyone being the wiser. Knowing Master Lenin, I'd say the key would be in his desk, on his person, or offsite." Moose slipped off her glasses and rubbed her eyes. "I can see if there's a key ring on him. Can you try to get into his desk?"

"Do you even know what this thing would look like? I don't think Master Lenin would just label it."

She shrugged. "I don't know. If you see a key ring, grab it."

I wanted to say no. I wanted to tell her that I was planning on Porting out of there the moment I mastered the stupid magical act. But she beat me to it.

"You're in this," she said in a low tone. "Like, right up to the ears in this. So, you're going to help me prove this. If not to figure out what's going on, then at least to save your own skin, ok?"

Not trusting my voice, I nodded.

"If we can't find the key, we'll have to be more creative," she added, although she didn't look to be a fan of that idea.

The clock chimed.

"We'll talk more later," Moose said, stepping back toward the gold doors of the greenhouse. "I'll see if the keys are on him and then we'll go from there."

"Moose."

She stopped just before opening the doors and stepping into the crowded hall.

"I'm sorry about your friend."

She nodded curtly. "I'm actually kind of glad to know the truth—as twisted as that is. She was my best friend. She'd never leave without telling me. And now I know it wasn't her fault. I guess as shitty as this is, I'm thankful for that." She pinned me with her sharp brown eyes. "You're doing the right thing, you know."

I said nothing. I just hoped she was right.

32

Down to the Master's Office

"Using your surgical scissors, cut the anterior end of your Bigalow squid.

"Please cut *only* the skin. If you pierce the ink sac, you'll be staying late to scrub it from your desk," the substitute said as she patrolled around the room. "Once you've made the longitudinal cut, pin the mantle open."

"Listening to sandpaper rub against itself would be more fun than her," Moose mumbled as she spread open the two halves of her squid.

The small creature was no longer than a finger and as bright as a yellow *Skittle* candy. Attached to the eight wiry tentacles were hollow needle-like barbs. Not for catching fish, as I had assumed at the beginning of the class, but to attach to tree branches and drink sap.

Thanks to the dry and humorless substitute teacher, Creature Studies was no longer fun. All around me students mourned the loss of their favorite teacher with slumped shoulders and disinterest in the subject material.

A row down and a couple chairs over, Clarence made his cut too deep into the squid. Ink, red as blood, leaked over the carcass and dribbled across the dissection mat.

Moose, witnessing the same thing, snorted.

The noise brought his attention around. A sharp flare of anger ignited in his dark blue gaze. He dropped his attention back to the ink now spilling across his desk.

I applied too much pressure to the scalpel and pierced the ink sack too. It wasn't as deep as Clarence's, but nonetheless, bright red ink dribbled from the small creature with a rich, metallic stench.

"Why is it red?" I asked, using the edge of the knife to scrape the ink back from the edge of the mat.

"It's supposed to look like blood to distract predators." Moose peeked over at my mat and wrinkled her nose at the mess.

"Any luck with getting the keys from Master Lenin?" I mumbled.

"I tried this morning," Moose whispered. "I practically gave the man a pat down and came up empty."

"How'd you manage to get that close to him?"

"At the beginning of the year, he named me the best in our class. I went to his office to thank him again and I gave him a hug."

A laugh stuck in my throat as I pictured Master Lenin awkwardly patting her back, oblivious to Moose's searching hands.

"Failed."

Once more our attention was drawn to Clarence a row below us. The substitute directed her wand at the mess before him. His squid vanished with a twinkle of gold.

Like a bloodhound, she turned her nose up and sniffed twice. Her gaze swung over to my bleeding creature.

Donning the same displeased expression, she aimed her wand at my mat. "Failed."

My squid disappeared, leaving a few streaks of ink behind.

"Both of you will be coming after dinner to clean up this mess." With a huff, she spun around to continue her patrol around the room.

Moose, much more carefully than before, continued cutting into her Bigalow squid. "There are no keys on him. Unless he keeps them in one of his shoes."

I leaned back into my chair. "Now what?"

"It's your turn." Moose continued to examine the squid's organs. "You'll have to check his office."

My stomach dropped. "And if they aren't there?"

"Then we'll need another way into the Records Room." She paused to look back down at Clarence. Our classmate was too busy doodling with the spilled ink to notice the extra attention. With the tip of his wand, he traced a crown on the desktop.

"I have an idea," Moose said. "But I'd rather not use it. Do you need help getting down to look through his office?"

I shook my head. "I got it."

She snuck a glance at me through the corner of her lenses. "You've done this before, haven't you?"

"Detention may have been my highest grade at my old school."

"I never pegged you as a troublemaker."

"Somehow I keep finding myself in the middle of it."

She sent me a sideways glance. "Like stumbling into a decades old killing spree?"

"Yep. Just like that."

Her lips curled as she turned back to her assignment.

When the clock chimed, we left the classroom and walked back to the mirroring staircases. We paused on the landing of the fifth floor in the rotunda. My next class was on the second floor while hers was on the sixth. This was the last time we'd see each other until dinner.

"When are you going to look in his office?" she mumbled as students rushed up and down the stairs.

"I was going to do it before dinner."

She nodded once. It was a curt movement that showcased just how nervous she was.

"Best of luck."

With my stomach in knots, I started downstairs.

I didn't pay much attention to my classes. My stomach was coiled so tightly, I wasn't able to eat lunch. I couldn't tell what I was more nervous about, going into Master Lenin's office to snoop or actually *finding* the key. That meant we'd have to go into the Records Room and then my crazy hypothesis would either be proven right or wrong. And I so badly wanted to be proven wrong.

Or did I? Moose said that if we proved this right, Master Lenin could lose his title and then I'd be free as a bird. Did that mean even Michael Kale wouldn't be able to keep his claws in me?

He'd probably be glad to be rid of me, I thought.

Before dinner, I went straight downstairs. Nervously, I clutched the strap of my bag as I made the descent.

The gatekeeper to Master Lenin's office sat behind her desk. Tessa Baker was dressed in her usual electric blue. She looked up and gave me a rehearsed smile. "How can I help you?"

Keep cool. "Master Lenin left a note for me this morning. He said he had a book for me."

"What's your name?" Her eyebrows drew together as she scanned her desk.

"Charlie Heart."

Her eyebrows rose.

"With an E," I clarified.

She twisted around and glanced toward the back room. "I don't have anything marked for you."

"He said it'd be in his office."

"Oh! Well, he's not here right now. He has a meeting with the School Masters in Australia. I can tell him you stopped by when he gets back," she chirped.

Australia? I had been so focused on Porting back to Kansas to get to Blake that I had never really thought that I could Port literally anywhere on the planet.

Focus.

"I actually need the book for class tomorrow morning. Do you think I could slip into his office and see if it's there?" I donned my most innocent smile.

"I really shouldn't—"

"I'll only be a second. I'll be out before you can blink twice."

Her teeth sank into her lip as she thought it over. All the while her eyes never left mine. After a moment, she nodded toward his office. "You have one minute."

My stomach lurched. It worked.

"Thank you!" I called over my shoulder. Moving quickly, I followed the curve of the hallway back to Master Lenin's office.

When the gold door with his name etched into the paneling came into view, my gaze swung to the other side of the hall. Directly across from Master Lenin's office was the unmarked door I noticed after my first visit to the School Master's office.

The Records Room.

Glancing over my shoulder, I confirmed the hallway was empty and reached my hand toward the gold door.

Trailing my fingertips down the smooth paneling, they prickled and burned with unseen magic.

Please let there be a key in his office. I turned away and pushed my way into Master Lenin's office.

The lights turned on as soon as I stepped inside. Rounding the desk, I pulled open the first drawer and shuffled around papers and opened files. I moved to the next one and pushed scrolls aside. Drawer after drawer, and all I got were paper cuts.

I pulled open the final drawer, hoping it would be empty and a glowing key would be at the bottom. Instead, more files greeted me, most of which were maps of arenas and budget sheets.

The click of expensive high heels echoed down the hallway.

I scanned the rest of the room. Bookcases lined the lower part of the wall. I searched the shelves for something to hide a key and found nothing. Not even a decorative chest.

Jumping to my feet, I rounded the desk. With trembling hands, I pulled a book from my bag.

Just as she rounded the corner, I held it up. "Found it."

Her artificial cheer was gone. Carefully, she scanned the office for anything out of place. My heart thumped against my ribcage. I never heard the last drawer shut. I stole a glance behind me. My heart nearly stopped when I saw it was cracked open.

"I'm sorry if I kept you waiting." I stepped toward the door, willing her attention away from the desk. "I got distracted by the pictures." I motioned to no wall in particular.

"He's very proud of his students." She stepped aside, letting me into the hall.

"Thanks for letting me get it," I said.

She nodded as she returned to her desk. As she sat in front of her computer her eyes locked onto me. I felt them drill into my spine as I moved up the stairs.

33

Promised Trouble and Lollipops

I took the stairs two at a time.

When I resurfaced on the main level of the school underneath the twin, spiraling staircases all classes had come to an end. A steady stream of students moved through the dining room doors. The buttery scent of pasta noodles permeated through the stairwell. Having barely eaten lunch, my stomach growled.

Moving through the dinner line, I looked over the room for Moose. My search found Daniel first.

He sat near the center of the room at a crowded table. His elbows were braced on either side of a bowl of pasta drenched in marinara sauce. He listened intently to an animated student on the other side of the table. His attention didn't stray from the storyteller, not even to indulge in his dinner.

Not for you, I reminded myself. Topping my bowl of pasta with a thick slice of garlic bread, I wove through the tables in my continued search for Moose. I found her on the other side of the room by one of the tall windows.

The night chill seeped through the glass making the outskirts of the room rather cold. Most of the students sat near the middle under the row of glittering chandeliers. Where Moose had chosen to sit, there were only a few students, most of which also wanted to be alone. Stacks of books and homework assignments took up most of the tabletops as a clear message of not wanting to be disturbed.

Moose found a way to get us some privacy in the middle of the school's busiest time of day.

Stepping over the bench, I sat beside her with a sigh. Moose looked at me with her mouth full of noodles.

"We're going to need another way in," I said.

Her nose scrunched with disappointment.

"I looked as thoroughly as I could," I went on. "But I don't think he'd keep the key to the most important room in the school right across the hall."

Moose cocked her head to the side as if to say, "You're probably right," as she continued to chew.

While she was occupied, I forked in a large bite of pasta.

Finally swallowing, Moose wiped a napkin across her lips. "Ok, so we defer to plan B."

"Which is?" I asked around the noodles.

"Miss Heart."

Moose and I jumped in our seats. We spun toward the voice and found the substitute from Creature Studies.

"When you're finished with your meal, I expect you back in my classroom to clean up all of the mess you made during the Bigalow dissection," she said sternly.

"Yes, ma'am."

"If I don't see you in ten minutes, I will go to Master Lenin."

"I'll be there," I assured her in a rush.

Without a nod of acknowledgment, she turned and prowled out of the dining room.

"I'm going to get plan B moving," Moose said, rising to her feet. "Come by my room when you're done. I'm in the Southeast Wing, room seven, thirty-eight."

She was gone before I could so much as nod. I devoured the rest of my dinner alone. I was still chewing when I stood up and put away my dirty dishes. Slipping my bag over my shoulder, I exited the dining room and made my way back up to the fifth floor.

As I climbed higher up the stairs, the sounds of the dining room fell to distant echoes. The hallway of the East Wing classrooms had a restful air to it as if after a long day of classes, the wing itself was catching its breath.

I pushed my way into the classroom and was met by a strong scent of cleaner that made my eyes water. There were a few students scattered throughout the room working to scrub out the last red smudges of the Bigalow ink.

The substitute stood at her desk with her dinner in one hand. She seemed unbothered by the fumes of the cleaning products.

"Here you go, Miss Heart." She nodded to the two remaining buckets before her. A pair of gloves were draped over the rim and a textured sponge floated among the suds.

I took the bucket and, careful not to slosh the cleaner everywhere, walked up the stairs to where I had sat that morning. I plopped the bucket on top of the desk and pulled the gloves up to my elbows. Just as I took hold of the sponge, the classroom door opened.

Clarence popped a final bite of garlic bread into his mouth. His dark blue eyes took in the room and landed on me. I dropped my gaze to the desktop and scrubbed the sponge back and forth.

"Mr. Hardy," the substitute called from her desk. "I've got a bucket here for you. You made the largest mess in the class."

I peeked at my classmate.

Clarence didn't respond, although the jab created a subtle effect to his countenance. A slight flush painted his cheekbones.

The substitute settled behind the desk and took out a book. Getting lost in the pages, she continued to eat her pasta.

Wordlessly, Clarence collected his bucket. She didn't spare him a glance as he made his way up the stairs to the red stained desk.

I turned my attention back to the pink suds before me and scrubbed a little harder. The textured sponge was making progress, but not fast enough.

"I'm surprised you're still here."

I looked down to the next row of tables. Clarence wasn't looking at me, but seeing as I was the closest to him, I assumed the statement was directed at me.

"Why's that?" I asked.

"Didn't you have an offer from the Academy? Or was that just to earn you bonus points with the golden duo?" He looked over his shoulder then. "Daniel and Moose."

"I decided to stay for a bit." I leaned my weight into the sponge.

"Pity."

I paused mid stroke. My mood jumped over annoyed and went straight for anger. "I didn't realize my presence impacted your existence here."

"It doesn't."

"Then why is it a 'pity' if I stay?"

"Not a lot of people would stay at the Magisterium. No one smart anyway."

"You're here."

"Because my father commands it," he said without bite or scorn. There was an underline of pride in his tone.

"Good for you." The woodgrain of the desk broke through the red stain. With an end in sight, I renewed my scrubbing.

Silence once more lapsed over the classroom. One of the students farther back finished and returned his dirty bucket to the front. The slamming door in his wake was the only thing to break the sound of scrubbing.

When the last smudge of red gave way to the cleaner, I soaked up the pink suds and tossed the sponge back into the bucket. Quickly, I made my way down the stairs and placed my bucket on the desk. I stripped the gloves from my hands and left the room without a glance back.

I added Clarence's name to the list of people to avoid.

Up two more flights of stairs, I headed down the Southeast Wing. When I came to room seven, thirty-eight, I knocked.

When the door swung open, I moved to step inside. But the person in front of me caused me to pause mid step. It wasn't Moose.

Ace Navarro, pale and lanky, barely filled the crack of the door. Her pale blue eyes watched me without emotion as she twirled a pink lollipop between her lips.

"Uh, hi," I said.

"Hey."

"Is this Moose's room?" I glanced at the number on the door to make sure I hadn't knocked on the wrong one.

Ace nodded. "Yep."

"Is that Charlie?" The door swung away from Ace to reveal Moose. "That didn't take as long as I thought it was going to. Come on in." She sidestepped out of the doorway.

Confused, I followed her in. Ace wordlessly walked deeper into the room and rounded the couch before the fireplace. Instead of sitting on the many open cushioned spots, she sat on the armrest and crossed her legs beneath her.

Beside her, Nirean waved. "Hey Charlie."

"Hi." I looked at Moose. "What are they doing here?" I hissed.

"They're plan B." She pushed the door closed. "Well, they're part of it."

"Why didn't you tell me that your plan involved bringing in more people?"

"Because we're out of our depth, we need help, and I didn't want to scare you off."

I ignored that last bit. "What can they do that we can't?"

"Get through the door. Ace has picked nearly every lock in the school. She doesn't come without Nirean, so I had to invite both of them."

"I don't like bringing other people into this," I said, keeping my voice low. "How do we know they won't run to Master Lenin or any of the teachers?"

"Why ruin the fun?" Nirean called from the couch. "Sorry, I was going to pretend that we couldn't hear you, but now our honor is being called into question."

"No offence—"

"None taken." Nirean rose to her feet in a single fluid motion. "What exactly is this about? You," she leveled a finger at Moose, "promised trouble, but all we've been doing is sitting." Nirean twisted to look over her shoulder, taking in the room. "Not that I'm not enjoying being in here. I think this is one of the few rooms in the whole castle that we haven't been in. Don't you think, Ace?"

Ace nodded.

"Have you been in my room?" I blurted.

Nirean grinned. "Would that bother you?"

My immediate thought was yes, but there was nothing out of the ordinary. The Porting books I stole from the library were hidden beneath the mattress. The getaway bag could be mistaken as a work out bag—if I was ever seen in the gym.

I shook my head. "If I had anything to hide, I guess it would."

Nirean's smile deepened. "Everyone has something to hide." She turned her bemused expression to Moose. "Take our charming Moose, for example. She's acted better than us in every way for four years. And now, here we are, indulging in her secret need to be reckless. Fate sure does have a funny way of force-feeding you your own words, huh?"

Ace snorted.

"Did you want a handwritten apology?" Moose asked dryly.

"No. But a box of chocolates would not be unwelcome."

A knock came then.

I turned back to the door. *Who else would Moose have invited?* Just before she opened the door, I wondered if it could be Master Lenin.

It wasn't. It was the third worst thing. The second being Michael.

Clarence sauntered into the room. When his dark blue eyes met mine, he grinned. "Surprised to see me, Red?" He gave my red streak a mocking tug as he passed by to the couch.

My sour gaze swung to Moose. "Really? Him?"

"Trust me, I'm not happy about it either," she said.

Cheese and rice. I wrestled my unease out of my chest and followed her to the couch.

"Well, now I am thoroughly invested," Nirean said, turning her attention completely to Moose. "If you've invited him, you must be looking into some serious trouble."

Ace's pale gaze was riveted on Moose.

"We . . ." Moose's eye flickered to me behind her lenses. She cleared her throat. "We would like to get into the Records Room."

Three sets of eyebrows rose, painting identical looks of surprise on Clarence, Nirean, and Ace.

"Like, Master Lenin's Records Room?" Nirean asked slowly.

Moose nodded curtly. "As it is the only Records Room in the school, yes."

Ace pulled her lollipop from her lips with a soft *pop*. "Why?"

"Yeah, it's not like you're going down there to steal test answers." Clarence's eyes brightened. "Unless that's why you've been so insufferable all this time. You're not smart, you're just a cheater."

Moose's previous nerves vanished in a blink. Fury lit her dark eyes. "I have never cheated on a test, nor will I ever need to cheat on a test. My brain can actually hold information."

Clarence leaned back into the couch cushions and kicked his boots up on the coffee table. "Then what do you want down there?"

"It doesn't matter," I said before Moose and Clarence could continue. "Can you get us down there?"

"It matters," Ace said.

"For sure," Nirean agreed. "Do we need to help you carry something out of the room? Are we just opening the door? Are we helping you destroy something?"

"That has to be the one." Clarence snapped his fingers. "What happened? Did a teacher write you up and you couldn't live with the embarrassment?"

"No," Moose said through her teeth. "We're going to look through transfer documents and death records."

Again, Ace lowered her sweet treat. "Why?"

At this question, Moose and I were both silent.

"Those are equally boring and useless." Clarence dug through the side compartment of his backpack and took out a tin mint container. He pried it open and removed a cigarette tinged blue and seafoam green.

"Do you have to do that in here?" Moose grumbled.

In answer, Clarence took his wand from his belt and touched the glowing tip to the end of the joint. It smoldered instantly, releasing a thin trail of blue smoke into the air which smelled more salty than the usual cigarette smoke.

"What is that?" I asked, crinkling my nose.

"Mermaid reed," Clarence drawled. "Want some?"

I shook my head, either to deny him or to shake the shock out of my skull—*did that mean mermaids existed too? At this point I shouldn't be surprised.*

"What do you want the records for?" Nirean prompted.

Moose glanced at me. I shook my head.

"Oh, come on. If you're worried about us tattling on you, our lips are tighter than an airtight container. Right, guys?"

"Mhmm." Ace nodded.

"Sure," Clarence said with a puff of blue smoke.

"Trust me. Last year, we . . ." Nirean looked at the others with a grin. "Never mind. My point is, we wouldn't be good at what we do if we told everyone."

"I heard you bragging about unlocking every door in this place in the middle of dinner rush last week," Moose countered.

Nirean lifted one shoulder to her ear. "At that point, Master Lenin already knew what we were doing. Might as well get some bragging rights out of it. So, what's all this for?"

Again, Moose turned her eyes to me. "Charlie thinks Master Lenin is killing students for their magic and saying that they transferred to another school."

"Cheese and rice, Moose." I buried my face in my hands.

"We need the records," she continued over me, "to confirm which students died on school grounds with the ones that were allegedly transferred away."

"Holy shit," Ace mumbled. Somehow, she managed to look even paler.

"You're serious?" Nirean looked between the two of us. "This isn't a joke?"

"Moose doesn't have a funny bone in her body," Clarence said. His cigarette smoldered between his fingers, momentarily forgotten. "How the hell did you come to that conclusion?"

"About a School Master, no less," Nirean added.

"Charlie saw Master Lenin leave the North Tower the night he was supposed to be helping Janet fill out the transfer paperwork—she's dead, by the way. Her mom said that she was killed in a fire. Charlie overheard Mr. Harrison say the same thing right before he was killed."

"*Holy shit*," Ace whispered.

"You're kidding," Nirean stated.

Moose popped her fists on her hips. "You think I'd invite you up to my room to tell a shit joke and then just wish you a good night and escort you to the door?"

Nirean blinked rapidly.

"We tried to find Master Lenin's key to the Records Room. If we were successful, you wouldn't be here. We need your help to get us into the Records Room. Can you do that?" Moose asked, pinning Clarence, Nirean, and then Ace with a stern eye.

"What's in it for us?" Clarence parried.

Moose took a deep breath as if she was preparing herself to climb Mount Everest. "Next year for our testing year, I'll let you cheat off my scores in *one* class of your choosing."

For the second time, Ace, Nirean, and Clarence were overcome by surprise.

"Any class?" Nirean clarified.

Moose nodded tightly.

Wordlessly, Nirean offered her arm to Ace who in turn pinched it with her black painted nails. Affirmed that she wasn't dreaming, Nirean sat back against the couch cushions. Her eyes glazed over as if she were trying to pick which class she wanted to use this reward for.

Clarence turned his gaze to me and cocked his head to one side. "So, what? You want to take down a School Master?"

I shook my head. "No, I just want to make sure he's not killing students for their magic."

"Oh, I guarantee he is. If I was losing a war for as long as he has, I'd do the same thing."

That's what I'm afraid of.

"If we agree to this," Nirean said, gesturing between herself and Ace, "we'll get you through the door and help you get your records, but we're out after that. Solving murder mysteries isn't really our thing."

Moose's keen eyes dropped to the pin on Nirean's shirt. "You're a Common Seven, just close enough to a Royal to be on his hunting list. I suggest you make it your thing."

"So quick to condemn the man who named you best in the school." Clarence clicked his tongue. "What fickle loyalty you have, Moose."

"Loyalty has nothing to do with it," she responded curtly. "There's a question I want answered, nothing more."

"Wait a second," Nirean mused slowly. "Didn't Holly Blackwell transfer at the end of last year and get hit by a car?"

Moose's cheeks were once again pink, but it wasn't from anger. She stubbornly held Nirean's gaze despite the fractures of grief that splintered throughout her own eyes. Her lips were pressed so tight they were almost bloodless. She nodded.

"You think she died here?" Nirean asked softly.

"I think she was killed here," Moose said. "She would never transfer so close to our testing year without telling me. There's no way."

There was a moment of silence between the five of us. Nirean and Ace shared a look full of wordless conversations. Clarence continued to smoke.

Finally, Clarence leaned forward and ejected two streams of salty, blue smoke from his nostrils. "I'm in. I'd do it for free just for a front seat to the sullying of your shiny record, Moose. But I'll take the peek at your scores as the cherry on top."

With a sigh, Nirean turned to Ace who still sat cross legged on the armrest. "Wanna go at the Records Room lock?"

Ace pulled the lollipop from her mouth. "Duh." She said it like she was offended Nirean had to ask.

On shaky legs, Moose sat in the armchair beside Clarence. "So how do we do this?"

Nirean leaned forward and grabbed for her backpack. She pulled out a large binder and dropped it on to the coffee table with a solid *thud.* She flipped open the cover and blueprints of the school, in the shape of a perfect compass rose, lifted from the pages like a pop out book.

The Magisterium sat in a bowl surrounded by jagged snow covered peaks. The West Wing was completely surrounded by towering pine trees, while the East Wing sat in the middle of a meadow. A river bumped into the North Wing and rushed under the East Tower before plummeting over a cliff beside the South Wing.

"Where did you get this?" Moose asked, leaning closer to the blueprints.

"Ace and I made it." Nirean flipped past the overall plans of the castle and went over each individual floor. She stopped at the plans of the basement.

The teachers' offices were in a large circle that outlined the middle of the compass rose. Each room—except for the one directly opposite Master Lenin's office—was labeled. The map didn't show the room it was connected to, just the door.

"This is the Records Room," Nirean said, tapping her finger over the door. "On the outside, it's guarded by Tessa Baker, a dozen teachers—if they're in their offices—and more often than not, Master Lenin himself. Ace and I thought about cracking it last year, but there were less complicated doors to check off first. The charm on the door will prove to be harder."

"There's a charm on the door?" Moose sighed. "Of course, there's a charm on the door. What does it do?"

"It's blood coded," Ace mumbled around her lollipop.

"If you don't share the same DNA as Master Lenin, it won't let you through," Nirean explained.

My heart fell. "How do we get past that?"

"We don't." Nirean grinned. "We go under it."

Moose squinted at her. "You want to tunnel through stone? Yeah, that won't draw any attention at all."

"Trust in the system, Moose." Nirean gestured between herself and Ace. "We've got it. The biggest problem is going to be getting past Master Lenin's gate keeper."

"I've got Baker." Clarence tapped his long middle finger against the joint, sprinkling purple ashes on Moose's carpet. "She handles all the student transfers. I'll just tell her that I'm thinking of moving schools. When she's helping me go through the paperwork, y'all sneak down the hall."

"I thought you were kicked out of all the other schools," I said.

"Not the Russian University. My father knows the School Master."

"So, that checks off the beginning and the end of this party." Moose ticked them off her fingers. "What about the middle—Master Lenin and the other teachers?"

"If we go after curfew all the teachers will be in their homes," Nirean answered.

"As for Master Lenin . . ." Clarence once more grabbed for his backpack and pulled open the main compartment. He took out a piece of paper, folded and horribly crinkled.

Smoothing it out against his knee, he said, "The old man really has no life. He has a School Master meeting tomorrow night and ain't expected back 'til Sunday. He has 'em every weekend until the school years' ends. Tuesdays he does record keeping. Every other Wednesday night he plays poker, and he meets with the teachers on Fridays. The rest of the time it's boring school management."

"What is that?" Moose peered over at the paper.

"Master Lenin's schedule for the month." He met Moose's astonished gaze with a shrug. "I like to know when the bastard is gone."

"How on earth did you get it?"

"I have Tessa Baker wrapped around my finger tighter than a wedding ring."

"If he's gone every weekend," Nirean said, getting us back on topic, "that seems like our best window."

"So, we break into the Records Room on a weekend after curfew." Moose wrapped her arms tightly around her stomach as if she was going to be sick.

At the mention of curfew, I remembered something. *Michael.* Every night at ten o'clock, curfew, I was transported to the South Wing to train with him. My stomach dropped.

I tried to think of a way to get out of the lesson. I could pretend to be sick but, knowing the jackass, he'd make me cast in between spells of vomiting. The one break he'd give me was if I were dead.

Maybe I could piss him off enough to end lessons early? No, if I pissed him off, he'd enjoy all the more whatever horrible lesson plan he cooked up. He'd probably just make the lesson longer out of spite.

So, I couldn't call in sick. I couldn't get out early. Then we'd just have to break in after the clandestine lesson. Because there was one thing I could count on and that was Michael's hatred for me. That very same hatred would propel him from the room the moment the clock struck midnight.

"We can't do it at curfew," I said. "I have to be in my room at ten."

"Why? Got a date with your lonely existence?" Clarence scoffed.

"I got in trouble a lot at my old school, so Master Lenin sends a tutor to my room every night to make sure I'm keeping up with my classes." Before any of them could ask, I added for good measure, "Don't ask. You really don't want to know."

"Actually," Clarence said, tilting his head, "I do want to know."

"So we go after midnight," Moose said. "Will Tessa Baker be at home?"

Clarence tore his curiosity from me to address Moose. "Maybe, maybe not. Sometimes she stays late."

"Ok, so we break curfew, Clarence distracts Tessa Baker, if she's there, Ace opens the door, and then Charlie and I copy the records and we get the hell out."

Nirean snickered. "I'm surprised you haven't broken into hives yet, Moose."

"Trust me, I'm dying inside."

Clarence raised the hand with the smoking joint. "Why are you copying the records?"

"So we can take them back here to look through. I figured the less time we spend in the Records Room, the better. Back here, we have all the time in the world."

"How are we going to copy all of that?" My hand ached just thinking of all the writing we'd have to do.

She gave me another amused look. "A simple copying charm should do the trick. All we have to do is bring the paper."

I shoved my hair away from my face. "So, when should we do this?"

Moose picked up Master Lenin's schedule. Gnawing her lip, she carefully looked over the packed itinerary. "Why not tomorrow night?"

Nirean threw her head back with a loud cackle. "I am *loving* this side of you, Moose."

34

Copy and Paste

The next day we took our lunches back to Moose's room.

"I can't believe we're doing this tonight," I said, setting my uneaten sandwich on the kitchen counter. "Does anyone else think we're totally unprepared?"

"That's why we're practicing." Moose dropped a stack of papers onto the middle of the table.

"Copying's easy, though," Nirean said. "I do it to your notes all the time."

Moose's eyes narrowed behind her glasses. "If you were copying me, your grades wouldn't suck."

"I purposefully guess wrong on a few of the answers, so I don't tip off the teachers."

"Thanks for tipping me off. I'm going to purposefully not take a single note in any class that we share."

Nirean smiled.

Ace chuckled.

"No, you're not," Nirean said. "You like winning too much."

Moose sighed. "I'm going to ignore this conversation for the sake of my sanity. You may be good at copying test sheets, but when we copy the records, they need to be perfect. We can't have anything misspelled or left out. Everyone grab a stack."

Ace hopped onto the table and curled her legs beneath her. With a green lollipop in her mouth, she took from the stack and placed the papers on her lap. No one commented on her sitting on the table or acted like it was unusual. Nirean just moved her chair over so she wasn't sitting directly behind her.

I took out my wand. "Alright, what are we doing?"

"It's simple." Moose held up a piece of paper with a sketch of a poorly drawn stick figure with a large tie. I think it was supposed to be Master Lenin. "Tap the paper and let your magic coat the surface. Then you hold it to a blank sheet and press the image onto it." She demonstrated the steps and held up a perfect replica.

"I can't believe I'm signing up for more work," Clarence muttered.

Moose ignored him.

I watched everyone point their wands at the paper they were given. Magic gleamed in the carvings on their wands.

My hands shook as I reached for the page with the drawing. This was the first time I was going to do magic in front of someone besides Michael. I pressed my wand to the sketched paper, watching as a golden sheen spread over the surface. Removing my wand, I pressed it to a blank page.

The image came in faint at first, almost like someone had drawn it with a dull pencil. I pulled on more magic. The lines darkened and before I could stop it, the page was one large inkblot. I flipped the page to the floor.

Clarence looked up at the movement. Like a cat, his eyes were drawn to the flutter of paper.

Moose put her foot on the ruined page and kicked it farther under the table, away from his prying eyes.

I grabbed a clean page, but the image came in too light again. I rolled the tension from my shoulders. *Come on, Charlie.*

I went through my stack of paper before anyone else. A stack and a half later, I found the right amount of magic to make a replica as perfect as the original.

Once everyone was making consistent copies, Moose stood up. "Alright. I'm going to get the supplies for tonight. Clarence, did you walk down to Master Lenin's office and time it?"

He nodded, rocking back on the legs of his chair. "From the apartments, it takes just under seven minutes to get down there. The old bat leaves his office around eight for dinner with Master Harlan. He ain't expected back till tomorrow morning. That gives us plenty of time to snoop around."

"Um, there is no *us*," Moose said slowly. "You're going to be distracting Tessa Baker."

He dropped his chair back on all four legs. "Not the whole time."

"Yes, the whole time," Moose stressed.

"Oh, come on," he groaned. "Why do you four get to have all the fun?"

"You'll be more useful where you are." I pocketed my wand.

His gaze hardened, but he remained silent.

Moose rubbed her hands together. "So . . . let's meet in the stairway at midnight."

Nirean jumped to her feet and helped Ace off the table. The pair was out the door with an excited pep in their step.

"Just curious," Clarence drawled as he collected his bag. "Do you hope you're right or wrong, Red?"

"Wrong. Obviously. Why on earth would I want to be right about this?"

"I hope you're right, just so I can see that self-righteous bastard knocked off his high horse."

"You want him to be a *murderer?*" Moose stressed with narrowed eyes.

"I want the world to see him crack." He shrugged. "I'll take it in any form I can get." Unbothered, he shouldered his bag and opened the front door. In the next second, he was gone.

"We can't let him inside the Records Room," Moose said in his wake. "I don't trust what he'll do in there."

I nodded in agreement.

Moose gathered the copied pieces of paper and took them to the fireplace. With a flick of her wand, the logs burst into flame and she promptly dropped the pages into the fire.

"You know, after you told me about how you grew up—without magic—everything makes so much more sense," she said as she returned to the table. "All of the questions you asked about Hunters and the war.

It makes sense why you didn't know it already." She reached under the table and took out the page nearly black with ink. "And why you suck at simple charms."

"Hey, I think I did pretty good for that being my first time."

Moose cracked a smile as she returned to the fireplace.

"Do you think the others will notice?"

She shook her head. "They're too self-absorbed to look too closely. I don't know if I would have ever put it together if you hadn't told me. You're a good liar."

Wordlessly, I dropped onto the couch and slouched into the cushions. It wasn't something I was proud of.

"Did you really not know that you had any magic?" Moose asked, watching the pages burn.

I shrugged. "I knew I was weird, but I didn't think it was *magic*. I didn't have anything to compare it to, so I didn't know it wasn't normal."

"Being a Royal Nine, you'd think there would be some tells as you grew up."

"I fell off a roof once and I practically bounced when I hit the ground."

Moose laughed. "No broken bones, huh?"

I shook my head. "I barely bruised."

She turned her back to the fire. "What's it like to have that much magic? I've always wondered."

I looked down at my hands, small and unassuming. "It's like walking around with a bomb and a livewire at the same time. I'm constantly worried that if I feel something too strongly, will my magic flare in response? If I get angry, will something catch fire? Will I hurt someone without meaning to? I thought I was cursed. Turns out I was just born a freak."

"Correction, you were born a Magic User. That doesn't make you a freak."

I smiled. I liked the sound of that better. "Did you always know about magic?"

"Oh, yeah. My mom likes to protect her manicures, so she uses her wand for everything—cooking, cleaning, the works. My brother, when he didn't want to play with me, would just levitate me into another room and close the door. My dad used it to Port when I was born and never come back."

"What was it like to grow up with magic?"

"Like you said, I didn't have anything different to compare it to." She paused for a moment. "Do you know anything about your parents?"

I thought about telling her the truth. She knew everything else, why not the last horrible lie? But this was a bit more dramatic. Lawrence Hart—just the sound of his name evoked reactions.

I shook my head. "I grew up in foster care."

"That explains how you flew under the radar for so long. Do you wish you were back there or are you happy you got all of this?"

"You mean am I happy that I was dragged into a war I knew nothing about as a secret weapon by a serial killer?"

"Ok, yeah, that was a dumb question," she said with a crooked grin.

"I was excited about it at first," I said, remembering the first time I used it. The *power* of it. "I used to think there was nothing worse than what I had in Kansas, but fate likes to screw me over."

"Well, after we figure this out and become global heroes, you can get a chance to enjoy it."

I liked the sound of that. "All of that hinges on our success with this heist of ours."

"Oh, come on, we have the smartest person in this school, the three biggest troublemakers, and a secret Royal Nine. What can go wrong?"

35

Five More Minutes

The rest of the day passed uneventfully.

It should have felt like a good sign. Instead, it felt like time was holding its breath. I took my dinner back to my room so I could practice the copying charm some more without prying eyes.

When that only added to my growing anticipation of the midnight hour, I put my wand away and took out the books on Porting. I had learned to turn off all the lights before I started so each failed attempt wouldn't burst all of the lamps in the apartment.

I was no closer to Porting to the other side of my apartment than I was a month ago. When the transporter beeped, summoning me to lessons with Michael, my chest hurt and my head pounded.

Taking up my wand, I grabbed the transporter and Ported into the classroom. Michael stood before me as still, dark, and expressionless as the stone around us.

His obsidian gaze dropped to my hand, confirming that I had my wand with me. He didn't nod approvingly. Instead, he crossed the room and leaned against the wall like a gargoyle returning to its gloomy perch.

"Levitate the desk." He nodded his head to the other side of the room.

I wiped the sweat from my palms and wrapped my fingers around my wand. After practicing magic for so long that evening, it slid easily into my wand and under the desk. I pictured expanding bubbles like last time and issued more magic beneath the desk.

Rising from the floor, it tilted sharply to the left.

"Ease up on your magic," Michael called. "Even it out."

I tried to make it even under the bottom, but my magic, egged on by my heartbeat and nerves, went from one extreme to the next. I wanted it to lessen on the right to level out the desk. The magic on that side diminished completely. When I tried to correct it by adding more magic to the falling edge, it flipped the desk over. The desk fell to the floor upside down with a *bang*. One of the corners splintered under the impact.

Michael's dark eyes flickered to my face. "Why are you so worked up?"

"I'm not." *I shouldn't have practiced copying* and *Porting.*

"Do your hands normally shake like that?" He nodded to my wand.

I tightened my fingers, stilling the tremor. "I ran to the transporter."

"You're that out of shape?" He muttered something, probably rude, under his breath. "Try again."

I took a deep breath before I drew upon my magic. Releasing the breath slowly, I drew magic from my core. The buzzing warmth that poured down my arm wasn't as urgent as before. When it left my wand, it encircled the desk and steadily lifted it from the floor.

Adding more magic, I levitated the desk above our heads as level as if it were on the ground between us.

"Good." Michael plucked a baseball from the bucket beside him and rolled it between his hands. "Pretend the desk is a crumbling building on fire. There are injured people all around and your job is to keep the desk—the building—suspended. Each ball that I throw is a person jumping from the burning building. For every ball that hits the floor, I'll add another five minutes to the lesson."

My eyes snapped to his face. *No. He can't add more time. I have to be in the stairwell at midnight!*

He gave me no time to process the scenario. He tossed the ball across the room. I spun around and threw magic beneath it. The ball stopped a foot above the floor. From the corner of my eye, I watched the desk dive toward the floor.

Magic flooded under the desk, catching it an inch before the ground.

"Multitask. If you can't save those under your command, you don't deserve their loyalty."

The second ball hit the wall and bounced to the floor.

"Five more minutes. You're using too much magic," he called as he grabbed another baseball. "If you continue, you'll pass out before the lesson is over." He threw the ball.

Cheese and rice.

Spinning around, I threw magic beneath it before it could land. I forgot the first ball and it fell to the floor.

"We're now up to ten more minutes."

No!

He grabbed two more balls. "Look at what you're doing. Remember my instructions." He tossed one toward the door.

The ball smacked against the door as he threw the second one. Just as I got the first one into the air, the second knocked another ball to the floor.

"Fifteen minutes."

I caught the next ten baseballs. When he threw the twentieth, I wasn't seeing straight. A slick, cold sweat covered my entire body. Breathing hard, I couldn't track where the ball went until I heard it hit the floor.

"Thirty minutes." He let out an exasperated breath. "If you pass out, I'm leaving you here. *Think.* What did I tell you to do?"

My mind could barely piece together a coherent thought. It swam with fragments of the Records Room plan, my failed Porting attempts—even Blake.

"You—" My knees almost gave out. Black dots started to bleed into my vision. "You told me to . . ." *Cheese and rice, what did he tell me to do?* The grip on my magic started to slip. "Levitate the desk. *You told me to levitate the desk.*"

"Then why are you levitating the baseballs?"

"You said for every one that hit the ground, you'd add more time."

"Your hearing has significantly improved. Now you just need to work on using your brain. Think through what I told you to do."

As his instructions played through my head, I heard another ball bounce against the wall behind me.

For every one that hit . . . so if I lowered one to the ground, would he add more time? Ah, what the hell? I'm already late.

Keeping my magic locked around the desk, I slowly thinned it from under the baseballs. Each one landed against the floor without making a sound.

Michael didn't utter a word.

Using significantly less magic, the black dots faded. My wand arm continued to tremble. My eyes refocused on the room just in time to see him toss another baseball in my direction.

This time I used as little magic as I could get away with. The blight of magic swirled around the base of the ball. Just as it neared the floor, I pulled up slightly, slowing its descent. It settled on the ground without so much as a bounce.

I looked over at Michael, fearing the worst. I couldn't be forty minutes late. I just couldn't.

But he said nothing. With a single nod, Michael bent down and took another baseball from the bucket. As soon as he straightened, he threw it across the room. I whirled around to catch it.

True to his word, Michael continued past midnight. Each minute past our appointed meeting time grated against my skin. I could hear Moose's sharp questions, feel Clarence's mocking gaze, and the curious eye of Ace and Nirean.

How am I going to explain this away?

"You're done," he said sharply. "You can lower the desk."

"Thank God," I mumbled. I pulled my magic back a little too sharply. The desk nosedived toward the black floor.

My heart leapt. I threw magic under it once more and caught it before I could do anymore damage to it. Carefully, I set it on the floor. Only when it was settled did I pull my magic back completely.

Michael grunted. He turned sharply on his heel and Ported from the room.

My shaking hands fumbled for the transporter in my pocket. As soon as I appeared back in my room, I threw the transporter on the bed and sprinted for the door.

Jumping into the hallway, I barely paused long enough to keep the door from slamming shut. The black stone steps passed in a blur beneath my feet.

"*About time*," Moose hissed when I hit the last landing before the main level. Ace and Nirean jumped to their feet at the exclamation. Clarence, leaning against the railing, looked up with annoyance pressing his lips tightly together.

"Where have you been?" Moose snapped, careful to keep her voice quiet.

"I'm sorry." I skidded to a stop before her. "My tutor wouldn't stop talking." I paused, sucking in a deep breath. "She wouldn't take a hint either."

"Are we gonna do this?" Clarence asked. "Or are we gonna keep chatting?"

Moose tore her heated gaze from me and turned to him. With a huff, she nodded. "Let's get this done."

36

The Records Room

Clarence straightened from the railing.

With long, casual steps he moved toward the downward staircase. "Wait a few minutes before you make your way down."

Without missing a beat, he strolled down the stairs. Not a minute later, soft murmurs of a conversation rolled up to us.

Moose stared at her watch without blinking. Her eyes followed the minute hand's slow progression between one marker and the next.

"Showtime." Moose pulled her wand from the pocket along the side of her jeans. Magic glowed in the handle, bright and golden, as she waved it over us. A layer of magic fell over me, Ace, and Nirean, dissolving us and our shadows from view.

Clarence and Tessa Baker's voices grew louder as the four of us moved down to the teacher's level. When we reached the bottom, Clarence leaned onto the counter. Idly his fingers played with the locks of hair at the base of his neck.

Tessa Baker was in a flurry. She gathered a few papers from the desk in front of her. Then she turned around and grabbed a few more from the filing cabinets.

As we tiptoed down the hall under Moose's charm, Tessa Baker didn't so much as bat an eyelash in our direction.

When we rounded the corner, Moose dropped the charm. Quickly we moved past empty offices until we were facing the unmarked door across from Master Lenin's office.

The Records Room.

Ace squatted in front of the handle and pulled a leather pouch from her bra. She chose a couple pins and stuck them in her mouth. With the grace of a spider, she poked several pins into the lock.

I glanced down the hallway, expecting flashing red lights or sirens. But nothing happened.

Ace carefully added another pin and clutched them all together. Twisting them to the left, a series of clicks tumbled through the door. Pulling the pins free, she pushed it open.

Large crystal chandeliers blinked on, filling an enormous round room with golden light. Dusty black shelves stretched toward the high ceiling. The front rows were filled with books that looked older than the ones in the library.

The doorway flared. Our small group jumped back as a gold sheen poured from the doorframe. Magic filled the doorway from top to bottom and in every corner. It was transparent enough to see through, but solid enough to remain a menacing presence.

Even a few feet back, I could feel the power of the ward. The air grew hot as if a bonfire roared from the doorway. It itched and prickled over the exposed skin of my arms and face. I flinched, rubbing my arms.

I noticed then that Nirean, Ace, and Moose didn't react. Ace, recovering from the sudden burst of magic, bent down to collect her lock picks. Moose glanced nervously down the hall.

Clenching my teeth, I forced my hands to fall limp by my sides.

Ace tucked her pins back in her bra as Nirean crouched on the other side of her. In unison the pair drew their wands. Together, they touched the tips to the floor at the base of the door.

Magic flared from their wands. It sparked against the black stone. With mirrored movements, they drew a straight line in front of the door. Then they drew the line over the threshold and into the Records Room. They made sure to keep their fingers away from the ward swirling in the doorway. They repeated their first stroke, creating a long rectangle the length of the doorway.

They pressed their wands to the corners in the hallway. Magic pulsed into the rectangle. Slowly they raised their wands. The black stone slab rose with them. The glowing, golden ward drew up with it, leaving the space beneath the cut of stone clear and magic free.

"Holy shit, it worked," Moose whispered.

Nirean flashed her a grin. "You doubted us?"

"A little."

Ace chuckled.

The pair stopped the cut of black stone halfway up the doorframe. There, with another spark of magic, they anchored it. The space beneath was just big enough for us to duck through.

Ace and Nirean stepped back. With a flourishing bow, Nirean gestured toward the opening. "Ladies first."

"I vote Charlie should go first." Moose stepped away from the door.

"Agreed," Ace said.

My gaze flew to Nirean. "It's safe, right?"

She shrugged. "Looks like it."

"That wasn't very convincing."

"I'm not entirely convinced."

I stared at her.

"What? We've never dealt with this kind of magic before. Your guess is as good as mine."

"You're kidding."

"Tick tock," Ace said.

"I'm with Moose. You think he's a serial killer, therefore you get zapped first so we have a chance to run." Nirean crossed her arms.

I faced the Records Room, eyeing the space beneath the teeming magic. Nothing looked out of the ordinary, but then again, I had never seen magic purposefully performed outside of a classroom.

Don't be a bigger coward than you already are, I scolded myself. *Michael is scarier than this and you face that jerk every night. Plus, if you die*—I smiled—*you'll never have to see him again.*

With that happy thought, I squeezed my eyes tight and, crouching low, ducked under the cut of obsidian.

On the other side, I cracked open an eye to see if I was looking at my afterlife. The Records Room was still there, and I was still breathing. "Am I a ghost?"

Moose shook her head. "Do you feel ok?"

I nodded. "Yeah. Do I look ok?"

"You look like you need to brush your hair," Nirean said.

Moose swatted her in the stomach. "You look fine." Taking a deep breath, she ducked under and joined me on the other side. Straightening, she quickly gave herself a pat down to make sure she was still in one piece. "It worked!"

Nirean and I instantly shushed her and looked down the hall. When no one came, we turned toward the bookcases.

"Alright." Moose took a deep breath. "Let's get this over with."

I followed her toward the towering bookcases. The library upstairs had covers of every color, height, and thickness. Master Lenin's private collection was made up of sets, each one consisting of one color and the same thickness. There were rows of what looked like identical books— bright gold, ruby, emerald, white, sterling silver, leather bound, and navy. Unlike the student library above, a thick layer of dust rested on the shelves.

Moose's eyes flew over the covers. I thought it was too fast for her to actually read the titles, but I was wrong.

She sprang forward. Reaching up on her tiptoes, she pulled out a thick maroon book. Propping it in her arms, she flipped open the cover.

"Bingo! Nirean get over here."

"What have we got?" Nirean asked as she shoved the bag off her shoulders.

"The transfer documents."

"Those are all transfer documents?" Nirean eyed the shelf Moose had pulled the book from. There were five books of equal size and color.

"Yep." Moose turned the book to Nirean.

"Are we copying all of them?"

"Only if you stop talking." Moose thrust the book toward her again.

Rolling her eyes, Nirean took out her wand and flipped to the first page where she pressed her wand to the yellow-aged paper. She held it there for a couple seconds, letting a faint golden sheen slip over the page.

After a couple of seconds, Nirean took an equal sized binder from the bag at her feet. She flipped to the first blank page and pressed her wand to it.

From the tip of her wand, words bled onto the page. Faint at first, then a rich ink black.

It was working.

"Charlie." Moose swiped the sweat off her upper lip. "We need the death records. You and Ace look for those."

"What am I looking for?" I asked, backing toward the other book-case.

"Your guess is as good as mine."

Ace beat me over to the other set of shelves. Her expression, usually upturned as if she were in on a joke no one else knew about, was as serious as I had ever seen it. Her pale eyebrows drew together as her barely blue eyes looked from one section of books to another.

I went to the other side and did the same. My fingers tapped nervously against the sides of my thighs as my gaze skipped from one title to the next. They passed in a blur of gilded letters some bright and others dull.

Trial Challenges.

There were twenty-three volumes with that title. The spines alternated the same pattern, gold, silver, black and then back to gold.

First Trial Themes and Castwork

Second Trial Themes and Castwork

Final Trial Themes and Castwork

In each of these collections there were just as many books. The first collection was gold, the second silver, and the third was black. After looking over a few shelves, I noticed that anything to do with those three colors was related. I soon skipped the colors all together.

Challenge and Arena Vendors

Contestant Selection Castwork

Judge Selection

Master Information

Titles and Accomplishments
Trial Theme and Challenge Suggestions
Contestant Contract Amendments
The Winner Chronicles and Places

My eyes flew over the shelves. I was just about to leave the rest of the collection for Ace to look through and head back to Moose when I spotted a spine no thicker than my littlest finger.

Fatalities

I jumped forward and yanked it from the shelf. I expected a black cover, decorated with skulls and headstones. But the cover was plain. It was bound in a dark leather that made it look more like a journal than anything else.

"I think I found it," I said.

Ace turned from her search and came to stand beside me. She read the simple title and nodded. She took the bag off her shoulder and yanked open the zipper. She tugged out a thick binder and held it open before me.

"Copy," she said, nodding her head to the book in my hands.

I thought back to my first attempt—the explosion of ink and destroyed pages. Nervous butterflies flew through my stomach.

"Did you want to do it?" I asked her.

She gave me a dry look. And in her usual short-spoken way said, "No." She pushed the book at me again.

Ok then, don't mess this up, Charlie.

My hand trembled as I opened the book to the first page. Two columns, one of names and the other of dates, divided the pages. The black ink swam before my eyes against the white paper.

Focus.

Breathing slowly through my nose, I took my wand into my hand. Magic swirled from my chest and down my arm. Spilling from my wand, it saturated the records of deaths. Keeping a firm grip on my magic, I moved my wand to the binder of blank paper in Ace's hands.

I squeezed my eyes shut and pressed my wand to the first page. *Please work.*

When my magic calmed, I peeked down at the binder. I expected to see an explosion of ink. Instead, a perfect copy sat before me.

Ace didn't give me time to celebrate. She turned to the next blank page and held it out to me. Moving with confidence, I copied and pasted the records into the binder with growing speed.

The book wasn't more than twenty pages long so we finished in a matter of minutes. When the last page was freshly copied in the binder, Ace snapped it closed and shoved it into her bag.

"Done," Ace called softly to Nirean and Moose.

Slamming my book closed, I winced as my finger slid across the edge of the page, drawing a thin line of blood. I stuck the abused finger in my mouth as I pushed the little book back on its shelf.

"How much more do you have to do, Moose?" I asked joining the others.

"We're barely halfway through this one." She swiped again at her damp upper lip. "Grab a binder and make yourself useful."

"There are other binders in there." Nirean kicked the bag at her feet. She turned to a fresh page for Moose.

Not wanting to push my luck, I grabbed for the empty binders before Ace could. I flipped to a clean page and held it out to her.

She huffed but didn't say anything. She grabbed the next volume of transfer documents and started copying them into the binder in my hands.

"Hey!"

My head snapped toward the door. My heart leapt when I found the doorway wasn't empty.

Clarence ducked under the lifted piece of floor and stepped into the room.

"What the hell are you doing?" Moose whispered harshly. "You're supposed to be distracting—"

"Master Lenin called Baker and said he was on his way back. I thought y'all would like a heads up!" he snapped.

He fired two small bursts of magic at either side of the slab of black stone. Unceremoniously it fell back to the floor. The protective ward filled the doorway completely, sealing our way out. When Clarence closed the door, the grand chandeliers dimmed.

"Hide, you morons!" he hissed as the light quickly faded, dropping us into a darkness so complete I could almost breathe it in.

We didn't need another prompt. Through the darkness, I heard someone grab the bag of binders. Curses and footsteps rounded the shelves. Feeling my way through the darkness, I bumped into a shelf. My hands whispered over the covers until I found the edge. Just as I pulled myself around to the other side, a key rattled in the lock.

37

Out and Up

I jumped behind the shelf as the door swung open.

The chandeliers flared brightly, once more filling the room with a warm golden glow.

I hunched down to the ground and pressed my back to the shelves. I clutched the copied documents to my chest, hoping to smother my pounding heart. My magic began to stir and warm my chest. Closing my eyes, I breathed slow and deep. I pressed my magic back tightly into my core, hoping the lights weren't already flickering.

Shoes clicked against the black stone. The steps were measured and clumsy, not the steps of a man on a mission to discover thieves in his protected room.

The stumbled steps drew closer and closer. His shadow slipped through the open slats of the bookcase beside my shoes.

I dared to turn my head and look up.

Master Lenin stood on the other side of the shelf that hid me. He swayed a little where he stood squinting at the row of gold books. Pursing his lips, he whistled a quiet little tune as he browsed. The rich scent of liquor followed his exhale.

I stopped breathing as he stooped down and retrieved a gold book from the shelf by my head. He scanned a couple pages before tucking it under his arm. He was about to leave when he squinted at the floor.

I followed his gaze and my heart plummeted to my toes. Right by his pointy shoe was a perfect drop of blood. My blood. If he touched it, he would know it came from me.

With a drunken hiccup, he shook his head. Mumbling to himself, he made his way back into the hall.

As soon as the door closed behind him, the great chandeliers once again started to dim.

In the fading light, I jumped from my hiding place and located the small drop of blood. As darkness fell, I swiped it up from the floor.

A bright flare of light burst over me.

I spun and landed on my back side.

A glowing orb of magic hovered over Moose's extended wand. "What are you doing?"

"I tripped," I lied, fisting my hand around the blood on my sleeve.

"Well, we need to *go.*" She turned back to the shelves. "Come on!" she hissed to the others.

Ace and Nirean ran out from the far shelf and into the circle of light cast by Moose. The four of us looked to the impenetrable darkness drowning the rest of the room. Nothing else moved or made a sound.

"Clarence," Moose whispered harshly. "Get your ass out here!"

There was no answer.

"I'm going to kill him," Moose said through her teeth.

"I'll get him." In three steps Nirean vanished into the darkness. A second later a similar burst of magic rose over her head to light her steps. She ran down the aisle dividing the room. Her head turned to the left and right in search of our final conspirator.

"Why would he go that far?" I asked when Nirean had shrunk considerably with the distance.

"Who knows?" Moose shook her head with a sharp sigh.

When Nirean passed a few more shelves her cast of light illuminated the fifth member of our party.

Clarence stood still.

His hands rested easily in his pockets as he looked down at his feet. He wasn't hiding. He was just standing in the middle of the aisle.

"What the hell is he doing?" Moose hissed. She looked to Ace for help, but she just shrugged.

Nirean took a hold of Clarence's shoulder and yanked him around to face her. Judging by her hand gestures and posture, she echoed

Moose's question. Clarence pulled himself from her grasp and started toward us. Shaking her head, Nirean followed after him.

"Any day now, Clarence," Moose called as loud as she dared. Unbothered as always, he took his time coming back to the front of the room. Nirean even outpaced him back.

"Are you done looking around?" Moose snapped.

"Not really—"

"I wasn't asking." Moose turned sharply, putting her back to him. "We only have a volume and a half, but I think we have enough to look through to answer our question. I don't want to push our luck by staying here."

"Agreed," Ace said with a nod.

"Then let's get the hell out of here."

Ace and Nirean took the lead back to the door. Quietly, Ace eased open the door and peered into the hallway. She waited there, still as a statue, for a few moments. When the coast remained clear, she opened the door as wide as it would go. The ward flared to life, a brilliant and gold warning to any trespassers.

Once again, she and Nirean crouched on either side of the door and drew their wands. They aimed at the glowing corners of the cutout and raised it from the floor. The ward lifted with it, leaving a space large enough for us to duck through.

Moose gestured for Clarence to go first. Rolling his eyes, he ducked beneath the slab of stone and stepped into the hall. Next was Moose and then me.

Stepping into the hallway, a load of tension dissipated from my chest. *This isn't over yet,* I reminded myself. *You can feel relieved when you're in your own bed and this whole mess is behind you.*

Ace, with her wand still aimed at the cut-out, slipped carefully into the hallway. Nirean did the same. When they were both outside, they lowered the slab back into place, once more filling the doorway with magic. Once the stone was where it belonged, the pair ran the glowing tips of their wands over the jagged edge. The cast of magic sealed it back to the floor, leaving no trace that it had been cut in the first place.

When that was done, Nirean waved her wand and the door swung shut with a soft *click.*

Ace reached into her shirt for the stash of lock picks.

Nirean shook her head. "Master Lenin didn't lock it on his way out."

Ace stuck out her lip, like she was looking forward to toying with the locking mechanism again. Regardless, she jumped to her feet.

Keeping our footsteps light, the five of us retreated down the hall toward the stairs.

As we neared the exit, Moose stopped at the front. I was about to ask why when I heard it too. It sounded like scratching. As we inched closer, I realized it was the faint sound of nails on a keyboard.

One by one, each of us looked around the corner of the curved hallway. Despite the late hour, Tessa Baker was at her desk typing at her computer. The worst of it was that she was facing our only way out.

My eyes flew around the room looking for anything that could distract her long enough for us to make a move for the stairs.

Nirean nudged Moose, but she gestured for her to give her some time to think.

That's when I got an idea. I pointed my wand at the steaming cup of coffee beside her and levitated it off the desk. I cut off the flow of magic and it fell to the floor. The cup crashed, sending coffee in every direction.

Tessa Baker jerked to her feet. Muttering something about "that damn ghost," she pushed away from her computer and strolled to the back of her office to get some tissues.

We didn't wait another second. In quick succession, Moose, Nirean, Ace, me, and then Clarence bolted around the corner and up the stairs. Despite her short legs, Moose kept in front of our pack.

Instead of running up the main staircase, Moose led us through the South Wing doors. Once everyone was through, she closed them behind us and ran toward the tower. Now that we were away from prying eyes, we didn't bother covering our footsteps. When we reached the tower, we climbed seven stories to the apartment level. Moose peeked out into the main stairwell and tiptoed to the Southeast Wing to her room.

Breathing hard, her hands shook as she took the key from around her neck and unlocked the door. Only when we were all inside with the door locked behind us did it finally sink in.

We did it.

I looked at Moose. Beads of sweat clung to her upper lip. A lively flush colored her cheeks and her eyes beamed with excitement. That light quickly dimmed when her eyes dropped to what was in my arms.

In our hurry to get out of the Records Room, I hadn't paused to put the binder back in Nirean's bag. I clutched it to my chest in one hand while the other still held my wand.

Moose sighed. "I'd suggest that we all reconvene back here in the morning, but I don't think I'll be able to sleep until we've looked through what we've taken."

I nodded. "I'd rather get it over with."

Moose turned to Ace and Nirean. "Are you staying?"

"This really isn't our thing—" Nirean started.

"Yes." Ace cut her off, simple and direct as always.

Nirean pinned her with a stern look, which Ace returned. They stood like that, having a conversation that no one else could hear. Finally, Nirean shook her head and turned for the kitchen. "I'll make some coffee."

"The coffee maker is beside the mini fridge," Moose called after her.

"Clarence?" I turned to the boy leaning against the back of the couch. "Are you in?"

"To ruin a Master?" He gave a wolfish flash of teeth. "All the way to the end, darlin'."

38

Matching Names

"While the coffee is brewing, we should at least make ourselves comfortable."

Moose took up Nirean's bag and turned to the private study off the living room. "Clarence? Charlie? Want to help?"

"No, thank you." Clarence threw himself onto the couch and kicked up his heels on the armrest. Completely horizontal, he crossed his arms over his eyes for a power nap.

"I'll help," I said, adding an extra bit of venom to my tone. Clarence didn't seem to notice. "What do you need?"

"We'll need more seating," she called from the next room. "Can you levitate one of the couches in here? I'll make room for it."

I knew exactly which couch I was going to move.

With the binder of stolen documents tucked under my arm, I aimed my wand at the couch that Clarence was dozing on. The golden glow wrapped around the legs of the couch and lifted it from the floor. I didn't bother trying to keep it level.

Clarence shot up as the couch began to tip. The motion of his startled awakening caused the couch to toss like a boat in a hurricane. I didn't use my magic to stabilize it. I continued to move the couch toward the study door.

The couch tipped and, with a startled cry, Clarence toppled off the cushions. He hit the ground with a curse that didn't sound like English.

I turned my back to him to hide my smile. Without him rocking the couch, it sailed smoothly into the study. I left Clarence glaring after me in the main room.

Moose's study was a disaster.

There were more books not on the shelves than there were on them. There were stacks on and around the desk. The precarious towers acted as a wall to the rest of the room. Anyone who sat behind the desk could effectively be hidden from the doorway.

The seats before the desk also held books, but these were open. Note cards stuck out of the pages. Other note cards were strewn about the floor. There seemed to be a color system for the notes; some of the cards were written entirely in pink, green, or blue ink. Others had passages highlighted in yellow, orange, or red. But from their scattered nature, there looked to be no reason to it at all.

"You can set it down over here," Moose said. In the short time it took for me to dump Clarence off the couch, she had swept the remaining books and loose pages from the back of the room into a pile in the corner.

She grabbed the back of one of the chairs and dragged it closer to the wall. The sharp motion displaced one of the books upon it. Note cards fluttered across the hardwood.

"I was thinking we can store everything in here too," she said as she bent down to collect her notecards.

"What about the cleaning crew?" I levitated the couch over to the space she opened up and carefully set it down.

"They won't come in here. They messed with my notes a couple of times last year and I couldn't find anything, so I told them this room is off limits."

"Can you find anything normally?"

"Sure." She stuffed the collection of note cards onto an empty bookshelf. "The desk is current assignments, the left chair is for future classes, the right chair is for fun research, and the back is when I'm bored with the other three."

I followed her finger and found one mess after another. I met her gaze and tried to keep my smile to myself, but I think she could see it in my eyes.

"It's not a mess. Messes aren't organized," she reasoned.

"I think you just proved that they can be."

Moose leaned to one side to yell at the door, "Are you done yet? Any day now would be great."

"You can't rush perfection!" Nirean hollered back.

Moose rolled her eyes. "It's boiled beans. Not casting science. Come on."

A moment later Nirean came in carrying a steaming pot of coffee. Ace wasn't two steps behind her with a tray containing five mismatched mugs—one of them was in the shape of a fish—a milk carton and a jar of sugar cubes. The coffee and tray were set on top of a stack of books at the center of the room.

Clarence came in last with a bag of chips. He shoved three into his mouth before sitting down.

"Where do we start?" Nirean asked, grabbing the fish mug and filling it with fresh coffee.

"We need to look through the transfer documents and the death records and see if any of the dates and names match." Moose took a mug with the Magisterium's black and gold compass rose on the side and passed it to Ace to fill.

"How long are we going to look?" Clarence asked around a wad of chips.

"I don't think it should take too long to figure out if we're right," Moose said, meeting my gaze.

Coffee was passed around and doctored. I declined a cup. I feared if I had any more energy, my hands would never stop shaking. Ace just took a handful of sugar cubes and popped one into her mouth.

When everyone else was sipping on the fresh brew, no one reached toward Nirean's bag.

Moose stared at it with half fascination and half horror. My grip around the other documents turned to one of white knuckles. I never wanted to be more wrong in my entire life.

Moose set her mug aside and pulled the bag toward her. The room was so quiet, that as she pulled the zipper it sounded as if it were happening right by my ear.

She took out the copied death records and dropped them on to my lap. Just as quickly she pried the binder out from under my arm and settled back into her seat.

She cleared her throat and opened the binder. In silence she flipped through the pages. Her lips were pressed tightly together. With each passing page, the more blood left her face.

"Holly Blackwell," she whispered. "Transferred October twenty-third."

Nirean's mug paused before her lips. Ace went as still as a statue. Even Clarence stopped inhaling potato chips.

Please let me be wrong.

I opened the cover to the death records and once more looked upon the two columns of information, one of names and the second of dates. A quick glance told me they were organized by last name, not date.

Please let me be wrong.

I turned a few pages to the B section. Running my finger down the names, the letters blurred together in intelligible masses of ink. I had to force myself to slow down and read each name.

And there it was.

Holly Blackwell, October twenty-third.

"Oh, wow." A rush of blood drained from my head. The world tilted so violently that I grabbed the armrests for support.

"No." Nirean lowered her mug.

"Is she in there?" Moose whispered.

I could hardly see, let alone form words. Was it shock or was it all the magic I used that evening? Nausea rushed from the pit of my stomach. Definitely shock.

Moose lunged forward, dumping the binder in her lap to the floor. She swiped the book from my hands and scanned the pages with fervor. I knew the exact moment she found the name. She went as rigid as a corpse. She certainly was as pale as one.

"Shit," Ace mumbled around a sugar cube.

"Please tell me you're just being dramatic," Nirean said in a small voice.

Moose slowly shook her head. "Her name's in here."

Ace and Nirean were on their feet in an instance. Nirean ripped the binder from Moose's hands. Finding the name, she turned her attention to the transfer documents.

"Oh, no. I did not sign up for this shit." Nirean tossed the binder down and fisted her hands into her curly hair. "You," she turned to Moose, "*you* said this would be nothing. Just a fun exploration where no student has gone before."

"Liar." Ace dumped her collection of sugar onto the tray.

Moose continued to stare at the book with her friend's name.

"What did you expect?" Clarence asked, grabbing for another chip.

"Not this!" Nirean grabbed the binder from the cushions. "We need to bring this to Master Lenin. He probably doesn't know what's going on."

That got Moose's attention. Her gaze broke from the binder and latched onto her terrified classmate. "We can't bring this to him. He might be the one doing it!"

Nirean shook her head, backing toward the door. The binder was still clutched to her chest.

Clarence pulled his wand from his back pocket and pointed it at Nirean's face. "Take one more step and I'll stun you into a coma for the rest of the year."

Ace's hand moved toward her wand.

"Make one move, weirdo. I dare you," Clarence said without looking away from Nirean and the binder.

"Clarence!" I jumped to my feet. "Put that away."

"Not until Nirean sits down."

"Don't be stupid—"

"Not until. She. Sits. Down." The messy markings on his wand sparkled with magic. He was ready to make his threat a reality.

Nirean slowly moved away from the door and perched on the edge of the couch. Only when he was sure Nirean wouldn't bolt for the door did Clarence lower his wand. Ace, with her wand drawn, slipped closer to her friend.

"This can be explained," Nirean said with a forced calm. Her dark brown eyes tracked Clarence around the room. "She tripped down the stairs or maybe she fell out a window."

"Yeah," Ace offered hopefully.

"If that were true," Moose said in a strained tone, "then why were there transfer papers issued the same day? You know she wanted to be a Master of the Casting Arts—she told everyone. She'd never transfer to another school."

"Maybe she didn't tell you everything, Moose," Nirean argued. "Maybe she felt so smothered by your dream to become Masters together that she filled out the paperwork behind your back."

"She'd never do that."

"You don't know that for certain."

"Her mom said she was *hit by a car.* She said nothing about her dying *here!*"

"Of course not. I'm sure Master Lenin didn't want word to get out that someone else died here."

"There's an easy way to solve this," Clarence piped up. He smeared the chip grease on the sides of his pants and set the bag aside. He took the transfer documents and death records from Nirean and casually skimmed through the pages.

His eyebrows rose at what he found.

"Spit it out," Moose snapped.

"Janet Raven, transferred February second," he read, flipping the records around. He dropped them to the makeshift coffee table. He did the same with the death records and announced, "Janet Raven, deceased February second."

Nirean collapsed onto the couch and stared unblinkingly at the pages.

"Care to explain that, Nirean?" Moose fumed. "She died the same night Master Lenin walked out of the North Tower. The same night she supposedly asked to transfer to another school. We were told she left the Magisterium and died in some freak fire *off school grounds.*" Moose pulled off her glasses and rubbed her eyes.

"Come on, Moose." Nirean was actually pleading with her. "You're going to accuse the man that crowned you best in our class so easily?"

"It doesn't add up. If you used the meat between your ears, you'd see that," Moose stressed. "You're just scared because this isn't as easy as your stupid game of stealing useless crap."

"Of course I'm scared! Messing around with Masters never ends well for Users without titles." Nirean crossed and uncrossed her arms. "Why would he do it? Masters have everything they could ever want."

"He's fighting a doomed war." Clarence resumed eating his chips. "He's probably stealing their magic for The Heel. Or maybe he's just a sick bastard."

While they argued, I picked up the transfer documents and grabbed a marker. I went through and circled all the names with a status between a Common Seven and a Royal Eight.

I took up the death records and hunted for matching names. I found one, and then three, and then five. As I continued to circle matching names, Nirean, Moose, and Clarence fell silent. All eyes turned to the book in my lap and the marker that darkened the page.

Of the fifty Commons and Royals I circled in the transfer documents, ten were found in the death records. And that was only going back through the last decade . . . we weren't even half of the way through the stolen documents.

"Now what?" Nirean asked. All the fight had left her.

"We still can't tie any of this to Master Lenin." Everyone turned to Moose. "It could be any of the teachers. We need a direct connection between him, these students, and the dates."

"I don't understand," Clarence said slowly. "Charlie saw him leaving the tower. And he signs all of the transfers personally. If that ain't a direct link, I don't know what is."

Moose shook her head. "Look around. We're a bunch of Commons—save for you," she pointed to Clarence. "But your knack for trouble would discredit anything that came out of your mouth." Moose glanced at me.

My stomach hardened. *She wouldn't.*

"Because of his rank," Moose continued, "Master Lenin can discredit everything we say. If any one of us were a Royal in good standing, we might be able to do something."

Which meant not me. As far as anyone knew, I didn't exist. Master Lenin made sure of that.

"We'd need solid proof not even a School Master can deny," Moose said.

"And where the hell are we going to find that?" Clarence dropped onto the sofa.

"The first victim of the tower, Blaine Willow. The more we know about her, maybe we can find a link."

"What makes you think she was the first?" I asked.

"All of this started right after she died," Moose explained. "If it's just a coincidence, then maybe she's seen something that can help us pin it to Master Lenin."

"Great idea," Nirean grumbled. "But you're forgetting that Hunters investigated that case and they didn't even find anything. What makes you think we'll do any better?"

Moose took a deep breath. "I know where we can get more information."

A beat of silence followed.

"Are you going to let us in the loop or are you just going to leave us hanging?" I prompted.

Moose shook her head. "It might be a long shot. Hopefully, I'll let you guys know tomorrow if it's any use."

"What do we do until then?"

She grabbed the forgotten binder and sank into the sofa. The leather rumbled as she shifted into a comfortable position. "We finish looking through the rest."

39

Valentine's Day

We found thirty-seven names before we ran out of documents to check.

The earliest matching name went as far back as thirty-seven years.

One name for each year.

No more, no less.

But there was no pattern or reason that we could make out for when the students were killed. Each event was scattered throughout the school year. The only consistent thing through all of it was the statuses of the victims. They were either Royal Eights or Common Sevens. He went no lower and, since I was the first Royal Nine to be born in some time, he couldn't go any higher.

After we finished matching the names, we sat in silence as if the circled names were between us like gravestones.

Ace held Nirean tightly in her arms. Clarence lit a joint of mermaid reed, but he didn't put it to his lips. Moose's eyes ran over the same name circled in both binders, over and over again. *Holly Blackwell.* And I . . . I stared at the window. The blinds were drawn against the midnight hour, but I could clearly picture the jagged mountain range with their evergreen coats in my mind's eye. The same desperate song thumped through my veins.

Run.

"Whether you like it or not, you're a part of this," Master Lenin said.

Janet Raven.

Run.

"We only ask that you try, to give us the hope to win."
Holly Blackwell.
Run.
"You could save generations."
Janet Raven.

On and on it swirled and churned. Each broken sentence knocked the wind out of me. Just when I gained a deep breath, it overwhelmed me again.

Right or wrong? Achilles Heel or the Crown? How could the question be so simple, nothing more than a few words, when the answer was knotted and tangled?

The Crown, Lawrence, had killed Deficients and Regulars by the thousands.

Achille's Heel, trying to stop him, was dripping with the stolen magic of thirty-seven Users—kids.

Had Master Lenin asked them to join the Heel's cause and when they said no, he killed them and covered it up?

The difference between good and bad was supposed to be as dramatic and sharp as white and black, day and night, life and death. But all I saw was grey.

I had one side telling me they were righteous and the other was led by the damned. But I heard from others that one was a misguided anchor, and the other was pruning for the future.

Maybe there were no good guys here.

Run.

I had half the mind to do it that night. To go back to my room and try to Port until I had no more magic. I would have done it too, if my eye hadn't been drawn to Moose.

Pinned on the right side of her dark sweater was her status pin. A seven gleamed from the center of the black and gold compass rose. That small, delicate pin placed her right in the sights of Master Lenin's war path.

I turned to Nirean, knowing I would see the same pin with the same number on her shirt. I found myself relieved when I saw that Ace's pin was graced with a six. The release of emotion was short lived when I was reminded that Clarence was a Royal Eight. And then there was me, a Royal Nine.

According to the documents between us, four out of the five of us had enough magic worth stealing.

Would Master Lenin take one of them next?

The very thought made it hard to breathe. Attachment is an anchor, and now I had four more keeping me locked inside a black stone coffin.

By the time any of us were able to move and go to our own beds, it was four in the morning.

I didn't go to sleep. I didn't even practice Porting. I just laid on my bed with the same cycle of questions rolling through my mind. I'm not sure where the rest of the night went, I just knew that the next minute it was morning and breakfast was starting.

With my head in a sleepless fog, I reached the dining room at the beginning of breakfast. The last time I did that was on my first day at the Magisterium.

All around the dining room large colorful hearts floated from table to table. They burst into a flurry of red sparkles above a student. In the midst of the glittery rain storm a card or bouquet of flowers floated down to the User. A tall vase sat at the center of each round table containing grand arrangements of roses and snow-white orchids. Bright, glittering letters hung over the stage. *Happy Valentine's Day.*

I couldn't have cared less.

In the doorway I looked around at my fellow classmates—more importantly the ones at the front near the stage.

How did Master Lenin pick who he was going to drain? The strongest based on their class scores? Or was it the trouble makers that no one would miss?

Making my way through the food line, I picked a few golden-brown waffles in the shape of a heart. I gave each a healthy splash of strawberry sauce. Just as I grabbed the whipped cream, someone wiggled into the spot beside me.

"Hey, no cutting!" a guy from my Wand Structure class yelled.

"Sorry!" Cornelia Montgomery waved with a bright smile. "I already ate. I just want to talk to my friend." She turned her bright blue eyes to me. "Hey, sorry about that."

"Uh, no problem." I topped each waffle with a small mountain of whipped cream. "What's up?"

"I was hoping to catch you before you sat down."

I don't like the sound of that.

"I was wondering if you wanted to eat breakfast with me and Daniel."

"Oh." I looked over the buffet to their usual table near the windows. Daniel sat in the morning sun laughing over his coffee. My eyes drifted to another table on the other side of the room.

Ace, Nirean, and Clarence had their heads together as an intense conversation bounced between them. Moose had yet to show her face.

"I already told some people I'd sit with them," I said.

Cornelia's smile dimmed. "I noticed you've been hanging around Clarence, Ace, and Nirean."

"Yeah." I replaced the spoon in the whipped cream. "We share a few classes together and we have the same mealtime block."

"That and," clearing her throat she stepped closer, "you sneak out past curfew with them."

I paused in front of the heart shaped strawberries.

She rushed on, "My room is right across from yours and I've heard your door shut past curfew a couple times."

She had no idea it was because I was coming back from lessons with Michael. She only had two dots to connect. Even though they were wrong, they were close enough to matter.

Trying to remain indifferent, I looked calmly back at her. "It could've been someone else's door."

She shook her head. "Not a chance. But that's not why I'm here. I'm a scholarship student too. So, I know how hard it is to get into this school without a high status backing you. I know Clarence is charming and that accent is adorable, but he's six kinds of trouble. He's gotten multiple people expelled. I really don't know where to start when it comes to Ace and Nirean."

She glanced over her shoulder to where they were sitting. "I guess what I'm trying to say is, if you ever want someone else to sit with, there's always an empty seat by me."

"Oh." At a complete loss for words, I nodded. "Thanks."

With another bright smile, she stepped away from the buffet. Before she headed back to her own table she hesitated. "Were you planning on going to the Valentine's party tonight?"

"I didn't really know there was one."

"It's a lot of fun. There's a thirty-foot-tall chocolate fountain and a live band. You should come!"

I looked back at my table. My heart shrank at the thought of diving back into this mess.

"I'll think about it." I was too tired to make the lie convincing. My smile wasn't even that warm.

But Cornelia's excitement didn't droop beneath my rain cloud. If anything, her smile brightened by a watt or two.

"Then I'll see you later!" She darted back to her breakfast and sat beside Daniel. He looked over his shoulder then and found me staring.

Quickly I turned my back. I took my plate of sugar over to the table on the other side of the room.

"Where's Moose?" I asked as I sat beside Ace.

She shrugged.

"She should be working on finding our direct link." Clarence reached across the table and took one of my waffles, leaving a trail of strawberry sauce behind it.

"Her deadline is tonight," Nirean said, before I could stab Clarence with my fork.

"I doubt she'll find anything." Clarence shoved half of my waffle into his mouth. "Hunters couldn't hack it. There's no way she will."

"If anyone is as smart as a Hunter, it's Moose," Nirean said.

Moose and I didn't share any classes that day. So, I didn't see her, not even at lunch. I searched for her between classes, but with no luck.

I went to her room, thinking she had gone back there to study, but my knocks went unanswered. After my last class, I went back to my room, exhausted.

I thought about chancing a nap before dinner. I could get away with putting off homework for an hour or two. Before I could fall face first into my mattress, there was a knock at my door.

I barely turned the handle before Cornelia burst into my room, pulling a suitcase behind her.

"Hello to you, too," I said, barely pulling my feet out of the wheel's way.

"Hey! Sorry. I tripped over the cord." She turned the suitcase to show the electrical cord hanging out of it. "I thought we could get ready for the Valentine's party together."

"Oh, I don't think I want to go."

"We'll, I've decided that you're coming." Cornelia nudged the door closed. "How was the rest of your day?"

I thought about kicking her out. I could fake a headache. It wouldn't be too much of a lie. I could feel the start of one building behind my eyes. But I had already blown her off for the first month I was here. Cornelia was as genuine as a spring flower. I didn't want my moody attitude to crumple her petals.

With a sigh, I moved away from the door. "I didn't have to cut anything open in Creature Studies or cut up garlic hearts in Potion Brewing. So I think it was a good day."

"My hands smelled for a week after we did that." She tossed a lock of blonde hair over her shoulder. "The only thing that worked was soaking them in daffodil oil, but then my hands were yellow." She shrugged. "Is it ok if we move into your room?"

"Sure!" I jumped ahead of her to open the door and to shove piles of clothes out of the way. "Sorry about the mess."

She laughed. "This doesn't even compare to my room." She dropped the bag on to my unmade bed. The suitcase popped open by itself. A train of bobby pins, hair products, and other clips rose into the air and hung suspended.

She patted the corner of the bed. "Have a seat."

I sat beside the suitcase and looked at the ends of my splitting hair. As my eyes moved to her silky waves, I was suddenly self-conscious. She'd probably be grossed out when she touched it.

Cornelia pulled out her wand and touched it to my roots. The uncontrollable fizzy that was my hair tamed instantly, leaving it straight and smooth.

My mouth dropped open.

She held up a satin lock. "Do you dye your hair?"

Speechless, I nodded.

She rolled the lock between her fingers. "What do you dye it with?"

"With . . . dye."

She burst out laughing. "Seriously? That's such a Reg thing to do." She touched her wand to my scalp and my hair bled to a natural shade of warm brown. My red streak disappeared but with a tap of her wand it came back. "Now your hair will grow in brown with the red streak. No more dye. You and your hair will thank me later. If you want to change your color, I can show you how."

I sat there, too shocked to say anything. Was this the end of bad hair days? I almost laughed at the idea. Touching her wand back to my hair, small sections started to spin into perfect curls.

"So . . ." *Think of something to say!* "How long have you been coming to the Magisterium?"

"Since I was fifteen. It's been kicking my ass since day one."

"Same here." I smiled up at her.

A can of hairspray fell from the air and hit the floor. I was about to pick it up when she stopped me. "I got it. Sorry. I didn't mean to make a mess." She cleared her throat. "Have you started thinking about what apprenticeships you want next year?"

My mind drew a blank. I couldn't remember Master Lenin mentioning anything about apprenticeships.

"Uh." *Could I ask her to elaborate and not draw suspicion?* "Not really."

"Me neither. You would think with our Testing Trial being next year that I would have some idea. I think I'll just see what I can get and then pick the best one."

I made a mental note to ask Moose about it later. "Same."

A tube of lipstick dropped.

"Cornelia." A hairbrush and coil of ribbon rolled across the room. "Is everything ok?"

"Yes! I'm just a little tired." She stooped to pick up the items and almost tipped over. Her lips were completely void of color.

"Tired—" I stopped. The bottles were held up by magic. I may have only been in this world for a couple months, but my guess was that she wasn't running low on energy, but magic.

"Cornelia, stop," I said jumping to my feet. "Whatever charm you're doing, stop."

She hesitated long enough for a spool of ribbon to drop to the floor. With a shaky breath, she pulled her magic back. The remaining items clattered to the floor and bounced across the carpet.

I ran into the kitchen and snatched a bottle of water from the fridge. On my way back to the bedroom I grabbed a container of chocolate covered raisins from the counter. Running back to Cornelia I fell to my knees beside her.

"Here." I pushed the water bottle into her hand. "Drink this. You should probably eat something too." I unscrewed the container and moved it to sit between us.

With trembling hands, she brought the bottle to her lips and downed the entire thing.

"Thank you," she said weakly. Her hand didn't shake as hard when she reached for the chocolate covered raisins.

I looked at the number on her chest. It said she was a Common Four. "Is that your real status?"

Her eyes snapped up from the floor. "I'm exhausted. I just did a lot of magic today in my classes. That's all."

Of course, she wouldn't admit a lie to a complete stranger.

She cleared her throat. "Please don't tell anyone about this, especially Master Lenin. I would hate for him to think—it's dangerous to be a Deficient these days. Users have been expelled, fired, and even evicted. That's not to mention the bullying."

"I won't say anything. I couldn't care less about magic status." I was walking on really thin ice here. "Besides. It's not really my place." Seeing as I was lying about my own.

She looked at me through her long lashes. Skeptical, she narrowed her eyes. "You really won't tell anyone?"

I shook my head.

"Why? You don't know me. I'm not even sure you like me."

I winced at that. "Sorry. About avoiding you. It's just . . . I wasn't planning on staying here long enough to make friends."

"I think you mean to say that I'm not your type of friend. You seem to be doing just fine with Moose, Ace, Nirean, and Clarence."

"We're working on a project together," I lied with a shrug.

She accepted my answer in silence. "You didn't answer my question. Why won't you tell anyone?"

I thought for a moment. "Because I'm lying about my status."

Her eyes dropped to my shirt. "Why?"

"I thought the extra status would help me get apprenticeships."

"What are you really?"

"A—" the truth twisted on my tongue. "A Common Five."

She sat there for a moment. Her fingers played idly with the bumble bee pendant at her throat. "I'm a Deficient Three."

"That's not so bad."

"I can hardly do anything." She gestured to the fallen bottles. "My parents lie about their status at work," she said quietly. "Last week a Deficient family was killed a block from where we live. We just want to be safe, you know?"

"Does that happen a lot?"

She nodded. "A lot more than the news reports. I'm not sure people really care as long as their status isn't being targeted."

"What about Achilles Heel? Can you go to them for help?"

"I don't think they have the manpower to do anything. Besides, everyone knows their objective is to kill Master Hart. Protecting lower statuses doesn't really fall under that."

Maybe that's why Master Lenin is stealing magic. I shook that thought from my head. His reasons were irrelevant. No excuse was good enough for what he was doing.

"No one's fighting for us," Cornelia mumbled sadly. "Because no one cares what happens to the weakest links of society."

"You could save generations," Master Lenin said.

"You're not weak," I blurted, trying to get Master Lenin's voice out of my head.

"That says otherwise." She gestured to the scattered items on the floor.

"Strength isn't always muscle—or magic. Surviving every day despite the cards fate dealt you—that's real strength."

"No one else sees it that way."

"No one has to."

She dropped her hand from the pendant around her neck. She looked at the container of chocolate covered raisins between us. "These really aren't good, by the way. I don't know anyone who willing eats raisins."

"They're covered in chocolate." That earned me a smile, which I gladly returned.

"That thin layer barely counts."

Laughing, I helped her back to her feet. "Are you ok?"

She nodded. Some of the color was back in her cheeks and her hands didn't shake when she brushed a curled blond lock from her eyes.

"Good thing I brought this." She stooped down and grabbed a curling iron off the floor. "Do you mind if we do this the Reg way?"

"Not at all. That's the way I'm more familiar with anyway."

She gave me a questioning look. "You're not like most Magic Users."

I shrugged one shoulder. "From what I know of Magic Users, I'll take that as a compliment."

Her smile widened. Moving slowly, she walked to the bathroom and plugged in the curling iron.

In the next hour she stuffed me into a short, flowy red dress and heels. She pulled some of my curls back with a ribbon. When she was done, I looked like someone who belonged at cocktail parties.

Before I could see if the image in the mirror was actually me, she looped her arm through mine and pulled me down the stairs.

The dining room had been transformed. The walls were draped with bright red curtains concealing all traces of black stone. Glittering hearts hung from the ceiling like stars. Some even floated around the room sprinkling chocolates as they went. Most of the lights were enchanted to cast a rosy glow over the room.

Just like Cornelia said, there was a towering, gushing chocolate fountain where the buffet usually sat. Surrounding the fountain were buckets of strawberries, banana slices, pretzels sticks, and marshmallows.

On the stage, a full-scale band of instruments played themselves while couples danced in the middle of the room. Behind the instruments, covering the wall from floor to ceiling, were tiny mailboxes.

"What are those?" I asked over the noise.

"Secret admirer boxes," Cornelia said, practically bouncing with excitement. "Each student gets one with their name on it and anyone can anonymously leave notes." Her eyes slid back to the chocolate fountain. "Now if you'll excuse me, I'm going to wash the taste of raisins out of my mouth with straight chocolate."

Somehow she had slipped into a dress five minutes before we left, and she still looked better than I did.

I cast a look about the lively room. Nirean and Ace were in the middle of the dance floor. The ends of Nirean's curly hair were as red as if they were dripped in paint. Decked out in her usual all black, Ace banged her head to the music.

Clarence lounged beside the chocolate fountain. His form of entertainment was taking freshly dipped chocolate coated strawberries and launching them at people who got too close.

Moose would've smacked the back of his head—if she were there.

I looked for a high ponytail and square glasses. Moose was never late to anything, yet the party was in full swing and she had yet to make an appearance.

Instead of loitering in the doorway, I moved farther into the party. Making sure to keep to the outer edges, I stayed away from the students concentrated at the center of the room.

A tray of flutes filled with a bubbling pink liquid levitated along the perimeter of the dance floor. It paused briefly beside me.

I plucked one from the edge. As soon as the stem lifted from the silver tray, it continued to float around the room without a carrier.

I brought the delicate glass to my lips and took a sip. Hints of honey and rose bubbled sweetly over my tongue. Taking a longer drink, I found an empty windowsill to hop onto. From this vantage point, I had a direct view of the dining room doors as well as a view of the dance floor.

Music thundered from the stage. I could feel the bass thumping through my chest as if an invisible force pounded on my ribcage. Enjoying my drink, I watched couples twirl around the floor or rock side to side without rhythm or concern. Every so often, I stopped people watching to scan the room for Moose.

"Hey Charlie."

I jumped, almost spilling the fizzy drink down my front.

Daniel huffed as he sat down beside me on the windowsill. "I think from now on I'm going to approach you head on. I'd hate to see you fall down the stairs just because I said hello."

"Don't worry. I've been told that I bounce back quickly." I set my drink aside to avoid further catastrophes.

Of their own volition, my hands simultaneously tucked a curled lock behind my ear and adjusted the loose fabric of my dress. I peeked at him from the corner of my eye. The rosy light of the room cast his features in a warm glow that seemed to concentrate on his cheeks. Angelic was too cliché of a word to use, but it was all that I could think of.

As was the theme of the evening, he wore a light pink tie dotted with red hearts. It stood out against his navy dress shirt.

Realizing I was staring, I quickly looked to the dance floor. "How's your evening going?"

"Oh, great." He leaned his spine against the cool pane of the window, looking as comfortable as a cat in a sunny patch. "Honestly, I don't know how anyone can have a bad time with thirty feet of melted chocolate."

I followed his gaze to the chocolate fountain. Clarence was still there, except instead of throwing fruit at passing students, he was shamelessly flirting with a Royal from our Enchantments class.

I snuck another peek at Daniel. Just as quickly to avoid his gaze, I looked around the students closest to us. None of the girls were looking over anxiously or with questions. Does that mean . . .

"Did you come with anyone?" I asked, hoping my voice sounded carefree.

"No."

My head snapped around. My heart tripped when I found him already looking at me.

He mistook my expression with a mocking roll of the eyes. "Surprising, huh? How could the Records Keeper be going stag to an event like this?" He laughed at his own joke. "The girl I wanted to take, uh, I never got the courage to ask her."

I was surprised by the sharp pang of disappointment that stabbed through my chest. *Why would that be me? I've avoided him for the last month. He probably thinks I don't like him. Besides, the moment I can Port out of here, I'm gone.*

That did nothing to squash the bite of chagrin plaguing my thoughts.

Taking hold of the conversation, I directed it to safer waters. "Well, at least your admirer box is getting a lot of attention."

He groaned. "You won't believe the things people put in there. I'm not sure I even want to read them this year. Have you gone to look at yours yet?"

"No." My curls bounced around my shoulders as I shook my head. "And I'm definitely not going to."

"Why not?" His grin turned mocking. "Are you afraid you'll have to fight off too many suitors?"

"Ha, or the depression when I find nothing at all. Which is more likely."

"You think it's going to be empty?" He slid off the windowsill and took my hand in his. "Let's take a look."

Butterflies ignited from his touch. My mind flashed to Master Lenin's pained face after he touched my hand. I almost yanked my hand from Daniel's, expecting him to be in pain. But his fingers curled around mine and his gaze remained as cheery as ever.

I vaguely remembered Master Lenin saying only higher statuses would be able to feel my magic. I took the foggy explanation and ran with it, because I rather liked the warmth and weight of Daniel's fingers around mine. I breathed slowly to keep the flush out of my cheeks.

Daniel immediately pulled me toward the stage.

"I really don't care." I tripped after him, passing Nirean and Ace who both wore amused expressions. "Really, Daniel, I don't."

"Humor me," he called over the music with another smile.

Weaving in and out of dancing couples, stepping on a few toes, and avoiding puddles of spilled drinks, we finally made it to the other side of the room.

He led me around a couple of students dropping off notes before we arrived at a small, black mailbox with my name printed in swirly gold letters. He gestured to it as if to say, *the honor is yours.*

A wave of butterflies moved through my chest. *What if it's empty? Would he laugh?* Kicking myself for being ridiculous, I pulled down the little door. A lump of disappointment dropped into my stomach when only shadows greeted me.

"Oh, look," Daniel said with mild surprise. "The kitchen staff is bringing out cream puffs."

Thankful for the distraction from the shadows inside the tiny mailbox, I followed his directing finger. But where he was pointing wasn't to a dessert table. It was to the middle of the crowded dance floor. The only table that could have even been close was still on the other side of the room by the doors.

I turned back to Daniel only to have something catch my eye. At the bottom of the mailbox was a heart shaped chocolate wrapped in red foil.

From the corner of my vision, I saw his hand return to his candy filled pocket.

A smile broke over my lips. I tried to keep it coy, but I had no such practice. The grin was broad enough to squint my eyes. I tried to salvage a shred of my dignity by ducking my head.

Get it together, Charlie.

The smile may have dimmed, but I couldn't do a thing for the flush warming my cheeks. I took the candy from the box and cradled it between my hands.

"I wonder who it came from," I said, still refusing to meet his gaze.

"Maybe it came from a guy who'll have enough courage to ask you to this party next year."

My heart skipped. Magic hummed through my chest. *He's talking about me. He's talking about me!*

Keep cool.

I slowly exhaled, coaxing my magic back into my core. "That's a whole year away. Can someone ask that far in advance?"

"I don't think there are any rules against it."

"A lot can change in a year."

"Maybe."

I dared to look up from the chocolate to meet his gaze.

"But I doubt it," he said in a soft voice that was barely heard over the amiable tune of the instruments.

He swallowed hard and straightened his shoulders. "Would you like to dance?"

This time my heart somersaulted through my chest. I wondered if all the irregular beating would make me pass out. I looked at the dance floor to the couples spinning expertly in formation and the ones standing intimately close together. The guy of the closest couple had his hands low on his partner's waist. Every time he spoke, his breath brushed by the hair on her forehead.

My fingers tingled. It felt as if sparks danced along my skin. It was so overwhelming that I barely registered the scar tissue across my back.

A flash came from the doorway. A brief glance of light off a glassy surface. It was just enough to snag my attention.

Moving from one side of the doorway to the other, a familiar high ponytail bounced into view.

Moose.

Just as quickly as she was there, she was gone, hidden by the doorframe of the dining room. The bright lights of the stairwell cast her shadow across the floor. Her shadow wasn't alone. Another, much taller, strolled beside her.

"Charlie?"

I tore my eyes away from the door. *Daniel.* He looked as if he were holding his breath.

"Sorry. Um." *Where is she going?* "Will you excuse me for a moment?"

He blinked in surprise. "Of course. I can wait for you here."

"No." I winced at how harsh that sounded. "I mean. No use waiting near an empty mailbox. I'll find you." His answer was lost as I bolted for the hallway.

Why did everything have to happen at the same time? Why couldn't Moose show up after *my dance with Daniel?*

Pushing through the crowd, I struggled to the other side of the room. Stepping out of the noisy party, I spun around looking for Moose.

The staircase was empty. The library ceiling wasn't glowing, so no one was in there either.

Where did she go? I spun again, taking in the stairwell. My eyes landed on the one thing out of place.

The gold doors to the North Wing were cracked open.

40

Into the Tower

No way.

I know she said she was going to get us a lead, but I wasn't thinking she would go to the one place in the entire school we were told to stay out of.

Moose wouldn't be that stupid, I told myself as I crossed the stairwell toward the ajar doors. *There's no way she would risk her standing in the school.*

Peering through the crack, I squinted into the darkness. Halfway down the hallway, the light from the stairwell glinted off the shoulders of two figures.

Cheese and rice.

Groaning, I pulled off my shoes and slipped between the doors. Keeping on my tiptoes, I silently followed their footsteps into the darkness.

"I didn't know the towers had keys," Moose said as they stopped outside the tower door.

"They don't. Blaine Willow loved this tower so much she installed the enchantment during her third year here."

Mr. While?

"You'd think an enchantment like that would have pissed off Master Lenin."

Mr. While chuckled. "Blaine was a Royal from old money. She could have painted the stairwell green and I doubt Master Lenin would have said anything other than compliment her castwork."

"Royals," Moose grumbled without her usual sting. "Where did you find that key?"

"In the kitchen cellar. I don't know what that says about the quality of food the kitchen staff whips up." Mr. While held up a rusty old key. "Would you like to do the honors?"

"Will it work? I thought the ghost keeps everyone out."

"You're correct, but she cast the enchantment on the tower doors, and she made the keys. She can't fight against herself—at least that was my theory. I never had the guts to test it out before you asked."

"Are you scared of ghosts?" Moose teased.

"I'd be a fool not to."

Undeterred, Moose plucked the key from his hand and slid it into the lock. The unlatching *click* echoed down the wing. She pushed the door open, letting a puff of ash into the hall. After they stepped inside, I counted to ten before sneaking up to the door.

I paused with my hand on the latch.

My skin crawled as if I were standing outside Denny's room. Every cell in my body knew not to go inside. But those thirty-seven names screamed around my skull.

Cursing, I pushed my way into the tower.

Ash covered everything from the black walls to the banisters of the curving staircase. The air was thick and stale as it entered my lungs. The only lighting came from the moon streaking through the dirty glass of the windows.

"Do you know if she hid anything in here?" Moose asked farther up the winding staircase.

"Since it's off-limits, no one has been able to investigate. But it's definitely a possibility."

Farther up, a door squeaked open as they traveled to the next level. With my heart in my throat, I followed them higher and higher.

My toes curled at the feel of the powdery char. Footprints belonging to Moose and Mr. While disturbed the layer of decay. There were other footprints too. But they were barefooted like me.

"Do you think she's still up here?" Moose whispered. "Blaine, I mean."

"Of course. She rules this tower. Did you see those footprints? They definitely aren't ours."

I looked back at the barefoot prints and swallowed.

"She was extremely stubborn when she was alive. It's no surprise she's the same way in death."

"You knew her?" Moose sounded as surprised as I felt.

"Hardly. She was a Royal and I was a Deficient so there was no room for us to interact." He almost sounded sad about that fact. "She was the smartest in our class, much like you. Her friends called her Whistling Willow. She would've whistled all day if she was allowed." He let out a quick, cheery tune that echoed down the stairs.

Each level of the tower was much like the first, charred and cloaked with ash. The seventh level had handprints covering the windows. The thin layer of ash over them suggested they had been there for a while.

I stared at a handprint the same size as mine and wondered who it belonged to.

"*Leave.*"

I jerked around so fast my dress flared around my knees. The word was no more than a whisper, a breath near my ear.

But there were only shadows behind me. On the floor, not more than a foot away from where I stood, were fresh footprints.

Moose and Mr. While stayed on the final level for a moment longer than they did the other levels. They spoke too softly for their conversation to filter down.

Finally, after what felt like an eternity in darkness, footsteps echoed down the stairs. Moose and Mr. While were coming back down and the only thing in their way was me, in a bright red dress.

Moose's temper was short, to the point of being non-existent. If she saw me following her, how would she react? Worse than that, how would Mr. While react? Would he tell Master Lenin I was there?

Wildly, I looked for an escape. A deep windowsill caught my eye. Without thinking, I jumped for it and hit the window with a thud. The sound echoed throughout the tower as ash tumbled on to my shoulders.

"I believe we've overstayed our welcome. Let's leave before we irritate her further." Mr. While flew by the windowsill with Moose a step or two behind. Their footsteps receded down the staircase and faded with each passing level.

I peeked out from my hiding place and looked down the winding staircase. They were gone.

I jumped back to the stairs. The ash covering the steps took the traction from under my feet and threw me into the railing. The drop to the next level made my stomach bottom out. Fighting the urge to kiss my savior, I released the rail and stepped back.

I was about to follow them down and out of the tower, but I couldn't stop myself from glancing up at the final level. I was exactly twenty-five steps from the top. An overwhelming impulse to see the final level of the tower filled me. I had come this far after all.

Moving up the last stairs, I stepped onto the final level. After seven floors of ash, the eighth, stretching high above the rest of the school, showed no signs of ever being set on fire. The seamless wall of windows displayed a moonlit panoramic view of the surrounding jagged mountains.

A whistle rang up the stairs.

Jerking away from the window, I spun to face the door. The shadows were unoccupied.

Inching forward, I peered over the railing. A shadow slipped into the seventh level.

I flattened myself against the wall. My heart broke into a sprint. Magic flared through my chest toward my shoulder. But I had left my wand in my room. Without it, my magic had nowhere to go, and I had no way to protect myself.

Calm down. It's probably just Moose and Mr. While. They probably figured out I was following them and they decided to give me a heart attack as payback.

Or it could have something to do with the fact that the tower is haunted. Remember that? I mentally kicked myself. *Master Lenin could be a serial killer, and I'm in his territory.*

My instincts told me to run, but in order to do that, I would have to head toward the shadow. The only other option was to throw myself out of the tower.

Muttering all the curses I knew, I forced myself down the stairs. I tried not to think about the other bare footprints that followed mine up to the top floor.

When I stepped onto the seventh level, I paused in the doorway. My heart raced around my chest as I looked around the rotunda.

It was empty.

Thank God.

I took two running steps toward the door. From the left came a flash seconds before someone slammed me into the wall.

My shoes clattered to the floor as I screamed.

41

In Over Your Head

The ghost of the North Tower stood six inches in front of me.

She wore a gown that belonged to fashion decades ago. Her hair was unkempt and loose like she had been tossed around. Blood matted her temple, trapping a lock of hair to her cheek.

Deep gashes marred her wrists. There was a matching small cut under the side of her jaw. Blood, frozen and black, painted the side of her neck and ruined the neckline of her gown. The worst was a gaping wound beneath her heart that stained the front of her dress.

Her nails dug into my arms as she pressed me against the wall. "You shouldn't be here."

Cheese and rice, I'm face to face with a ghost. Am I even breathing?

"What?" She tilted her head, bringing her face closer to mine. "Cat got your tongue? How did you get in here?"

"I—I followed—" I gestured clumsily toward the stairs. "Holy shit. You're Blaine Willow."

She arched an elegant eyebrow. "You thought I was the main star of a horror story." Her grip tightened. Her nails broke through my skin sending drops of blood running down my arms. "Does that feel real enough for you?" Shoving me back into the wall, she spun away taking her sharp chill with her.

"I'm Charlie."

"I don't care." She turned to the shadows.

"Wait!" My heart tripped over itself as it tried to keep beating. "I need to know who killed you."

"Your words are ones of courage, yet your voice trembles." She turned to me with a flare of her skirt. "Need is a strong word. Why do you *need* to know?" she asked mockingly.

"Because . . ." A couple lies spun across my tongue, but for once I forced them down my throat. "Because I was pulled into something, and I want to make sure the men I'm working for aren't as evil as I think they are."

Interest sparked in Blaine's eyes. "Aren't you a little young to be dealing with evil?"

"Life likes to screw me over."

Blaine looked at the blood on her fingertips. "No kidding."

"I think whoever killed you might be one of the men I'm working for," I continued slowly. "If it is, we can destroy your killer and set me free. Two birds with one stone."

"Get lost, kid. You're in over your head."

"I usually am. Please, I need to know if I'm helping a murderer or if I'm on the right side of this war."

"War?" Her eyes squinted. "You look a little young to be dealing with life and death."

"Please," I said. "I need your help."

"Even if I did help you, you can't handle him. He's clever and resourceful. On the night I died, I hit my head." She gestured to the hair stiff with blood near her temple. "Instead of going for help, he took my magic, cut me into pieces and then threw me into the river. To keep the Hunters off the scent, he poured cleansing potions into the river to erase the evidence of blood."

"Hunters—do you mean Michael Kale?"

Blaine shook her head. "Enough. Just because you're a Royal doesn't mean you can handle this."

Seeing my shocked expression, she gestured to my scratched arm. "You can tell a lot about a User from their blood. And yours is very interesting." Blaine crossed her arms. "He will kill you, steal your magic, and then you'll end up in his collection. That's how it works."

Goosebumps rose over my skin. "Death doesn't scare me."

"Huh." Her eyes narrowed. "You actually believe that."

"There are worse things."

"You don't have to tell me." Mindlessly, she traced the wounds on her wrist.

I dared to step away from the wall. "Who did this to you?"

Blaine shook her head causing her messy hair to fly around her face. "He cursed my words. I cannot tell you. I cannot write it down. If I think of his name, pain explodes through my mind."

"What if I gave you a name? Could you confirm or deny?" I lined up Master Lenin's name on the tip of my tongue to spit out the moment she answered.

But she shook her head. "His curse is thorough. I wouldn't be able to nod, give you a thumbs up, or a wink."

Damn.

"There has to be some way you can help," I pressed.

"What makes you think I want to help?"

"Because even after you knew how much magic I have, you told me to leave instead of throwing me down the stairs for him to kill." I crossed my fingers hoping I was right. "You want to stop him just as much as I do."

Her bloody eyebrow arched.

"Ok, fine. You want him stopped more, but you know what I mean." I paused, giving her time to voice any objections. When she didn't, I asked, "There has to be something you can do."

Her grey eyes stared at me, unblinking. As the night wind whistled by the windows I couldn't tell if she was considering answering me or throwing me down the stairs. The char-covered room grew colder the longer we stood still.

Finally, she sighed. "You're not the first person to come here demanding that I tell them what I know. I have something." She rolled her eyes. "If I had known how much trouble that diary was going to be, I would've burned it. At least then—" She slapped her hands on her head and let out a small, muffled scream.

"My diary," she continued after a moment, "has an account of my time here. Inside are the clues to put together his identity. He knew this and practically destroyed my room trying to find it."

Hope sparked in my chest. "But you hid it."

"Of course. I'm not an idiot." She kept her eyes closed for a few seconds. "I hid it with a powerful enchantment. I left instructions for my friend hoping she would find it and give it to a School Master or someone with enough authority to do something, but her brain function wasn't what I hoped."

In a blink, she appeared inches from my face. "I'll only say this once," she whispered, "for I fear he might overhear. I will be by your side every second of every day. If you try to tell him my cursed words, I'll rip out your throat. He can't get his hands on what is in there. Or else what is happening here will happen everywhere."

She moved so close that her chill sucked all the warmth from my body. I knew her lips were right by my ear but I didn't feel any breath with her next words.

"A blue-lined notion will guide you to a piece of shining night. The north beacon will tell of my lover's curse. He craves the radiant taste of control. But the very thing he hunts has turned him black."

Cheese and rice, I suck at solving riddles. "A blue-lined notion?"

"In the place I loved most. This tower may have been my hiding place, but it was never my favorite."

Blaine stepped back, taking her horrible chill with her. "Trust no one, for you know not who you can trust. He's powerful enough to have ears in the walls and eyes in the shadows. Don't come back here. He's always watching. You were lucky tonight because he was preoccupied."

"What if I need to talk to you again? The door is locked."

She laughed a beautiful, silvery laugh that didn't belong in dark, ashy towers. "No one enters this tower without permission from its lady. Whistle and the locks shall spring. Now go, before he comes back."

She sprang forward. Before I could flinch back, she grasped my shoulders. The cold that emanated from her body soaked through her fingers and into my skin. It crystalized over my bones, stilling my blood and breath. Struggling to breath, I squeezed my eyes shut.

Just as quickly as she had grabbed, she let me go. The bitter cold, however, receded more slowly. Sucking in a deep breath, my eyes sprang open. My breath clouded the air before me as I spun around looking for the woman in grey.

She was gone and so was the tower.

I was at the far end of the North Wing beside the gold doors leading to the stairwell. Eerily, music from the dining room crooned softly through the closed doors.

I turned my back to the stairwell and faced the darkness hiding the door to the North Tower. My shoes sat upright by my feet. Blaine managed to transport me six levels down and across an entire wing without so much as ruffling my hair.

With my mind reeling, I collected my shoes and stumbled through the North Wing doors into the stairwell. The lights were so bright they actually hurt my eyes. The music, conversations, and clicking shoes of the party were deafening compared to the silence of the tower.

I scanned the crowd for Moose's ponytail, but she was nowhere in sight.

Standing on my tiptoes, I hopped from one foot to the other trying to locate one of the people from our investigating group. The closest was Clarence who was levitating a cup of punch over to a low status classmate. With a look of pure boredom, he prepared to tip it over the student's head.

I was about to run toward him when I actually looked down at myself. My feet were black with soot. The bright red fabric of my dress was splattered with ash. Bloody crescent moons from Blaine's nails were mirrored on each arm. Going in there looking like that would draw more attention.

I looked around for something to throw at him to get his attention. In one hand I had my shoes and in the other I still had the chocolate Daniel gave me.

I took one of my shoes and hurled it at Clarence. A small sting of magic shocked my fingertips as it left my grasp. The shoe tumbled end over end and smacked him in the middle of his back.

He spun around looking for a fight. That died quickly when he saw me waving for him. Rolling his eyes, he picked up the shoe and walked over.

"Damn, Red, if you don't approve, you don't have to stone me with footwear." He stopped when he got closer. He took in the ash and smudged blood on my arms. Quickly, he pulled me from the doorway. "What the hell happened to you?"

"I got it! I know how to find a link to Master Lenin."

"Keep your voice down," he snapped. He roughly brushed his hand across my forehead, trying to remove some of the ash. "Now, what are you going on about?"

I batted his hand away. "I followed Moose and Mr. While into the North Tower—"

Shock lifted his eyebrows and widened his eyes. "You did what?"

"I saw her, Clarence. I saw Blaine Willow. She's still there. She's a creepy ghost, but she's still there."

His Adam's apple bobbed. "You saw the ghost of the tower? That ain't a good thing, Charlie. People who see her end up hurt."

My excitement stalled. "What?"

"During my first year, a girl ran around saying she saw the ghost. A month later she was found at the bottom of the East Tower unconscious. It was a coma she never woke up from. Stuff like that's been happening ever since she took up residence. Why do you think Lenin closed off the entire wing?"

Chills raced over my skin. "It doesn't matter."

"Fine. If you die, don't come back to haunt me."

"Will you stop for a minute?" He opened his mouth, but I rushed on. "She gave me a riddle. If we solve it, we can find her diary, which will tell us who killed her."

Interest ignited in his eyes. "Are you serious? What did she say?"

I shook my head. "I think everyone should hear it at the same time."

He looked me over. "You can't go in there looking like that. Call it a night and I'll tell the crew to meet in the library in the morning."

I nodded, already moving toward the stairs. I made it to my room with ten minutes to spare before my lesson with Michael. I was still covered in ash. But I couldn't clean up yet.

I dove for my school bag and ripped open a random notebook. I flipped past potion brewing temperatures till I found a blank page.

I jotted down the riddle so fast my handwriting was barely legible.

Tossing the notebook aside, I tore off the ruined dress and rinsed off the stench of smoke clinging to my skin. Having a lot of practice, I wrapped Blaine's fingernail marks tight with gauze and pulled a long sleeve shirt over my head. As soon as the transporter beeped, I grabbed it.

Michael froze when he saw me. I guess it was his version of startling. "I never thought I'd see the day you were on time." He smirked, but only for a second. "Miracles do exist."

"I have to keep you on your toes."

"Don't give yourself too much credit. You're still dull as a rock." Unzipping his leather jacket, he reached beneath his arm and tugged his wand from the holster strapped across his shoulders.

"Come on." He nodded to the wand in my hand. "Let's go."

I so badly wanted to tell him that his impatience was the most annoying thing about him but I didn't want to piss him off. He'd probably lengthen the lesson out of spite, and I couldn't have that.

I had things to do.

So, I bit my tongue, pulled on my magic, and got to work.

42

The Records Keeper

The next morning I ran down the last flight of stairs into the library.

It was so early Mr. While wasn't even in. No student in their right mind would be here before breakfast, which meant the bright blue line on the ceiling pointing toward the back belonged to my accomplices.

I followed the light to where tables were laid out for intense studying. Walking past rows of computers, I found my group near the back wall.

"There better be a good reason why I'm awake this early. And why I'm in the library," Nirean groaned. She had thrown herself across a table with her arms crossed over her face.

"It ain't that early." Clarence glanced down the main aisle toward the door. "Where's Ace?"

Nirean dropped her arms. "Her *parents,*" she spat, "picked her up this morning. They decided to transfer her to Aquarius. They're keeping her home until the paperwork goes through."

"You're kidding." I dropped into the seat across from her. Seeing Nirean by herself was like looking at a puzzle without the edge pieces. She was incomplete. Not to mention lonely.

"Why?" I asked.

"Something about them wanting her to change the focus of her studies. But really, they're scared of her being around Master Lenin."

"You can't blame 'em," Clarence muttered. "This school is a shit show compared to the others."

"But they don't know that!"

"They know it's haunted and that the School Master is working with a Master Hunter. That's not even mentioning that a teacher died here last month."

Nirean rolled her eyes. "But out of all the great schools, Aquarius? She's practically albino! She can't tan to save her life." She crossed her arms back over her face. "And she hates the ocean."

"I don't see why you're so bent out of shape," Clarence said. "I'm sure you can call her any time you want."

"There's a twelve-hour time difference and Master Lenin limits the time we're allowed reflective calls," Nirean said.

Clarence shrugged, obviously not affected nor sympathetic to our party losing a member.

"Where is Aquarius?" I asked, hoping the answer wasn't well known in the magical world.

"Somewhere on an Australian coast," Nirean grumbled.

"I'm sorry," I said softly. I cut Clarence a scornful glance, before looking back at Nirean. "Did you get to say goodbye?"

"Barely. Her mom didn't even let her pack. They're sending someone to get her stuff later today."

Moose skipped around the corner and plopped into the chair beside me. "Good morning!"

"I hate morning people," Nirean grumbled.

"I barely slept once I got Clarence's message," she said, pulling her book bag into her lap. "I didn't know which was more impressive, the fact that you called a meeting or that you knew where the library was."

Clarence grinned tightly.

"Where's Ace?" Moose glanced around the library like Clarence had.

"Working on her tan." Clarence nodded at me. "The floor's yours, darlin'."

I had no idea where to start. Everything I wanted to say flooded into my mouth. I fumbled in my pocket and handed the riddle to Moose.

As she read it over, her eyebrows pulled together as questions collected in her eye. "What's this?"

"It's going to lead us to Blaine Willow's diary," I said. "She documented her life, so we should find the name of her killer inside it."

"That's convenient," Nirean said slowly.

"I'll take convenient if it gets us out of this mess sooner." Moose pulled the paper closer. "It doesn't make any sense. Where'd you get it?"

"Uh . . . I got it in the North Tower. I followed you and Mr. While last night."

Nirean sat up to look down at her. "You were with the Book King?"

Moose's gaze lifted from the page. "*You were spying on me?*"

"She was making sure a sketchy situation didn't turn into a stupid decision," Clarence defended me. "You should thank her for giving a damn."

"He wouldn't have done anything."

"You don't know that. Until we confirm that it's Master Lenin, any teacher could be the killer."

"He's a Deficient. Every victim so far has been a Royal or a High Common. It's impossible for a Deficient to overpower that kind of magic." Moose crossed her arms. "He physically cannot be the killer."

"That doesn't mean you should go sneaking around with a goddamn teacher."

"For your information, I went with him so I could see what he knew about the tower and Blaine Willow. That's more than you've done." She lifted up the paper. "So where did this come from?"

"Blaine Willow gave it to her," Clarence stated flatly.

Moose was out of her chair and in my face within a second. "Are you serious? You should've started with that. What did she look like? What did she say?"

"All that matters is that we have a riddle to solve." Clarence leaned back against the bookcase. "One that can give us a direct link to Master Lenin."

"Why did she give you a riddle instead of just telling you where she hid it?" Nirean asked.

"She said something about him cursing her words," I explained.

"She didn't happen to say who 'he' was, did she?" Moose asked hopefully.

I shook my head. "Every time she thought of saying his name, she got a headache."

"Of course, this couldn't be easy." Nirean flopped back on to the table. "Well, what's the first line say?"

"As much as I want to hang around and solve the damn thing, we can't." Clarence glanced at his watch. "If we miss breakfast all together, someone will notice."

Moose looked pained to be agreeing with him. "Let's make copies. That way we can work on it on our own time." She took sheets from her notebook and started pressing her wand to the different pages.

"Just a second." Nirean ripped Clarence's copy from his hands. "If we're going to do this, we need to be smart. You don't get one."

"Why the hell not?" Clarence reached for the paper.

Nirean slid further into the middle of the table. "Your apartment gets searched once a week and sometimes more because of the mermaid reed found there two months ago. If the cleaning crew found this and handed it to Master Lenin, we'd be screwed."

"I won't label it *secret tower riddle*." Clarence made a reach for it again.

"I agree with Nirean," Moose interjected. "You can help someone with their copy but you don't get your own."

"Oh, come on! You can't be serious."

"I'm dead serious." Moose turned to the rest of our group. "If you think you have a breakthrough with the riddle, alert everyone. The sooner we get this decoded, the faster we put this behind us."

"I *could* help with the faster part," Clarence said dryly.

Ignoring him, Moose handed the original copy back to me. "In the meantime, we need to learn everything we can about Blaine Willow. What classes she took when she was alive, who her friends were, what clubs she was a part of. Anything that can help us solve this." She flicked the copy in her hand.

"Ace and I can start going through the yearbooks," Nirean said. Her mood soured. "I can see who she hung out with."

An idea popped into my head. "Would the Attendance Records have which classes she took?"

Nirean groaned. "Please tell me we aren't going back into the Records Room. We can't do that without Ace."

Moose slowly nodded. "Yes, and what clubs she was a part of, but Nirean's right. We can't go back in there. I don't think we're lucky enough for a second go."

"I wasn't thinking of breaking in." The thought of doing that again made my empty stomach churn. "Daniel Phillips maintains the records for Master Lenin."

A laugh erupted from Clarence. He laughed so hard he ran out of breath. "You wanna ask Einstein for help? He'd never let you in— not with that stick up his ass."

"If Charlie asks him, he might. He was flirting pretty hard with her last night," Nirean said, with a broad smile. She glanced to her left but didn't find Ace's snickering face to back her up.

My cheeks flamed bright red.

"I thought you weren't going to be here long enough to see the end of this," Moose said with a small smile. "It almost sounds like you're finally owning a bit of this."

"Einstein is a long shot," Clarence drawled. "He's been kissing Master Lenin's ass longer than Moose has. How do you think he became the Record Keeper?"

"Oh, I don't know," Moose said dryly. "Maybe by working hard and *not* being a pain in everyone's ass?"

"He'll never bring you down there," Clarence said to me. "He'll run straight to Master Lenin the moment you ask. He follows the rules as if they were gods."

"I thought the same thing about Moose and then she helped us break into the Records Room." Nirean turned her tired eyes to Moose. "I thought for sure you would back out or pass out. You did pretty good."

Moose struggled to remain unaffected by the compliment. She scrunched her lips together to keep a smile from blooming, but she couldn't do anything about the glow in her eyes.

"Long shot or not, ask Einstein," Moose said. "Meanwhile, I'll see if I can get anything from Mr. While. He went to school with Blaine. He might know some school drama that didn't translate into school records." She folded up her copy of the riddle and headed down the main aisle toward the stairwell.

Yawning, Nirean dragged herself off the table and followed after her.

"Stupid Common," Clarence snarled at Moose's retreating figure. "I can help."

"She's right to be careful. Especially with a School Master involved."

Clarence rolled his eyes. "Whatever. I can help, but if you want to drag this out, be my guest." Pushing away from the bookcase, he shook his head.

"Good luck would've been just fine," I mumbled, stuffing the riddle back into my pocket.

Walking out of the library, I smoothed my hair back in place. Whatever Cornelia had done to it somehow survived last night's adventure and a shower. Taking a deep breath, I walked into the dining room and zeroed in on my target.

Daniel was already looking at the door when I walked in. He smiled and waved. The guys around his table looked over and mimicked him. Only when they did it, it wasn't as charming.

With my stomach full of knots, I walked over. Daniel did a double take when he saw me heading toward his table.

The same warmth from the night before spilled into his gaze.

My steps faltered. In the library, it was easy to talk about him as a next move, the dotted line from what we needed and how to get it. But looking at him, I was reminded that he was just a young man who showed kindness to a total stranger on her first day and then, despite being avoided for a full month, had extended the same quiet affection to a girl standing alone at a party.

Janet Raven.

Holly Blackwell.

Remember why you're doing this, Charlie.

"Good morning," he said cheerfully when I reached his table. His bright mood acted like a kick to the gut. He should be cold or at least wary of me for leaving him, but he just smiled up at me.

"Morning." I pushed my guilt to the side as best as I could. "Can I talk to you for a minute?"

His friends around the table chuckled. One wagged his eyebrows at me.

"Of course." Daniel collected his breakfast plate and stood. Before I could change my mind, I moved to an empty section of the dining room.

"I owe you an apology," I blurted. *Come on. Keep it together.* I took a deep breath to settle myself. "Last night I just left you by the mailboxes. My headache turned into a migraine. Whatever Helen gave me knocked me out for the rest of the night."

"Don't worry about it." Daniel waved his hand in a placating gesture. "I'm glad you're feeling better."

My stomach tightened with guilt. Half of me wanted to leave it at that, but I kept going.

"I want to make it up to you, somehow, but everything I think of doesn't make up for abandoning you." The lies tasted bitter on my tongue. "I'd offer to help you with your homework, but I'd probably do more harm than good."

He actually smirked at me. "My grades are fine, thanks."

I shifted my bag from one shoulder to the other. "What about the Records Room? Do you need any help in there?" My heart started to run like a hamster on its wheel.

"It's fine, Charlie."

"Are you just saying that though? Because I don't mind helping."

A smile tugged at the corner of his lips. He was too polite. There was no way he was going to accept. I could see the artfully crafted excuses bubbling to the front of his mouth.

"How about this?" I offered. "I meet you here after dinner and then I can help you with whatever until curfew?"

"I'm not really supposed to let people in there," he said slowly.

So, he was considering it! Hope filled my chest. He just needed a little push. "I'll be careful. No one will ever know I was there." I clasped my hands in front of me. "Please? I know it sounds like I'm asking, but I'm really not."

His smile grew. "You really feel that bad?"

"I feel awful."

Sighing, he put down his cup of juice. "Fine. After dinner I'll grab you."

"Perfect. I'll see you then. And if I don't see you after dinner, I'll just end up outside the Records Room and that will be hard to explain to Master Lenin."

"Ok, fine." He laughed. "I won't back out."

"Good." Spinning around, I walked to the breakfast line. Passing Moose and Nirean, I gave them a thumbs up.

The knots in my stomach followed me throughout the rest of the day. I was used to lying to people; it was practically my second language. But I hadn't done it to someone who didn't deserve it. With Blake, I always told myself it was for his own good. But with Daniel no matter how I tried to justify it, the excuse felt weak.

You're leaving as soon as you can. So why does it matter?

I couldn't put my finger on it. I just hoped Daniel never found out about any of it. The hurt look that would fall over his face, the coldness in his eyes when he looked at me— *He won't look at you because you'll be gone.*

I spent the rest of the day trying to figure out how I was going to look back decades into the records without making Daniel suspicious and appear to be helpful at the same time.

When dinner rolled around, I could barely get the food down my throat. It was like swallowing rocks.

I dropped my fork with a clang to my plate. Running my hands through my hair, I tried to block out the sounds of silverware scratching against plates and the clatter of students.

Get in, play nice, and get out. Get answers and run.

Someone tapped my shoulder.

Taking a deep breath, I put on a smile fake as plastic and turned. "Hey you."

"You really don't have to do this," Daniel said. "I think a coffee at the glasshouse would be just as fine."

I shook my head. "I've already made up my mind." Grabbing my bag, I jumped to my feet.

Daniel smiled. "Do you have gloves?"

"No. Should I?"

"You can borrow one of mine. You won't believe how dry your hands can get from touching so much old paper." He grabbed my bag and slung it over his shoulder with ease.

"Speaking from experience?" I asked as we left the dining room.

"My hands cracked so much that I was bleeding all over my homework." He pulled a worn leather glove from his back pocket and handed it to me.

With that mental picture, I tugged the glove onto my dominant hand.

As we descended to the lower level, he turned his curious gaze my way. "So, what's your story?"

"What makes you think there is one?"

"A mysterious girl transfers to a taboo school in the middle of the year with a single red lock of hair and no legacy backing her." He arched his eyebrow at me. "There has to be a story."

I knew I was going to have to lie to him again. And I hated myself for it.

Just as I opened my mouth to answer, he held up one finger. "Hold that thought."

We stepped off the last step onto the teacher's level. Tessa Baker looked up at the sound of our footsteps.

"Good evening, Mr. Phillips," she said with a smile. "And Miss Heart. What can I do for you?"

"I'm just going to finish up the records for the year." Daniel propped his elbow on the high edge of the desk. "Charlie was going to keep me company."

"No unauthorized Users are allowed in the Records Room," Tessa said without losing her professional politeness.

"I know that." Daniel nodded his head. "But you see, I double booked myself. I was supposed to be prepping her for finals this evening, but I also told Master Lenin I'd be done with the records tonight."

"Then it seems that you need to learn time management, Mr. Phillips."

"So my mom keeps telling me," Daniel chuckled. "I figured I could do both."

"Miss Heart is unauthorized." When her eyes flickered toward me, I donned my sweetest, most innocent smile.

"I figured since Master Lenin *himself* brought her into the school that that might sway you."

Tessa shook her head.

My fingernails bit into my palms. This was going sideways fast.

"I'll watch her the whole time," Daniel assured her. "If anything happens, I'll take personal responsibility for all of it. I'll even tell Master Lenin that you had nothing to do with it. It was all my idea."

No. It was all my idea.

Tessa sighed. "Master Lenin will be back by curfew. I suggest you be done by then."

"We'll be done well before then." He drummed his fingers against the desktop. "Thank you!"

"Don't make me regret this."

"I wouldn't dream of it." Daniel placed his hand on my lower back and guided me away from the desk. I could feel the heat from his palm even through my thick sweater.

Focus. I forced myself to step away from his touch. "Did you just lie to her? I didn't think you were the type."

"Does that mean you've been thinking of me?"

Heat flooded my cheeks. "What? No! I mean—"

"Have you been trying to figure me out?"

"No. It's just—everyone calls you Einstein. They treat you like the gold standard of the school."

"They call me Einstein because I'm smart. You can be smart and duck under rules." He grinned. "But you're getting us off topic. I stopped you earlier from answering." He twisted his wrist in a gesture that told me to continue.

Right.

"I was born and raised in houses all over Kansas. My mom is MIA, and my father isn't interested. I went to a small school until Master Lenin gave me a scholarship here." Time to get the spotlight off of me. "What about you?"

"That was extremely vague."

"I hate to break it to you, but my life's just not that interesting. Are you avoiding my question?"

He shot me a smile. "I'm a native to Camden, Maine where my mom and stepdad live. My actual dad is in London. I have an older brother, Sam, and a younger sister, Erin." His smile grew. "She's already stressing about which school she wants to attend."

I shook my head. I had no idea what it was like to have a family that you smiled about. Envy curled around my chest. How could some people win the family lottery, while others only drew blanks?

My train of thought was interrupted when the Records Room came into view.

Walking up to the door, Daniel shrugged off his bag and dug out a large set of keys.

"That's a lot of keys," I noted nonchalantly.

"There's a key for every door in the school." Obviously familiar with the ring, he selected the right key and placed it into the lock.

As he pushed open the door a wave of uneasiness flooded my stomach. Did Daniel have a key to the North Tower? How old was he? He looked my age, but magic could alter how you looked.

Remember, anyone who can get into the tower could be the killer.

As the golden glow of protective magic filled the doorway, Daniel selected another key. This one he pressed against the wall of magic. The moment the key and ward touched, the gold glow swirled away from the doorframe and settled into the key.

Daniel stepped inside and the chandeliers filled with fire, illuminating the large, round room. Without pause he walked confidently down the aisle.

The last time I was here I hadn't bothered to look past the first row of shelves where the death records were stored. Not that I really had time to.

Daniel led me deeper into the room until we reached an intersection. The school's crest, a compass rose encircled by the school's name, was etched into the obsidian floor.

I looked back at the door and judged the distance from when I was last there. Was this where Clarence disappeared too? I looked down at the school crest. It looked just like every other engraving or pin I had seen.

"So, what's the plan?" I asked, pulling my gaze up from the floor.

Daniel set our bags beside a deep cart partially filled with scrolls.

"I was hoping you would sit there and just keep me company."

"Not a chance. How can I help?"

His dimples appeared again. "Each student signs one of these scrolls at the beginning of the year. After they're signed, they come down here where I alphabetize them on those shelves." He gestured to the shelves surrounding us.

There were four distinct sections of shelves. Instead of holding books, the shelves were divided into slots just big enough for a single scroll. Under each slot was a gold plate with a student's name.

Perfect.

"I'm usually done by this time of year," Daniel said. "But a couple classes have proved to be more challenging than I thought."

"Can't you use some kind of magic to put them all away for you?" I asked, looking at the number of scrolls in the cart.

"I wish. Unfortunately, for security reasons, only minor charms can be used down here." He moved to the opposite side of the cart. "I can't even use a levitation charm. Without it, I guess I'd be out of a job and my resume would be shorter."

"What's in the scrolls?"

"Everything." He pulled open a random scroll. Running his finger down the paper, he pointed. "Name, birthday, home address, status, grades, room number, classes, teachers, and a bunch of miscellaneous stuff, like where you hang out and every offense you've had in school. It's almost scary how much they know."

I laughed, but for an entirely different reason. This was too easy. "So, what do I do?"

"You really don't have to—"

"What do I do?"

With a sigh, he reached into the cart. "Just grab a scroll and put it on the correct shelf. Each section is alphabetized so it's easy." He was already moving toward the back with a scroll in hand.

I grabbed a scroll and rolled it open. Maxwell Charles.

Damn. Blaine's scroll would be in the Ws. The Cs were about as far from the Ws as it could get. It would be too obvious if I took the scenic route to the Cs. I'd have to wait for a W or something closer.

"Have you ever looked at your own record?" I called to Daniel as I climbed a ladder and stuck the scroll in its empty slot.

He rounded the corner and helped me down. "I did once, when I first started as Records Keeper. I was paranoid for a week wondering if someone was watching me. But when I came back here, I saw how much dust was on them. I figured they hardly check them."

"Have you ever been tempted to look at anyone else's?" I asked as we headed back to the middle of the room.

"Of course, but I never have." He plucked another scroll from the cart. "I'd hate it if someone went snooping through mine and knew everything about me."

I found myself smiling at him, then quickly stopped myself. I tried to remind myself that no man is that good. The scars on my back proved that much, but that didn't stop every nerve in my body from being attuned to where he was.

"I hate to pry," he called from another shelf. "But what happened to your mom?"

"No clue." I stood on my tiptoes and pushed a scroll into its new home. "She's either dead or running around somewhere."

"So, you were raised by your dad?"

I wonder what that would've been like. I shook the chills off my skin. "No. They dumped me in a trashcan the first chance they got." I froze in front of the cart. The only person I had told that to was Blake.

"Did you grow up with another family member?" He came around the shelves and stopped beside me.

Unable to meet his gaze, I fished around the cart for no scroll in particular. "No, I actually grew up in foster care."

"And you landed a spot in one of the greatest schools anyway." He smiled. "That's impressive. Most Users in your position would've stayed in low grade schools."

My cheeks heated at his words. No one had called me impressive before. *Stop it, Charlie. He's not complimenting you. He's complimenting the lie Michael and Master Lenin gave you.*

"Have you ever thought about wanting to meet them?" he asked. "Your parents."

"No. I figured if they didn't want me in the beginning, they wouldn't now. After the way that I grew up, it didn't matter if they ever changed their minds. They lost their chance."

His expression was soft and sincere. "It's their loss."

I couldn't help but smile back.

Reaching into the cart, he grabbed an arm load of scrolls. "I mean—" he cleared his throat. "You got into a prestigious school without them. That says a lot."

"That was pure dumb luck." I reached into the bin and picked up a scroll.

"No one gets into the Magisterium without connections or supreme intelligence. Since you don't have connections . . ." He trailed off, leaving me to fill in the blank.

I dropped my gaze to the scroll in my hands. Little did he know I did have a connection.

Unrolling the scroll, I froze at the name artfully scripted at the top.

Boone Augustus Watson.

Butterflies assaulted my stomach. I had my window.

"Do you have any idea what apprenticeship you want?" he called over his shoulder. With his arms full of scrolls, he strolled toward the back.

I really need to start a list of questions to ask Moose.

"Not really. I'm kind of just waiting to see what will come my way." I grabbed a few extra scrolls, adding to my cover, and headed in the opposite direction as Daniel.

Once out of sight I stuck the other scrolls under one arm and took out a blank piece of paper I had grabbed for this purpose. Deep in the Records Room, the W section towered over me.

"That's smart!" he said. "You don't get your hopes up and you keep your options open. I wish I had the same flexibility."

"What about you?" I called back. "Do you have one in mind?" I hoped that was the right question to ask.

Trapping the paper between my teeth I quickly scaled the ladder. Willow . . . I ran my fingers down the nameplates, passing Whatts and Wills.

"I'd like to apprentice with a Master of Criminal Law or maybe a Master of Languages. But I don't know."

My heart squeezed in my chest as my fingers touched Willow. Glancing both ways down the aisle I pulled it into my hands.

I unrolled it and read, *Blaine Francis Willow.*

With shaking fingers, I took out my wand and touched it to the scroll. My fingers tingled with magic as I quickly rolled it up and put it back on the shelf.

Taking the paper from my teeth, I called back, "Why don't you?" I touched my wand to the paper and pulled on my magic. The moment all the information pooled on the page, I stuffed it back into my pocket and hid my wand.

"My dad—my biological dad—has strong objections. He already has a path laid out for me to Master in the magical arts."

Untucking the other scrolls from beneath my arm, I scampered into another aisle and put them away. All the while my heart knocked heavily against my ribs.

Dropping off the ladder, I went back to the middle of the room. "I'm guessing you don't like those plans."

Daniel turned away from the bin and leaned back against it. He was completely oblivious to what was in my pocket.

"I'm not against them. I just don't know if I want to follow in his footsteps." He rushed on before I could vocalize my curiosity. "I don't want to dominate your evening. I think you've served your sentence. But first," he tossed me a scroll, "these are the last two scrolls. I'll race you."

I looked at the name. Katherine Smith. What could it hurt? I might be able to run off some of the nerves shaking my hands. "You're on."

We lined up behind the school crest in the middle of the room. My toes covered the very edge of the intricate compass rose. Putting one foot in front of the other, we set to launch into the maze of shelves.

"On my mark," he said, with mischief glittering in his hazel eyes. "Get set . . . GO!"

I bolted into the shelves counting them in my head as I passed. I could hear his feet pounding on the obsidian floor not too far behind me.

Almost flying up the ladder, I ran my hands down the names. I plopped it in its slot and jumped off.

Running as fast as I could back to the cart, I rounded the corner and stopped.

He was leaning against the bin with a smirk of satisfaction. "Well, aren't you the slowest person ever."

"What name did you have?" I panted.

He hesitated. "Frank Adams."

I smacked his shoulder. "Your name was closer. I had Katherine Smith!"

He shook his head. "Excuses, excuses. I still won." He grabbed both our bags and headed for the door.

We chatted effortlessly as we walked up to the seventh floor. I forgot about the riddle or the information in my pocket. Daniel had me completely captivated.

<h1 style="text-align:center">43</h1>

<h1 style="text-align:center">Blaine Willow</h1>

"Thank you for helping," Daniel said when we reached my door.

He pulled my bag off his shoulder and offered it to me. "That's probably the most fun I've ever had doing that." He cleared his throat. "Can I count on another race?"

I found myself smiling. "As long as you don't cheat." I stretched my arms over my head. "I'll start training to kick your butt."

"Good luck. I've got years on you, new girl." His eyes flickered over my shoulder. His playful gaze turned curious. "Did you leave your door open?"

"What?" Turning around, my blood stilled when I saw my door was open a crack. My hand dropped to the wand in the pocket along my thigh.

"Hey," Daniel said softly. Gently taking my arm, he pulled me behind him. Setting down his bags, he nudged open the door. His tense shoulders sagged. "Uh, hey Clarence."

"Clarence?" I stepped into the room and found the southern spitfire sitting on my couch like it was his apartment.

My eyes snapped to Daniel. The playful spark in his eyes had given way to a jaw stiff of annoyance.

The way Clarence had made himself at home—his arm stretched across the back of my couch, the smug curl of his lips—I knew Daniel could only assume one thing.

My stomach dropped.

I shouldn't have cared what Daniel thought of all of it. But I did. I so did.

340

"Daniel—"

"About time you showed up." Clarence pushed the books off his lap. "I was starting to think Einstein locked you down there."

Daniel's expression became bored. "Thanks, man."

"How did you get in here?" I asked.

"I snagged your key from your bag this morning." He nodded to my coffee table where my keys sat. "So, was it as boring as I think it was? Did he bore you with equations and pop quizzes?"

"It was actually a lot of fun."

Clarence's eyes narrowed. "Your lips are saying one thing, but your eyes are saying another. If you're in distress, blink twice."

"What are you doing here?" I snapped.

"We're study partners, remember?" He gave me a pointed look.

The information in my pocket burned against my leg.

Clarence turned his smug look to Daniel. "This is where you leave, Einstein."

Turning his back to the intruder on my couch, Daniel dropped his voice. "Are you ok with him here? I can stay if you want."

Warmth glowed through my chest. "I'm good." That warmth fizzled out with the lie that tumbled effortlessly from my lips. "We're working on a paper together. I told him we'd work on it before lights out."

Daniel looked uncertainly over his shoulder. Clarence waved sardonically at him.

Biting back his annoyance, Daniel nodded. "Well, have fun with that. I guess I'll see you tomorrow." Offering me one last dimpled smile, he pulled the door closed behind him.

The sound of the door clicking shut shot through my heart like a bullet. How had we been laughing not a minute ago? And now he was gone and the night ruined.

You're leaving. What does it matter anyway? I didn't know the answer to that. I just knew that it did.

"If he was wound any tighter around your finger, I think you'd lose a digit," Clarence said.

"Do you ever get tired of hearing yourself talk?"

"Nope."

I dropped my bag on the kitchen counter and finally took out the paper containing Blaine Willow's information.

As I unfolded the page, Clarence cocked his head. "What? Did he give you his number?"

"It's Blaine Willow's student record," I answered with an edge. Clarence was off the couch in an instant, knocking his books to the floor.

"You actually got it?"

I nodded. "It wasn't hard."

I walked over to the couch and sank into the spot he just vacated. Plopping into the seat next to me, he looked over my shoulder.

Name: Blaine Francis Willow, Female
Date of Birth: February 17, 1974
Room: East Wing, #732
Residence: Brest, France
Magic Status: Royal 8
Highest Grade: A+
Lowest Grade: C+

Classes:
• Laws and Boundaries of Magic, Carmel
• Techniques of Magic Use, Geyer
• Wand Structure and Anatomy, Jung Advanced Wards, Myers
• Creature Studies, Harrison
• Royal Magic Control, Leatherwood
• Advanced Counter Wards, Penne User Anatomy, Solas

Extra Curriculars:
• Wand Shaping
• Badminton Girl's Club
• Chess Club
• Records Keeper
• Library Assistant

In-school Offenses: breaking curfew, trespassing outdoors, detaining library books

Choice Places: North Tower, South Tower, Library, Glasshouse

"Judging from her classes, she was studying to be a Master of the Magical Arts." Clarence scratched his head.

"Is that a good thing?"

He shrugged. "Most of the sorry saps in here aspire to get that title. Most of them change focuses in their third or fourth year. Those locations will be helpful." He pointed to the bottom of the paper, *Choice Places*.

"You think she hid her diary in one of them?"

"If you wanted to keep something secret, wouldn't you hide it in a place you knew really well?"

He had a point.

"Her being a Royal actually helps us. Back then statuses weren't allowed to mix. That limits who she would've been around."

"Meaning we don't have to look at the whole school, just her status group."

He nodded. "I bet Moose and her new friend Richard While could track down photos from her years here. Since Royals get all of the attention, I bet anyone around her was photographed."

"That's good for us."

"That's more work for us."

44

That Wasn't Subtle

A week passed.

Exactly seven days from the night we ventured down to the Records Room. Six days since I came face to face with a ghost. Five days from when I got Blaine Willow's student record.

And we were no closer to Blaine Willow's diary or confirming Master Lenin's involvement in the covered-up deaths of thirty-seven of his students.

I collapsed onto a bench in the dining room. My head dropped into my folded arms like it was severed from my neck. My eyelids were so heavy it felt like I was fighting with myself to keep them open.

My stomach rumbled, but I was tempted to ignore it. *If I don't get breakfast, I could steal a few more minutes of sleep before the clock chimes.*

"Say hi to Charlie."

I lifted my head just enough to peer over my arms. Nirean turned her phone to show Ace. She was sitting on a beach beneath a large blue umbrella. Her knees were pulled tightly to her chest as if the sun would flash fry her.

"Hi," Ace waved.

I lifted my fingers in a halfhearted wave. "How's Aquarius?"

She shrugged. "Hot."

"She got sunburned from head to toe on her first day." Nirean laughed. "Some of their classrooms are near the surface so they're basically sitting outside for a full hour."

Ace nodded. "Yep."

Nirean turned the phone back around. "Did you get that sunblock I sent you?"

Clarence tapped the butt of his fork against the back of my head. When I didn't move, he did it again.

"Knock it off." I swatted his hand away.

"If you ain't going to eat this, then I will." He shoved a plate across the table and into my elbow. "Moose got it for you. But if you don't want it—"

The buttery aroma of pancakes made my stomach rumble again. I pulled the plate toward me and grabbed the nearest fork. I hacked off a chunk of pancake and shoved it into my mouth. I thought about closing my eyes while I ate, but I was worried I'd actually fall asleep with food in my mouth.

During the daylight hours, Nirean, Moose, and I went about our normal routine. Breakfast, classes, lunch, classes, dinner, homework, and curfew. Clarence did whatever he liked, as was character for him.

However, after my late-night lessons with Michael, I'd sneak to the Southeast Wing to Moose's room. There I'd find Moose, Nirean, and Clarence nearly buried in notes and theories of ways to decipher Blaine Willow's twisted words. Clarence gave reports on his strolls through Blaine's choice areas—the North Tower, the South Tower, library, glasshouse—and if there were any places someone could stash a diary for a couple decades. He hadn't had much luck.

We called it a night around two or three. Then the cycle would repeat all over again.

"Dammit." Moose scribbled something into her notebook.

"What's eating at you?" Nirean asked over her phone. Tapping her thumb across the screen, she flipped the camera so Ace could see Moose's hunched shoulders.

"This part about shining night," Moose mumbled.

I almost flipped the table when I saw what she was working on. "Are you insane? Put that away!"

She pulled it to her lap and rubbed her eyes. "I think I might have something."

Nirean leaned closer, dropping her voice. "If anyone sees you—"

"They're too ignorant to know it's anything special." Moose sighed. "I might have a lead."

I scooted across the bench to sit next to her. "What do you have?"

"Blaine said her words were cursed. So I thought, maybe, these aren't the words she wanted to use. I've been swapping some of them out so they're easier to understand." She pointed to the first line. "Notion is another word for thought. Beacon could be referring to a signal or sign."

"Sounds like you still ain't any closer to solving it." Clarence leaned his elbows against the table.

"It's better than what we had last night." I turned to Moose. "Can you make me a copy? Maybe I could switch out some words you haven't thought of."

She shot me a skeptical look.

Ace's scoffing laughter bubbled from the phone, putting a smile on Nirean's face.

I rolled my eyes. "I'll use a thesaurus."

"I found something else," Moose said, handing me the fresh copy. "After looking through the yearbooks, I started collecting pictures of every name we found in the death records."

Nirean went green. "Why would you do that?"

"Yeah." I didn't have to see Ace's face to know her expression matched Nirean's.

"I was tired of them just being names." Moose shook her head. "Anyway, they all have something in common."

"We already knew that. Their statuses." Clarence took a pancake from my plate. "Why else would he bother?"

Moose looked down at the riddle in her lap. "All the girls look the same."

"What do you mean?" I asked.

"They all had dark hair and a pale complexion. They're even the same height, give or take a few inches."

My mind instantly jumped to Blaine Willow. When I saw her in the tower the moonlight glowed off her skin. Her hair, displaced and dried with blood, was as black as an oil spill. Janet Raven shared both of those characteristics.

"Holly was a blonde though," Nirean said softly.

Moose shook her head. "She dyed her hair a week before she died. She wanted it to be brown, but the charm she used was too strong and it turned black."

"But that doesn't make sense." Nirean cast a look around. "If Master Lenin is killing them for the war, he wouldn't be targeting them based on looks. He'd do it based on status, right?"

Moose nodded. "That's what I was thinking."

"You said all the girls looked alike," Clarence pointed out. "What do the fellas look like?"

"They're all over the place—blonds, brunettes. The only thing they have in common is they're either Royals or High Commons." Moose took off her glasses and rubbed her eyes.

"Why does this make less and less sense the more we look at it?" I asked.

"Seriously," Ace agreed through the phone.

Moose slipped her glasses into place. "I don't know."

The clock chimed.

All around the dining room, students rose from their seats almost in unison. The impending day halted our conversation. Nirean said goodbye to Ace and, with no choice but to gather our bags, we walked to class.

In Creature Studies, Moose headed right for our usual row in the middle of the room. She pulled out the riddle and hid it between the pages of her textbook. This was the first time I'd seen her not pay attention in class.

Still in the doorway, my gaze moved over the rows of tables and empty chairs until I found Daniel a couple levels up. He was already looking my way when our eyes met.

With a dimpled smile, he waved.

I looked at the empty spot beside Moose. It was where I usually sat. Maybe it was because I was tired to the point of a breakdown or maybe I just wanted a break from *everything*—the riddle, the lies, the war—but I found myself passing the row where Moose was hunched over the riddle.

Two rows up, I scooted behind a couple of occupied chairs until I stood beside Daniel.

"Is anyone sitting here?"

His dimples deepened. "You, if you'd like."

Grabbing the back of the chair, I dragged it away from the table and took a seat. Butterflies fluttered around my stomach. I forced myself to move with care as I took out my books and set them before me. When I was settled, I tried to keep my attention forward.

My left side, closest to him, felt as if the small rift between us was charged with electricity. At any moment, tiny bolts of lightning would flash from his skin to mine.

The teacher came in, closing the door behind her, and the class started instantly.

Just once, I gave in and peeked at Daniel from the corner of my eye.

He was leaning onto the table. His pen was poised over a half-filled page of notes. His warm brown eyes flickered between the teacher's chalkboard and the notepad in front of him. For a few scribbled notes, he didn't even look down.

Then he glanced over at me.

When our failed clandestine glances met, his pen stilled in the middle of a word. A soft smile played across his lips.

I hadn't realized I was holding my breath until he focused back on the black board.

With five minutes left before the clock's call, Moose sat upright.

The change of posture was so abrupt that it drew the attention of the students around her.

Hunching back over her notebook, her hand moved sharply over the page.

Is she scribbling out the riddle?

Moose straightened again. This time she raised her hand and waved it through the air. The teacher was too absorbed in her own lecture to notice.

Leaning into the desk, I squinted down at her notebook. I was too far to see exactly what she'd done. But I could see that she had blacked out the entire first line of the riddle. The scribbles on top must have been where she rewrote the passage.

The teacher sighed. "Yes, Miss Moose?"

"Can I be excused?" Moose ask in a rush. "I'm not feeling well."

Moose was bailing in the middle of class? What on— My eyes dropped back to the notebook. *Did she solve it?*

I jumped to my feet. "Can I go with her?"

"Miss Moose, you may be excused. Miss Heart, you don't have a reason to leave, therefore you will stay." Then she launched back into her lecture.

Moose didn't bother putting her books back into her bag. Stacking them on top of each other, she tucked them under one arm and her bag under the other. She rushed down the row and stopped just before the door.

She glanced back at me with an intensity that shocked me. Without a word, she was out the door.

"Is everything ok?" Daniel asked when I sat back down.

I nodded. "I'm sure everything's fine."

The moment the clock chimed, I slammed my book closed and rose to my feet. I scooped everything off the tabletop and headed for the door.

"Charlie!" Daniel carelessly collected his stuff and stumbled after me. "Uh, did you want to sit with me at dinner? Cornelia will be there too," he finished in a rush. "It won't be just us. Unless that's ok and then, I don't know." He winced. "Dinner? Are you game?"

The butterflies in my stomach broke free and swirled around my chest. I wanted to break into a smile, maybe even giggle like a kid walking through the gates of Disney World, but all I could think about was Moose.

Did she solve it?

I glanced at the door. "Yeah, sounds good."

He broke into a grin. "Brilliant. I'll save you a seat."

"See you then!" Before he could say anything else or be any more adorably charming, I darted from the classroom. Weaving in and out of the crowded hallways, I ran up the stairs to my next class.

But her seat was empty.

Taking the stairs two at a time, I sat next to Nirean. "Have you seen Moose?"

"Not since breakfast," she said with a glaze of boredom.

"Where's Clarence?" If anyone knew where she was, it would be him.

She shrugged. "Probably smoking in the greenhouse."

"Good morning, everyone," Miss Mullen chirped from the front. Like always, her eyelashes were so long they cast shadows on her cheeks. "We're going to jump in where we left off with daphne sap. Open your books to chapter fourteen and we'll get started."

I pulled out *Magical Plants: Enchantments and Potions, Volume 3*. A pale pink flower with four pointed petals awaited me in chapter fourteen.

"The sap and berries are mostly used in potions that affect the mind. The silvery sap can be found in potions like *Vous Oubliez*." Standing on her tiptoes, she wrote the name on the board. "This potion erodes the mind, stealing memories and habits through headaches and delirium. Most victims die because they forget not only who they are, but how to perform the basic functions of life, such as breathing and eating. In most cases, they don't remember how to wake up."

I slumped low into my seat. I couldn't have cared less about this flower or what it was used for. Over and over my mind played through what Moose said at breakfast. Whatever she found, I wasn't seeing it.

Nirean slapped her hand over my fidgeting hand. "You need to chill."

"Sorry." I hadn't realized I was drumming my fingers on the desk. "Moose found something."

Her eyes bulged. "Did she say what?"

I shook my head, glancing at the clock. "She just ran out of class."

"Damn." Nirean settled back in her chair. "I've known Moose

since my first day. She's only missed one class and that was because her grandfather died."

That didn't reassure me. "I don't understand why she didn't say where she was going. Or leave a note. *Something.*"

"That's the thing about Moose. Her brain moves so fast her mouth doesn't stand a chance to keep up."

"Perhaps Miss Knowles can tell us what potions the daphne berries are used for." Miss Mullan glowered from the chalkboard.

Nirean didn't miss a beat. "Can they put me out of my misery from this boring class?"

A few students tried to stifle their laughter without much success. Miss Mullen's eyes narrowed. I wondered if she could see through her eyelashes. "Not another word, Miss Knowles, or your grade will drop lower than it already is."

Nirean slumped lower in her seat. "Then it's a good thing I don't want to be a Potions Master." But for the rest of class, she didn't say another word.

As soon as the clock chimed, I was out of my seat and running down three flights of stairs to Clarence's class.

But he had the same answer as Nirean. No one had seen Moose since Creature Studies.

Could she have found the diary? She would've told me if she had . . . right? Doubt clouded my mind. I skipped lunch and wandered around the school looking for her. I went to her room and pounded on her door a couple times but each time there was no answer. I would've skipped my afternoon classes, too, but I didn't want Master Lenin to hear I'd been playing hooky.

By dinner, she still hadn't shown up.

If she found it, she would come get me. There's no way she'd read through it by herself. Maybe she really didn't feel well and was laid up in bed. But I remembered the intensity in her eyes before she left Creature Studies. That wasn't a look of sickness, lightheadedness, or pain that I knew of.

I waited outside the dining room with my eyes trained on the stairs. She had to eat sometime. When she did, she'd have to pass right by me.

"Charlie!"

I spun toward the cheery voice.

Cornelia left the dining room with a plate of chicken pot pie in her hands.

Right. I told Daniel I'd eat with them. Crap.

"We have a seat for you," she said, drawing closer. "Whenever you're ready."

"I was just on my way in." I looked back at the stairs. They were nearly empty now that the majority of the student body was in the dining room.

Where are you, Moose?

Reluctantly, I turned my back to the stairwell. "Where are you guys sitting?"

"Over there." Cornelia pointed just to the right of the center of the room. "Daniel already got you a plate."

"Oh. Great." I turned away from the buffet and followed her to the table. Every few steps, I looked back to the door.

When Daniel spotted us a few tables over, he jumped to his feet. With a bright smile, he waved to us.

"Hey," he greeted. "How was the rest of your day?"

"Uneventful." I looked back at the door. For good measure, I sought out Clarence and Nirean. They sat at different tables, and, much to my disappointment, Moose wasn't with either of them.

"I got this for you." Daniel settled back on the bench. He reached for the two plates before him and took the one with the larger slice of pie. "The line was moving so slow, I thought I'd save you some time."

"Thank you." I stepped over the bench and sat down between him and Cornelia.

"Did you want something to drink?" He moved to get back to his feet.

"I'm good. Really. Sit down and eat."

He dropped back to the bench but made no move to pick up his fork.

"So," Cornelia said, filling the pause, "you've been here for a couple months now. Does that mean you've chosen to stay at the Magisterium?"

"Uh, yeah, for the time being."

"That's great! We can use some fresh blood around here."

At the mention of blood, my gaze was pulled back to the doors.

"Have either of you seen Moose?" I asked.

Daniel shook his head. "Not since Creature Studies."

"I think I saw her at breakfast." Cornelia twisted to follow my gaze. "I'm kind of surprised she's not here already."

"She left in the middle of class," Daniel said.

"Really?" Cornelia's eyebrows jumped up.

"I'm sure she's somewhere studying." Daniel nudged me with his arm. "She does this all the time. She gets too caught up in one of her assignments and forgets the time. She'll turn up."

"Oh, you know what I just remembered?" Cornelia tapped her forehead. "I have to call my mom. I have to get her signature to sign off on an assignment. It's the one with the, uh, enchantment and stuff. You know."

Daniel shook his head slowly. "I don't think I do."

"You know." She gave him a pointed look. Just barely her head tilted toward me.

Was she trying to bail?

"Oh." Daniel's confusion evaporated instantly. "Right. For Mr. Sanderson."

"Right!" Collecting her plate, Cornelia got to her feet. "I guess I'll see you two later. Good to see you, Charlie."

"Yeah, you too."

Just as she was about to turn from the table, I caught her winking at Daniel. In a matter of steps, she was out of view from the table. And Daniel and I were alone.

He sighed. "That wasn't subtle."

"It really wasn't," I laughed.

"She volunteered to leave, by the way." He twisted on the bench to face me head on. "I didn't ask or kick her out. It was her idea."

"Sure."

"I'm serious. You can ask her."

"I would, but," I gestured to the empty spot where she used to be, "she's gone."

He grimaced. "Of her own volition."

"So you say."

"I'm not going to live this one down, am I?"

"That depends. Did you ask the entire dining room to leave or just her?"

He threw his head back with a laugh. "I didn't—"

"Right, sorry." I held up my hands between us. "Did they all *volunteer* to leave?"

"Not that I know of." He stabbed a potato with his fork and popped it into his mouth.

I'm not sure how he managed it, but as we picked at our food, I completely forgot to check the door for Moose. In fact, all thoughts of Moose, the riddle, and her potentially solving it, vanished from my mind.

Daniel held my attention. He transformed it into a fascination. I had to catch every detail. When he laughed nervously, he ran his fingers through his hair. Which was different than when he was truly tickled. That barking laugh was accompanied by a single clap. He often rocked forward and back until the amusement ran its course. His polite laugh, a low sound in the back of his throat, came with a wide smile.

There was a fearlessness about him. When I talked, his gaze held mine as if I were the only one in the room. I found myself looking over his head, at my fidgeting fingers, or our dirty plates. But every time I looked into his face, he stared back. As he listened, his fingers drummed against his thighs as if they played the invisible keys of a piano.

For the briefest moment, nothing existed outside of the little bubble at that table.

45

The Price of the Riddle

Daniel dropped another glance at his watch.

It was just a flicker of the eyes. It was so quick I wondered if he actually saw the time. Not a minute later, he looked again.

"What time is it?" I asked.

He winced. "Sorry, I didn't mean to be rude. I was trying to be cool, but I have homework due tomorrow that I haven't even started on yet."

"Don't worry about it." I rose to my feet as if coming out of a slumber.

For the first time, I noticed how empty the dining room was. Most students had moved to other study locations. Only a few tables were occupied. Judging by the number of notebooks and textbooks on the table, the classmates left were part of study groups. The windows lining the room were almost undisguisable from the black stone of the walls.

My heart jumped. "What time is it?"

"Just a little after eight," he said pulling the strap of his bag over his head.

Thank God, I'm not going to be late for lessons with Michael.

"I should get going too."

"Let me walk you up." Stepping over the bench, he fell in line with me. Together, we left the dining room and headed up the stairs.

"Do you have any plans for this weekend?" he asked.

I shook my head. "Just homework."

"Well, if you're up for it, Cornelia and I were thinking of going to the ice sculpture exhibit in Iceland. Have you ever been?"

"I had never left Kansas until a couple months ago."

"Well, then you have to come with us!" His excited voice echoed around the quiet stairwell. "The enchantments last year were amazing. They get better every year."

"They enchant ice?"

He nodded. "Last year Maria Horacio enchanted her carving of a Pegasus to actually fly. She should have won but she came in behind Plihoff Flamite and his orchard. He wins every year."

If Daniel Ported me out of the school . . . could that be how I get out of this castle? My mind raced forward with the intoxicating idea of getting the hell out of here. The weekend was the day after tomorrow. Could I be gone that soon?

And then you'd be trapped in Iceland, reason spoke from the back of my mind. *Because you can't Port, remember?*

My moment of excitement quickly died. That wasn't to mention that if I did run, that would turn Michael's attention to Daniel. The Master Hunter already had one of my friends under his proverbial sword. I wouldn't give him another.

The realization of that thought shocked me. I liked Daniel, significantly more than I should. The thought of running from the Magisterium and never seeing him again put a rock in my stomach.

But I had to run. I couldn't stay here and be sharpened into a weapon for Achilles Heel. I had to get out and get Blake. But that would mean leaving Daniel.

Attachment is an anchor.

"So, what do you say?" Daniel asked excitedly. "The festival also has the world's largest collection of hot chocolate stands. I have yet to try them all."

"I'll have to ask Master Lenin." I already knew the answer. There was no way he was going to let me out of his black stone cage. "Since I'm not an official student, he's got me on a short leash."

"I can put in a good word for you." Reaching the seventh floor, he paused at the top of the stairs. "Thank you for joining me for dinner."

"Thanks for the invite."

He opened his mouth, probably to say something charming or sweet or a potent combination of the two. He already had me doubting my plan to run. I couldn't give him any more weight to keep me here.

"I'll see you at breakfast?" I asked, cutting him off. For good measure, I stepped back toward my room.

Whatever he was going to say, he swallowed. Despite the interruption, he didn't lose his smile. "See you at breakfast. Have a good night, Charlie."

I turned my back before his dimpled grin could sway me farther. "You too," I called over my shoulder.

Moving quickly, I retreated to my room and locked the door behind me. Most people ran toward good things and here I was running away. I really was messed up.

I dropped my school bag on the couch and continued to my room. I closed the door and locked it. Crossing the carpet, I reached under the mattress and pulled out the books on Porting.

I used a hair tie and a piece of scrap paper to mark where the instructions were. I flipped open to the marked sections and stepped back from the bed. Taking a deep breath, I closed my eyes and drew upon my magic.

Please work.

With a low hum, the burning flood of magic spilled from my chest. It swirled down my legs and arched through my skull.

Breathing as evenly as I could, I pictured the other side of my room. I had done this so often that I didn't need to concentrate much. The window, closet door, nightstand, and piles of clothes effortlessly filled my mind.

Holding my breath, I turned on my heel.

My feet twisted out from under me as my magic flared. The overhead light sparked and almost went out as I fell on my side. The rush of magic made my vision blur—or that might have been because I wasn't breathing. The failed attempt and fall knocked the wind out of me.

Of course. I was starting to wonder if I'd ever be able to Port by myself.

I laid there until I could breathe right. Slowly, I dragged myself back to my feet and tried again. At the end of the hour, my insides felt as if they had been scraped raw and exposed to an intense flame.

Unlocking myself from my room, I limped toward my school bag on the couch. I dropped onto the cushions and pulled out my homework.

A loose piece of paper fluttered to the floor.

Written in Moose's tight handwriting with her favorite blue pen was the riddle she copied for me at breakfast.

A blue-lined notion will guide you to a piece of shining night. The north beacon will tell of my lover's curse. He craves the radiant taste of control. But the very thing he hunts has turned him black.

In the first line, a few of the words were scribbled out, this time with a red pen, and rewritten.

A blue-lined thought will guide you to a fragment of glowing darkness.

Cheese and rice. It was a whole new riddle and it made as much sense as the first one. Grabbing a pen, I leaned back into the couch.

Moose said the words Blaine used might not have been ones she intended, thanks to the curse on her tongue.

A piece of shining night . . . I looked out my window at the dark evening sky. Night doesn't shine. A star twinkled at me.

A star! A star is a beacon north . . . like the North Star?

The north beacon will tell you of my lover's curse.

What did that even mean? I tried rearranging the words and even changing some of them. But it only made it more confusing. Soon my page was filled with more scribbles than words.

But the very thing he hunts has turned him black. Was he hunting a creature? Moose could probably name every creature that turned you black as it killed you.

My eyes drifted back to the first line. The North Star.

The first time I saw the North Tower door, there was a star branded into the metal. Could the North Star be referring to the North Tower? The riddle said a beacon north and the North Tower was definitely pointing north.

Was the diary in the tower? I looked back at my scribbles. *The north beacon will tell of my lover's curse.*

What better place to hide something than at the scene of the crime? Maybe that's why I saw Master Lenin leaving the North Tower. He narrowed it down to the tower and was trying to find Blaine's diary.

Did Moose figure out the same thing? Of course, she did. She found the diary and got lost in *reading* it! The North Tower was the perfect spot to read without being found or accidentally interrupted. Creepy as hell, but secluded.

My gaze flew to the clock over the microwave. It was a quarter to ten. I had time to dart down and snoop around the North Tower before lessons with Michael.

Stiffly, I got back to my feet. Just in case I wasn't going to be back in time, I grabbed the transporter from my bedside. Then, quietly, I left my room.

In the stairwell, I looked around, scanning the staircase to see if anyone was watching me. Confirming I was alone, I crept down the stairs. On the third landing, I grabbed the railing and swung myself over. After a brief moment of flight, my feet slammed into the floor.

I pivoted toward the North Wing and darted forward on bare feet. Grabbing the large handle, I leaned back with all my weight and tugged open the doors. As soon as there was a gap large enough, I slipped inside.

Complete darkness greeted me. The late-night silence was heavier here. I could feel it crowding into my ears as the doors closed, sealing me into the abandoned wing. My breath became shallow as I waited for something to disturb it.

But nothing did.

"Moose?" I whispered. "Are you down here?"

My words darted down the hall, echoing softly against walls, with no reply.

Moving away from the doorway and the only source of light, I stretched my hands in front of me until I touched the wall. Using it as my guide, I crept farther inside.

In my head, I counted the number of classroom doors. With each one that passed, I roughly knew I was coming upon the tower.

"Moose?" I whispered again.

A soft splat accompanied my question. Something cold and thick pushed up through my toes.

I jumped back with my heart in my throat.

I stood there, waiting, but there was no other sound.

Keeping one hand on the wall, I crouched down and trailed my fingers along the smooth black stone. The same cold, wet substance met my searching hands. I sniffed the air but couldn't make out anything over the smell of char from the tower.

With my clean hand, I reached for my wand. Michael hadn't taught me how to cast light, but it couldn't be that hard, right? Every time I drew upon my magic it glowed like molten sunlight. So that's all I had to do.

Before I could pull my hand free, a sharp ring came from my hip.

The loud shrill acted like an icicle piercing my chest. My lungs froze, my heart just about burst as the silence shattered. Losing my balance, I pitched forward and landed on the floor with a *splat*. Just as the cold liquid soaked into my sweater, something popped out of my pocket.

The transporter, glowing brightly, rolled over my hip and bumped into my elbow. As soon as it touched my skin, I was ripped off the floor and Ported to the other side of the school.

The cold, dark hallway was traded for the brightly lit training classroom.

Squinting against the change of light, I found Michael standing over me. His lips curled around a phrase that never reached his tongue. The words died the moment his eyes locked on to my hand. For once his gaze wasn't riddled with mockery or barely contained rage. He looked shocked.

It was such a contrast to his normal expression that I followed his gaze to my hands. My entire body went cold.

It was blood.

<h1 style="text-align:center">46</h1>

<h1 style="text-align:center">The Aftermath</h1>

"Oh, my God."

Far from the rich scent of smoke, the metallic stench of blood burned up my nose. My stomach rolled. I tore my gaze from the vibrant red on my fingers. It covered my shoulder. It was on my foot and in between my toes.

A shadow descended upon me.

I flinched back just as Michael crouched in front of me. "What the hell happened?"

"I—I don't know."

"Are you hurt?"

"No."

"Then who's blood is this?"

I stared at the ruby smear covering my fingers.

"Hey." Michael ducked his head to meet my gaze. "Whose blood is this?"

"I couldn't see—" My stomach bottomed out, taking my heart with it.

Moose was gone all day.

Moose wasn't in her room or at dinner.

If she solved the riddle, would she have gone back to the North Tower?

My gaze leapt up to his. "The North Tower. She's outside the North Tower."

Without hesitation, Michael jumped to his feet and Ported.

You're wrong. This isn't Moose—she's fine.

But I needed to see for myself. Jumping up from the floor, I sprinted across the room and through the door. The cold blood seemed to burn against my skin as I ran down the South Wing.

I flew across the stairwell, around the clock tower, and rammed my shoulder into the infirmary doors. They flew open with a bang.

And there she was.

Moose.

She was on her back. A thin, delicate line cut her throat almost from ear to ear. What skin wasn't painted in blood was dark purple—like the bruises I had seen on Michael so many nights. For the first time since I met her, Moose's keen brown eyes were empty. There was no scheme or clever thing to quip in them. They were lifeless with a dull sheen. Her diamond shaped glasses, splattered with blood, sat crooked on her nose.

I choked—caught between a gasp and a scream.

I doubled over as my heart felt like it was trying to claw its way out of my chest. No matter how hard I tried, I couldn't look away.

"Oh, God—Moose!" I stumbled forward on weak knees. My vision blurred with tears.

Michael Ported in front of me.

Taking ahold of my shoulders, he Ported us away from the doors, deeper into the room. He slammed me back against the wall of potions. The smell of ground sage barely covered the rustic stench of blood. The bottles rattled and clinked against each other from the impact.

"What the *hell* were you doing in front of the North Tower?" His dark eyes glared down at me with a level of fury I hadn't seen before.

"I—I—" I watched Helen flutter around Moose's still body. *This isn't happening.*

He sharply pushed me back into the wall. A bottle teetered off the shelf and shattered by my feet. "Don't look at her. Look at me. What happened?"

"I found her," I blurted.

"What was she doing?" When I couldn't get my tongue to work, he yelled, "What was she doing?"

This isn't happening.

He rammed me back into the wall. "Answer me."

"Master Kale, release her."

Master Lenin came into focus over Michael's shoulder.

My heart, which felt as if it hadn't been beating since I entered the room, broke into a full gallop.

Did he kill her? Did he know she had the riddle?

My eyes flew over the School Master, looking for blood splatters, a single hair out of place, literally anything that said he was outside the North Tower. This late at night he had removed his tie and jacket. His dress shirt and pants had a couple of creases, but that could have come from being worn all day. There was no blood. Not even a stray hair clung to his clothes.

Michael pried his fingers from my arms with a curled lip of disgust. Without him pinning me against the wall, I slid to the floor.

This isn't happening.

"What happened?" Master Lenin asked, walking over to him.

"She Ported into the room like that." Michael didn't take his eyes off me. "She told me where to find—" he looked at Helen for assistance.

"Aanya Moose," Helen said softly. Master Lenin's eyebrows shot up.

"She was dead when I got there," Michael finished. "Has been for a few hours."

A few hours.

I doubled over my knees, suddenly finding it hard to breath. It was as if there were holes in my lungs.

I had been looking for her all day. And she was *right* there all along.

I squeezed my eyes shut against the onslaught of images of Moose on the bed. The slit across her throat. The deep red on her blouse. The pinpoint splatters on her diamond framed glasses.

She bled out alone.

Why did I say anything? Why didn't I brush her off? If I hadn't opened my mouth, we never would have looked for the diary.

My head went light as my magic swarmed through my chest like a hive of bees on fire. Around the room, the lights glowed too big for their containers. The glass vases started to melt as the fire grew brighter. The potion bottles rattled on their shelves.

"Miss Heart, take a deep breath." Master Lenin kept his voice even.

"I told you she was unstable," Michael said.

"*Enough*." Master Lenin moved around Michael. Softening his voice, he said, "Just breathe. In and out. Nice and slow."

I tried to scoot away from him, but I only managed to push myself back into the shelves of potions. A sob ripped through my throat as I tangled my hands into my hair.

"Tell me what happened," Master Lenin said.

For all I knew, he was the one who killed her. "Why don't you tell me?"

"I was not there," he said gently. "I need you to tell me so I can explain to her mom what happened tonight."

At the thought of her family, I hugged my knees to my chest. *Why didn't I keep my mouth shut?*

"Miss Heart," Master Lenin prompted.

"I hadn't seen her all day." My voice was as hollow as the rest of me. "When she wasn't in her room, I tried looking for her." I hugged my knees tighter.

"Would Miss Moose have any reason to go into the North Wing?"

I squeezed my eyes shut and shook my head.

"Can you think of any reason why someone would want to hurt her?" Michael asked.

"The entity of the North Wing isn't fond of visitors," Master Lenin said sadly. "She's injured a couple of students who have gotten too close." He paused to look over his shoulder. "But never like this."

"What about her classmates?"

"I crowned her the best of her class at the beginning of the year, earning her interviews with at least ten different Masters this summer. Any student beneath her could have a motive based on that alone."

It was astounding how well he said all of that. Effectively, he moved the suspicions away from himself. My stomach churned with anger.

"I want a list of everyone in her class," Michael told him.

"I highly doubt it would be another one of my students," Master Lenin insisted. "Blaine Willow is to blame here."

"Then why not ward her out?"

"She's a magic entity with the status of a Royal Eight. There is very little that can remove her other than her own choice," Master Lenin said coolly.

Michael considered this for a moment before looking back at me. "Did anyone or anything see you go into the North Wing?"

My gaze flickered to Master Lenin. "Why?"

"If whoever did this thinks you know anything, they might try to tie up loose ends. Or you just pissed off a territorial, bloodthirsty ghost."

This wasn't Blaine. My eyes snapped up to where Master Lenin stood. *Why hasn't he killed me already? Maybe he doesn't want Helen to know what he's up to.*

"Master Kale, take her up to her room please," Master Lenin said. "Make sure there's no one there. I'm going to speak with Helen." Master Lenin turned toward the curtain.

Michael grabbed my elbow and hauled me to my feet. Pulling on his magic, he Ported us from the infirmary to outside my apartment.

Dropping my elbow, he mumbled, "Stay here."

Opening the door, he passed inside. He returned a moment later and gestured for me to come in. I moved by him and stood in the middle of my room, unsure what to do next. I looked at my blood-coated hands.

My stomach dropped and rolled.

I barely made it to the bathroom before I threw up everything from dinner. When my eyes opened, my hold on the toilet seat was smudged with blood. A sob tore out of my throat.

"Shit."

I jumped at the sound of Michael's voice behind me.

He pulled me up from the floor again and deposited me into the bathtub. Reaching over my head, he turned on the water. The hot spray splattered blood against the white tile walls.

"What are you doing?" I called over the water.

"Would you rather go to bed covered in blood?" he quipped. In a less-snappy tone he asked, "Can you get undressed and washed by yourself?"

I nodded, thankful for the break from his usual harshness.

He stepped back and pulled the shower curtain closed. I pulled off my sweater and watched the water darken. I tossed my ruined clothes over the shower curtain, not caring that they would probably stain the bathmat.

Filling the body scrubber with soap, I scrubbed my skin as if I could scrub the memory right out of my body.

Only when I was raw did I turn off the water. After drying off, I quickly pulled on warm clothes and stepped into my bedroom.

The smudges of blood on the toilet bowl and the drips on the floor had been cleaned up. Michael was also gone.

Barefooted, I climbed into bed. I was so numb I couldn't feel my wet hair beneath my cheek.

I squeezed my eyes closed. Why couldn't I keep my mouth shut? Who cares what Master Lenin was doing? I was getting out soon and never looking back. Because of me, Moose found the diary and she was killed for it. Michael would probably investigate.

I sat bolt upright.

The records.

All of them were still in Moose's room. If Michael or Master Lenin found them, they would know we were onto him.

47

Missing Pieces

I threw off the covers.

As soon as my feet touched the ground, I bolted out of my room. With my heart hammering in my throat, I paused before the apartment door and cracked it open. Upon seeing an empty hall, I ran to Moose's room. I readied my wand to blast open the door but it was already open.

I slowed to a stop in the middle of the hallway.

Shadows swam between the door and the frame. I paused to listen, but nothing sounded on the other side.

With my wand raised before me, I pushed the door. Soundlessly it swung open.

The whole room was trashed. Furniture was flipped over and tossed aside. Pictures hung crooked on the walls. The couch stuffing was strewed around the room. All of the kitchen cabinets were open. Glass and tupperware were scattered across the hardwood.

Did Michael get here first?

No. The chaos of the room wasn't from someone who was just looking. Whoever did this was frantic, mad. *I don't think Michael did this.*

My blood went cold. After he killed Moose, what if Master Lenin came up here to look for the diary.

The records!

Scrambling over broken furniture, I stumbled into her study. I sighed with relief when I saw the binders of stolen records. They'd been shoved off the shelf, but they were still intact.

Stepping over Moose's study notes, I collected the stack of stolen records and the scattered pages that had come loose. Hugging them to my chest, I looked around the room for Moose's backpack. The riddle she had been working on that morning would be in it. I looked through the study, the living room, and the bedroom, with no luck.

She never went anywhere without that backpack. She must have had it with her when . . .

One problem at a time. I can't let Michael find these.

My heart ran nervously around my ribcage as I darted from Moose's room to mine. Kicking the door closed behind me, I looked around the living room for somewhere to put the records.

I couldn't put everything in the study like Moose. Maybe Master Lenin had someone search my room as they cleaned. Or worse, if Michael came by for an unexpected visit. The ceiling was solid with no tiles I could move like my old school. Under my bed was too cliché. I stopped when I saw the fireplace.

Making my way over, I stuck my head up the chimney. The flue created a ledge big enough for the books.

Carefully I arranged the binders on the ledge. By the time they were successfully stowed away, I had soot in my hair and determination in my bones. Twisting my wet hair into a knot at the top of my head, I once more left my room.

Eleven chimes rang up the sleepy stairwell. Grabbing the railing, I propelled myself to the North Wing. I barely paused to shove my way between the gold doors. This time I drew my wand. I wasn't going in blind.

Magic flooded down my arm and filled my wand. The molten glow cut back the thick tendrils of darkness to gleam across the black stone. I had never seen the North Wing in so much light before. A thick layer of dust coated the floor and walls. It hung from the chandeliers like knotted locks of hair.

My bare feet carried me down the hallway with hardly a sound. As I neared the end, a figure slowly came into view.

Her grey complexion drew me to a stop. *It wasn't . . . it couldn't be . . .* I squeezed my eyes tight, finding it hard to breathe.

When I looked, I found Blaine Willow.

Her grey eyes scanned the floor right where Moose had been. It was the only spot on the floor wiped clean of dust and loose ash. There was no sign of blood or that Moose had ever been there.

I looked at the shadow of the girl before me with her frozen wounds and grey skin. Her proud posture had been reduced to slumped shoulders and a melancholy turn of her lips. For a moment, I got a glimpse of what she must have gone through year after year: frozen, unable to do anything other than watch as student after student was taken and killed.

My thoughts turned to Moose. *Would she be condemned to the same fate?* My heart broke at the thought, but I needed to know.

"Is Moose . . ." I cleared my throat. "Is she here?"

Blaine shook her head. "No. I don't let any of them stay. One person in this hell is enough. She was stubborn about it, though. If she had more magic, she would have won." Her shoulders drooped farther. "They're saying I did this, aren't they?"

Unable to look away from the clean spot of stone, I nodded.

"He hasn't killed like this before. He never wastes magic." She grimaced as the curse on her mind forced her quiet.

I had questions for her, all of them important, but none of them seemed to matter over the one at the forefront of my mind. "Why did he? He's already stolen magic this year."

"She found it."

My heart leapt. *The diary.*

Blaine met my gaze. "And she wouldn't give it to him."

"Her backpack," I said in a rush. "If she solved the riddle, then it's in her bag—"

"I took care of that," she said coolly. "By now it's miles downriver."

My heart screamed at the thought of Moose's bag being lost. I found that I couldn't have cared less about the riddle inside—the bag was just *Moose.* Her whole personality was in that bag—the Reeses peanut butter cups that she had every afternoon, her color-coded notes, an ever-changing book for light reading, and a pen collection that bordered on ridiculous. All of it was gone.

"She put the diary back," Blaine continued. "She knew that this was bigger than her or you. I trusted you with that riddle because you said you could stop this."

"I've been trying," I snapped. "If you just told me where to look—"

"I did," she said simply. "It's not my fault you're not smart enough to figure it out. Because of your slow mind, you've gotten someone killed."

"*No.* Your stupid diary did this."

"I told you this would happen if you pursued my mind. This," she gestured to the floor, "is on you." In a blink she was in front of me. "It'll only be a matter of time before he finds out about your real status. Then you'll get your answer, and you'll be just like me." With a flash, she was gone.

"I'm not done talking to you," I snapped to empty air. I grabbed the door handle and pulled but it refused to even creak. Digging my heels into the floor, I pulled again and only ended up on my tailbone.

Getting back to my feet, I slammed my fists against the door. "Open up!"

Silence was the only response.

Now I was pissed.

She was the one that gave me that stupid riddle and it killed Moose. And now, *she* wasn't going to answer the damn door?

I closed my eyes and tried to remember the inside of the tower. There had to be another way in besides the door. On the main level there were windows all around and they touched the ground.

Retreating down the hallway, I pushed my way into an abandoned classroom. This far down the wing there were actual desks in a level classroom instead of chairs and rows of tables.

Layers of dust covered everything like grey snow. I crossed to the far side of the room and pushed up one of the windows. Cold wind whipped through my damp hair as I crawled onto the windowsill.

Dropping to the ground, I nearly slipped on the wet stones. I didn't realize how dark it was. The sliver of the moon barely cast any usable light.

When the darkness eased, I located my goal. The river washed right up against the tower windows.

Stumbling over river rocks, I almost rolled my ankle and fell into the river. Cursing as the cold water soaked my feet, I stepped onto the window ledge. The ash covered glass prevented me from seeing inside. The midnight darkness wasn't helping either.

Running my hands along the side, I felt for the hinges. The windows opened inward. I pushed and, just like the door, nothing happened. I lurched forward, slamming my shoulder into the pane. It didn't even groan.

Taking a step back, I slammed my foot against the window seam. It shook but remained closed. Shaking off the ache in my leg, I kicked it again. The damn thing showed no signs of budging.

Reaching down, I grabbed a large river rock. I didn't care if anyone heard, not that anyone would. The entire wing was abandoned.

I walked up to the window and slammed it into the glass. It bounced off without leaving a crack or even a chip.

Magic boiled in my chest. Just as I drew my arm back for another blow, a pair of hands grabbed me. I was spun around and slammed against the side of the tower.

Even through the darkness, I could see the pair of black eyes glaring down at me.

48

Consequences Be Damned

Michael didn't say anything at first.

His jaw clenched as he dug his fingers into my arms. Very slowly he took a deep breath and released it. His warm breath curled into a cloud between us.

With barely contained rage, he asked, "What are you doing here?"

"Sleep walking?" That sounded stupid, even to my ears.

"Try again."

"I was curious—"

"Curious means going in once. Three times equals stupidity."

How the hell did he know that?

Seeing the shock on my face, Michael pried his fingers free from my arm. He took up my wrist and brought it up between us. The silver bracelet that Master Lenin gave me a month ago glittered in the low moonlight. I had forgotten about it until then. It fit just enough that it didn't move much to draw my attention.

"This bracelet is infused with a tracking charm."

My stomach dropped to the river rocks under my feet.

"I didn't have a reason to follow your movements through the castle until tonight. And what do I find? You *in* the North Tower. And then in real time, I find you *trying to break back in.*"

He closed his fingers around the bracelet, pressing it painfully into my skin. "Do you even know what happens around this tower?"

"Yes."

"And you're here anyway. What the hell is wrong with you? If you wanted to die, I would've saved you the trouble."

"I wasn't trying to—"

"Oh, really? Because from where I'm standing, in the dark, just outside a cursed tower, it sure looks that way." He stepped so close I had to crane my neck to look him in the eye. "I could carve your brain from your skull and dissect it before your eyes for the answer, which would be an incredible waste of my time and skills. So, do us both a favor and tell me. Why. Are. You. Here?"

Magic flared as I rose up on my toes to snap in his face. "To talk to Blaine Willow, because apparently only the dead tell the truth."

"What the hell are you talking about?"

"I don't trust you. I don't trust a single person in this damn place. All of you are liars. You've proven that much. From what I've seen over the last few weeks, you're no better than Lawrence Hart."

He lurched forward at those words, backing me into the side of the tower. "Say that again. I dare you."

"I know Master Lenin is killing students in this tower and then covering it up by saying they transferred and were killed on their way home. I guess when you're fighting a war alone, you'll stoop as far as you can go to win."

For a moment he just stared at me, letting my words echo around us.

Finally, he shook his head. "Explain. What makes you think Lenin is killing students?"

"That night in the library, I heard Mr. Harrison talking to Mr. While. He said that once a year a high-status student transfers to another school, but they never make it there alive. He said Master Lenin was killing them for their magic to use for your war."

"That's teacher gossip."

I grew bolder. "Then why did I see Master Lenin in the library before the attack? Why did I see him sneaking out of this tower the night he was supposed to be helping one of his students fill out transfer paperwork on the other side of the school?" He remained quiet, so I continued. "I guess you know I was in the Records Room."

He gave a sharp nod.

"I copied the death records and transfer documents. It was just like Mr. Harrison said. Once a year a high status student dies on school grounds the same night they fill out the paperwork to transfer from the school."

After a few seconds of contemplative silence, he asked, "What does Blaine Willow have to do with this?"

"She was the first student Master Lenin killed for her magic."

"Blaine Willow told you this?"

"Well, no," I admitted. "Her mind is messed up. She said her words were cursed so she couldn't name her killer. She said her diary was the key to everything. Moose found the diary and she was killed because she wouldn't share it."

"You think Lenin slit her throat?" he asked slowly.

"Who else would it be?"

"Literally so many other people," he said. "Where is the diary now?"

My stomach went cold. "You're working with him, aren't you?"

He ignored my question. "How did your friend find it?"

"Over my dead body."

"Don't make me ask again."

I bit my lip to keep it from quivering. If Moose could hold this information, so could I.

He lashed forward, pressing me tightly against the siding of the tower. Ripping his wand from his holster, he sent a blast of magic into my forehead.

Everything went still: the air in my lungs, my limbs, even the blood in my veins. Worse, I couldn't stop what he was going to do next.

Reaching into his jacket, he pulled out a clear stone and pressed it to my forehead. Magic surged through his wand, into the stone, and then into my head.

I had grown used to the burning in my chest when I used magic. But having it swim around my skull was excruciating. If I could, I would've screamed.

With a flash, the stone spat out a scroll of images into the air between us. Leaning back, Michael scrolled through them. Ice slid down my spine as I realized they were my memories in rewind.

I was running down the hall, then up the stairs, and back to my apartment. I was hiding the records in the fireplace and then in Moose's room.

The infirmary and finding Moose's body flashed by too, along with the evening spent with Daniel sorting records. Pain rippled through my skull as Valentine's Day whipped past and I was back in the tower talking to Blaine Willow. Finally, he pulled the stone from my forehead.

I fell to the riverbed.

I took in such a deep breath I thought my lungs would pop.

Michael stood there; he idly fiddled with the stone as he stared at the tower. With a frosty sigh, he stooped down and dragged me back to my feet. River rocks clattered around my stumbling feet as he tugged me to his side. Before I could form a thought to run, he Ported to my apartment.

Roughly, he shoved me into an armchair.

Without a word, he walked to the fireplace and pulled out the binders of stolen records. He deposited them onto the coffee table. Lastly, he disappeared into my room and returned with my notebook.

I sat there, unsure what to do, as he sat down and spread everything out in front of him. He examined every page, sorting the papers into piles.

When he got through the records, he finally shook his head. "Shit."

"You didn't know about any of this," I asked. "Did you?"

His eyes never left the pages in front of him, but his silence was enough of an answer.

If he didn't know, then he wasn't working for Master Lenin. He wasn't going to kill me over this. Maybe.

He closed the binder with a snap and stood up. "You're under house arrest."

Hold the phone. "What?"

"I don't know who might've seen you go into the tower, tonight or any other night. If whoever killed your friend saw you there, you just helped him paint a target on your back." His eyes locked on mine. "You'll go to breakfast, then straight to classes. After dinner, you'll return immediately to this room."

"But—"

"You'll do as I say. And if you don't, I'll know." He glanced pointedly at my wrist.

The bracelet seemed to grow heavier under his sharp gaze. "What are you going to do?"

"That's none of your business."

"Are you going to tell Master Lenin?"

"As far as he's concerned, this doesn't involve him until I can make sense of it." He took out his wand. With a wave all the loose papers and records disappeared, leaving the room as clean as it was before. "Meanwhile, this situation no longer concerns you."

"Like hell it doesn't!" I walked around the coffee table and glowered up at him. "My friend got killed because of this. There's no way I'm stepping out now."

"Listen Heart." He said my name with such curtness it felt like a slap across the face. "I didn't ask for your opinion, nor do I give a damn. I'm not going to let your stupidity ruin our chance to win this war by getting yourself killed."

"I don't give a damn about your war!"

His expression hardened. "You should. It's the only thing keeping me from scraping the idiocy from your veins with my bare hands." He zipped up his leather jacket and headed for the door. "If I see you anywhere near that tower, I'll personally make sure you can't walk for the rest of the year."

The door slammed behind him.

I plopped onto the couch and glared at the bracelet around my wrist. I grabbed the clasp and gasped as it singed my fingers. Quickly I released the enchanted metal.

He may have taken all the papers, but I still had the riddle memorized. And there was no way he was going to stop me from working on it. I was going to solve it and find that diary before he did.

Consequences be damned.

49

A Blue-Lined Notion

I was still seething the next morning.

The dining room was quieter than I had ever heard it. Most conversations didn't go above a respectful whisper. At least half the students were on cellphones. Some were speaking into enchanted mirrors.

As I walked to my table, I heard a student assure his mother, "Everything's fine. It was just an overzealous Common who got too close to the tower. No, Mom, I'm staying away."

"Charlie!" Nirean's voice echoed around the room. Jumping to her feet, she ran past dozens of curious eyes and met me in the middle. Clarence followed a few steps behind with a waffle in hand.

"Tell me it's not true," Nirean demanded, crowding into my personal space. "Tell me Moose is at home with a cold. Tell me Master Lenin is full of shit."

I couldn't even get my mouth to open.

Her hope dimmed. "Was it Master Lenin?"

"I—" *Cheese and rice, I didn't want to talk about this.* My chest was still raw. "I didn't see who did it."

Clarence choked on his waffle. "You were there?"

I shook my head. "I just found her."

"It has to be Master Lenin," Nirean said. "Moose found something and—"

"Hey." Clarence shot a barbed look at a student who was clearly eavesdropping. "Does this conversation pertain to you?"

Taking me by the arm, Clarence yanked me into the stairwell. "Half the student body thinks another student did it while the other half thinks our tongue-twisting ghost is to blame."

378

"Total bullshit," Nirean snapped. "What happened?"

"We got played, that's what happened," Clarence said. "We'll need a different approach."

"He *killed* Moose. They should be able to find something on her." Nirean's voice broke. "Something that will tie him to her, right?"

Clarence shook his head. "He's got the infirmary head and a Master Hunter on payroll. No one will find anything on her."

Nirean cursed.

"I'm not so sure it was Master Lenin," I found myself saying. Clarence and Nirean's gazes snapped to my face.

"Last night," I shook off the phantom chills of the infirmary, "he seemed genuinely shocked."

"He's been alive for over five hundred years," Clarence said dryly. "I think he can fake a basic emotion."

I shook my head. "The way he acted . . . he was more concerned with telling her family than he was about questioning me."

"But you saw him leave the North Tower," Nirean said. "You saw him eavesdropping on Mr. Harrison and Mr. While."

My stomach churned. "We're missing something."

"With a dead student under his roof, we can draw the eyes of the other School Masters and get his title stripped," Clarence said.

"He'll just bat his eyelashes and shift the blame away from himself," Nirean said, dejected.

"Not if we call in the right people."

"And tell them what?" I asked. "All we have is hearsay, stolen documents, and my word against his."

"And a Common's word at that," Nirean added.

Unconvinced, Clarence shook his head. "If we apply the right pressure, he'll crack."

"That was never the point of this!"

"Maybe not for you."

"I thought we were doing this for Holly and Janet," Nirean said slowly.

Clarence cocked his head with an incredulous look. "And I thought this was about taking out a School Master. *This*," he gestured to the North Wing doors, "could change things. What did you think was going to happen after we proved that he was behind this?"

"I—" Cheese and rice, I didn't know. If Master Lenin was killing his students for the war front, my plan was to run as fast and as far as I could. I never thought what that conclusion would *mean,* and I certainly didn't think about what would happen to the people I left in the aftermath.

"I don't know," I reluctantly admitted.

The smugness in Clarence's expression tripled. "That's one of the problems with Commons." His gaze dipped to the six pinned to my shirt. "You're all too near sighted."

"No, asshole," Nirean said through her teeth, "Charlie just has a soul and gives a shit about someone other than herself."

Nirean had no clue I was planning on jumping ship the moment I learned how. Her vote of confidence and brisk compliment ignited a wave of guilt through my stomach.

Clarence's lips curled. "That's one of her greatest weaknesses."

"Is everything ok over here?"

Our trio turned.

Daniel stood with a cinnamon roll in one hand and a steaming drink in the other. Cornelia hovered by his elbow. Her wary eyes watched Clarence like she expected him to pull out his wand.

Daniel glanced back and forth between Clarence and Nirean before landing on me. "Is he bothering you?"

"There's no need for your knight in shining armor act." Clarence stepped away from Nirean and me. "I was just leaving." Spinning sharply on his heel, he slammed his shoulder into Daniel's causing his beverage to slosh over the sides. Cornelia jumped out of the way as he returned to the dining room.

"What was that about?" Daniel asked, watching him go.

Nirean shook her head. "Does he need a reason?" She turned to me. There was more she wanted to say but couldn't with them there. Tears welled up in her eyes. Swiftly, she turned and headed for the stairs before they could fall down her cheeks.

"Is everything ok?" Cornelia winced. "Sorry. That was a dumb question. Obviously, everything's not ok. I'm so sorry about Moose."

When I didn't answer, Daniel cleared his throat. "I thought you were going to miss breakfast, so I got you this." He offered me the cinnamon roll and the steaming cup. The rich aroma of the hot chocolate did nothing to soothe my insides.

"Thank you." I wasn't hungry, but I took it.

"You should take the day off," Daniel said. "I'm sure Master Lenin would understand. I can take notes for you in Potions Chemistry."

"And I can take notes during Casting Techniques," Cornelia added.

I looked between the two of them, wishing I had spent the last month sitting at their table. I doubt either of them would have broken into the Records Room with me or even entertained the thought of a School Master killing students for their magic. Moose would still be alive.

I shook my head. "Thank you, but I can't just sit up there all by myself. I'd rather do something."

Cornelia nodded earnestly. "Well, if you need anything, don't hesitate to ask. I'll save you a seat in Techniques." At the last second, she pulled me into a tight hug. The warm smell of her vanilla perfume only added to the level of comfort.

Quickly she pulled back and darted up the stairs.

"Which class do you have first?" Daniel asked, wrapping his hands around the strap of his bags.

"Wand Anatomy with Mr. Sterling."

"You'll want to get *Structure Materials for Wands* by Alexander Morris from the library. Mr. Sterling didn't add it to the syllabus, but he references it throughout the lesson."

"Thanks." I looked down at the gooey cinnamon roll. My stomach hardened as if to say, *"Don't even think about it."*

"I'll see you in class," Daniel said. "Let me know if you need anything." With a soft smile, he headed down the East Wing.

Crossing the busy stairwell, I made my way to the library. Stopping in the doorway, I looked up at the ceiling. I had the book title that Daniel told me already at the front of my mind.

A blue light hovered over me, waiting for me to direct it.

A blue-lined notion.

My lips parted. *Cheese and rice.*

As soon as the translation of the first line of the riddle popped into my mind the line pulsed and the rest of the lights dimmed. I almost dropped my breakfast. *Was it really that simple?*

"Blaine Willow's diary." The words were barely audible to my own ears.

My stomach was hard as a rock as the line glided over the ceiling. I shot a look over my shoulder to the stairwell. The current of students was headed up the stairs and into the main wings of the school. I bolted after the light.

It led me in a perfect line all the way to the back. I was so enthralled I didn't notice the studying table before it was too late. My knees slammed into the edge. I slowed only long enough to curse at the furniture and put down the hot chocolate and cinnamon roll Daniel gave me.

The light stopped at the back wall. There was no bookcase or alter with a key on it. There was just an old dusty painting of a black star. The bottom point was elongated, like every depiction of the North star.

A blue-lined notion will guide you to a piece of shining night.

If night could ever shine, it would be as a star.

The north beacon will tell of my lover's curse.

Wasn't the North star *the* ultimate beacon North?

He craves the radiant taste of control. But the very thing he hunts has turned him black.

That last bit didn't make sense to me in the moment, so I shoved it aside. I could decipher that later.

I grabbed the picture and pulled it away from the wall. Nothing marred the black stone behind it. I straightened it on its hook and glanced around.

"Are you kidding me?" I muttered.

It was probably just a magic malfunction. Can magic malfunction? *I'm missing something.* Through the library entrance, framed between the gold doors was the greenhouse.

I turned back to the painting. It was a picture of a star with an N stamped in the middle. The school was in the shape of a compass rose. Each wing pointed in a different direction and this painting was pointing north.

The north beacon will tell of my lover's curse.

My mouth went dry as I set my bag on the floor. "I want to read Blaine Willow's Diary."

Nothing happened.

Maybe it appeared behind the picture? I moved the frame again and found the wall was still blank.

I crossed my fingers. "Reveal your curse."

The reaction was immediate. The painting rattled against the stone. The star glistened and then started to bleed. Black paint dribbled over the frame and down the wall. The small trickle grew into a steady stream until the painting was a dull brown.

I jumped back as the paint collected on the floor. It swirled on the carpet, moving as if something swam inside it. Then it started to rise and shrink together. The paint hardened and when it stopped moving a book sat at my feet.

With shaking hands, I scooped it off the floor and flipped open the front cover.

The Belongings of Blaine Willow

Cheese and rice, I found it.

I spun around. The library was empty behind me. Dropping to my knees, I couldn't stuff the book in my bag fast enough.

Slinging my bag over my shoulders, I barely controlled myself from sprinting up the stairs. Keeping my gait casual, I joined the flow of traffic. Splitting away from the student body, I went up to the seventh floor. Once out of the stairwell, I sprinted to my apartment.

I dead bolted the door and sank into the couch. With nervous hands, I pulled the diary from my bag. I lifted the old cover and turned the delicate pages to the first entry.

50
The Belongings of Blaine Willow

Diary,

Tomorrow will be my first day at the Magisterium of Magic. Father informed me of everything there is to know about this place. He talked of little else for so many years. I thought for sure I would walk in and be familiar with it all. But it's still strange.

I wish to go home to the warm breeze and laughing faces of my family. Or at least to another school. One that isn't so dark. At least one that lets me outdoors. But it's useless. I'm doomed, trapped here until summer, per my father's wishes.

Thankfully, I'm not alone in my damnation. During my exploration of the castle, I met a boy, R.W. He's the same year as me. He has glasses. Anyone with a respectable amount of magic would've fixed their sight.

He's a Deficient, which explains it. I've never met a Deficient before. From the way Father portrayed them, I thought they were all dull and incompetent. R.W. was perfectly charming and by far the most intelligent in our class. He has already started planning for our testing year.

In Father's grand speech of expectations, he made it very clear to keep the company of Royals only or High Commons if I had to stoop for better company.

I've always been around Royals and never got along with them. While I inherited my father's status and my mother's disposition, I never adopted their prejudice of status.

R.W. asked to meet me at breakfast tomorrow to explore the castle before orientation. I said yes, because I plan to make my days in this cold, dark school as pleasant as possible. And that isn't going to happen if I'm surrounded by people my parents approve of.

It was a mystery how this book was so small and not the size of three dictionaries stacked together. Blaine wrote every night.

During her first two years at the Magisterium, she made friends quickly, keeping detailed records of all their statuses. She only ever referred to them by their initials. Her reason was if the diary was ever found by her father, he wouldn't be able to tell who she was spending her time with. At least not easily.

She fell in love with R.W., which according to her was the scandal of her life. When she wasn't with him, she studied like her life depended on it. From what she wrote about her parents, it was a good thing she did.

It wasn't until her third year that things started to change. The entries about R.W. grew less frequent, and when his initials did appear, her words were sad. Entries about her father's wrath and disappointment became longer.

Diary,

I have two years left in this place. Whatever happens, it will never be as wretched as this past summer. I look forward to the space between my father and me. He's still outraged about me wanting to change my title focus. I know when he comes home from work because the lights flicker in announcement to his annoyance. Mother has yet to speak to me.

I thought I would be happier at school and away from them. I too am shocked that I was looking forward to returning to black stone and no fresh air.

Since R.W. didn't answer a single letter I wrote, I decided to put my elaborate plan into motion. I managed to corner the fool outside the dining room. For a moment I thought I snagged the wrong person.

R.W. changed. I know I sound ridiculous by accusing him of changing. Everyone changes. I'm certainly not the same shy girl that once entered this school, but this is different. He gelled his hair back like all the boys we made fun of last year. He isn't wearing glasses and he acted like he doesn't need them.

And there's something else. I can't believe I'm even saying this. His status has changed, which is impossible, I know. But when I touched him, I felt it. I touched him nearly an hour ago and my hand is still tingling!

A Deficient Two does not shock! Normally you cannot feel it! Only a Royal or a High Common can give off such a reaction. You can't increase the status of magic you were born with.

Should I report it to a teacher? Maybe I'm being foolish. After all, R.W. is far too smart to get himself in any sort of trouble. But I can't help but wonder what he has gotten himself into.

I stared at the initials R.W.

That entry rang a bell . . . There was a way a Magic User could increase their status . . . but how? *Cheese and rice, was that my first lesson with Mr. Harrison?*

I hardly remembered the class. So much had happened between my first day and now. It almost felt like it belonged to another calendar year.

A binding curse. It allowed a User to steal another's magic into their core. It was dark magic because it used outside materials like herbs and potions to exceed the limits of a cast with a wand.

At the start of all of this, none of it made sense. Master Lenin, Janet Raven, the transfer documents. The further we dug, the more pieces we unraveled, it just didn't fit—the similarities in the girl's appearances and now this.

R.W.

Not only were those not Master Lenin's initials, but he told me that he was a Royal Eight. He could have been lying—but he said at the beginning that only high statuses could feel my magic when they touched me. I remembered our conversation right after I tried to run away. He took my hand and told me that it stung.

He could have faked it.

But R.W. was a student. At the time Blaine was in school, Master Lenin was still the School Master.

But why did I see him leave the North Tower the night Janet died?

In the library, I saw him right before Mr. Harrison was killed.

For the first time since all of this began, I started to wonder if he didn't know any more than I did. Michael didn't know anything until I showed him the transfer documents and death records. Why would Master Lenin leave his number one man, a Hunter who reveled in bloodshed, on the side lines? Even if Michael didn't agree with draining magic, he wanted Lawrence's head above all else.

And then there was what Blaine said to me last night. *"It'll only be a matter of time before he finds out about your real status."*

Master Lenin already knew. He created the lie pinned to my shirt. Could Master Lenin be trying to fit the pieces together like I was?

The dates on the pages gapped. A whole month went by without her writing a single word. In her next entry, just by looking at her writing, I knew something was wrong.

I don't know what to say. My mind seems incapable of developing a complete thought.

I guess I should start from the beginning. Maybe words will find me along the way.

R.W. snuck out. He has been for the last couple weeks. It's stupid to go out past curfew. My father would have a heart attack if he heard of this, but I followed.

I shouldn't have, I know. Being caught could impact my good standing, but I had to see what he was doing. I thought maybe he was meeting someone. A new girl or one of his new friends.

R.W. went to the North Tower. He was on the highest level talking to himself. And his eyes were red.

Even as I'm writing this it sounds ridiculous. I wouldn't believe it myself if I hadn't seen it with my own eyes! The only mutation that could happen in a User to cause red eyes is the demon transformation.

He always complained about how low his status was. He always looked at others with envy, but everyone does. It's just how things are.

I keep trying to convince myself that R.W. would never be foolish enough to try to raise his status. But the evidence explains everything. The dramatic increase of magic, his violent mood swings, and his complete change of character. Now, I fear only the darkest parts of him remain.

Why would he be so foolish to do something like this? Many students in this school are mocked for their low status, but I don't see any of them trying to change it! Let alone perform dark magic to achieve it. But I can see it in their eyes. They would do anything to be equal to those around them.

I left after I saw his eyes. I was afraid I was going to be sick all over the stairs. But my adventure wasn't over.

I was flustered to the point of hysteria. I thought he might be following me. I drew my wand, searching the shadows, and I made my way to the stairwell.

I startled over a reflection from my magic. The light caught in the gold of the clock tower. I was so scared that it was R.W.—that he might have seen me watching him and came to silence me—that I fired. The cast struck the clock. I nearly broke the thing in two.

And then it started to regrow.

I've seen magic repair broken things, but that always requires the broken pieces to be fitted together and fused in place. Even then, another enchantment must be placed on top to cover the cracks. This wasn't that.

This was creation. The broken pieces dissolved into the floor and the clock reformed itself. The inside cracks of the mending pieces were magic. Pure magic.

I sent another cast at the clock, this time to break it to the stem. And there, teeming in the floor was a well of magic, so bright it looked like I had been transported into the middle of the day.

I think the school is not made of obsidian as it looks, but it's made of pure magic.

Mr. Carmel once taught our class of a myth that the world runs on magic, like a lamp runs on oil. He explained it like there was a lake of magic under our feet and at certain places this lake branched off. Most were sealed up, by nature or User, but some remained hidden.

If I'm right, then the Magisterium is one of those access points and it has a direct line to this lake. Unlimited power.

I have gotten myself in the middle of something I don't know how to get out of. If R.W. or the monster he has become discovers this, I can't imagine the kind of darkness that will cover this world.

The diary dropped to my lap but the sound didn't pierce my ears. My eyes were locked on the wall in front of me.

A demon. That was the side effect of using a binding curse. The act of dark magic caused a User's magic to kill them from the inside out. It mutilated their core to where their status could increase over what they were born with.

And that wasn't even the most shocking bit of it.

My mind's eye pictured the clock tower seven floors below. An entire school made of magic.

In a war, that would be like a ship load of nuclear bombs. Now I understood why Blaine said that this was bigger than knowing a ghost's secret. This would change the outcome of everything. The next entry was the shortest, and the last. Tear stains splattered the page, smudging the ink.

I should have told the Master, but love ties my tongue with loyalty. There's no mercy for demons. If I uttered a single word, R.W. would be executed. I chose to ignore him and let him slip out of my life, but he confronted me after class.

He admitted everything. He stole the magic so he could be someone I could be proud of, someone my parents would approve of. The selfless nature that drew me to him in the first place drove him to condemn himself to darkness.

He saw me that night in the stairwell. He saw the magic in the walls. He told me he tried to access it himself, but his casts weren't strong enough to break the barrier of stone. He wants me to help him.

I told him no.

The love that drove him to steal magic for me dissolved into a feverish envy. He threatened that if I didn't help him, he'd kill my family.

If I do this, it won't be just my family that will be threatened but everyone else. I know he'll kill them if I don't help, but I can't live with the knowledge that I fed a monster instead of destroying one.

When I leave tonight, I'm going to hide this. My only hope is that my beloved friend, Jaclyn, will find it and hand it to the authorities. Then the evil that has become my love will be taken care of.

I know R.W. is going to kill me tonight. Surprisingly, I have no fear. I pray, Jaclyn, that you find this and do what I could not.

That was the end of Blaine Willow's diary.

Closing the cover, I stood with it clutched firmly in my hand. Walking over to the fireplace, I looked down at the flames. I had so many questions that empty words couldn't answer.

I released the book into the fire. The flames eagerly slipped between the cover and ate away at the old pages and ink.

The first thought that came to mind was Michael. I should've told him. Actually, I should've shown him the diary before I burned it. Or maybe not. Would he use Blaine's secret for his war?

I looked at the clock. I had less than an hour before war lessons. But I still needed answers. The only person who could give them was trapped in the one tower I was forbidden to enter. Not to mention the door was locked.

Whistle and the locks shall spring, Blaine said.

I ran to the door but stopped at the sight of the bracelet on my wrist. The last time I touched it, I got blisters on my fingers. I was no stranger to pain. That wasn't even on my scale of torment.

I grabbed the clasp.

Searing pain shot through my fingers as my skin sizzled like bacon. I jerked them away with a curse. The heat clung to my skin, lingering just beneath the surface.

I tried again.

This time it felt hotter, and the stinging became sharper with every move. Gritting my teeth, I pushed the bar through the loop and the bracelet slipped to the floor.

With my fingers screaming in agony, I pulled open the door. I made sure no one was around before I quietly closed it behind me.

I kept looking over my shoulder, making sure no one was there. Dropping off the last step of the stairs I stared at the clock at the exact center of the school.

A school made entirely of magic.

I walked around the clock tower and headed right to the North Wing. Checking again that it was just me, I slipped inside.

Blindly walking through the darkness, I reached the gold door of the tower. Taking a deep breath, I let out a whistle.

With a groan, the door creaked open.

51

How Far Could I Fall?

Against every instinct, I stepped into the smoky tower.

My heartbeat raced as I nudged the door closed.

With a rustle of fabric, Blaine Willow appeared in front of the stairs. Her eyes widened with surprise. "Do you have a death wish—"

"I found it."

Her mouth clicked shut. She stared at me with grey, unblinking eyes. Then she stiffened. "Where is it? Does anyone know you have it?"

"No, I burned it. No one knows I had it."

"Oh, thank God." For a moment I thought she was going to faint. "Thank you, but you have to leave."

"Wait." My hands fluttered at my sides. "I need to know who did this."

When she looked back at me, I was shocked to see her eyes dilated with fear. "You've come at the wrong time. I thank you for helping me, but you have no idea what you've walked into."

The sound of scraping metal cut me off. Blaine shoved me into the shadows just as the door swung open. The faint moonlight illuminated the outline of a man. He pulled a body off his shoulder and dropped it to the floor.

Cornelia's pale, sleeping face was lit by the pale moonlight.

"Hello, my lady."

Everything in me froze. I knew that voice, but it wasn't the one I was expecting.

It belonged to Richard While.

Blaine stood with her back proud and straight. Her head dipped as her gaze dropped to the unconscious girl on the floor. "I thought you got enough magic from the last one."

"The ritual didn't go as well as I hoped," he answered softly. Shoes scuffed across the floor as he stepped closer. I pressed deeper into the darkness of the tower. "I lost half her status in the transfer."

"Why a Deficient? That girl can't give you what you want."

"I'm afraid people are noticing the high statuses I've been taking. This Deficient won't be missed. Besides, my king is going to kill her kind eventually. I'm just saving him the trouble." He started up the stairs, his footsteps echoing through the empty tower. "Watch her for me, will you?"

I waited with trembling hands until the sounds of his feet grew faint.

Run.

As soon as I couldn't hear him, I sprang through the door and ran as fast as my feet could take me.

Michael could stop this, save Cornelia, and then this would just be a very, very close call.

I slammed to a stop in the middle of the North Wing.

Cornelia.

I spun around. She was still on the floor guarded by a ghost who couldn't do anything while Richard While did only God knows what five floors up.

"Go!" Blaine mouthed, shooting a panicked look over her shoulder.

I looked at Cornelia sprawled motionless across the floor behind her. There was no telling if I could get to Michael in time. I wasn't going to lose someone else over this. Ignoring the chant to *run* that thundered through my veins, I charged back into the tower and grabbed Cornelia under the arms. I dragged her through the ash toward the door.

The door creaked and slammed shut behind me.

"Well, this is interesting."

Dropping Cornelia, I spun to face the man on the stairs.

Mr. While meandered his way down the last few steps with a

smile. When I had first met him, I would have described him as soft. There were no sharp edges on him, or at least none that his oversized sweaters would show. He was the definition of unassuming.

But in the North Tower, lit by the harsh light of the moon, there was nothing soft about him. The intensity of his gaze hit differently. He wasn't interested in what I had to say; he was starving. His posture wasn't casual, it was poised, ready to pounce.

"I would say I'm surprised," he said coolly. "But now it just makes sense."

"Richard, let her go," Blaine pleaded.

"Silence."

Her mouth snapped shut.

"You killed Moose?" The words slipped from my mouth.

His forehead furrowed. "That was an unfortunate event, I assure you. I never would've done it if she'd simply cooperated. I need that diary to correct my ills."

"You mean to increase your status."

He shrugged. "A darkness is coming, one that will burn everything. When it does, I need to be ready for what my king asks of me."

"But why kill Blaine? You loved her."

"And I always will. Killing her was an accident. When she ran from me, she fell down the stairs. I took her magic so she'll always be with me." He tapped his chest right where his core sat. "You sure know a lot."

Blaine shook her head wildly, willing me to shut up.

Mr. While watched her scared reaction. His lips parted when he put two and two together. "You read her diary."

All carefree amusement was gone in a blink. "Blaine told you where to find it, huh?" His eyes filled with rage causing her to cower into the shadows. "I've been trying to get the answer from her for decades. Don't be as stupid as Aanya. Tell me where it is."

"At the bottom of my fireplace in a pile of ashes."

His hand lashed toward my throat. Just as his skin touched mine, he jumped back with a yelp. He stared at his hand before he turned his wide, green eyes back to me.

In two quick strides he trapped me against the gold door. He placed both hands on either side of my face.

With horror, I watched his eyes darken to a ruby red. They glowed from their sockets casting his cheeks in a strange light.

"You're full of surprises, Miss Heart." A hungry glaze clouded his eyes as his thumbs brushed over my skin. "What status are you?"

"S—six."

He slammed my head back into the door, causing my eyes to water. "Don't lie to me. I know what a Six feels like. This is higher than an Eight." Closing his eyes, he pressed his forehead to mine. "Now I understand why Master Lenin brought you here."

"Get off me." I planted my hands on his chest and shoved him back.

"Richard, please!" Blaine was in front of him in an instant. "Leave the girl alone. Too many bindings this close together will kill you."

His eyes softened. Some of their natural green started to seep back in. He placed his hand on Blaine's cheek. "My sweet girl, always watching out for me."

"Please." She placed her hand over his. "Stop this, my love."

"You know I can't. My king needs me." Once more, red claimed his eyes. "Leave us."

With a flash of silver, Blain was gone. Then his eyes locked onto me. I fumbled for my wand pocketed at my side. But he was faster. He pulled out his wand and shocked mine from my stiff fingers before I could aim it. My wand disappeared into the shadows of the tower.

"I can put you to sleep," he offered. "Then you won't feel a thing."

"You don't have to do this." I held up my shaking hands as he drew closer.

"I'd be an idiot to pass up a status like yours."

The back of my heels hit the stairs. My escape options dwindled down to one.

Up.

Spinning around I took the stairs two at a time. Halfway to the second level, he Ported in front of me. His hand wrapped around my throat as his eyes glowed even brighter.

I didn't have my wand, but I grabbed for my magic out of instinct.

Magic roared out of my core. In my panic, I pulled on it harder than I had ever done before. It filled my entire body to the point where I thought I was going to burst. I thought of the safety of my room—why had I left? I tried to pull out of his grip, but I only managed to twist my heel off the edge of the step.

I fell backward, pulling Mr. While with me. In midair I tried to twist around to catch myself on my hands.

With thoughts of my room, my magic acted. It flared like it did every time I tried to Port, but this time it wrapped around me.

The smoky air of the tower vanished.

I tumbled across the floor of my apartment. I sat up, completely astonished. *I Ported!* I must have not pulled on enough magic all those other times before.

I didn't have time to celebrate.

Mr. While was on the floor beside me, dazed and wheezing. He had been holding me by the neck when I Ported. My magic pulled him with me.

The transporter blared in the next room. *Michael!* I never thought I would run *toward* the man in black but I was laughably out of my depth.

I pulled back my foot and kicked Mr. While in the face. His glasses crunched under my shoe, cutting his cheeks and eyebrows. Scrambling to my feet, I lunged for my bedroom door.

A ward knocked into my shoulders. I lifted off my feet and landed on the coffee table. It shattered beneath me.

The transporter beeped louder. Shaking wood chunks from my hair, I pushed myself to my knees. Another ward sent me over the couch. With a wave of his wand, the couch flew out of the way and crashed into the opposite wall. The windows cracked under the impact.

Mr. While grabbed me by the hair and Ported us back to the tower.

He tossed me to the cold, ashy floor. Just as I rolled on to my back he fired a ward to my chest.

My muscles relaxed and went limp. Panic drowned me. I was unable to move, only blink and breathe.

He wiped the blood from his cheek. Reaching into his back pocket, he took out a petite, leather book.

"I appreciate you coming to me," he said, trailing his fingers across the faded cover. "Usually, I have to lure my prey. With Janet, I fed her vanity. With Aanya, I played her ego. Everyone has a weakness. Once you find it, you have the perfect bait for any creature." He sighed. "With your magic, I'll be free from this never ending cycle of death. My king will finally see me."

Bending down, he took both of my hands in his and placed them around a knife. Unable to move my head, I didn't see where he got it.

"Thank you for your contribution to the reshaping of history." Quickly he pulled the blade from between my hands, cutting both palms. I couldn't open my mouth to scream. I could only squeeze my eyes shut and feel the tears stream into my hair. Hot drops of blood fell to my chest.

Pressing my hands back together, he put a glass vile under the stream of blood. When the vial was full, he set it aside and took a small bundle from his pocket.

He moved out of sight. In the silence, my ears were attuned to every move he made. His footsteps were followed by the striking of a match. The smell of something burning, metallic and meaty, wafted through the air.

My eyes flew around the room. There was nothing in this burnt tower that could help me. Not when I was magically paralyzed.

Blaine was banished. Cornelia was unconscious. Master Lenin, Michael, Nirean, Clarence, and Daniel had no idea where I was. My wand was six floors below me.

The smell of cooking meat grew stronger. I strained my eyes trying to see what he was doing. From the corner of my vision, I watched him levitate the vial of blood over the burning plants.

When the plants were smoldering ashes, he gathered them and

poured them into the blood mixture. He shook the remaining items from the bag into his hand. Out tumbled two coins, each the size of a half dollar. Taking the bloody knife, he sliced his own palm open.

He closed his own bleeding hand around one coin. Magic glowed through the cracks between his fingers. Then he dropped both coins into the vial and gave the dark grey concoction a stir.

Then he came back to me. My heart was racing so fast that I was out of breath. A scream filled my head as he grabbed my wrists and dragged me to the center of the room.

Something hot and wet seeped through the back of my sweater. He straightened my legs and spread my arms open wide, palms up.

Tears streamed down the sides of my face. Sharp pain slashed across my wrist, first the right and then the left. Blood glided over my skin and collected beneath my hands.

He knelt by my face and turned my head so I was staring straight up. His hands were wet too, but it wasn't my blood. It was his. His wrists were dripping just like mine.

He ran the knife under the left side of my jaw. I watched as blood seeped through the high neck of his sweater. He was receiving matching wounds. Whatever happened to me, happened to him.

I squeezed my eyes shut, knowing what was coming next. Each wound he inflicted matched the ones I had seen on Blaine. The only one missing was the fatal wound to the heart.

He put a hand on my ribcage as if to steady himself. Then he thrust his hand *into* my chest.

My eyes flew open. The air froze in my lungs.

A glow moved up his arm. He groaned as my magic sank into his chest. He pushed his hand deeper. The glow grew brighter until his whole arm was highlighted.

I tried to pull it back. It was *my* magic. I commanded it, no one else. My magic flared, filling the lights around the room, but it traveled up Mr. While's arm, as if pulled by a magnet.

Black dots filled my vision. I struggled to breathe. Exhaustion leaked into my body, replacing the magic he took. My head started to ache. My limbs trembled from the loss of magic. *No, no, no!*

A whistle rang through the tower.

Mr. While jumped, yanking his hand from my core. Air rushed into my lungs as he spun toward the door.

"Blaine?" he called. "I thought I told you to leave." He stalked through the door and down the stairs.

Hope flared through me as my hands moved to clutch the wound at my side. Blood poured through my fingers.

The freezing charm was broken.

The world spun as I struggled to my feet. I gathered my magic to see if I could Port out. Instead of the mighty burn, it was a lukewarm rumble. Weak, my magic slipped from my grasp and slid back into my core.

Mr. While's footsteps sounded up the stairs.

Gasping bloody breaths, I grabbed the railing and stumbled up to the final level in the tower. Every breath was like inhaling shards of glass.

A laugh sounded from behind me. "Where do you think you're going?"

The laughter spurred me on. My foot caught at the top. Tripping, I skidded across the obsidian floor.

The door slammed shut by itself.

With a dull flicker, Blaine appeared beside me. "I'm so sorry."

I struggled to get my feet back under me. My shirt and jeans were soaked in blood. My hands and legs shook. I fell against the door and sank to the floor.

Mr. While banged his fist against the door, shaking me where I leaned. "Don't do anything stupid, Charlie. Your soul is bound to mine. Your magic is mine."

"I'll do my best to keep him out," Blaine said. The outline of her body flickered. "He won't be able to Port in here."

"And then . . . what?" I wheezed. "Can you get someone and . . . bring them here?"

She shook her head. "I'm too weak. He's trying to cast me out. Since my magic is in him, it'll work."

"Charlie!" Mr. While shoved his shoulder against the door. "You're ruining my binding!"

"And I'm really sad for you about that," I spat. I looked back at Blaine. "Help me."

She knelt beside me. Before, her gaze had always been cold and sharp. The gaze I met then, there was a flicker of humanity.

"When he's done with you, he'll bind your friend," she said softly. "But he has to finish harvesting from you first. If you were to sever the link before he could, you can save her. You can avenge everyone he's done this too."

"How do I do that?" I rasped.

"Two souls bound together are like a coil of rope. You can't cut one without severing the other."

Her words sparked a memory from long ago. I saw what happened when he cut me. His skin opened as well.

So that was it. I looked past Blaine to the clear glass of the windows. It was such a beautiful night, cloudless and sparkling. The moon, as bright as a lighthouse, shone from the navy blue sky.

I wiped the tears from my cheeks, smudging blood across my face. With labored breaths, I pressed my weight into my heels and pushed myself up the door inch by inch until I was standing.

I limped toward the far window. Before I could touch it, the window sighed open—Blaine's last attempt to end the horror that started with her. I looked over the edge at the drop that ended at the mercy of the river.

How far could I fall before I broke?

This was higher than any of the landings in the stairwell. Unlike last time, I was hoping it was too high.

I thought of Blake then. Of his candy apple green eyes and his graphic t-shirts. I thought of his hot chocolate and the music he played. I thought of the hug he gave me right before I got on the bus.

Blaine flickered and disappeared. The moment she vanished, the door shrieked open. Mr. While burst into the room, his wand ablaze with magic—*my magic.*

He chuckled. "This high up, you won't survive the fall. Magic can't fix everything."

A rush of wind blew through the window, bringing with it a strange sense of relief. "I don't need to survive. If I die, you die."

I stepped over the ledge. I caught a glimpse of his panic-stricken face as I plummeted through the air.

Fear unlike anything I had ever felt spiked through my chest. I screamed as the ground rushed toward me. My magic exploded once more from my core, but with no wand and no direction, it could do nothing more than react.

It tore from my chest.

The magic flare rushed to the lanterns at the top of the tower. Just like all the cars on the interstate not so long ago, the rotunda exploded with flames. And my stolen magic responded in kind.

Through the ruby flames, I watched my magic flare from Mr. While's chest. The force of it tore his ribcage apart. Mr. While's screams filled the night as I hit the water.

52

A Ghost's Thank You

I was drooling.

My eyelids were heavy with the need for more sleep. Stiff clean sheets felt like cement over my aching legs. Yawning, I winced as the skin under my jaw stung.

Blindly reaching up, I felt the skin on my wrist scream in unison with my palm. Opening my eyes, I found my palm and wrist tightly taped. The infirmary came into focus behind my lifted hand.

Scenes from the night before fogged my mind like fragments of a bad dream.

Cornelia.

Mr. While.

The binding curse.

The jump.

Rising on my elbows, I looked around the infirmary and saw I was the only one in a bed. Did that mean Cornelia was okay? Or . . .

"I was wondering when you were going to wake up." Helen rose from her seat beside me. "You're the deepest sleeper I've ever met. I dropped a tray of bottles an hour ago and you didn't even move." Helen walked to the bedside table and lifted a silver dome off a plate of food. She picked it up and placed it on the mattress beside me.

"My friend—Cornelia. Cornelia Montgomery—she was in the tower with me. Is she ok?"

Helen's smile deflated the anxiety in my chest. "She's fine. As far as she remembers, she passed out in the library after an exhausting day of classes." She nodded to the plate beside me. "I don't want to see a single crumb left over."

"I'm—" I sucked in a breath as the cut under my jaw burned. Barely moving my lips, I said, "I'm not hungry."

"Miss Heart." She smiled sweetly. "Just eat it."

I struggled to sit up without the use of my hands. No matter what I did, I ended up angering one wound or another. The one under my ribcage complained the loudest, bringing tears to my eyes.

When I was finally in the sitting potion, I pulled the tray toward me. On it were scrambled eggs, two pieces of toast, bacon, and a tall glass of orange juice. The bandages encasing my palms made it difficult to grab the fork. After several failed attempts, I ended up using my fingers.

As I ate, Helen went to the back wall and collected a few bottles. She brought them to my bed and set them up on the now empty bedside table.

When my plate was clear, she moved the tray to the floor. She dragged a stool from under the bed and sat in front of me. "Alright, let's see how those hands are healing."

She gently took my hands into her lap and started to unwind the bandages. The closer to the skin she got, the redder they became.

I winced as an angry, red gash came into view. "Not that I'm complaining, but how am I alive?"

"The binding curse placed on you acted as a shield. Anything that happens to you, transferred to the casting User. When your heart stopped, so did the casting User's. Luckily, I was able to get yours restarted. There wasn't much left of your attacker to do the same."

My palms and wrists ached under her words. The slice beneath my jaw and under my ribcage hissed with healing fire. "But every time Mr. While cut me, he got the same wounds."

Helen's hands froze in a tangle of bandages. Her gaze snapped up to my face. "Richard did this?"

I managed a small nod.

Placing a hand to her heart, she leaned back. "I never thought— he was such a nice man."

"Trust me, he wasn't in the end."

My words acted like a bucket of cold water to the face. Helen blinked rapidly and shuddered. Dropping her hand from her heart, she took up the bandages. "Of course. I'm so sorry."

She motioned toward my chest. "Lift your shirt, please."

I didn't want to see this one. Doing what I was asked, I stared at the black wall behind her. I tried not to wince when she pulled the gauze away. She cleaned and applied a potion to the wound and taped it back up.

"Why did he get cut when he cut me?" I asked, needing a distraction from the feel of her fingers probing my torn skin. All too well, I could remember Mr. While's hand sliding against my ribcage toward my core.

"From what I've been told, demons like the pain of the transfer."

The food in my stomach churned. "Will they scar?"

"I'm afraid so." She uncorked a small vial of yellow liquid that smelled of pistachio pudding. She dabbed it on a cotton ball and glazed it over the cuts. Underneath the cloudy goo, my skin pulled together and dulled in color. She quickly wrapped them up again.

"Is there something that can get rid of them?"

She shook her head. "They were inflicted by an enchanted blade. The only way to cover them is with a potion or enchantment."

Great. Now I'll have scars on the front as well as the back.

"You can put your shirt down." Helen reached behind her and grabbed more clean bandages. "Tilt your head back for me."

Looking at the wall to my right, I clenched my jaw as she worked the bandage off my neck.

"Most Users don't survive an encounter with a demon. Let alone a binding curse." She grabbed a clean cotton ball. "You should wear these scars with pride.

"This one," she lightly touched the one under my heart, "is a victory tally. Death tried to take you by force. You need to display them for anyone who tries to do the same."

"I don't think I can pull it off. Michael can."

She smiled as she put the bandage over my neck. "Master Kale is a great example of a victory tally. Why do you think he keeps the scar on his cheek? It's not because it improves his looks. It's his proclamation that your father tried to kill him and failed."

I balked. "My father gave that to him?"

She nodded. "He did."

Maybe that's why he hated him so much. With a scar like that, the battle it must have come from would've been to the death.

"Why?"

"That's Master Kale's story to tell." She tipped my face to look at her. "A demon tried and failed to kill you. That's quite a feat."

"But I killed him."

"That's the price of surviving, I'm afraid." Helen patted my knee and stood. She recapped the jar of thick yellow potion and handed it to me. "Make sure you put this on every night. If you don't, they could tear open and get infected."

I nodded and slipped the jar into my pocket.

"I'm going to let Master Lenin and Master Kale know you're awake."

I winced, already imagining the lecture that was on its way. "Do you have to?"

She glanced at the clock on the other side of the room. "I can give you five minutes."

I slouched with relief. "Thank you."

With one last smile, she pulled a bag from under the bed. My light blue hoodie peeked out from the gap in the zipper. She gathered the used bandages and disappeared behind her usual door in the back.

I soaked in the silence and for the first time since I arrived in that black stone castle, I just breathed.

All too soon, the gold doors flung open. Closing my eyes, I absorbed every last second before the yelling started. Heavy boots pounded across the stone and stopped in front of me.

I took a deep breath of patience and looked up.

Michael stood before me with Master Lenin slightly behind him. The glare on his face ruled over all the others he had given. All around the room, the lights dimmed as if they were shrinking away from his glare.

"Morning," Michael said tightly. "Did you have a good night?"

"I'm pretty sure I've had worse." I tugged the shirt away from the throbbing wound on my ribcage. "How about you? Did you sleep well?"

His patience snapped. It held out a lot longer than I thought it would.

"For the love of God, I have never wanted anything more than to rip out your tongue."

"Master Kale, please refrain from making those comments." Master Lenin sounded as if he had gone a million years without sleep.

"I'm really interested to hear what you have to say about all of this." Michael gestured to my bandaged hands.

"Actually." He raised his hand, halting me from speaking. "Let me start and then you can let me know if I missed anything."

Master Lenin sighed and started kneading his forehead.

"Last night when you were late to your lesson, as always, I came to your room. Not only did I find it trashed, but I found this on the floor." He tossed my tracking bracelet onto the bed. "I thought to myself, where would one incredibly obstinate girl go if she didn't want to be tracked? Obviously, the one place I told her not to go.

"When I got to the tower, I found your classmate unconscious on the floor with your wand. In the next second, you go flying by the window and the tower is being ripped apart by a magic flare. You nearly tore your core in half. It took Helen three hours to put it back together." He crossed his arms and growled, "Did I miss anything?"

There was no way to lie my way out of this, so I didn't even try. "I solved the riddle."

"You found the diary?"

I nodded. "And before you ask, I burned it."

Michael's nostrils flared. Before he could erupt further, I rushed on.

"The diary didn't have anyone's names, only initials. So, I took off the bracelet to ask Blaine. I didn't think it was Master Lenin, but I needed to know for sure."

The School Master startled at the sound of his name.

"Mr. While walked in with Cornelia before I could ask," I finished.

Michael's eyebrow moved up another inch. "Richard While?"

I nodded. "He went to school with Blaine." I watched his face closely now. "He was a demon."

Michael nodded. "I know."

"What? How?"

His eyes narrowed. "Because I solved the *entire* riddle."

"So did I."

"No, you solved the bit about where to find the diary. 'Radiant taste of control' is a lengthy way to describe magic. The last part about the thing he hunts turning him black is an old expression for the demon transformation."

Michael paused. His dark eyes searched my face. "For fuck's sake, you knew he was a demon before you ran into the tower. *And you went anyway?*"

"I didn't know he was going to *be there!* I thought I'd just pop in and confront Blaine and then leave. But Mr. While came in with Cornelia. Either way my question was answered."

"What made you think that I was behind this?" Master Lenin asked softly.

"I saw you leave the North Tower the night you told the school you helped Janet Raven fill out the transfer paperwork. And I saw you eavesdropping on Mr. Harrison and Mr. While in the library the night Mr. Harrison died."

"You think I attacked them?" Master Lenin looked like he was on the verge of swearing and breaking his air of professionalism. "Why on earth would I do that?"

"To shut Mr. Harrison up before he said too much." I braced my hand against the pulsing wound on my side. "I don't know."

"I would never—"

"Yeah, well, I wasn't really giving you the benefit of the doubt after you blackmailed me."

Master Lenin nodded thoughtfully, but remained silent.

"What were you thinking?" Michael demanded. "If things didn't pan out the way they did, While could still be walking around and no one would be the wiser."

I rolled my eyes. "I couldn't just sit around while you took your sweet time figuring it out."

"I told you to back off."

"I didn't know if you were helping him get away with everything." I gestured to the School Master and winced as the tender skin pulled on my side and wrist. "Students were being killed and no one even knew about it. I thought he was covering it up so he could drain the magic for your war like Magee suggested not a month ago *about me.* Neither of you have been remotely truthful with me, so I just added it to the list."

A long, uncomfortable pause followed.

"If it's any consolation, I didn't know." Master Lenin turned his gaze to the snow falling out the window. "Not until last year anyway. Holly Blackwell was one of my most prized students. I was coaching her for her testing year. When she suddenly transferred without warning, and I learned that she was dead, I found that I recognized the sequence of events with a handful of other students.

"When I saw Janet Raven's paperwork come through, I picked up on his pattern and waited in the tower for him. I missed him. Even in the library, he somehow made the ward that killed Mr. Harrison to look as if it came from his victim."

"You could've asked him to help out." I nodded to Michael, refusing to meet his glare. "Isn't that what Hunters used to do?"

"I thought I could handle it on my own. His attention was better spent on the war." He removed his gaze from the window and placed it on me. "Do you remember the diary?"

I frowned. "What?"

"What did the diary say?" he repeated. "Do you remember?"

I opened my mouth to tell him to shove it sideways.

What did the diary say?

A big, fat blank filled my mind. I read it. I knew that much. I could picture myself sitting on my couch with it in my lap. Every time

I tried to remember the words on the page, my mind emptied. *Why couldn't I remember?*

My eyes shot between the two of them. "What did you do to me?"

Master Lenin slid his hands into his pockets. "Obviously, what was in Miss Willow's diary was important. My father, and his father before him, and every Lenin who has ever been the Master of this school has kept the secret Miss Willow uncovered. I placed a cap on that memory so it can only be unlocked by me."

Michael's jaw pulsed with displeasure.

"Why didn't you just erase them?" I asked, too confused to be angry.

"One day, that information will be useful." His face flushed with his next question. "Did Mr. While say why he was doing this?"

"He said something about wanting to please his king."

Master Lenin jerked his eyes to Michael. "Why would he plant someone in my school?"

"We suspected this when you declared your side of the war," Michael replied calmly. "You're lucky he was only here to observe."

"How do you know that?"

"While was killing students for his own pleasure. He didn't do anything to you."

Master Lenin pressed the palms of his hands over his eyes. "Oh, my God."

"Relax. This was a stupid place to plant a spy. There's nothing to report other than the number of students transferring away from you. I'll have my team look at the rest of your staff so there are no more surprises."

A spy? Then it clicked. Lawrence was the king Mr. While spoke of. I was that close to someone who worked for my father? A chill rolled down my spine.

Master Lenin turned his sad gaze my way. "Miss Heart, I was hoping your time here would be uneventful. Please accept my deepest apologies for what you went through last night. If I had known . . . I'll give you a chance to rest. When you're ready, I'd like to hear about your encounter with Mr. While." To Michael he asked, "I assume I'll see you shortly?"

"I'll head down in a moment," he answered.

Oh, great.

Before he moved away, Michael handed him a small black book. The smell of smoke rolled off its ash-dusted cover. *Was that Mr. While's?*

Without another word, Master Lenin walked out of the room and the gold doors clicked shut behind him. Reaching into the bag at the end of the bed, I grabbed my hoodie and carefully pushed my arms through the sleeves.

"I have a question," Michael said, breaking the cold silence. "Why did you jump from the tower? You couldn't have known the binding curse would save you."

I regarded him for a moment. "I didn't plan on being saved. I just knew that if I died, he wouldn't be able to hurt Cornelia."

His eyes narrowed, but he remained silent.

My turn. "I have a question. Why didn't you just steal my magic and get on with the war? I doubt training me is a good use of your precious time."

He rolled his eyes. "Has anyone ever told you that you talk too much?"

"Has anyone ever told you that you're a pain in the ass?"

"If you paid attention in your classes, you would know the art of stealing or draining magic isn't natural. That's not a line I'm willing to cross."

He's a good man, Master Lenin said at the beginning of the year. *He just forgets that sometimes.*

"Charlie—"

My head jerked up. *Did he just use my name?*

"If something like this happens again, you need to tell me. I can't help you if I don't know anything is wrong."

Ha, that's a joke. "That would require trust."

His leather jacket rumbled as he crossed his arms. I think it was a way for him to keep himself from grabbing his wand. "You should've come to me when you solved the riddle. If you had, you wouldn't have those scars. I was trained to handle situations like this."

I gingerly got to my feet and poked him in the chest with an accusing finger. "I didn't trust you. Hell, I still don't. You gave me no reason to. For all I knew, you were helping Master Lenin steal the magic."

"I would never—"

"Words don't mean anything," I said. "Most of my life I've been around people who talk out of both sides of their mouth. You want me to trust you? Show me why."

He sighed harshly. "What I'm trying to say is, this can't happen again. You have Lawrence's status, which means . . ." He bit his tongue, struggling with the words in his mouth. "You could be useful."

"It's like you wanted to say something nice, but then your personality got in the way. Did anyone ever teach you how not to be a jackass?"

He rolled his eyes. "My mother tried."

I laughed at the thought of him having a mother. He probably sprang out of a haunted house like a summoned demon.

"I meant what I said. You've brought hope to Lenin's doomed cause. I want your word that if something like this happens again, you'll say something, if not to me then to Lenin."

I had no idea how long I was going to fight with him, but I had a feeling it was going to be a while. My instincts told me to raise my middle finger. But without him, a future of my own would never be mine.

So, for reasons beyond me, I nodded. "Fine, I will."

With a curt nod, he turned to the door. Over his shoulder, he called, "As soon as you're ready, head down to Lenin's office."

I rolled my eyes. "Of course, Master Kale."

He paused with his hand on the door.

"You're the only person stupid enough to call me Michael in a long time." He yanked open the doors. Just before they closed behind him, he said, "Don't stop now."

Shaking my head, I pulled the bag of clothes toward me. That man was as confusing as a platypus.

Snatching up a pair of socks, I quickly tugged them on to put a barrier between my feet and the cold floor. My palms stung as I moved my fingers to slip them over my heels. When I was done, my palms and wrists ached to the bone.

I grabbed my wand from the bottom of the bag and limped toward the doors. The wound under my heart made a point to punch me every time I took a step.

With a flash of silver, a familiar face stood in front of me.

"Blaine?" I stopped in my tracks. I thought since all of this was over, I would never see her again. I hoped I never would. "What are you doing here?"

"I wanted to see if you were ok." Her eyes dipped to where my hand clutched my side. "I also wanted to say thank you for doing what I was unable to do."

I didn't have a response to that. I knew she loved Mr. While, that much was obvious in her diary. How could I say, "Sure thing, you're welcome" for killing someone she loved? Even if he was a demon. He was good once. Just a sweet boy who wanted to be worthy of his lover.

The road to hell is paved with good intentions. I used to think that was bullshit, but I was looking at the aftermath of it. Richard While was burned, and Blaine was a mere shadow of herself, each trapped in their own little hell.

"If it was up to me, I would let your kind die out. But you ended my torment, so I came to warn you." She stepped closer, bringing her horrible chill to my skin. "I know what you are, and I know who your blood ties you to."

Shock rocked me back on my heels. "Wha—"

"I knew from the moment I touched your blood." She dropped her voice. "This war won't kill you. The men you're fighting to save will. If you win their doomed war, they'll end your life. They can't risk a rerun of what's happening by having another being with as much power as you walking this earth."

My head reeled. "Who?"

"Achilles Heel, Michael Kale, Henry Lenin—whomever. They'll never let you see the world heal itself."

I stumbled to the nearest bed and dropped onto the mattress.

"How do you know?"

"I hear everything that goes on in this castle. The night you came here, Master Lenin gave the order to Master Kale. Run while you still can."

In a flash, she was gone.

I sat there, too shocked to move. I wish I could say that I was surprised. But I was just too tired. Michael tried to kill me at the New Year's Festival and threatened it multiple times. What would stop him after I helped him?

Nothing.

They hid the war from me in the beginning. Why wouldn't they hide their end game as well?

Lies upon lies upon lies. Where did it end? With me beneath a tombstone? Or me turning my back on this altogether?

How was I in the exact same position I had been in back in Kansas? Anchored in place, with no hope of escape.

Only this time, there was no one to get me out of it.

No Blake.

No bus.

No window to crawl out of unless I wanted to die in the woods.

There was no one . . . but me.

I thought back to that moment in the North Tower when my magic seared my insides from head to toe and *I Ported.*

Run.

Run.

Run.

I wasn't the same girl as I was in Kansas. I had magic. I had fallen out of a tower, faced a demon, and *lived.* What could the fists of men do to me?

Maybe I wouldn't be able to run for long.

Maybe Michael would catch me in a few days.

Or maybe I'd vanish off the face of the earth.

Maybe I'd remain out of reach.

Maybe . . . my life would be my own.

I rose to my feet, barely feeling my wounds. When I pushed

through the infirmary doors, it was the first time I was moving forward without fear pushing me.

I felt free, like a balloon without a string. Like every tether that had every been bound around me was suddenly cut.

Stepping into the center of the school, I turned my face up and looked past the clock tower, between the two staircases to the glass ceiling. Bright sunshine poured over me, flooding the stairwell.

Through the glass was a sky of pure blue. It felt as if I was at a crossroads, but instead of just four avenues to choose between, there was a hundred thousand. A world of possibilities was at my fingertips. All I had to do was pull on my magic and think.

When I took a deep breath, it was the easiest one I had ever taken. Magic rushed from my core. The burning hum thundered down my bones, filling every vessel and cell.

Just when I felt like I was going to explode, I turned on my heel and Ported.

End of Book One

The lies continue
in the second installment
of The Royal Trilogy,
The Master's Trial.

Acknowledgements

First, I'd like to thank you, the person holding this book at this exact moment, reading these exact words.

Thank you for starting this wonderful journey, The Royal Trilogy. Thank you for welcoming this story into your home, for listening to these characters, and getting lost in their world with me. Thank you for making it to the end! Or maybe you're like me and you like to take a peek at the final pages— if that's the case, get out of here. You have work to do.

One day, I hope to say all of this to you in person with a big hug. But in the meantime, reach out and let's fangirl together.

I hate to be cliché, but I honestly have no other way of phrasing it—it takes a village to put something like this together. Thank you to Jodi Keller at NY Book Editors for challenging me to stray away from what is simply convenient. It was painful, but worth it. Thank you to Mary Weber and her team at Cherry Pie Author Services for making me look like I know what I was doing.

I am forever grateful to my parents, who let me slack off in high school so I could write down my daydreams.

In no particular order—Kimberly, Deanna, Laurel, Matthew, Lauren, Paige, Franklin, Kristen, Caleb, Bethany, Paolo, Annemarie, Jessica, and Caitlin. You read this book first. You saw through the typos and discrepancies—and there were many— and you loved it anyway. Thank you for your countless reactions and encouragements. Without you, I truly believe this story would still be locked in the vaults of my mind, never to see the light. I love each of you with all my heart and soul, with each breath and fiber of my body.

Last, but not least, Jess. You saw a star where I saw an overcast sky. For that, this book is for you. And for you, I am eternally grateful.

With much love,
M

Photo by *Laurel Anne Creative*

Michelle lives in Colorado Springs, Colorado, covered in cat hair and always with a cup of tea in hand. When she's not writing, she's either daydreaming up the next scene or sketching something from her world.

Instagram –
Connect with me | @michellenhagood
Series Updates and Fangirl Fuel | @_theroyaltrilogy_
Website | www.michellenhagood.com